More praise for Dylan Schaffer's *Misdemeanor Man:*

"A terrific read—the best legal fiction I've read in years, hands down. Thrilling, funny, and heartrending in turn. A totally unique, genre-smashing page-turner."—**Barry Scheck, professor of law, Benjamin N. Cardozo School of Law, and coauthor of** *Actual Innocence: Five Days to Execution, and Other Dispatches from the Wrongly Convicted*

"If you're tired of the conventional legal thrillers that overflow book-store shelves, do yourself a favor and try something with personality and panache."—*Chicago Sun-Times*

"The thinking man's John Grisham. For a guy who isn't me, Dylan Schaffer can really write."—**Kinky Friedman, author of** *Roadkill*

"San Francisco lawyer Dylan Schaffer's superb debut pits an engaging public defender against a stacked legal system in a case that shouldn't see the light of day. With a winning protagonist and a fast-paced plot, he is a fresh new voice in a crowded and highly competitive field. It makes you hope that he can take time away from his law practice to focus on writing a sequel. Highly recommended."—**Sheldon Siegel,** *New York Times* **bestselling author of** *Final Verdict*

"A terrific debut. With wit, compassion, and tremendous humor, Schaffer has created a lovable reluctant hero in Gordon Seegerman. *Misdemeanor Man* is the rare legal thriller that never forgets to tell the most compelling stories?—those that occur outside the court-house."—**Alafair Burke, author of** *Judgment Calls* **and** *Missing Justice*

"Those who like quirky comedy mixed with mystery will feel right at home here."—*Booklist*

Misdemeanor Man

I Right the Wrongs
Dog Stories

Misdemeanor Man

a novel

Dylan Schaffer

BLOOMSBURY

Published by Bloomsbury Publishing, New York and London
Distributed to the trade by Holtzbrinck Publishers

All papers used by Bloomsbury Publishing are natural, recyclable
products made from wood grown in well-managed forests.
The manufacturing processes conform to the
environmental regulations of the country of origin.

The Library of Congress has cataloged the hardcover edition as follows:

Schaffer, Dylan.
Misdemeanor man : a novel / Dylan Schaffer.—1st U.S. ed.
p. cm.
ISBN 1-58234-460-4 (hc)
1. California, Northern—Fiction. 2. Attorney and client—Fiction. 3. Indecent
exposure—Fiction. 4. Public defenders—Fiction. I. Title.
PS3619.C315M57 2004
813'.6–dc22
2003022603

First published in the U.S. by Bloomsbury in 2004
This paperback edition published in 2005

Paperback ISBN 1-58234-569-4
ISBN-13 978-1-158234-569-7

1 3 5 7 9 10 8 6 4 2

Typeset by Hewer Text Ltd, Edinburgh
Printed in the United States of America
by Quebecor World Fairfield

For Alfred and Flip and Alan

Some of us will end up to be lawyers and things.
—*Bob Dylan*

1

NOVEMBER 14, 2002. Duke Abramowitz—misdemeanor supervisor, boss-in-theory—stands in my office doorway as I saunter into work at eleven on a Friday morning. I squeeze past him. He tosses a thin file, hitting me, not unpainfully, on the back of my head. Admittedly there is a small bald spot back there, a target of sorts, but still.

"Good morning, Duke," I say, not looking (or needing to look) around to see the expression of disgust etched into his face. He is tall and exceptionally skinny and has a cross manner. He has a comb-over and a large, sickeningly three-dimensional mauve mole on the tip of his aquiline nose. After extensive observation, and thanks to my familiarity with reports in the *National Enquirer*, I've concluded the apparent mole is, in fact, a space alien that controls Duke's body.

"Blow me." He remains, staring at me. I pick up the file and pitch it back.

"Come on, Duke, I'm full up," I say.

He looks at his watch. "You have an arraignment in three hours."

"I busted my ass for six weeks to clear out my calendar."

There are thirty-six assistant public defenders in my office, nine who deal misdos full-time. Anyone but me, any time but now.

"You still getting a paycheck?" The file lands on my desk.

"Have I been dreaming, or did we have a discussion about this?"

He begins to croon, to the tune of the Barry Manilow hit "I Write the Songs": "You write the briefs that make the judges laugh, you don't take this case I'll cut your salary in half." He exits, chuckling.

"Can I at least get the highlights, then?" I yell, hoping he'll fill me in on the new assignment.

Nothing.

"I appreciate that, Duke," I bellow from my tiny, windowless, mold-beset, ash-color-carpeted, gray-walled basement office. My office, with its single adornment: a nearly life-sized poster of Mr. Barry Manilow (aka MBM).

"Not a problem," Duke whines from the hall. Then he deepens his voice to that of a TV announcer and says, "It's just the case forrrrrr—*Misdo-Man.*"

I open the file. Dunn, Harold. Arrested last evening. Penal Code Section 314, lewd exposure in public. Three witnesses, including an eight-year-old girl. Arraignment and bail hearing at two P.M.

We call defendants in 314 cases willy wankers, which is a not altogether accurate description of the crime. Dunn could have violated Section 314 without touching himself at all. It's the exposure that counts—the public display of the willy. The wank, if there is a wank, is like icing on the cake. Or something. In Dunn's case, as it happens, a wank is alleged. The report says Dunn held his erect member in his hand, smiled, and said to a witness, "So, what do you think?" Lovely. A wanker looking for affirmation.

A Detective Hong filed the report. Odd. Hardly a detective-sized crime. I think to pick up the phone to call my pop, but he's probably sleeping. No use rousing the monster unnecessarily. It would thrill him to remember, bring him back momentarily. But if it isn't there, the frustration and confusion would clobber him like a surprise left hook.

In his less foggy days, my father was a bit of a Santa Rita luminary. He was the lead detective in series of high-profile cases. Shortly before things began to fall apart, he was appointed acting deputy chief. But that's where it ended. When they finally got around to forcing him out

2

of the department, his legendary career had been reduced to a disheartened shake of the head and a lewd joke.

Hong. I don't recognize the name. I don't know too many of the cops investigating serious crime in Santa Rita these days because, well, because I don't do serious crime. I'm Misdo-Man. I do deuces and petty grabs and possession for fun. I do frat boys shooting guns at no one in particular, and drunks pummeling each other because they've nothing better to do after last call. And I do wankers. I suppose I might have graduated from misdos—misdemeanors—a long time ago, to a better office, to a higher caliber of criminals. But I like it in the basement. It suits me.

I didn't intend to end up here. I finished high school because I didn't want to be a bartender—I spent too much of my childhood waiting for my dad in bars, watching bartenders mop up vomit. I went to college to avoid becoming a cop, which is what everyone expected of me. And I went to law school because there aren't too many jobs other than cop and bartender available after an undistinguished college career. In the end I became a public defender. Now I spend much of my time with cops, in bars, where, it turns out, I feel most at home.

I could have been a prosecutor, I suppose; that would have driven my dad less crazy. But why would anyone want to be a prosecutor?

I'll be appearing shortly with Harold Dunn at the afternoon master calendar—a court appearance characterized by a crowd and a noise level worthy of a mosh pit—so I decide to go meet him first, explain how things will go from here. I walk the two blocks to the jail from the PD's office, sign in, and look over the file until my client shows.

The case seems simple, and unwinnable, which comes as a great relief. There couldn't be a worse time for me to take on an innocent client or a case that might be triable—to attempt any actual lawyering. My band, Barry X and the Mandys, is in the final stages of preparing for the most important gig of our lives—the show at which Barry Manilow himself will appear, if we are incredibly lucky. And if we are even luckier, and play our hearts out, MBM will let us record some of his songs.

I worked nights and weekends for months to clear out my calendar, and I'm not keen on any distractions. So, Harold the Willy Wanker will make bail, take the standard offer, and plead out in a few weeks. And I'll be free to focus on the music.

The rest of the band members fell for MBM relatively recently and their nervousness about meeting him, about playing for him, has turned me from bandleader into mother hen. Terry and Preet, who have been best friends since they were nine, almost came to blows at the gig last night over a minor costuming question. And Maeve? On a good day, on a low-stress day, on a day not a few weeks before the day she will drum for Barry Manilow, Maeve speaks constantly, loudly, rapidly, and profanely, has a microscopic fuse, and sports a paranoid streak that precludes her from driving, using a stapler, or eating foods that cannot be purchased in sealed, and preferably vacuum packed, containers. These days? You can imagine.

The Mandys. I care for each of them as I would for a beloved pet— perhaps the kind of pet best kept in a cage in the yard except on very, very cold nights, but they are my best friends and without them Barry X would still be getting booed off the stage at open-mike nights. If we get this deal—if MBM shows and signs off on our record project—it will be because they shared my vision.

As for me, I am not unsettled at all by the thought of performing for MBM himself. His music was the soundtrack of my childhood. My mom was the original Mani-lover. One of my earliest memories is of riding around in the tiny backseat of her Corvette convertible, clinging to the red leather seats with my fat five-year-old hands, squealing while she belted "Mandy" with the radio.

In 1976, she developed breast cancer. She was in and out of the hospital over the next four years—but the music never stopped. MBM got bigger and bigger as she wasted away. In the last months of her life I'd come home from school, tiptoe upstairs, and sit by her bed. She'd say, "Sing to me, Gordy," and I'd hum "Can't Smile Without You" or "This One's for You" in my squeaky, prepubescent soprano until she fell asleep. Barry on the car radio, Barry on the stereo. My dad escaped to work or a bar, my brother, King, to his friends' houses. Mom and Barry and I stuck it out together until the end. I was eleven when she died. After the funeral, our house filled with friends and family, I sneaked upstairs to her bedroom and removed the huge poster of Barry from her bedroom wall. The poster that hangs in my office today.

I knew then, as I know now, that I will meet him, that our paths will one day cross. I know that MBM will appear at our gig, that he will love the band, that he will shake my hand and say, "Yes, do it. Make me proud." I know these things just as I know Harold Dunn is a man who, best intentions aside, cannot keep his pecker in his pants in public. Some things are simply so.

2

I'VE BEEN WAITING ten minutes for my client to show. His arraignment is in less than two hours, so he ought to be in the jail's basement, waiting for the bus to take him over to court at the Santa Rita Hall of Justice. No reason it should be taking this long. I check in with the desk deputy, who tells me Dunn is in the High Power unit, which is where they keep the really bad guys—the gangbangers and red shirts (defendants charged with murder), and the high-profile defendants who might be targets for violence in the jail. Hardly the place for a willy wanker.

"You're kidding. On a misdemeanor? Any idea what he's doing upstairs?"

The deputy stares back, bored and faintly fed up. He says nothing.

"So, is he on his way or are you waiting for the snipers to get in position before bringing him down?"

He gives me a long look.

"Seegerman, right?"

They must give special instruction at the academy on how to say my last name, how to draw it out with a perfectly dismissive blend of pity and reproach. It's my dad, I know, his less than unblemished history. But it's like dog crap wedged into the sole of my shoe.

"That's right," I say. I leave him no room to follow up with a sniggering comment about Pop. If I thought he might have something original to offer, I'd consider waiting, but I'm confident this guy—a year out of the academy, stuck checking visitors and lawyers into the jail—doesn't have the brains to disrespect my father novelly.

"He's on his way." He grins slyly. I brace for the remark. "I seen you at Ted's."

This I am not prepared for. A minimally literate deputy sheriff at a Barry X show? The scene at Ted's—where we have performed two nights each month for more than a year—is distinctly Santa Rita hip, distinctly gay, urban, downtown. And distinctly not law enforcement.

"Oh, yeah? I've never seen you."

"You're pretty good. I ain't much of a Barry Manilow fan, but I liked it all right."

A fan. I slip into Barry X mode.

"Thanks. Thanks a lot."

He looks around, no doubt to make sure none of his comrades see him chatting amiably with a member of the shamed Seegerman clan who happens, in off hours, to double as the front man of a Barry Manilow cover band. He looks relieved when his radio crackles. The wanker Dunn will arrive shortly.

I read over the police reports, looking for an explanation for Dunn's high-security housing. But the incident seems unremarkable. One of the witnesses, Marjorie Styles, thirty-two, sees Dunn a couple of different times at a Cullen's outlet, one of those huge discount clothing stores. She thinks maybe he's stalking her, because she's in the women's apparel area and Dunn doesn't appear to be trailing a wife or daughter. Later she comes out of a dressing room and there's my client, his member firmly in hand. Dunn smiles, looks at her calmly, and says, "So, what do you think?" No doubt rendered speechless by the enormity of the affair, Styles walks away to find a manager.

After she leaves Dunn turns around, his pecker still very much at large, and up walk Lorraine Dykstra and her eight-year-old daughter, Callie. The mother is focused on shopping—she later identifies Dunn,

7

says she sees him in the women's dressing area, but does not see his privates. The kid does, though. Talk about freeing Willy. Unbelievable.

Dunn walks off, but for some reason doesn't leave the store. Security guards, led by Styles, find him browsing in Men's Shoes. It happens that a Santa Rita police detective—Martin Hong—is standing next to Dunn when the guards pop him. Which explains why a detective, whose beat tends to murderers and rapists rather than wankers like Dunn, ends up taking the witness statements and filing the report.

There is no rap sheet in the file. Good news. Dunn's not a chronic wanker, so the DA might be willing to deal the case for less than the standard offer. And bad news, too, because the client will probably be completely freaked out by jail and worse, might insist on his innocence and force me to try what will almost certainly be a complete loser. If the guy had been through the drill before, we could settle the case quickly and painlessly. A newbie I'd have to massage through the system, which means more time playing lawyer and less time playing Manilow.

The deputy directs me to a small, windowless interview room. Harold Dunn sits at attention. There is a panic button on the wall. I've never used it. Every time I go in to speak to a client I wonder whether this will be the time—the psychotic break, the attempted strangulation, the stabbing with a sharpened toothbrush. Did you know inmates are forbidden to possess Jolly Rancher candies in the Santa Rita jail? A year ago an inventive prisoner amassed quite a few candies, dissolved them in his mouth, spat the liquid into a tinfoil form, and made a blade, which he then used to slit the throat of his cellie. Then he attempted to eat the weapon but choked to death in the process. True story.

Dunn is about forty years old, tallish, thin, though a bit less thin around the middle, pockmarked face, greasy, stringy, longish hair

8

slicked back behind jutting ears. His head is enormous, twice the right size for his frame. He wears styleless glasses, lenses as thick as the porthole of an ocean liner, and the suit of orange pajamas provided free of charge to all inmates. He looks up but does not get up when I walk into the interview room. I extend my arm and introduce myself. We shake awkwardly because of the cuffs around his wrists. He does not speak.

"I'm sorry we're meeting under these circumstances, Mr. Dunn."

I scan around the cage—which is what we call the claustrophobia-inducing interview rooms—hoping he will sense I've been here a thousand times before, that he can trust me. I give him my usual rap. The system's imperfect, but I believe in it. After eight years, I know what I'm doing. I'm not here to judge or to punish. I don't care whether you're innocent or guilty. The thing that counts, the only thing I'm interested in, is the evidence the DA can bring into court. My job is to be your advocate, to walk you through the maze, and work hard for "the least restrictive outcome."

That is the phrase I always use. It sort of means something, and sort of not, and that's what I intend. Make him trust me, but confuse him enough to make it clear he's in over his head and he might as well do what I tell him. Which, in this case, will be to take the customary offer, do the six months, and for crying out loud, quit displaying his pecker in public.

Dunn says nothing. He hardly moves. His eyes, magnified like fish in a glass bowl, follow mine. A few times he follows my hands, which I wave around recklessly. Otherwise he remains still. His cuffed hands rest on the table, motionless.

"So we'll go into court today and get you bailed out, and then in a couple of days we'll meet and talk about the case. Look at the reports. See what we can do. Okay?"

He nods.

"Bail should be around a grand, maybe fifteen hundred. Can you make that?"

9

He shakes his head no.

"Is there a reason you're not speaking, Mr. Dunn?" His eyes dart back and forth. Oh no, no, please, let this one be halfway normal. I don't have the time for a psycho. "You know, the cops can't listen in here. There are rules protecting you when you talk to your lawyer. And now I'm your lawyer." I smile. He does not. "You could tell me you killed Princess Diana and they couldn't use it."

He does not respond, which is strange because, frankly, I think that's a damn good line.

"You didn't kill Diana, did you? Because I sort of had a thing for her."

Nothing. I can't tell whether Dunn is paranoid, otherwise mentally ill, mute, or simply so intensely embarrassed after getting busted with his weenie on display that he can't think of what to say.

"You're going to have to talk to me eventually, Mr. Dunn, otherwise I won't be able to do my job." He understands, I think. "So, you can't make a thousand dollars' bail. You only have to come up with about two hundred dollars, for the bond, you understand that?"

It seems like that might work, that he gets it, but who knows?

"I'll see if I can get you out on your own recognizance. But you have to make your appearances. Otherwise the judge'll tear my head off. Right?"

He nods.

"I can't tell you how many clients I have who get arrested for relatively minor stuff and then make their lives a lot worse by failing to appear for their hearings. It makes the judges feel unloved. So please, come back after you get out, okay?"

Another, almost imperceptible nod.

"Normally this is where I ask if you have any questions. You want to write something down?" I push a pad across the table. He takes my pencil—I think of the scene from *Silence of the Lambs* where Hannibal Lecter jams a pencil through the hand of his jailer—and writes "GOD."

Oh, God. My stomach flips. God, no. Suddenly things get complicated. My client is a religious nut, perhaps floridly psychotic, which means motions and shrinks and special hearings. So long Mandys, hello law library.

"God," I say.

Frustrated, he shakes his head. Then he points to the first letter, G. Then to the second, O.

"God?" I pause. "Not God."

He looks crushed. I gather I ought not to have uttered the almighty's name aloud. Would "Yahweh" be acceptable? I curse my lack of religious training. And I figure I better get out of there before he gives me an unambiguous indication he is a wacko. Maybe I can plead him out before anyone notices his defects.

"Let's worry about this later, all right? Time for court."

He sticks out his bound hands and I shake them.

3

DEPARTMENT 10, JUDGE Garnett I. Reasoner, afternoon calendar court. The zoo.

One reason I like performing as Barry X so well is that in other areas of my life, chaos reigns nearly unchecked. Onstage, if the Mandys and I have done our work, things should and often do proceed just as we intend. We control the energy flow, we control the mood. And if we decide to take things to the edge, we do so knowing it's our room and we can pull back if necessary. We're in charge. Not so at home. Definitely not so at the afternoon master calendar.

At two each afternoon, every person arrested in Santa Rita County—which includes the city of Santa Rita and five smaller, suburban towns to the north, south, and east—in the past twenty-four hours stands before the master calendar judge, who arraigns the defendant, sets bail, and then sets preliminary hearing and trial dates. From jaywalkers to serial killers, they all have to pass through Department 10. Also the master calendar judge schedules hearings, takes pleas, and imposes sentences. In a courtroom intended to hold, say, a hundred people, there are, at any given time during the session, which typically extends well into the evening, that many lawyers, that many defendants, and twice that many sheriff's deputies, court clerks, law students, court reporters, translators, probation officers, friends, and family members.

Hence the resemblance to a mosh pit. Not only because of the crowd and the din. There is also the issue of body odor, mostly the fault of the defendants, who aren't permitted showers too regularly, but also, sometimes, of the professionals in the room. And then there's the constant head-butting, intellectual and otherwise.

Judge Reasoner was once an unflappable, fair, decent, and intelligent judge who managed his courtroom expertly. So I have heard, anyway. The judge first climbed the three stairs to his wooden chair behind the bench sometime around the Civil War. By now, as you might expect, his synapses have retarded considerably. He is as effectual at controlling the master calendar as Mr. Rogers might have been at officiating a pro wrestling match. His temper is violent and unpredictable. His rulings are regularly unintelligible, often legally wrong, and always proprosecution. Reasoner particularly does not like me, probably because of my last name.

I sign the appearance list and sit back with a newspaper to pass the time. Shortly before the clerk calls the room to order a deputy district attorney named Silvie Hernandez takes the seat next to me. She is, as my grandfather would say, "a very nice piece of fish." Dark hair, blue eyes, Cuban-German, booty like two water balloons filled to the bursting point. Tough and brilliant with a dark and ripping wit. She was my girlfriend for four years. She was my musical partner before the Mandys, my biggest fan, and the only thing I've ever done that my father publicly approved. Then we split and she married a rich frat boy and abandoned Barry.

I have no heart. Have I mentioned that? Silvie Hernandez has it.

Silvie took a big-firm job after law school, made a bunch of money, burned out, and then joined the Santa Rita District Attorney's Office a few years ago. She's been one of the office's most ambitious and successful felony prosecutors and looks likely to graduate to the big time—the murder beat—soon. I do my best to avoid Silvie, and because I handle misdemeanors exclusively, our paths don't often cross.

"Silvie," I say, continuing to stare at my newspaper, but not reading a word.

"Hey, Gordy."

"What's happening?"

"Not a whole lot. What's up with you?"

"Not a thing."

"How's your dad?"

"Confused. Except when he's sleeping."

"You want to see something sort of interesting?" she says.

"Interesting how? Like intellectually interesting or amusing or—"

She places a district attorney's case file in my lap. The tab at the top says "Dunn, Harold: Penal Code 314." "Why do you have that file?"

"Because I'm doing Dunn."

"Dunn can take care of himself, thank you very much."

"Gordy."

I look up at her. I have yet to figure out the precise nature of the hold this woman has over me. Pop used to say she's like my mom—same external polish, same intensity. Maybe that's it. It's been years since we broke up and still, in her presence, I feel like I've just been run over by a truck. I know she's married and I know she's not coming back. I just can't seem to shake her. Probably because the split was my fault; her decision, but my fault.

"You've got to be kidding me. You get demoted?"

"No."

"You don't do misdos."

"I do this misdo."

"That's wonderful."

A minute passes. I return to staring at the same headline, listening to Judge Reasoner rant at one of my PD colleagues.

"We off the record?" she says.

"I figured we were permanently off the record."

"I'm getting bumped up to homicides."

"Big freaking bully for you. What's that got to do with Harold Dunn?"

14

"You could at least pretend to be happy for me."

"I'm still trying to get past the shock of learning we have a case together."

"Fischer asked me to do this one as a favor." Garland Fischer. Santa Rita's elected district attorney. And a candidate for mayor.

"Fischer asked you to do this one as a favor. I am definitely missing something. He say why?"

"No."

"No, you can't tell me, or no?"

"He just asked me to handle Dunn as a favor. Then I move up to homicide."

"All right, fine. I suppose I can overlook the intense awkwardness of this situation, momentarily, in the interest of resolving the case. What's the offer?"

Usually at this point the deputy district attorney pretends to review the file and then makes the standard six-month-county-jail plea offer. Silvie does neither.

"There's no offer."

"Silvie." I put my hand on her arm. The feel of it is both familiar and startling. "Maybe you've been prosecuting real crimes for too long. This is a misdemeanor. So, the way it works is you make an offer, I say no, we go back and forth a bit, and eventually we agree to something pretty close to what you wanted to begin with."

"He can plead to the sheet if you like."

In other words, plead guilty and throw himself on the mercy of the court, without any commitment by the prosecution to a sentence.

"To the sheet, in front of Reasoner? He'll get the death penalty." My volume is rising.

"I'm all right with this, with us handling this together. Are you?"

"This has nothing to do with— How can there be no offer? Is this from Fischer?"

"There's just no offer."

15

"Throw me a frigging bone here, will you. What difference does it make?"

"He pleads to the sheet or we go to trial."

"Okay, fine, we go to trial."

"Fine."

"Silvie, my guy will plead to being Jack the Ripper for fuck's sake. Give me something. I'm gonna look like an idiot."

"We're adding an enhancement for a prior and a 647.6."

"Wait a second." She has slipped into bust-ass mode. I am losing her. "What prior?" She hands me a sheet that shows a decade-old exposure conviction from Oregon. The old case means Harold is eligible for state prison time. "Why no rap sheet with the reports?"

"I don't know. The detective had some trouble running it last night. I just got it a few minutes ago."

"Ten years old. You're going to try to send this guy to state prison for a wank and a ten-year-old prior? You've lost your mind. And the 647.6?" Penal Code Section 647.6—annoying or molesting a minor.

"The eight-year-old," Silvie says.

"How do you get a molest? Fine, he whips it out. Call the freaking feds. It's not like he asked the kid to hold it. You sure she even saw it?"

"Oh, she saw it all right. Your guy's exposure is three years state."

"Three years in state prison."

"Three years," she says, in the self-satisfied "I'm doing justice, you're defending scum" manner of aggressive DAs. Only I'd woken up next to this DA for years thinking she was the only person I'd ever love. Which may still turn out to be true.

"Please, educate me."

She counts it out on her fingers. Thin, long, delicious fingers.

"A year state, minimum, for the 314 and the prior on the first witness—Styles. A year for the 647.6 on the kid. And a year for another 314 on the mom."

"It's all one crime, Silvie, your basic wank. He pulls it out, he does a year county. And if the prior sticks, you get a year state, *if* you can convince a real judge that sending my guy to prison is remotely justified. Not three. The mother doesn't even see his weenie."

"That's our view of the case." She stands up. She dumps my heart out of her briefcase onto the floor, spikes it a couple of times with her heel. Then she kneels down and stabs it repeatedly with a ballpoint pen. The blood squirts all over the gallery. "If he decides to take the sheet, come see me."

"You don't want to strike the prior for old times' sake?" I say.

"There's something about this one," she says. "Fischer wants this guy. Don't ask me why, because I don't know."

"Is all this why Dunn's in High Power?"

She laughs. "High Power? Are you serious?"

"This is turning out to be a remarkably bad day."

"We'll be seeking substantial bail, too."

I've had enough and wave her off. She doesn't budge.

"The sheet, huh."

"Sorry, Gordy."

4

I WALK OVER TO Dunn, who is sitting in the jury box where the in-custody defendants, shackled together, await their turn before Judge Reasoner.

I put my hand on his shoulder and whisper, "You okay?" He nods. "Things have become slightly more complicated. A couple of extra charges. Nothing we can't deal with." He stares ahead, mumbling or perhaps humming quietly to himself. "So you've been through this drill before. Ten years ago. Oregon."

He swings his big head slowly from side to side, in the manner of an elephant, and grumbles.

"Don't worry about it. Let's get through today. All right?" He is agitated and pale. "We still have a while before they call us. You want to talk?" I wave over a deputy, who frees Dunn from the chain gang in the jury box and leads us into an interview room.

At first, our exchange is much like the one we had in the jail. Dunn sits. I spew generalities about the master calendar, Judge Reasoner, the deputy district attorneys. For an uncomfortable few moments we sit in silence. Then he asks me to come closer so he can whisper. I have reason to believe the man suffers from a serious mental defect. I can hardly be expected to be thrilled with the idea of placing my head within striking distance of his teeth. I swallow my reluctance and lean in.

"Selmer Godfrey," he says.

"Selmer Godfrey," I say.

"Selmer Godfrey," he says, again, as if it is an incantation.

"Ohhhh, Selmer Godfrey," I say. He nods his head slowly. I have just been let in on a secret of immense significance. "Mr. Dunn, I have no idea what are you talking about."

He looks straight into my eyes for several seconds.

"I wonder if any of it makes the slightest difference now."

"Any of what?"

"How should I know how far it's gone?"

"Mr. Dunn, speak English, please. I don't have time for this."

He pauses another few moments. Our eyes remain locked. I notice that one of his eyes is brilliantly blue, and the other is a murky green-gray.

"I was only trying to do my job. Can you understand that?" It is an entreaty.

"Uh, actually, no," I say.

He speaks rapidly and without interruption for the next few minutes, in a barely discernible mutter, while I hold my head down, my ear inches from his mouth. He speaks in the timbre of one who has spent his adult life with his lips wrapped around a bottle, who has smoked many thousands of packs of cigarettes. Even at a tiny volume his voice is intensely crusty. But I can tell I am not speaking with a dummy. A loony, yes, a wanker, no doubt, but not a dummy. There is something else, too, an eagerness, a touch of mania maybe, that speeds him up and makes it exhausting to listen to him.

"I'm an accountant," Dunn says. "I used to be a CPA. Now I'm a bookkeeper. I've always been an alcoholic. I was an alcoholic before I had my first beer. I was born an alcoholic."

He's been sober and working for the past five years for a local nonprofit called Giving-Out-Dinner, founded by an ex-nun named Mary Godfrey. G-O-D, as it is commonly known, got its start in the 1980s, delivering hot meals to the elderly and infirm. The group soon expanded into other charitable ventures—drug and alcohol rehabil-

19

itation, clothing and furniture distribution, after-school programs for disadvantaged kids. G-O-D could not be more highly or widely respected. Mary Godfrey is Santa Rita's own Mother Teresa.

Dunn says Godfrey saved his life. After drying out, and graduating from the rehab program, he worked as her assistant and eventually became the head bookkeeper in the group's business office.

But, according to my wank-happy, number-crunching, big-headed, elephant-eared client, a couple of years ago Godfrey ceded control of G-O-D's day-to-day operation to her son, Selmer, who rapidly turned it into a criminal enterprise. So, if Dunn is to be believed, the county's most successful and admired do-good organization has morphed into a racketeering syndicate. Money laundering is the thing. Dunn claims the group has some high-level county politicians on its payroll, judges too.

G-O-D has hired the Mandys and me to play its holiday bash in a few weeks. I don't bother to tell Dunn this. Given his paranoia, I suppose the information might result in a complete mental collapse. Best to avert psychotic breaks by clients in tiny concrete rooms.

Dunn says Mary Godfrey, now well into her seventies, has no idea what has become of her organization. And Dunn hasn't let on to Selmer or anyone at G-O-D that he knows what's going on. But he thinks the junior Godfrey might have set him up after becoming concerned that Dunn would blow the whistle.

"You are telling me you were framed."

"I don't know what to think. I was in that store looking for shoes. That's all."

"They have"—I open the file to emphasize the point—"three witnesses, one a child. The stories are fairly consistent."

"I'm not asking you to believe me. I'll work it out."

"The old conviction is a bit of a problem. Under California law the jury will most likely hear about it."

"I was drunk for twenty-five years, Mr. Seegerman. Believe me, I did

20

worse than that. Not this time, though." He cracks his knuckles furiously and taps his fingers incessantly against the table. "I was shopping for shoes and the next thing I know I was under arrest. Go talk to Mary. She'll tell you they have the wrong person. But please don't mention anything about Selmer. I don't want to do anything to hurt her."

"Any theory on how Mr. Godfrey convinced three people who happened to be in the store, including an eight-year-old girl, to tell a police detective that they saw you with your penis in your hand?"

"I don't know. I really don't know."

I feel suddenly guilty about the dejected look on his face. His story makes little sense, but he seems almost to believe it, and to be anxiously looking to me for affirmation. All I can think is that a crazy client means a competency hearing and shrink reports and maybe the guy gets sent to the state hospital, where God only knows what happens to him. If he'd only kept his pecker properly corralled. What is it about these people that makes them want to show it off? I am a reasonably screwed-up person and I have never, ever contemplated unwrapping my package in a shopping mall.

Dunn continues. "Selmer knew about my history. Everyone did. Step Five, you know, admit to God, to myself, and to others the nature of my wrongs. I didn't hide anything about my past. I don't know what I did to worry him. But it sure looks like he wants me out of the way."

"And Selmer Godfrey, I suppose he paid off the detective who arrested you, and maybe Judge Reasoner, too. What about me, Mr. Dunn? Why have you decided I'm trustworthy?"

"What choice do I have? None of it makes any difference, anyway. If you *are* working for Selmer, tell him he never had anything to worry about in the first place. I'm no rat."

"Anything else you'd like me to communicate to Selmer?"

He has no idea what to make of me. He opens his mouth, but

21

nothing comes out. I don't let him stew too long, because as crazy as he must be, as much as I believe none of his story, and as pissed off as I am at Duke Abramowitz for handing me this piece-of-shit case, I already kind of like the guy. He's a nerd, that's it. And a nerd with an active imagination.

"That was a joke, Mr. Dunn. I'm going to be very frank with you here, because you seem like a nice person and we should get back into court. I look at this police report and I see a whole lot of evidence that you're guilty of a relatively minor offense. I've been around for a while, and usually—not always, but usually—these"—I hold up the reports— "don't lie. I think we can probably settle this thing without—"

Dunn cuts me off in an uncharacteristically firm tone. "No deals, Mr. Seegerman. I didn't do anything wrong and I won't say I did. I've made some mistakes in my life, and I've paid for them. I won't let Selmer Godfrey or anyone else turn me into a liar. They want to send me to prison, fine. I won't do it for them."

"Who said anything about prison?" Other than Silvie, of course.

"I won't plead."

We sit in silence for a long moment. Even if it is true—Dunn's frame-up theory—no judge would let me use it in front of a jury without the kind of proof that almost certainly does not exist—say, a videotape of Selmer Godfrey bribing the detective who pinched Dunn. He really ought to be a nice guy and plead out and do his time and try not to ruin my life.

"Tell me, Mr. Dunn, what do you think of Barry Manilow?" He looks at me as he might at a tax return completed, in purple crayon, by a five-year-old.

"What?"

"Barry Manilow. Like him, hate him?"

"I don't understand."

I stand up to return to the courtroom. "I'll see you in there."

*   *   *

22

On August 23, 1978, a month after my ninth birthday, my mom took me to see Barry Manilow at the Concord Pavilion, an outdoor amphitheater about twenty minutes east of Santa Rita. Fog billowing in from the Pacific can chill the summers here, but over the hills, in Concord, August is hot and dry, made for evenings under the stars, eating fried chicken and cherries, and listening to Barry. Two of her friends came. She laughed rowdily with them. And when she did, her mouth was a cavern, her silver fillings glistening like gems. She seemed invincible. Not sick.

They rooted for Barry and sang together. They sat forward as I stepped behind them, from one folding chair to the next, trying to see over the crowd. I danced for them and they cheered. They bought me onion rings and Dr Pepper. The crowd went bonkers. I have never felt so much at the center of anything in my life.

It is not possible to truly appreciate MBM's genius without seeing him live. More than any other singer, maybe more than any singer ever, he knows how to turn a five-thousand-seat arena into a small club; he knows how to look at, to reach, to touch, every member of the audience even while his eyes are blinded by spotlights.

He sang directly to me and for me that night. He knew my mother was dying. He knew my father and brother had evaporated. He knew I'd just had a birthday and felt like this might be the best night of my life, and the beginning of the end. And he cared. He sang as if I were on his lap the whole time. By the end of the show he was my best friend in the world. I vowed I'd always remember the favor. Barry X was born.

5

I WALK OUT INTO the courtroom, into the gallery, and sit behind Silvie; I lean over to whisper in her ear. The smell of her neck is enough to make me weep.

"My guy says he was framed."

She smiles, feeling sorry for me I suppose. "Are you going to 1368 him?"—in other words, invoke the competency statute, declare in open court that my client is a nut.

"Absolutely not." Not today, anyway. Tomorrow? Probably. "I have no reason not to believe him."

"Keep me posted on that."

An hour later the clerk calls Criminal Number 1534–02, *People of the State of California v. Harold Dunn.*

Silvie and I enter our appearances and I waive formal arraignment. Dunn pleads not guilty.

"Will Mr. Dunn be waiving time, counsel?" Judge Reasoner asks. The question is whether we will insist on a quick trial, within forty-five days, or whether we will seek more time to prepare. It is November 14. Keeping in mind our date with MBM on December 20, I figure I might as well get it over with. Anyway, the case is bound to settle, and a rapidly approaching trial date tends to light a fire under a recalcitrant client.

"No, your honor. I'd ask that a trial date be set within the statutory period."

"And the trial will consume how many court days?"

"Two, maximum," Silvie responds.

"Two sounds right," I add. Not that my opinion has any significance. Still, one does like to hear the sound of one's voice.

"Trial will be set for December 18. Pretrial December 16."

"I'd ask the court to set bail according to the schedule," I say. No use trying to get Dunn out on his own recognizance now that I know Silvie intends to oppose even the scheduled bail.

"Ms. Hernandez?"

"Your honor, as you can see from the amended complaint, Mr. Dunn has a prior conviction of this nature from Oregon. Also, the misconduct in this case involves not only the 314s, but also a 647.6 against an eight-year-old girl. Under the circumstances, I think a considerably higher bail is appropriate. Mr. Dunn is a danger to the community."

"Your honor, I just learned about the enhancement and the additional charge this morning."

"I'd be happy to continue this matter, counsel." Meaning Dunn sits in jail a week while I do what? The charges are the charges.

"That won't be necessary."

"Good. Now, have you something intelligent to say on the issue?"

"The scheduled bail is more than appropriate. Mr. Dunn informs me he has been employed as a bookkeeper and administrative assistant at the Giving-Out-Dinner project for five years. He has lived in the same apartment for an even longer time. There is simply nothing to suggest that he will not abide by this court's orders and make all his appearances. Ten years ago he was a chronic alcoholic who made some very bad decisions and served time in another state as a result. Thanks to Mary Godfrey and the remarkable work that the folks at G-O-D do, Mr. Dunn has been sober for many years. He has gained the confidence of that organization and I understand he works closely with Ms. Godfrey herself. He has pleaded not guilty and is presumed to be not guilty until the district attorney proves otherwise. Although

Ms. Hernandez has chosen to stack the complaint with an old conviction and various charges relating to the present incident, in fact Mr. Dunn is alleged to have committed a single misdemeanor. If he is convicted, he will go to jail, but in the meantime it would be a grave injustice to impose bail above the scheduled amount."

Reasoner does not hear a word. He shuffles papers on the bench during my argument.

"Is that all, counsel?"

"Yes, your honor," Silvie says.

"Submitted," I add.

"Bail is set at ten thousand dollars. The matter is assigned to Department 26 for trial."

"Your honor, Mr. Dunn is charged with—"

"The matter was submitted, Mr. Seegerman. I have always understood that to mean closed, kaput, done, no longer subject to argument, as eloquent as yours always is. Anything else?"

"Yes, your honor. Despite the minor charges in this case, Mr. Dunn is presently housed in the High Power unit at the county jail. I have reviewed the file and I can't see a reason for that. His placement is a hardship with regard to visiting and so forth. I'd ask the court to direct the sheriff to place Mr. Dunn in the general population forthwith, unless it can show cause for the present arrangement."

Silvie relents for a moment. "The People have no objection to such an order, your honor."

"Denied. Please call the next case, Madam Clerk."

Denied. It's a word a defense lawyer becomes accustomed to hearing over the years. Denied, rejected, overruled, viewed with and occasionally held in contempt, identified with one's client's crimes, and despised by right-thinking, law-abiding citizens everywhere. Like the meter maid and the clerk at the Department of Motor Vehicles and the IRS auditor, the criminal defense lawyer is first stunned by the opprobrium, then saddened by it, but finally wears it as badge of honor. Eventually you crave it and it impels you to act—in the interest of your client, in the interest of justice always—like an imbecile.

"Your honor, if I might be heard." Dunn takes a step back, shrinking from the scuffle about to occur. The courtroom hushes. A hundred pairs of eyes, moments before wandering and listless and impatient, now focus on the back of my head, waiting, hoping for a moment of comic relief in which the defense lawyer brings the ceiling down upon himself.

"Counsel, if you'll turn around you'll see there are others who have business before this Court."

"Judge, I have appeared here many times and I am aware of the demands on the Court. Nevertheless, something inexplicable has occurred here and I wish to make my record."

"Everyone is waiting, Mr. Seegerman."

"With all due respect, Mr. Dunn is charged with a misdemeanor."

"A wobbler with the enhancement, I think," the judge retorts. A wobbler is an offense that can be treated either as a misdemeanor or a felony, as Dunn's 314 charge could because of the old conviction.

"Very well, a wobbler. In my experience no person in his position has ever been required to post ten thousand dollars' bail. It's a violation of due process."

"I look forward to seeing your writ papers. Anything else?"

"Yes. Unless circumstances truly require it, no one in his position has ever been placed in the extraordinarily restrictive High Power unit without good cause. All I ask is that the court seek an explanation from the sheriff."

"Now are you done?"

I look over at Silvie. She seems tense and shrugs.

"Yes."

"Yes, what, counsel?" He is looking for the "your honor," but I am way past there.

"Yes, I'm done."

"Denied. May we have the next case, please."

I turn around, but Reasoner isn't through with me.

"By the way, Mr. Seegerman, make the check payable to the Clerk of Court. Five hundred dollars should do."

"Excuse me."

"Excuse me, what, counsel?"

"Excuse me, *your honor*."

A smile creases his sagging face. "Now you've got both feet on deck, counsel. Five hundred, to the clerk of court."

"I am being held in contempt."

"With all due respect, Mr. Seegerman, whatever microscopic quantity of respect that may be, that is correct."

6

I GO TO GRAB a sandwich. By the time I get back to the office, word of my spin-out in court has spread. Aineen O'Connell, our chain-smoking receptionist, smirks when I walk in. She is twenty-four. Her cheekbones are angular; her short spiky hair is dyed blond. She dresses only in black, has a metal rod through the skin above the bridge of her nose, and a tattoo of a circle on her right biceps and a square on her left. She is small, but lifts weights daily and so has lavish musculature.

Maeve O'Connell—Aineen's mother, and the drummer in my band—sits nearby, painting her daughter's fingernails. She does not acknowledge my arrival. She is the public defender's office manager.

"Mr. Abramowitz has been asking for you," Aineen says.

"Tell him I've expired."

"Retired?"

"Yeah," I say, walking down the long dark hallway toward my office, flipping through illegible messages. "That'll do."

Aineen is her mother's aide-de-camp, chief enforcer, heir apparent, and number one snitch. She spent most of her adolescence and early twenties in a drug-addicted stupor from which she has only partially emerged. I believe she is the least competent office worker on the planet. In general, her demeanor at work is that of a guest at a spa.

I stand outside my office. Terrence Fretwater has his feet up on my desk. Duke approaches from around a corner. I shut the door, loudly, and lie on the floor behind my desk.

"What happened?" Terry says.

"I'm having an exceedingly bad life."

"A minor setback, I'm sure. You were absolutely on fire last night." Terry is my bass player. He is also the best investigator in the office.

"Because I was focused on the music, T. Like a laser. Now I have issues." I stick the Dunn file up in the air.

"What?"

"Duke set me up. I told him, no new cases until the gig. He has eight other lawyers, but he has special powers. He knew this case was going to require"—I raise my hands in the air and form quotation marks with my fingers, which, from behind my desk, are all Terry can see of me—"special attention."

"Are quotation marks really appropriate here, I mean, strictly speaking?"

"Was I in the middle of something? Jesus."

"Sorry."

"He knew. It's like he's psychic or something. I'm minding my business, and before I know it, Reasoner flips out on me. He set bail at ten grand for a freaking wank job."

"And you didn't feel that was appropriate?"

"Correct. And the client's psycho."

Duke barges in, towers above me. Even from six feet below, the mole looks otherworldly. "The office isn't paying that fine, Seegerman," he snarls.

I stare up at him. "Are you through?"

"You have to do a report."

"If I'm paying the fine, why—can you see I'm in a meeting here?" Duke slithers off. "Why does a guy charged with a misdo end up in High Power?"

"Profile, usually. Or he's a snitch."

"No and no. He's an ex-boozer who popped out his weenie in a Cullen's outlet. That's it, except a really old out-of-state prior."

"And your guy doesn't know what he's doing in lockup?"

"Oh, believe me, he knows."

On the way over to the jail to see Dunn I fill Terry in on Dunn's story, the G-O-D conspiracy, the setup.

"You'd think something that big, I'd have heard a noise before this."

"Terry, the reason you haven't heard a *noise* about it is because it's complete bullshit. The guy's wacko. There's got to be a logical explanation."

"Why no offer, though? That doesn't fit."

"That could just be Silvie."

He gives me a bent look. "What?"

"Why?"

"I don't know. She misses me? She wants to spend time in trial with me? She wants to destroy me in front of a jury?"

"That I buy," he says.

"She told me Fischer asked her to handle the case as a favor. It makes no sense. Why stick it to him on the misdo?"

In jail, as before, Dunn at first refuses to talk, waves his hands around pointing out all the places the cops might have a microphone, writes furiously and incomprehensibly on my yellow legal pad. But Terry gets to him—flips some confidence switch I couldn't find or had no idea was there—and Dunn's tense, brittle bearing slackens like a junkie after his first shot of the day.

I've seen this happen a hundred times. Terry is a gorgeous man, with the sort of perfect body a two-thousand-dollar suit hurls itself off the rack at, hollering, "Take me, mister, you're the one for me." Loose dreads shot through with streaks of sienna sprout from his skull. And he has the kind of harmonious face that ought once and for all to explode the fiction that the bass player is always the ugly one in the band. I figure about half of the folks who show up at a Barry X gig couldn't care less about the music; they've come to ogle the Adonis.

But until you watch Terry Fretwater do his job—until you sit next to him as he interviews a trio of crank-addled bikers in a double-wide outside Fresno, or a society maven in San Francisco, or the thirteen-year-old sister of a murdered gangbanger in West Santa Rita; until you realize that unlike a cop, with his badge and gun and implicit threat of arrest, Terry can't *force* anyone to talk to him; until you watch him flip from role to role, as appropriate, from son to brother to shrink to bartender to boyfriend to priest; and until you watch the witnesses, no matter how initially dangerous or crazy or reluctant, act as if they've forever been waiting for this moment, to unload—you'll never appreciate the guy's genius.

Dunn prattles for a half hour—about his drinking days, about getting straight, about the evil Selmer Godfrey, about the big frame-up. Terry takes notes.

"Good luck." He chuckles as we walk down the jail steps and into his mint-green 1968 Mercedes convertible.

"Take me home so I can be with the lunatics who love me," I say.

"One of two things is true. Either Dunn's psycho—"

"You know what I'm going to do—"

"Or you're in the middle of some heavy, *heavy* shit—"

"I'm going to do nothing. All I have to do is my job, right?"

"I suppose."

"I'll go see Mary Godfrey and see what she says. I'll see if I can get Silvie to go back to Reasoner on bail. You'll take a whack at the witnesses."

"Wait, wait. I didn't say anything about—"

"I'll do a couple of bullshit motions. I'll try the case. And I'll lose."

"Nothing to be ashamed of. You're doing your job."

"This is my point. Dunn can live in his mentally deficient little wanker's world. Should there be any truth to Dunn's allegations, that's not my problem."

"Other than the bit about me interviewing witnesses, it all sounds very reasonable."

"I stay focused on Barry. Like you said," I say, slapping the dark red leather dashboard, "a minor setback."

We drive in silence for a few minutes. Out of downtown Santa Rita, with its dense collection of high-rises and civic buildings—the courts, city hall, the jail—all lacking the slightest architectural charm. This was the heart of the city when Santa Rita was a destination, something more than fifteen miles from San Francisco. The downtown isn't so much dead or even dying as it is permanently disabled—in the sixties by radical politics, in the seventies by an economy in free fall, in the eighties by crack and the gang wars it inspired.

In the nineties, the city—eager to join the economic carnival taking place across the bay—shined its shoes, put on a tie, and went looking for suitors: businesses and developers, and the sort of residents who could and would contribute to the ballet and the art museum. We elected a white mayor for the first time in thirty years, which was quite a concession to the business community. *See*, we said, *we know what it takes to join the big time in America.* For a while, Santa Rita felt like the place to be. The real estate market went through the roof. Quite a few businesses located here during the rise of Silicon Valley and the Internet.

But the crash came early and hard to Santa Rita. By the end of 2000, before the bears took over Wall Street or the disasters in New York and Washington knocked the last wind out of the boom, the techies and builders in this county had their bags packed. And the murder rate, which had declined steadily after crack finally killed the last of its habitués and lost its charm among the white wannabe gangbangers in the hills, was on the rise.

We drive past the Pyramid Theater, an Art Deco–era auditorium restored during the boom, but rarely used. My grandfather played the

Pyramid in the thirties and forties, its façade shimmering with white light, limos emptying movie stars and cigar-chomping gangsters onto the carpeted sidewalk. The mob controlled the town then—Santa Rita had the busiest docks on the West Coast, and the rackets have always had a special fondness for the import-export business. My grandfather says Jimmy Milano, the patriarch of the Milano family and the guy who effectively ran Santa Rita until the sixties, used to sit in the front row and blow cigar smoke at him on the piano until he could hardly read the charts.

Although we are a city of more than a million people, larger by a third than San Francisco, one of the most ethnically diverse cities in the nation; although it is our harbor where the trucks, from Tulsa and Tucson, wait for DVD players and cell phones shipped from Asia; and although our football and baseball and basketball teams are world class, because we are a black city, a yellow city, a brown city, because we are a murderous city, and because we are a poor city, we are forever viewed by the rest of the world as in decline. We are not even a suburb. We are a national symbol of failure. I wouldn't think of living anywhere else.

Terry drives up Broadway, through neighborhoods of small, struggling businesses, single-story houses with puny, tidy front yards, and restaurants—Korean, Vietnamese, Mexican, Indian. Then up into the hills. I've lived on this five-mile-wide ridge between the California coast and the start of the Central Valley for more than thirty years, and I've never quite become used to how rich and white and clean it becomes the minute the car points its nose up Santa Rita Avenue. Just fifteen minutes west are some of the worst slums and poorest people in California. And here, where my father and my grandfather and I live, it is as peaceful and safe as Bel Air.

Once inside my house, however, all is rarely peaceful or safe.

7

I PUT MY KEY in the gate, open it, close it behind me, and take one
step into the front yard. The area, about twenty-five yards across
and fifteen to the house, is tiled with rust-colored Mexican paving
stones at the edges and is otherwise covered with a lawn desperately in
need of mowing. This is grass to fall in love on, velvety and plush. Not
the bristle and stubble Californians are used to. There is a large
fountain in the middle of the yard which attracts many birds I cannot
name.

Across the lawn our house, a brown-shingled Arts and Crafts–style
mansion, sits impassively, immutably. A mountain is not permanent,
and neither is an ocean. Life and love, justice, money: all of these are
evanescent, fleeting. Yet our house, with its scaly, moldy roof and its
peeling paint, will always be here. I believe this because my mother,
who was a dreamer but not a liar, told me so. The fact that the house
sits above the most dangerous fault line in the United States has
sometimes led me to question my mother's claim. But in the end I
accept it because I need the consolation. So much in the life of my
family has been flimsy and unsure, it is reassuring to have faith that
4200 Candlewood Lane will not forsake us.

I take several deep breaths before going inside. Then I hear whining
from above me and see S.'s—my dad's naked backside in an open
second-story window. Then his front. His face, which must be close to
the top of the double-hung window, is masked by a yellowed shade. In
my father's arms is my wriggling, cinnamon-colored, four-year-old

Dachshund, LeoSayer. S. bends his knees slightly and dumps the dog out of the window as if emptying a bag of trash into a garbage chute. That may be precisely what he thinks he's up to.

The dog dribbles over the windowsill, bounces off a lip of roof, and tumbles into the air. The customary "No!" or "Don't!" does not pass across my lips. Rather, as if I am nine and we are playing catch—something we might well have done, but in fact never did—I bolt toward the house, trip, and collapse onto the lawn. The dog bounces off the backs of my legs and scurries off. S. hollers from behind the window, where, still, all I can see is his bare midsection: "Next time . . . lucky you're . . ."

The voice, shuddering, is barely intelligible.

I carry the spooked but seemingly uninjured LeoSayer into the house, set him down, and begin climbing toward the second story that is S.'s dominion and jail. Still naked, perched at the top of the narrow stairwell, he balances against a rickety banister with its many layers of paint flaking off in patches.

"Hi, Dad."

"Gordon." That is all he says. But a cognitive triumph it is. My father recognizes my face.

"Should I ask what you're doing up here?"

"Waiting for you," he says. Half statement, half question, like almost everything my dad says these days that is at all intelligible. He seems essentially lucid, able to see my face and tie it without much exertion to my name, to the fact that I am his second son, the one who lives at home. Tonight the clouds have parted and my dad's brain is, momentarily, marginally, operational.

I welcome his words. When S. can't remember, he stops talking altogether, and a vexing silence descends over the house. Without intending to, or having any particular goal in mind, the rest of us abbreviate our sentences and speak quietly.

"Do you want to get dressed?" I reach the top of the stairs. LeoSayer follows closely behind. S. looks down and seems shocked by the sight of his own nakedness. And slightly confused as to what to do about it. I walk him into his bedroom.

"That's what I was doing when your dog attacked me." He is on the verge of tears, pointing at my overweight and sluggish bratwurstlike canine. "Does he have to follow me everywhere?"

S. tries to kick at the dog, but loses his balance and falls onto the bed.

"He's fine, Dad. How are you feeling tonight?"

He looks for a moment as if he might take a chunk out of my thigh with his teeth. A glimpse of the old truculent, cantankerous S.

"Fine."

"You know a detective named Hong, Martin Hong, out of Central?"

"No."

It is like walking blindfolded on the edge of a cliff, asking my dad to remember. It is good for him to keep trying, but painfully frustrating if he cannot. And it is impossible to predict which questions will help him access his past and which will draw the gate to his memory closed with the permanent and menacing clang of a jail cell shutting behind a new inmate.

"He's probably new." I tell him something about the Dunn case. "Martin Hong, out of Central."

"I don't know. Sounds familiar, maybe."

"What about Selmer Godfrey?"

"No."

"How about Uncle Sam?" He smiles quickly, still sharp enough to catch a softball.

I watch S. struggle to remember which dresser drawer contains which items of clothing, and what to do with each of the garments. He gets it all right and then goes to the mirror to check and smooth down his full head of hair. Cognitive deterioration aside, S. remains a handsome and profoundly vain man. I follow him down to the living room where he collapses into a frayed armchair.

"Did Lillian make soup?" I say, asking after the Filipina nurse who cares for my dad three days each week.

"I think so."

With his memories have flown off his sense of humor and his bad attitude. I miss them. When I ask my dad about dinner, what I really want is for him to yell back, as he might have done at my mother, "I don't want effing soup. I want an effing martini." When I ask him how he is, I want him to say he feels like Joe DiMaggio the first time he screwed Marilyn. He was a complete prick, my father, but it was easier to take, and far more entertaining, than this.

A few minutes later my grandfather Ferdy returns from his evening walk. The man walks obsessively. He stashes his metal cane by the front door. He doesn't need it for support, but I suppose it might come in handy in the pitched battle with the police he's been counting on.

"Evening, son," Ferdy says, stopping in the middle of the living room. S. greets his sprightly eighty-eight-year-old father and looks enviously at him. "Nice to see how much that dog loves you. He's about the only one who can stand you anymore."

LeoSayer has leapt onto the ottoman and nuzzled a small space between S.'s legs. My dad lacks the energy to shoo him away. And his defenestration notwithstanding, he appears resigned to the dog's affections. LeoSayer, for his part, is unbothered by S.'s abuse. Ferdy walks behind the armchair, smooths a few strands of hair away from his son's face, and rubs his shoulders briefly.

"I'm dying, you know," S. says. "In case anyone hadn't noticed."

The comment paralyzes Ferdy. I walk out of the kitchen to see what is next. This is as visceral and coherent and momentous a statement as my father has uttered in months.

Then the front door bursts open and my brother, King, lumbers into the living room. He is cursed by our family's tendency to stubbiness.

He is short, like me, but he is also fat. He wears a reckless beard and his hygiene is inexact. His attire this night consists of blindingly white tennis shoes, black sweat pants, and a stained sweatshirt.

"We know that, Dad," I say. "We're doing our best."

"What's going on?" King says.

"I think your dad's scared of dying," Ferdy says.

"Oh."

We stand around for another minute, seeing if my dad wants to add anything, to yell, to cry, to lament, to make some sort of final comments before he climbs permanently inside his own head. But S. says nothing.

My father has, and will die from, a particularly nasty variant of Alzheimer's called Early Onset Familial Alzheimer's disease. As I understand it (and, to be honest, I don't, really), if you were to look very closely at a portion of S.'s fourteenth chromosome—14q24.3, to be precise—you'd find a mutated and otherwise screwed-up presenilin gene, PSEN1, also known as S182, an anomaly passed on from his mother, who had the good sense to die young. While most Alzheimer's shows up in old people, Early Onset AD began to wreck my dad's brain in his late forties or early fifties. He was lucky. It can strike much earlier.

As a result of his ruined and ruinous PSEN1 gene—although it is not at all clear how this occurs—my dad's brain suffers from cerebrocortical atrophy, neurofibrillary tangles, senile plaques, granulovacuolar degeneration, and neuropil threads. None of these are good things. Because of them, he often has no idea what to do with a fork. Because of his mutant PSEN1 gene, S. cannot recall my mother's name.

And because the mutated gene is dominant, there is a 50 percent chance that the child of a person with early-onset familial Alzheimer's will get the disease. Toss a coin in the air. Watch it flip and twirl.

39

Watch it crash to the pavement, spin for a moment, and finally collapse. That is my life.

At some point very soon, I will or will not forget where I put my keys. I will look my friend Terry in the face and realize I have forgotten his name. I will think it is December 1 when, really, it is June 7. I will become depressed, irritable, and possibly psychotic. Seizures, incontinence, hallucinations, mutism. I will slowly become unable to read, identify common objects, or speak coherently. Ultimately, I will be entirely unable to care for myself. Unless, as it turns out, I am heads, not tails. To be sure, I will die. But there is only a fifty–fifty chance I will die from complications of Early Onset Familial Alzheimer's disease.

There is a test I could take to see whether I will end up like my dad. It's been seven years since we discovered the root of his burgeoning confusion. Which means more than two thousand, five hundred mornings waking and wondering whether this will be the day I get tested, the day I discover my fate. And two thousand, five hundred mornings waking up and wondering whether this will be the day I realize I needn't bother, the day a forgotten name or a missed appointment or a wrong turn confirms what I assume to be true— that Alzheimer's will, shortly, abscond with my brain.

King tested within weeks of my dad's diagnosis. He never considered waiting. He thinks I'm a fool for living in the space between knowing and not. He is negative.

Although more than five million people in the United States have AD, the sort that runs in my family is pretty rare and unusually vicious. For example, most old people with the disease do not suffer from myoclonus, uncontrolled muscle twitchings and spasms. S. does, so he gave up feeding himself a while ago.

We eat around the television news, as is our habit. I kneel on the floor at my dad's side, feeding him small portions of stew that has been cooked for so many hours and stirred so vigorously that it has the color and consistency of a chocolate milkshake. S.'s head jerks while I feed him. Bits of beef fall onto his pajamas and the armchair. LeoSayer arrives quickly to clean up the mess.

8

"IS IT MR. Seegerman or Mr. X?" Mary Godfrey greets me with a strong handshake in G-O-D's administrative office, which looks like the command center of a *Fortune* 500 company. She is tall, six feet, thick-boned, with a helmet of unmoving, spray-encrusted, silver hair. Is "bouffant" the word? She has a plain face, small dark eyes, a large nose, and a bit of a mustache. If I passed her on the street I might think, "Transvestite?"

"I was wondering whether you'd make the connection," I say. "How about Gordon?"

Since its founding in the early eighties, G-O-D has taken over both sides of a city block in West Santa Rita, a ruined square mile at the edge of the city. The campus is close to the docks. Moist, salty air from the bay mixes with diesel fumes from tractor-trailers and container ships to form a permanent, low-lying haze. Nearby, the mammoth elevated track for the train to San Francisco stands arrogantly above, whisking commuters to their homes in more lighthearted climes. Its roar echoes through the neighborhood every few minutes, a reminder that this ground is impoverished, untouchable.

Although the surrounding streets are mostly deserted, with half-burned buildings and vacant lots, the structures occupied by the charity—two facing rows of Victorians—have been meticulously restored. The area is an oasis, a sanctuary. Women and children fleeing from abuse, addicts retreating from the substances that harry them, Santa Ritans struggling to climb out of a hole of illiteracy and poverty: they all find refuge here. The place is downright cheery, which is a bit unsettling given the devastated surroundings.

"Gordon, then. I'm looking forward to your performance. Come, let me show you around."

It is perfectly clear to me within minutes of meeting Mary Godfrey that Harold Dunn's story is nonsense. Sister Mary, as everyone calls her (though, like G-O-D's most successful clients, she left her habit behind years ago), has an iron grip on G-O-D's operations. She knows everyone—employees, volunteer staff, clients—by name and goes on for some time about the group's accomplishments. No way she'd let her son assume control of G-O-D. And that she would jeopardize her two decades of work, or let anyone else do so, seems not simply unlikely but inconceivable.

She leads me on a tour of the facilities—a huge kitchen, where G-O-D proves itself worthy of its name, churning out hundreds of meals each day for Santa Rita's elderly and infirm; a counseling center; a job-training facility; a bicycle repair shop run by teens; a women's shelter—and I keep wondering when she will turn to me and break into "Climb Ev'ry Mountain."

There are one or two odd notes to the scene. Two large men follow several steps behind us until we end the tour in Godfrey's office. She says there have been some threats over the years, and her son insists on the protection. Given the location, and Godfrey's very public verbal assaults on Santa Rita's highest-profile drug dealers over the years, the bodyguards make sense. Although I doubt they are necessary. Godfrey is the sort who could karate-chop a gun-toting attacker into submission while tending to a needy five-year-old and throwing together a bouillabaisse. To be sure, none of it would budge her bouffant.

Also, there is something to Mary Godfrey, beyond the halo that hangs above her, that smacks of despotism. Her dedication to G-O-D's mission, to alleviating suffering among the poor and abused and ill and forlorn, seems nearly obsessive. Somehow I feel as if I am following a slightly insane general around a conquered city. I keep glancing back over my shoulder, smiling nervously at the bodyguards, listening to Godfrey spout off about G-O-D's achievements, and thinking "What exactly am I doing? I'm here to talk about Dunn. Why am I being treated like a potential donor?"

When we reach her office, Godfrey introduces me to her son. After Dunn's story, I suppose I'd imagined a more imposing figure. Selmer Godfrey is a homunculus—a little, misshapen man, perhaps forty-five, with a swollen face; wisps of black hair are painted down the sides of his small, pointy head. He has no neck to speak of, and turns his entire body when he looks to either side. He leans precariously to his left when upright. His smile, which appears to be indelible, is positively infectious. Despite his gnarled features, Selmer Godfrey seems to be among the most jovial and least menacing men I have ever met. Further evidence that my client is out of his mind.

I explain my purpose for the meeting—to get a better sense of Dunn, to see if they have any insight into the offense, or any idea how I might help him. They cannot explain the behavior, though they are both aware of his history.

"Harold is a wonder with the books," Mary Godfrey says, looking to her son, who supplies the required confirmation. "To tell you the truth, before he got here we'd had some problems, money missing, some employees we had to let go. He'd been through the program and had been sober for quite some time. He has always appeared to understand the importance of the work we do here, and the sacrifices we must all make to achieve our goals."

"And his job performance? No problems?"

"Our accountants think very highly of his work. We had no reason to believe anything like this would happen."

"What about recent stresses?" Neither knows of any. "What I can tell you," I say, "is that for some reason, probably because there was a child present, the judge has taken a very hard line on the issue of bail."

"Did you know that Mr. Seegerman is the leader of the band for the holiday party?" the elder Godfrey asks her homunculus. His smile grows even wider, which threatens to split his head in half.

"I did not know that. That's wonderful."

"I hope that doesn't pose a problem? I keep my two hats—"

"Not at all," Selmer assures me. "We are all looking forward to it. I could not be a bigger Barry Manilow fan. That was the music I fell in love to."

Hard to imagine.

"We try to expand on it a bit, but I'm sure you'll recognize the songs."

God strike me dead if Selmer Godfrey, all sixty-one bent inches of him, smile never leaving his face, does not stand up and begin to belt out "Mandy." This is hardly the first time my interest in MBM has transmogrified me, helplessly, into a bartender at an all-Barry karaoke bar. And, frankly, it is not the worst version of "Mandy" I've ever heard.

The mother, embarrassed, cuts off her boy. "Selmer, will you please?"

I shake my head agreeably. "We'll be sure to do that one for you."

They both stand. The meeting is over. I came to ask them to help me get my guy out of jail and I haven't even posed the question. There doesn't seem to be any use.

Halfway back to my office, my cell rings. Selmer Godfrey. It sounds as if he is calling from a mobile phone.

"What was the figure you mentioned, for Harold's bail?"

"Ten thousand. A bond is—"

"And you believe Harold won't be able to raise the funds?"

"He says no."

"Thank you for your time, Mr. Seegerman." He hangs up. It is the same chipper voice, the same cordial tone. It is as if he'd called to tell me I'd forgotten my umbrella.

*   *   *

45

I call Terry into my office and give him the rundown. No conspiracy, no bad guys at G-O-D. An unpleasant truth is quickly emerging: Dunn is a nut job and I will be derelict if I do not inform the court. I tell Terry I'll take another shot at settling the case, before the status conference set for the next afternoon. And I ask him to do a couple of hours on the witnesses. Check the addresses, knock on their doors. See if anything seems out of whack.

If it all checks out, as I am sure it will, and Silvie won't budge, I will declare a doubt as to Dunn's competency and off he'll go to the state hospital for a few weeks of observation. I don't favor that approach, and Dunn will hate it, but my hands are tied. I have no defense, an apparently psychotic defendant, and a recalcitrant DA who, I should add, possesses a more than passing ability to ruin my day by just showing up in a room.

Then Duke walks in. He does not knock.

"You settle that wanker yet?"

"The case came in the door five minutes ago, Duke. We haven't even interviewed the witnesses."

He studies his metal clipboard. Duke's clipboard contains a multi-page list of the cases in his division. His highest purpose in life appears to be to make thick black lines through once active matters. He does not care how we make the cases go away, but he cares deeply about how long it takes us to do so. The sooner we make the cases go away, the sooner he gets to make his lines across the clipboard.

"So when are you gonna resolve it?" Duke asks.

"I don't know when I'm going to resolve it. Perhaps I won't resolve it for several years. Who can say?"

"Is there a problem?"

"I don't know, Duke. Because I've only just got the case and I haven't done any *work* on it yet and as you may recall from that one case you tried ten years ago, sometimes it takes doing some *work* on a case before you can settle it."

"Doesn't the guy want to settle?" Terry laughs a little, and I would too, but the alien is still standing there looking like we are having a meeting, not joking around.

"What is so hard to understand? My guy says he's innocent of the crime charged. I realize this doesn't happen very often around here, but it looks like this is a case I'm going to have to actually work up. Does that make sense?"

"I guess."

"Maybe we'll even do some investigation. For example, Terry here might go out and talk to a couple of witnesses for me. Just in case they have something interesting to say."

Duke looks stunned. Investigation is something the real lawyers do. If I were to ask a server at a Taco Bell for a Ketel One martini, straight up, he might give me a look like the one on Duke's face.

"You'll need authorization for that."

I laugh. He does not. "Okay. So, Duke. Looks like I'm going to need to do some investigation on this Dunn case. All right if Terry here goes out and talks to a couple witnesses?"

"Fine," he says, finally leaving. "But don't reinvent the wheel."

Here is one unambiguous indication that Duke is no human being. Although he claims to be a native English speaker, he often uses phrases like this in a nearly, but not exactly appropriate way, like he's grabbing idioms out of an Alien-English dictionary.

9

SATURDAY NIGHT WE play an insurance company's holiday party in the ballroom of a hotel in San Francisco. Terry spent the morning looking into the Dunn case. While we set up and sound-check in the nearly empty room that afternoon, he reports back.

Witness 1, Marjorie Styles. Thirty-two, looks like she might have been around the block several times. Lives with her boyfriend, who looks like he might have been the one chasing her around the block. Definitely substance happy, both of them. Old car, beat-up apartment. Says she works for Merry Maids Cleaners, but Terry couldn't find the listing. One mangy kid.

Styles happily discussed the incident with Terry, confirming the statement she gave Detective Hong. She told Terry she could describe Dunn's package if he'd like. He declined. She also seemed perfectly pleased to reveal she'd been through the G-O-D treatment program twice, and that she thought of Mary Godfrey as a mother to her. Styles has a G-O-D bumper sticker on her 1978 Toyota Corolla station wagon, silver. Terry's take is that the witness is as unsophisticated as she is believable. In other words, very.

"Dunn said that." I look up from a tangle of wires.

"What?"

"That Mary Godfrey is like a mother to him."

"So?"

I shrug.

Witness 2, Lorraine Dykstra, and her husband, Phil, live in my neighborhood, although their house, according to Terry, is in a considerably better state of repair than mine. Fancy house, fancy cars, fancy people.

"My dad did the guy's knees," Terry says. His father is African-American, a former profootball player turned orthopedic surgeon. His mom is a former model, not African-American, from Italy. Did I mention Terry's a looker?

"That's wonderful. How are they holding up?"

"Apparently pretty well. They've gone golfing several times."

"Your father and Phil."

"Apparently. The witness, Lorraine, knows my mom, too. Some kind of neighborhood thing."

"My client is screwed."

The eight-year-old girl was at home, but the parents refused to let Terry talk to her. Lorraine told Terry, as she had Detective Hong, that she didn't see Dunn do anything wrong, but she did see him in the area shortly before the kid said she saw the goods. She also said the kid was pretty upset by the whole thing and had never made up a story like this. The parents believe her. The cops believe her. Terry believes her.

"Any G-O-D connections?"

"Not that I could see. They don't look like they need their meals delivered."

"You ask?"

"They've heard of it, that's about all."

"The husband?"

"Phil."

"What's his deal?"

"Frat boy type, early fifties maybe. Pressed jeans. One of those creases in his chin that makes it look like a little butt. Tucks in his T-shirts."

"Nice detail."

"Thanks." He looks at his notepad, to which is stapled a business

49

card. " 'Senior Vice President, Santa Rita Mutual.' He looks pretty proud of himself."

I point at Terry's head. "Say that again."

"He looks pretty—"

"The guy works for Bartholomew Setz."

"He does?"

"I don't believe it. Bartholomew Setz. The name doesn't ring any bells? Silvie?"

"Your Silvie?"

"Silvie is married to Bartholomew Setz, Junior. This Dykstra dude works for the father. Dunn may be a wanker, but I think I just figured out why Silvie is taking no prisoners in this case. I can't believe she tried to lay it off on Fischer."

"Lay what off?"

"Silvie said Fischer asked her to handle the case and to refuse to deal it, although she couldn't explain where Fischer was coming from. Mystery solved, don't you think?" I say.

"Right." As in, "Perhaps you'd like to sit down for a moment, Gordy, while I rustle up some Valium."

"Terry, Mr. Good-as-New Knees Dykstra is pissed off because his kid gets a surprise anatomy class. He goes to Setz, Setz goes to Junior, Junior goes to Silvie, and boom, my guy goes to state prison."

"Ladies and gentlemen," Preet trumpets into a microphone from behind a door to the ballroom, which empties into a parking lot. We hurry him, freezing our butts off. We've been standing outside for fifteen minutes waiting for the crowd to settle at their tables. The majestic first chords of "I Write the Songs" pipe in over the speakers. "Open up your heart, put your hands together, and welcome, please, a worldwide symphony, Barry X and the Mandys."

"Thank merciful *Gawd*," Maeve says.

She pushes us through the door into the dark room. Maeve's face is

tabula rasa white, unblemished, unfreckled, creamy. She is preterna-
turally profane. Her nose is long and sloping, like Richard Nixon's.
Her lips are elastic and typically painted bright pink. She is forty-three,
from South Carolina, with the accent to prove it. She is, as she often
tells strangers within thirty seconds of meeting them, a "lez-bean." She
is buxom and full-bellied and thick-thighed and can put her whole fist
in her mouth. We ask her to do this quite often, as it helps her not to
speak. Maeve has some difficulty not speaking.

We rush onto the makeshift stage and begin our show. Like MBM's,
our performances are thoroughly orchestrated, and carefully sculpted
to match the venue. We've done enough of these corporate affairs to
know not to go too far outside the box. At Ted's, we'll take a standard
Manilow tune—"Weekend in New England," for instance—and
tweak it until it is nearly unrecognizable. But for an insurance
company's holiday party, we're basically a Barry cover band. Some
of the numbers we soup up so the crowd can dance. "I Write the
Songs" turns into a funky reggae tune after the first verse. We rock up
"This One's for You" and "Can't Smile Without You." But we don't
go too deep into the albums—we stick to the hits, play for an hour and
fifteen minutes, tell a few jokes, and turn it over to the DJ for the rest of
the evening. At Ted's we often play a few of Preet's songs in a set. But
these people have come to hear Barry, to dance, to ignore us and sing
across the table to one another, their mouths filled with rubber chicken
and bad wine.

I always feel a little cheapened after these gigs. I'm not an im-
personator, I'm an interpreter. I don't look like Barry Manilow, I don't
sound like him. Barry X and the Mandys is homage, not a dress-up
band. We play this music because we believe in it, and because we feel
strongly that it has never been adequately appreciated, particularly by
the types of people who wouldn't think of standing in line for Barry
tickets—the intelligentsia, the literati, the critics. But we decided a
long time ago that exposure is exposure, and money is money, and

until we get the record done, until we expand beyond our loyal Santa Rita audience to the national scene, until we get the cover of *Rolling Stone*, we'll play the Christmas and July Fourth gigs. And, to prevent turning the audiences against us, we won't play, for example, a ten-minute punk version of the lesser-known MBM ballad "Seven More Years."

The show goes well. The crowd loves us. We have been in a definite groove for some time, and though we do not discuss it, we are all praying the magic will last until after the next Ted's show. There, unless something goes terribly wrong, Barry Manilow will appear. With luck, he will smile upon us and sign off on our record project. Not a tribute album, although our adoration will be obvious. A reimagining. I have faith that MBM will be proud of what we have done. Because he is, and has always been, first and foremost, a composer and an arranger. Long before he was an icon, long before he sold his fifty millionth record, he was a musician. He will see the value in reaching new audiences, in making the case for the versatility of the songs, for their distinction.

We do not speak as we pack up. Superstition, I guess. We all know how good we were. No reason to rip it to shreds.

Several people, a few who are a martini or two past their limit, come up to say hello. We are polite, but busy. And anxious to get out of there.

I have my back turned when a female voice says, "Why the Mandys?"

A Barry Manilow ignoramus. Not enough to make me turn around.

Terry drops his bass into its case and sings to himself: "She came and she asked without thinking, please send her away, oh . . ."

"Don't you agree the name is a bit emasculating?" Preet asks, wrapping a guitar cord around and around from his elbow to his hand. "Frankly, I've always felt uncomfortable with it."

Preet Singh, our Theosophist electronics wizard, whose real name is Charanpreet, meaning "One Who Loves the Lord's Lotus Feet," is short, round, with a single eyebrow, a soft, carefully trimmed, shiny black beard, and unnaturally large feet and hands. His face is fleshy and inordinately mobile. His family are Sikh. Preet's head is always wrapped with a turban. Tonight the turban is emerald colored. I play piano; Terry plays bass and guitar; Maeve plays drums. Preet plays orchestra, and everything else.

"It's news to me you had any balls to begin with." Maeve cannot control herself.

"Please try to ignore them." I have my back to the voice, my hands tangled in wires. "It's from one of Barry Manilow's first hits." I turn to face the voice and quickly have the feeling that my nose is too large, my hair unruly, my breath sour; that I am not smart enough or good-looking enough or talented enough; that I am deeply and fundamentally unworthy.

I stick out my hand. "I'm Gordon Seegerman."

Fifteen minutes later Terry, Preet, and I finish packing Preet's van. We stand around sharing one of Maeve's cigarettes. A postgig ritual.

"Hello, I'm Gordon Seegerman." Preet offers his hand to Terry, sounding serious.

"Wait a minute. *I'm* Gordon Seegerman," Terry answers, shaking enthusiastically.

Maeve joins in. "Excuse me, *I'm* Gordon Seegerman. Are those your real tits?"

Preet now: "Hello, I'm Gordon Lightfoot."

Terry: "Hello. I'm Flash Gordon."

For some reason my extremely brief, unremarkable interaction with the insurance company employee, whose name I can hardly recall, results in this inane interchange.

"What?" I say.

"I was going ask you if you needed any help scraping your tongue off the floor," Maeve says.

"I'm going home."

"You get her number?"

"No."

"No?"

"Gimme a break. She said she liked the show."

"What's her name?"

"Myla and something Slavic I can't remember."

Maeve looks at Terry with a smirk. "I'll be referring to her as Ms. Hair."

Maeve lays eyes on Myla's perfectly straight, satiny blond curtain and seconds later she comes up with the perfectly dismissive nickname. The woman is a genius of sorts.

"No number?" Terry says.

"*No.*" Yes.

10

"**YOUR HUSBAND DOESN'T** happen to work with a guy named Phil Dykstra?" Silvie walks up, looking harried and not particularly happy to see me.

"Hello, Gordy. What are you talking about?"

"Ah hah."

"That clears it up."

I am sitting outside the chambers of Judge Rufus Heymann, who drew the trial assignment for the Dunn matter. We'll meet with the judge off the record before the initial status hearing this afternoon.

What typically happens at these chambers meetings is the judge yells at the lawyers and tells them to settle the case. Judges don't like to try cases any better than lawyers do. Trials take time. Trials cost money. Trials involve jurors, and jurors are almost always unhappy to be there. Trials also necessitate rulings, and rulings require judges to act like judges, which is hard for them because judges, beneath their robes, are almost always prosecutors. And also rulings sometimes lead to reversals by the Court of Appeal, and no judge likes to be told, by three other, more senior judges, that he or she is an idiot. So I expect Judge Heymann to tell Silvie to offer me something, and I intend to take it.

"Aha, aha," I respond.

"I don't have time for this. Is Heymann in?"

"Lorraine Dykstra is your witness?"

She looks at the file and speaks without looking up. "This may be difficult for you to grasp, but this case is the least of my problems right now. Can we go in?"

"Lorraine Dykstra."

"The mother."

"Married to Phil Dykstra. Father of your kid witness, Callie Dykstra."

"Is this leading somewhere?"

"And Phil Dykstra just so happens to be a big wig at Santa Rita Mutual." That gets her attention. "Holy conflict of interest, Batman."

"What conflict? So maybe Bart and the father of my witness are colleagues. I've never met the man. I've never even heard the name."

"And this little co-inky-dink has nothing to do with your 'plead to the sheet' position in this case."

"No." She looks surprised, though.

"Well, you better tell Fischer I smell a rat." She laughs for several seconds. A response that not only lacks respect for my position, but also shows no regard for the memory of our long love affair.

"I am going to say exactly that to Garland Fischer—that you smell a rat."

"You do that."

Judge Heymann is thought by most defense lawyers to be a pretty decent draw. Unlike ninety percent of his colleagues, he never worked in the district attorney's office. He spent twenty years at a big firm before being appointed to the bench five years ago. I've never tried a case in front of him, but he has a reputation for intelligence and fairness. He is a rare creature in the Santa Rita Superior Court—a real live honest-to-goodness judge.

He waves us into his chambers and opens the file. I've never heard him speak and I nearly fall out of my chair when he does. He is a tall, thick-set man with broad shoulders and a close-cropped, graying beard. He is African-American, with a handsome face, dressed off the bench in luxuriously tailored suits. And, he sounds a hell of lot like Mickey Mouse. I swear, I think about checking to see if someone is under the desk with Heymann's nuts in a vice. The man positively squeaks.

"Ah yes, Mr. Dunn." He shakes his head. "Couldn't quite keep the family jewels in the safe."

"No, sir," I say, digging a pen into my palm, trying not to laugh.

He looks at me. "I'll be glad to go on the record later, counsel, but I thought we might as well tee this one up right away. I have substantial conflicts in this case. And I'll tell you right now that if you or your client has the slightest doubt about my impartiality, do us all a favor and speak up. I'd hate to get down the road and have to send you to another department."

"I understand, your honor."

"To begin with, my good friend and former client is Bartholomew Setz, Senior, Ms. Hernandez's father-in-law. My firm was and, as far as I know still is, outside counsel for Santa Rita Mutual, Mr. Setz's company, although I have no continuing economic interest in that work. I officiated at Ms. Hernandez's wedding, and was proud to do it. I am fond of her husband. He played ball with my boys. And, perhaps most important, I had a working relationship with Phil Dykstra, who is married to one witness and is the father of another. I cannot remember meeting Lorraine and I am quite sure I never met the child. There you go, counsel. You say the word and I'll call Judge Reasoner right now for a reassignment."

I pause a moment, but only for effect. "No. I appreciate your candor, Judge. My client will proceed in this department."

Given Heymann's rep for being a halfway decent judge, and the other choices at the Hall, I figure I might as well stay put. It rarely makes sense to jettison a judge with serious conflicts. All judges have biases, and often those biases are against criminal defendants. The only difference here is that Judge Heymann has put his prejudices on the table. Having done so, he will, I am confident, go out of his way to be fair, which means I might actually win a ruling or two. If we move, I'd be appearing in front of one of Heymann's colleagues, most likely a former DA, who'd be certain to take revenge for my having suggested—by dumping Heymann—that he could not act impartially. There is no choice, really. Heymann is our guy.

"Very well. What's the offer, counsel?" He looks at Silvie.

"Your honor, we feel that due to the prior and the child involved that an appropriate outcome in this case would be the legislative mid-term and no less."

"There's no offer?"

"The offer is the sheet."

Judge Heymann studies the charges. "Which amounts to—"

"The mid-term would be three years state prison."

"Three years state prison."

"That is our position."

"Why would we take that deal?" I speak up.

"Looks like your guy could do five under the aggravated term," the judge says.

"That may be, your honor. But there aren't any aggravating factors here. This is a wildly overcharged misdemeanor case. The guy should do nine months county, max. Somehow, probably because of the color of my tie that day, Judge Reasoner set bail in this matter at ten thousand dollars. At the very least I'd ask you to reduce that to fifteen hundred—something reasonable."

"I didn't mention bail. Did you hear me mention bail?" Judge Heymann asks Silvie, who shakes her head.

"I apologize. As you might imagine, my client would prefer to go to trial, then plead for no benefit whatsoever."

"It does seem to me you're overdoing it, Silvie, but if you want to try the case we'll try the case."

Wait a second. This is when Heymann's supposed to turn blue and tell her he's not going to waste two days of court time over a silly exposure case. I suppose he's too busy remembering the enchanting nuptials. I'd give a limb to have been there with a truckload of paint balls.

"I think 'overdoing it' is an understatement. The prior is more than ten years old. Despite the profusion of charges, there is a single culpable act. One. Three years state prison is silly."

"That's an interesting question. If your guy exposes himself on a street corner and over the course of an hour fifty people walk by, how many crimes has he committed?" Oh, Jesus, I'm back in law school.

"I haven't researched that issue, your honor, and I will certainly do so. But in any event, given the circumstances here, three years?"

The judge is done. He closes the file.

"Talk to the legislature counsel. Ms. Hernandez wants to practice her trial skills, who are we to get in her way?" This is as close as Heymann is going to come to beating on Silvie.

"I think I could convince my client to take a state prison term, but not three years." I'm begging.

"Silvie?"

"Can't do it, your honor. It's the girl. Off the record?" The judge and I shrug. "My sense is Garland wants to look good on these kid cases. We've lost a few high-profile ones over the years and one of his consultants says it's a weakness. Dunn should have waited until after the election."

"Politics, law, it's all fun and games until someone loses an eye," the judge squeaks, escorting us out of his office. "See you folks this afternoon."

I get back to my office to find a handwritten note from the recently released Harold Dunn. "Thanks for everything." And a number. I call over to the jail to ask about the bail. The deputy says a man in a suit, with ten thousand dollars in cash, came in this morning. The wanker went free before noon. I call Dunn's number, but there is no answer.

11

DUNN'S RELEASE SEEMS like good news.

Jail has its purposes. I have had clients who were unmanageable, unreachable outside such a highly restrictive setting. But in most cases, particularly for a guy like Harold, who is inexperienced with incarceration, and who appears to reside on the brink of mental collapse, jail screws with his reasoning skills. Confinement, the constant risk of assault, the bad food, the infantilizing—inmates find themselves with bed and bath times, dressed in bright orange pajamas—it all so strips some people of their humanness that they lose the ability to think clearly about their lives, about their choices.

I figure Dunn will get out and he'll relax a little. He'll come back this afternoon for his hearing and see that it's all not going to just go away. His problems—his legal problems, at least—are real and require him to make the tough decision.

There is no way to try the case. Given Silvie's position, my advice to Dunn, and his logical choice, will be to plead to the sheet and rely on Judge Heymann not to hammer him too badly on the sentence. Probation is a possibility. The DA will oppose it, but my sense is Heymann sees nothing about the case that makes him cringe. And even if Dunn gets state prison time, I figure he'll get the mitigated term, a little more than a year with credits. Not the end of the world.

As it turns out, Harold Dunn's release is not good news. As it happens, I figure incorrectly.

Silvie and I arrive back in court that afternoon. Since we had settled nothing earlier other than my lack of objection to Heymann's presiding over the case, it is now time to put matters on the record. This is the way justice is done. The lawyers and the judges hash things out in chambers, and then the defendant and the public get a watered-down version in court. Heymann's afternoon calendar is not as crazy as the master calendar, but there is a long line of lawyers waiting to get in and out of there. The clerk calls our case first. I look around. No Dunn.

"Your honor, Gordon Seegerman, assistant public defender, appearing for Mr. Dunn. I don't see my client, Judge, and I'd ask you to pass the matter. He unexpectedly bailed out this morning and there may have been some miscommunication about the appearance."

"I'd be happy to issue a bench warrant, have the sheriff pick him up. That would save you the trouble."

"That's very big of you, Judge."

"It's my pleasure, Mr. Seegerman."

"No, thank you. I don't think that will be necessary. I'll find him. If you could just pass the matter. I'll inform the clerk when he arrives."

"Next." He is not pleased. Silvie has to be elsewhere. I go to call Dunn.

The number rings and rings. I call my office to see if he's been in, but no one has heard from him. I try Mary Godfrey's office. She is out. I know virtually nothing about this man. His address is in the file, a photo of his driver's license. I should let the court issue the warrant. Why is this my problem? Silvie is waiting for me outside the courtroom.

"I'll go find him," I tell her.

"You should have 1368ed this guy while you had the chance."

"If you'd have been remotely reasonable, we'd have settled the thing already. But noooo, you're concerned for the child. Mark my words. She'll look back on this as a valuable learning experience."

"Find Dunn. I'll have my cell on."

I turn to leave.

"Gordy."

"Yeah," I answer.

"If he's gone, I want to know, soon. Seriously. I have to protect my ass here." So many possible rejoinders, if only we were still sleeping together. I am dumbstruck with the sheer potential of it. "Hello, Gordy? We understand each other?"

"Okay, okay. The guy just got out of jail. He might have more important things on his mind than a status conference. I probably forgot to tell him. You know me."

"That's not funny."

"I'll call you, I promise."

Silvie Hernandez broke my heart. That is true. She left me and Barry, she married the Junior Setz. She abandoned all that is good and right in the world and went to work as a deputy DA. But I have given you the wrong impression if you think Silvie dumped me.

My dad developed Alzheimer's symptoms early, in his late forties, although for years he and everyone else assumed it was the drinking. Pop was an alcoholic for sure, certainly after my mom died, but he was an extraordinarily functional drunk. He still worked like a maniac and had a reputation as one of the best detectives in the Santa Rita police department. The cops respected his ability to drink like life was an unending wake, and to do his job so effectively anyway. "The guy had balls of steel." How many times have I heard that, some bombed cop blabbering on about the great S. Seegerman? The metaphor is mutable, of course. Sometimes his balls are concrete. Sometimes they are lead. They are almost always likened to a hard, dense material.

He wasn't much of a factor at home. Ferdy was there, and a slew of housekeepers. My dad could be found, when he was needed to sign a check or a school form, at a bar or on the job.

Then, in a relatively short time, it all fell apart. He made some serious mistakes at work and eventually lost his job. The diagnosis came years later.

I was twenty-six years old. Silvie was my girl. We appeared together as Harry Loves Ethel (a reference to one of MBM's first musical partnerships), at open mike nights, in cafés. I'd been in the PD's office for a year. She was making big money at a corporate firm and we were having the time of our lives spending it. My dad's illness was a strain, but, frankly, not that big a strain. We'd never been that close, and Ferdy seemed to have matters in hand. I wasn't around the house much.

Then the doctors discovered the genetic basis of my dad's cognitive deterioration, and King and I learned there was a fifty–fifty chance we'd get the disease. Silvie said she was in. It made no difference. She'd be with me whether I chose to get tested or not, whether I developed AD or not. She was in.

What happened to us is as simple as it is sad. I left. I thought about it and believed it was the right thing to do, that I shouldn't saddle Silvie or anyone with my catastrophe. I sat her down one sunny afternoon in the apartment we shared and told her that the risk of losing my mind made it impossible for me to commit to a relationship. That is what I thought. I told her I loved her. I told her I was sorry. Then I walked out, closed the door behind me, and moved back in with my dad and Ferdy.

A few weeks passed. Then I changed my mind. I went back. She said no. I returned again and again, with flowers and poetry and tears and anger and regret spilling out of my ears. Nothing worked. I had broken whatever spell she'd been under, and now she wanted to move on. She said she now believed what I said, that it would be too hard for her, that it was too much of a burden to take on. But that was a fib, for sure. The real reason she wouldn't take me back was because I'd left, because I'd proven myself too weak, too scared, to stay.

*   *   *

I sit in my office for an hour, becoming angrier and angrier at Dunn. I drive by the address in the file. He lives in half of a duplex in a rotten part of town not too far from the G-O-D complex. No one is home. I speak with a neighbor who says she heard some noise in the apartment earlier in the day, but nothing recently. She says Dunn's car is gone. I wonder whether the guy offed himself.

While I am speaking to the neighbor, a white van pulls up, across the street from the building's small front yard. The man driving stays put. I do not recognize him. The passenger door slams and I see another man, large, dressed casually, walk purposefully toward Dunn's door. I push the neighbor a step into her apartment so he cannot see me. The man bashes his fist against the door of Dunn's apartment repeatedly, and then peers in the front window. I am watching with my head around the corner. No doubt Dunn's neighbor thinks I am insane, perhaps criminally so. She begins to speak. I shush her. The man takes several steps toward us. I duck inside the apartment and pull the door almost closed. The neighbor and I are almost face to face. I grin. She does not.

"Can I—"

I put my index finger to my lips to quiet her. The footsteps begin to recede. I look out the door and the man is walking to his van, which quickly screeches off. On the back I see the G-O-D emblem.

I back out through Dunn's neighbor's door, hoping she does not begin to scream. "Thank you. Sorry. Thank you."

Back at the office I call Silvie and we return to court, toward the end of Heymann's calendar.

"Mr. Seegerman, please enlighten us."

"Your honor, I am certain this is my mistake. And I apologize to the court. As you know, Mr. Dunn's bail was set at a very high level, and I don't think either of us anticipated that he would be getting out. I assumed he would be in custody, and I cannot swear I told him about the appearance. I believe G-O-D, Mr. Dunn's employer, generously provided the bail money. I am certain Ms. Godfrey, who directs that organization, would not have done so if there were any chance at all my client would seek to leave the jurisdiction."

"Is this your way of informing us that Mr. Dunn is not here?"

"Depends what you mean by 'here.' "

"Yes, I suppose it does. Bench warrant will issue—"

"Please, your honor, I feel very bad about this. I truly believe I failed to inform my client about the status conference, and it will damage my relationship with him if as a result of my mistake he is rearrested." I turn to Silvie for help, but she stares straight ahead. "I have no reason to believe he has fled. I would ask the court to reset the matter for tomorrow morning. He will be here."

The judge turns to Silvie. "Counsel?"

"I'll submit it, your honor. I'm concerned. Mr. Dunn was informed about this status conference at the last appearance. But perhaps there has been some miscommunication. Mr. Dunn deserves a chance." Silvie looks at me when she says the last words, and I can see the pity in her eyes. Miscommunication, my ass.

"Nine A.M., counsel."

I leave the courtroom and sit on a bench. I try Mary Godfrey's office again. Phone to my ear, I wave thanks to Silvie as she walks by, wagging her finger.

"Mr. Seegerman, what can I do for you?"

"I seem to have misplaced my client. I was hoping you might have seen him."

"No. Isn't he in jail?"

"Not since this morning. He bailed out, thanks to you."

"I don't understand."

Uh-oh.

"Well, someone posted bail for him. Someone with ten thousand dollars in cash."

"And you thought that was me?" She laughs. "Heavens no. I am very fond of Harold, but ten thousand dollars."

"Could it have been Selmer?"

Now she laughs hard. "Oh, no, I don't think so."

"Now I'm very confused."

"I'm sorry," she says. She doesn't sound particularly sorry.

"If you see him, please let him know it's very important that he reach me."

"I could use a few words with Harold myself. Perhaps if you see him you might tell him the same from me?"

"Absolutely. Sorry to bother you."

Before I can properly say good-bye my cell phone beeps. Another call.

"Yeah."

"Gordon Seegerman?"

"That's me."

"This is Officer Sokolow at Central." Oh, Jesus. Dunn's done himself in. Or wanked himself back into jail. At least I won't have to go chasing after him. I'm supposed to be in rehearsal tonight. "I was wondering if you could come down and pick up your father?"

12

THIS ISN'T THE first time my dad has escaped, gone wandering, half-dressed, half-cocked, fully out of his gourd. But the timing is not good. I call King and leave him a frustrated message. Why do I always have to be the one to get these calls? Ferdy doesn't drive anymore, which is happy news for the public's safety, but bad for me at the moment. I head over to Santa Rita police headquarters.

"I'm Gordon Seegerman. You have my dad somewhere?"

"See-ger-man." The name. A normal name, no? Unremarkable. But when the cops say it, it's like someone is drawing a broken piece of metal slowly across a chalkboard. The desk officer looks down at his roster. No luck.

"You know what the arrest was for?"

Now he is baiting me. Everyone in the department knows or knows of my dad, his story, his undoing. The bit about him suffering from a serious illness, about that having most likely been the cause of his ruin, seems not to have played as widely or as well.

"An Officer Sokolow called me not fifteen minutes ago. My father is Detective S. Seegerman. If you call that officer you might be able to locate him."

A few minutes later Sokolow leads S. down the hall. He looks well, though he was found wandering, shirtless, in a light rain, a mile from my house. S. objects to my taking him into custody. Sometimes my dad plays this game intentionally, to preserve what's left of his will. Sometimes recalcitrance or obstreperousness is his way of making clear he's not quite ready to surrender. But today he simply cannot figure out why the police want to turn him over to a complete stranger.

I thank Sokolow and drive us home.

"Where were you off to, Pop?" Nothing. "You know, I like hanging out with you and everything. But you could just call and say you miss me. You don't always have to get my attention by acting out. All right?" I look at him. He is staring straight ahead, just like a chastised teen might. "Anyway, I'm sorry if you feel neglected. It's just a little crazy at work right now. Remember I mentioned that detective, Hong? Anyway, the guy he busted, who I now represent, missed his court appearance, and between us, I'm a little worried I spaced out telling him."

"Where's King?"

"I have no idea. I would have been happy if he came for you, but I couldn't reach him. How come you took off again?"

"To get out of the house. I like to walk."

"That's fine, but could you wear a shirt next time? And take LeoSayer. He needs more exercise."

I chat at him until we make our way back to the house. We find Lillian, S.'s part-time caretaker, busy with her soaps. She thought S. was asleep in his room the whole time. She crosses herself repeatedly, apologizes profusely, and threatens to beat my father with a broom if he attempts to bolt again. While she hustles him upstairs I call my office. No word from Dunn.

My dad lies in his bed, staring into space. I watch through a crack in the door, wondering whether there is relief in his haze.

Ferdy walks up behind me and puts his hand on my shoulder.

"Quit beating yourself up. It's not your fault."

"I'm starting to think King's right."

My brother has been lobbying us to move S. someplace where the care is more reliable than we can offer at home. The thought sickens me.

Ferdy is at home some, but he spends a lot of time cruising around Santa Rita with his gang of octogenarian rabble-rousers. I have work. King comes for dinner a few nights each week. Lillian handles my dad brilliantly, but we have insufficient cash to keep her around full-time. On her off days I drive my dad to a day program and pick him up in the evening. S. objects no matter what—to being left alone with Lillian, to leaving the house, to being kept in the house. He resents the old folks at the day program, he resents my grandfather for having a reliable brain, he resents me for leaving him every morning and for coming home every night.

There is no happy solution. We have barely enough money to place him in a decent home for a year or two—money left over from my mom's estate. Probably after that we'll have to sell the house. I suppose that is why I resist. S. isn't going to get any easier to handle. Soon enough, his needs will exceed our caretaking skills. But the minute he moves out, the clock starts ticking on the Seegerman family's occupation of 4200 Candlewood. My mom's ghost lives in the house and I am not keen on leaving her alone.

Back at the office. Late afternoon. Still no Dunn.

"How you doing?" Maeve wanders into my office to kill some time. Her official title is something like administrative director, but "office despot" better describes her role.

"I suck. My client has disappeared. How are you?"

"Perfectly aflutter. Got me a date with a fine young lady this evening. Barely made it out of diapers." Maeve is proud of the forty pounds she has on me.

"You're diseased."

"You got a minute to talk about musical matters?"

"No."

For the next ten minutes Maeve rants, lectures, and harangues on the subject of Preet's orchestration of her numbers. Too lush, too rich.

"Can you say 'Liberace?' If Preet wants to drown himself in syrup it's okay with me, but not on my songs." She is through, for the moment.

Terry arrives. "We practicing tonight?"

I have completely forgotten.

"I'll let you know. Dunn's split and if I don't get him into court tomorrow Heymann's going to issue a bench warrant. I don't know when I'll be able to get out of here."

Maeve laughs. "Look at this, Terrence. The little man is concerned about his child-molesting client. You want me to have Aineen make some calls? Hospitals, that sort of thing."

Aineen is as likely to successfully complete such a task as Maeve is to simultaneously renounce tobacco, bourbon, and married and under-age women.

"He's not a child molester, and I'm just worried I spaced out telling him about the appearance." They understand the implications of me forgetting anything, ever. "Anyway, I doubt he's in the hospital. Something else is going on here, and Harold Dunn decided not to stick around to find out how it ends." I stand up and put on my jacket. "A misdemeanor defendant ends up in High Power, tells me he can't make fifteen hundred bail, then makes ten thousand. The whole thing makes no sense. You guys want to go for a ride?"

A clerk at the county jail had given me the name on Dunn's bail receipt: Gerald Fitzgerald. Mr. Fitzgerald was in such a rush to hand over his ten thousand dollars to the Santa Rita sheriff that he left no phone number. He did fill out the address section on the receipt, someplace fairly close to Dunn's house. Good, I think. We'll find this friend and get a line on the wanker.

I have no problem with the guy taking off, which will have the same effect on my life as his taking a deal. He flees, the case goes away, and I get back to MBM. No Dunn, no prep, no trial, no mess. On the lam, he's the cops' problem, not mine. But I have to make sure the whole thing isn't my fault, that I haven't forgotten to tell him about the appearance. I figure before I let Judge Heymann order the cops to pick him up, the least I can do is make an effort to find him.

Terry knocks. An elderly Chinese man cracks the door half an inch.

"Good afternoon, sir. My name—" The door slams. We hear loud voices. We hear the word "police" several times. In my opinion, the manner in which the word "police" is used in this case does not suggest that the people inside the house are major contributors to the SRPD's benevolent fund.

"Not police. No police here. Mr. Fitzgerald?" Terry says loudly.

The door opens again, wider. A wall of a man, Samoan or from someplace else in the South Pacific, towers above us.

"May I help you?" He quickly catches sight of Maeve's physique and loses sight of Terry and me. Maeve has enormous breasts. It is impossible not to notice them. But I sense our wall-man has the whole Maeve in mind. She is a consequential woman, just the sort of full-figured, hip-swinging gal Mr. Samoan could proudly take home to Mama. Of course, Maeve, upon arrival at Mr. Samoan's house, could be trusted immediately to start hitting on his teenage sister. I can feel his heartache already.

"We have this as the address of a Mr. Fitzgerald. Gerald Fitzgerald."

The man yells at the top of his lungs, without taking his eyes off Maeve.

"Gerald Fitzgerald. Would a Mr. Gerald Fitzgerald come to the door." No one appears. "It seems you're mistaken." The man pronounces his words attentively and softly. I am desperate to know what is going on in that house. But he does not invite us in.

"You want to check around back?" Terry asks.

"No. It's bogus. No phone, bad address. Dunn's history. Let's forget it."

I turn back as we walk away from the dilapidated house. The

71

curtain in the front window splits open. Wall-man watches, with a wistful look on his face, as true love slips from his grasp.

Before going home that night, I stop by the jail. The clerk remembers Fitzgerald—big guy, dark hair, mustache, nice suit, late thirties maybe. A businessman or a really well-dressed chauffeur. Never took off his sunglasses. She still has the pile of cash in her drawer—one hundred crisp Ben Franklins.

"He say anything? Make any conversation?" Nope. Stood there like an obelisk. Until she handed him a copy of the bail receipt. Then he said thank you, and left. He may have had a Southern accent.

The deputy at the front desk—the one who'd been at the Ted's show—seems pleased to see me.

"Seegerman, right?" The edge is gone.

"Good memory."

"You'll never believe this, but my girlfriend saw you play the other night."

"Really," I say, skeptically. Someone must be wearing a wire. "Where was that?"

"You played at her company's holiday party."

"That's amazing. You guys are almost like groupies now."

"She loved it. She says you're a genius. Seriously."

"That's very nice." I am so pleased and my head is ballooning so dangerously fast, I nearly forget my purpose. "Hey, maybe you can do me a favor."

I spend the next half hour leafing through the public visitors' logs. No one came to see Dunn. In the week he was in custody, no friend or family member dropped in to wish him well. I think maybe I can figure out where to find him. But what I learn is that Dunn was, and probably still is, alone.

"Thanks a lot," I say.

"You find anything?"

"Not really. You remember my guy, Dunn?"

"The faces kind of blend together."

"He was in High Power. You had him upstairs for some reason, even though he was in on a misdemeanor."

"Skinny white guy. Greasy looking. Really big head."

"That's him. He bailed out and I can't seem to catch up with him."

"Lot of action on that guy."

"How's that?" I wonder.

"Attorney visits."

"I'm his lawyer. I only came twice."

"Don't ask me. I just remember processing him over and over." He calls up a screen with a list of official visitors: those, like me, who can come at any time and who are entitled to private, interview-room meetings with the inmate. My name appears, twice. Below it is the name of another person, identified as Dunn's lawyer, who visited several times in the past week. Gerald M. Fitzgerald.

13

NEXT MORNING. BACK in front of Judge Heymann, who looks unhappy to see me sans client.

"Your honor, I must apologize to the court. Mr. Dunn has apparently disappeared. I have no explanation."

Heymann issues a warrant for Harold Dunn's arrest.

Silvie, waiting outside the courtroom, is pissed.

"This comes as a complete surprise to you?"

"The guy told me he couldn't make fifteen hundred. I had no reason not to believe him. He lives in a shithole in West Santa Rita. I have no idea where he got that money. I can tell you this, though—it isn't from G-O-D. As far as I can tell the guy just walked out of jail and disappeared."

That is, with the assistance of one Gerald M. Fitzgerald. I wasn't about to hand Silvie or the cops that lead. My job is to help Dunn. If I can give him a head start, without landing in jail myself, why not? Dunn doesn't seem likely to be a threat to public safety.

"You told Heymann Mary Godfrey came up with the money. Is that now incorrect?"

"That is incorrect."

"Well, what is correct?"

"If and when I find that out, I'll let you know."

"Please do. Fischer's gonna freak on this," she says, feeling sorry for herself.

"It's not your fault the guy made bail. Jesus, he should have OR'd."

Had Judge Reasoner been more reasonable, he would have released Dunn on his own recognizance, without insisting on bail at all.

Silvie suddenly becomes snippy. "No, he should have been 'no bail,' because as we now see, he was a flight risk."

"As they say, hindsight is twenty-twenty."

"As *they* say, if this guy shows up, I'm going to grind him into a soupy mush and feed him to my dog."

My heart plunges into my stomach. When did you get a dog?

The news thrills Duke. Although not officially a dead case—it has not been settled, dismissed, or tried to a verdict—boss-in-theory can, logically, mark it off his list. Dunn split. There is nothing else for me to do. The cops have a warrant for his arrest, but by now he is in Brazil or New Jersey, someplace he can start a new life. His small crime will hardly lead to roadblocks or a Tommy Lee Jones–led manhunt. Dunn's name goes into the computer; if a cop somewhere stops him for rolling through a stop sign, and if the cop thinks to check for warrants, the wanker will be back in the county jail a few days later. But until then, he is forgotten.

Terry and I sit in my office batting around the odd circumstances in which Dunn made bail and then evaporated. I do a Web search for Gerald M. Fitzgerald. A guy by that name wrote an article on Indian nudists in 1935. That fits, in a way. Maybe Dunn's the leader of a cult of wankers who worship South Asian naked people. Also, Gerald Fitzgerald was the fifteenth Earl of Desmond, but at nearly five hundred years old, I cannot see how he could be Dunn's pal.

Duke draws his black marker carefully across the front of his clipboard. "Seems like she's a dead one. Suki"—the preliminary hearing supervisor—"needs some help. She has a couple of people out."

I stand up and wave Terry to join me. "Sorry, Duke. I'm booked." We walk out. Duke comes after us, but I ignore him. No new cases until after the MBM show. I have plenty of little things to keep me busy at work, and as S. seems to be deteriorating, I feel I deserve a break. I thank Dunn for taking a powder.

Which doesn't mean I'm done with him entirely. I am still a little concerned and a little curious. I sort of like the guy. And I worry about him. The kind of like and worry you might feel for a flawed but engaging character in a book. Someone has ripped fifty pages from the middle of my novel. I can't help but try to piece them back together.

Terry and I drive over to Dunn's place. Through a crack between tattered curtains in the front window I can see the place is a mess, but it doesn't look abandoned. I knock on the neighbor's door and explain the situation, tell her I'm concerned for Dunn's safety. Her eyes on Terry the whole time, she offers no resistance and shows us to a rock where she has seen Dunn stash a spare key. But we don't need it. When I push the key into the deadbolt, the mechanism falls off and the door swings open. It isn't clear whether the lock was purposely broken or is simply in the same state of disrepair as the apartment itself.

The unit is drab. The walls empty, the paint peeling from the ceiling. Old newspapers, takeout containers, a mangy stuffed animal I choose not to touch, a rotten armchair and stained rug, a few dirty dishes in the sink—all of it looks like the set of a movie about a lonesome ex-alcoholic wanker. It could not be drearier.

"What am I looking for?" Terry asks.

"I don't know. Wanker manuals, trench coats, kiddie porn. The usual."

I wander around and keep blabbering to cover up the unpleasant feeling that slowly overtakes me inside the apartment. Harold Dunn is in trouble.

He's been here, that much is clear. He must have come by after he made bail. Yesterday's *Santa Rita Journal* is on a small table in the kitchen. The sports section is the only one that has been opened.

"You notice anything weird about this place?" Terry bellows from another room.

"What?"

"You see a telephone?"

We cross paths looking for a phone, but there is none. I end up in Dunn's bedroom.

You can tell a lot about a person from his bedding. I remember my mother's during her final days, piles of white comforters and down pillows with flowered cases. Eventually she withered and disappeared into them, so that all that was left of her was her sickly sweet smell, something like the orange-colored sauce on sweet-and-sour pork. Dunn sleeps in a single bed. The blanket is dark green, and thin, though the place is not well heated. There is one ratty pillow. An unplugged television sits on the floor in the middle of the room. Some polyester short-sleeved dress shirts hang in the closet. A small tattered suitcase is stuffed into a shelf.

Dunn hasn't fled. Razors, shaving cream, and a bottle of sleeping pills remain in the bathroom cabinet. A framed picture of Dunn and Mary Godfrey at Dunn's graduation from rehab hangs on his bedroom wall. A dresser is half filled with clothing. The wanker is close enough to stop by every so often, to replenish his supplies. But for sure he is scared of something—Selmer maybe, or getting sent back to jail, or God knows what else, real or imagined.

Terry walks into the bedroom with two phone books—one residential, one business—in his left hand and a tall trash can in his right. "You want the garbage or the phone books?"

I take the less disgusting job, and start flipping through the book looking for the loose pages—the ones most used—and any circled or underlined listings. Thirty minutes later, we know Dunn has ordered pizza from nearly every delivery outfit in Santa Rita. We know he eats a ton of oranges. In the margin of yesterday's sports section Dunn, or someone, handwrote a list of two-digit numbers. Terry fishes a week's worth of junk mail out of the garbage and flips through it. Dunn must have trashed the week's accumulation and taken the personal mail with him—if the wanker gets any personal mail.

"He really shouldn't turn down all these credit card offers," Terry says. "That's the way you build credit. You don't have to use them."

"But there's the yearly membership fees to be considered."

"True, but many companies will waive the fee after the first year."

"If you use the card."

"True."

"Dunn seems like a cash-and-carry sort of guy."

This wholesale invasion of Dunn's privacy goes on for another hour. We look at a local map, folded improperly and stuffed into a drawer in the bathroom, to see whether Dunn has circled any meaningful locations. We scour his medicine cabinet and his dresser drawers and a few books for clues. There is nothing. He works for G-O-D. He reads the paper. He eats pizza and oranges.

There is a knock on the door. We freeze. Then another.

"Hello?" A woman's voice, but not the one who showed us the key. "Anyone home?" We do not respond. Then something lands on the living room floor with a thwack. After a minute Terry stands, quietly, and peeks around the corner. Then he strides out and returns with Dunn's mail, which includes a cellular phone bill.

"Nice timing," I say.

He tosses it at me. "Better you commit the federal offense."

The bill lists every outgoing and incoming call for the thirty days preceding Dunn's arrest. Very accommodating of the wanker, to get busted at the end of a billing cycle. I count eleven different phone numbers on the bill. There are several calls from and to some of the numbers. One is the main number at G-O-D. One is Moviefone. Three are food-related. One is disconnected. One is a dentist's office.

Which leaves four unidentified numbers, all local. At the first a woman answers the phone "Foghorn Trading." She happily gives me the address of the business, which I scribble on the bill.

At the next number, there is no answer and no voice mail.

At the next a man answers.

"Yo."

"Hi, my name is Gordon Seegerman. I'm a friend of Harold Dunn's and—"

"You got the wrong number, buddy." He hangs up.

I call back.

"Yo."

"Hi, I'm sorry to—" And again, he hangs up.

"The wanker has at least one very rude friend." It's obviously not a wrong number: Dunn logged perhaps twenty calls to the same listing, some lasting many minutes.

At the final number a machine answers. The voice is the sort you might expect on a phone sex line. Not that I've ever called a phone sex line, but it just seems like that kind of voice. "Hi there. You've reached Golden Girls. Leave your message and we'll get back to you soon." I hang up.

From the car, Terry calls Preet, whose lair behind his family's store looks something like the command center at NORAD. If it involves silicon and ones and zeros, Preet is your man. He does not appreciate being called a hacker. He prefers "computer sleuth." We have phone listings. We need names, addresses.

While Preet is running the numbers, we drive over to G-O-D. Selmer Godfrey meets us in the waiting room. He seems no less happy to be alive now that Harold Dunn is out of jail. He behaves amiably. He evinces no fear of Dunn or nervousness about his disappearance. I mention the name Fitzgerald, but it has no meaning to him. As far as he knows, Dunn has not called or spoken with anyone at G-O-D, including his mother. He agrees to let me know if Dunn should call or show his face.

When we leave Terry says, "That is the happiest ugly person I have ever seen."

We drive over to the address the receptionist at Foghorn Trading gave me. It turns out to be the Santa Rita Mutual building. Where the Setzes and Phil Dykstra work.

We take the elevator to the fifteenth floor. The address leads us to a glass door emptying into a suite of offices. The door says Foghorn Trading, Inc. A friendly receptionist tells us she has never heard of Dunn and that no one by that name has called any time recently. Gerald Fitzgerald doesn't sound familiar. I ask if she can tell me what kind of foghorns they trade.

"No," she says. "But I can have someone call you."

"Sure, why not?" I say, and hand her my card. "You better tell them I'm broke. Don't want to raise any false hopes." She takes the card without acknowledging my repartee.

I look up and an attractive, expensively dressed man about my age appears from a hallway and, without noticing us, walks into a conference room behind the reception area. The room has floor-to-ceiling windows with a view over the city, and the bay, to San Francisco. The man ignores the view. He sits at the conference table and stares at an open file.

Bartholomew Setz, Jr. I've seen his face in the paper. Not a bad-looking guy. Better than me. Can he sing, though? Can he pound the keys and sing and make a room full of cynical and wearied souls ache to fall in love for the first time, all over again? Silvie has settled, that's for sure.

I close the suite's door behind me.

"Junior Setz," I say.

"Really? Interesting."

I leave Terry in the lobby of the building to use the restroom. I find my brother, King, at a urinal.

80

"Hello, brother."

"The hell are you doing here?" He seems appalled to see me.

"Uh, urinating? What about you?"

"I was supposed to meet a guy." He looks up at the ceiling. "Nice bathrooms over here, huh?"

"Stunning."

"What about you?"

"I'm trying to find my client."

"He work here?"

"In this bathroom? No."

My brother's face is mostly invisible. His beard climbs nearly to his eyes. His hair is wild about his forehead. His eyes are intensely bright, though. I believe his latest job is distributing organic dog food. But with King it's better not to delve too deeply.

"How's Dad?"

An uncomfortable three moments, in which both of us think of S., of our disparate views of our responsibilities to him, of King's good fortune in avoiding Alzheimer's and my recalcitrance about testing, of our shared experience—Mom's death, Father's ignominy and illness—and the discomfiting way it has linked us.

"We should talk about Thanksgiving," I say.

He zips up. "I'll call you."

He tries to shake my hand—before washing his.

"Dude!"

He grins sheepishly and flees.

14

PREET HAS NO luck with two of the remaining three numbers—the one at which no one answered, and the wrong number that isn't a wrong number. The third—at which the answering message lady referred to something called Golden Girls—is under the name Stone Van der Geist, at an address south of the business district, near the bay, in a neighborhood called the Downs. The area used to be exclusively warehouses and a wholesale food market, the kind of place that's bustling between four and nine A.M. and otherwise all but dead. In the nineties, developers put up some lofts, and a few decent restaurants and cafés popped up, displacing the artists and garage bands that had coexisted merrily with the meat packers and machine shops for years. For worse or better, the crash destroyed the real estate market in this part of town, and the old scene is quickly re-forming.

Ted's is here, in a glove factory closed in the seventies. Since then it has had several incarnations—a furniture warehouse; a studio for a group of light artists, who painted every surface black and cut several holes in the ceiling, thirty feet above. Since 1992 it has been Ted's. Terry and I stop by on the way to see Mr. Van der Geist.

Ted, the owner, manager, lead bartender, booking agent, and chief bouncer, lives upstairs with his two bulldogs and his Thai wife, Songsuda. His official résumé contains vague references to his having been a roadie and sound guy for various bands. He knows the industry, that is for sure.

But, in fact, for twenty years Ted was perhaps the most prolific and successful importer and distributor of Southeast Asian marijuana in the country. He grew up in Los Angeles and learned to sail before he shed the training wheels from his bicycle. By the early eighties, he was sailing multi-ton shipments from Thailand to Oregon, for distribution to the entire continental United States. The difference between Ted and almost everyone else in the industry is that he saw the war on drugs— the enormous increase in potential prison sentences, the stepped-up interdiction, the cooperation with foreign governments—coming, and got out. Because the statutes have run out on his offenses, because he never got into coke or heroin, and because he doesn't flaunt his wealth, which must be considerable, the feds leave him be. He retired to Santa Rita, bought the old glove factory, and established the finest live music venue in the San Francisco Bay Area.

Ted, in his late fifties, has a long gray-blond ponytail, a leathery face, and a white mustache. He is not a large man, and he is not a loud man. His bearing is solid, and his manner measured but unequivocal. He is as close as we—the band—have ever come to a manager. He believed in us when we sucked, and he is pushing for us now that we don't. We trust him.

"Yo, T."

"T, yo." Terry and Ted pound fists and complete some kind of ultra-hip, hand-sign-based greeting that is beyond my comprehension.

Behind the bar with Ted is Max Lichter, the number two man at the club. Max and I were in the same high school class, though we traveled in different circles. Actually, Max was part of a circle of one. Then, I knew no one who had ever spoken with him. He was the sort of person one hoped not to find oneself alone with in a bathroom.

He is an enormous and menacing-looking man with a shiny, shaved crown and a remarkable volume of metal stuck into his skull. He has, too, angry-looking prison tattoos smeared across his arms, torso, and neck. After high school he drifted for a couple of years and then joined the Army. He served in the first Gulf War. After his discharge, he became addicted to crank, a habit he financed by burglarizing houses and cars, and ended up in San Quentin for two years. Then he cleaned up and went to work for Ted, who hired him less for his bartending skills than to discourage his (Ted's) former narcotics-business associates from encroaching on his new, law-abiding life. Somewhere along the line, Max fell in love with Aineen O'Connell.

"Any word?" I ask as I walk up to the bar. We are relying on Ted—his industry connections, his experience, his quiet charm—to get Barry to our show. From there it will be up to us to wow him.

"Yup," Ted says, cleaning glasses behind the bar.

"What?"

"How's your dad?"

"He's fine. What's the deal?"

"And Ferdy?" My grandfather comes to all our gigs with his crew of wilding alter kockers, invited or not.

"Fine. How's Songsuda?"

"Excellent, thanks for asking."

"Good. Now would you please—"

"It's a go. They heard the demo. They saw the clippings. They agreed Barry should hear it. He's heard it, and he's intrigued. He also has a charity gig or something in Tahoe that Sunday. So he's in town anyway."

"Yes." I pound the bar.

"Don't get too excited," Ted warns. "His guy said they'd confirm that week."

The album, tentatively called *Manilove*, is our ticket to the national scene, but we're pitching it as a fund-raiser for Alzheimer's research. Ted has agreed to finance the studio time and produce. We've had a few bites from major retailers, assuming Barry signs off. No one will touch it unless he's on board. The guy sells a phenomenal number of records, and no one wants to piss him off, no matter how worthy the cause. If the album sells, we'll do a tour. I'll take the Mandys national and never look back. We'll win over a whole new generation to the wonders of MBM.

"We should sit down and talk about the set list," Ted says.

"Can you imagine how nuts this place is gonna go when Manilow walks in? It's going to absolutely explode," Terry says.

"Relax, gentlemen. Don't start shooting into space on this thing yet."

"You think he'll sit in?" I say.

"Duuuude," Terry says, a silly smile on his face.

"This is way too huge," I say.

"You ought to think about bringing your dad," Ted says. "Put him right up front. Maybe introduce him."

"You want me to exploit my father's illness for personal gain? I'll do it," I say.

But I'll have to put a rope around S. and drag him behind the car. As much as my mother worshiped Barry and adored his music, my father couldn't stand the sound or the sight of him. The only thing my dad detests more than my playing in a Barry band is my being a defense lawyer. Tough cop, S. Too tough to appreciate the music. Too tough to see the difference between representing a bad guy and being one. Too tough to admit he'd fall apart without me. Not too tough to lose his mind, though.

We head over to the address we have for Van der Geist. It turns out to be an auto body repair shop, although it looks like it hasn't been active for a while. The place is deserted. We walk around the side of the building and through a gate. Across a yard scattered with engine parts and beer cans we see a man, at work on a vintage BMW motorcycle, a cigarette with a long ash hanging off his bottom lip. He is short, wearing a dark green trench coat, and a head of close-cropped raging-red hair. We walk toward him.

The gate slams behind us and a man with a sawed-off shotgun, a short, bearded, fat biker type, walks slowly toward us from behind. I see him first and stick my hands up in the air. This strikes Terry as comical, until he sees the weapon. Then he drops and lies spread-eagle on the dirt. I look down at him. What is he doing? Clearly the appropriate response in such a situation is to raise one's arms.

"We're looking for someone," I manage to mumble. Terry props himself up on his elbows, but remains prostrate.

"Who are you?" the man without the shotgun says, not looking up from his work.

"Public Defender's Office."

"I have a lawyer."

The gun is now about a foot from my neck. I wonder whether this would be a better, a less messy, a more heroic way to die than shrinking from consciousness over years as I will if my life-as-coin-toss comes out the wrong way.

"Actually we're looking for my client, a man named Harold Dunn."

"Never heard of him."

"The number here shows up several times on his phone bill. Now he's missing."

"That is unfortunate."

"We're very sorry to disturb you. Mr. Dunn has disappeared. We were just trying to make sure he's okay."

"Yeah, but the thing is, now you *have* disturbed me and you know where I am so the smart thing to do would be to shoot you both and bury you out back." He looks up, smiles, and waves off his friend with the sawed-off, who retreats to his position by the gate. "Fuckin' A, you guys look terrible," Van der Geist says, with a note of pity. He introduces himself. Terry stands up and dusts off. My hands remain in the air.

Van der Geist walks inside a shack at the back of the property. I look back at the gunner, grin embarrassedly, and drop my arms. From the outside, the structure looks about to fall over. But from the yard I can see the place is nicely outfitted: a couple of computers in what looks like an office, a leather living room set. A middle-aged woman with bleached hair—Van der Geist's mother, perhaps? The phone sex lady on the answering machine?—works two phones. She smiles at Terry. Van der Geist walks out with a slip of paper.

"No cops. Cops come to see me, I come to see you. Get it?"

"That's fine."

"Not a problem at all," Terry adds.

"I got no problem with Dunn. Always paid his bills, treated my staff like a gentleman. Generous man, Mr. Dunn. I'd hate to think something unpleasant might have happened to him. That would be bad for my business."

"We understand completely. We're just concerned for his welfare."

"I can't say I've seen him, but if you go to this restaurant"—he points to the slip of paper—"someone there may be able to help you. Ask for Don."

"Don."

"If you see Dunn, tell him we've started a frequent-flier program." Van der Geist looks Terry up and down. "You're a good-looking guy, my friend. You thought about escorting?"

"Not really." Terry takes his card.

"Give me a call any time. Easy money, my man. Easy money."

Perhaps it will come as a surprise that in my eight years as a public defender, though I have represented some bad people, and though I have been verbally abused and threatened with a violent end on numerous occasions, I have never before had a sawed-off shotgun pointed at my head. I have been spat at with some regularity. One time someone tried to stab me with an umbrella after I cross-examined his girlfriend. But never a sawed-off shotgun.

I will simply say that for the person at whom the sawed-off shotgun is aimed, it might as well be a nuclear bomb. It is a weapon of obliteration. It aims not simply to shoot, to poke bloody holes, but to erase. When the gate closes behind us, and Mr. Van der Geist is out of sight, I begin to shake.

"I know what you're going to say, so just don't," Terry insists.

He gets in the car and turns on the engine.

"Am I permitted to speak now?"

"Fine."

"Dunn is not my problem. I admit I felt slightly responsible. Now I don't. Don is the name of a hit man. Don is a knuckle-dragging bloodthirsty enforcer. I don't want to talk to Don."

"Are you done?"

"Yes."

"Good." He pulls away from the curb.

15

"**D**ON" TURNS OUT to be short for "Madonna." She looks nothing like the pop diva. She looks like a porn star of an Asian variety. She is perhaps five and a half feet tall. She has long straight black hair and perfect, perfectly spherical breasts. She wears a skirt and blouse that might adequately have covered a ten-year-old. Her red vinyl boots rise to mid-thigh. Her lips are painted neon orange. What we have here is a very beautiful, and probably very expensive, hooker. And, unmistakably, a man.

"You're looking for Harold." Van der Geist must have called. She seems pleased to see us.

"Yes."

"We were over at my apartment this morning. He's fine."

"Does he know there's a bench warrant for him?"

"He didn't mention it. He *has* been acting kind of nervous for a couple of weeks. He didn't want to talk about it, though."

Don says Dunn has been in town all this time. They spent the prior afternoon together. He showed up again this morning. He contacts her through her service—in other words, Golden Girls. They always meet at her place, downtown. She says she knows very little about him.

"He's a sweetheart. Kind of lonely. Never violent. Never touches alcohol. Very generous. Sometimes he gets kind of crazy, like can't stop talking about stuff, big stuff, the way everything in the world works, all that kind of shit. A few times I slipped him a Valium because he was going so fast."

"Do you mind me asking what a typical, uh, you know, how much would an encounter cost?" I say.

Don saves me: "We call them dates." I knew that. For crying out loud I'm a public defender. The nitty and the gritty are my business. But still, the word sounds so seventies-television, so Kojak, I'm embarrassed to use it. "With a tip and everything, around fifteen hundred." I raise my eyebrows. "You don't think I'm worth it?"

"I'm sure you're worth every penny," Terry puts in. "We just didn't figure Dunn for that kind of money."

I ask her to pass along the message to contact me, and about the warrant.

"Do you think he'll come by again?" I say.

Don frames her lovely face in her hands and says, "He can't resist. He'll call."

Maeve is waiting for us back at the office. When we walk in, she waves a fistful of phone messages around like winning lottery tickets. She has a distinctly gleeful look on her mug.

"Problems, problems, problems."

Silvie, Phil Dykstra, and Mary Godfrey.

Silvie first.

"What's up, Silvie?" She begins to yell. I remove the phone from my ear and speak into the mouthpiece at a distance. "Jesus, calm down. I cannot begin to make out what you're saying."

"Your damn client is everywhere, Gordon." Gordon. Uh-oh.

"Dunn."

"He called Styles. He went to the Dykstras' house. He tried to talk to the kid."

"That's not good."

"Phil Dykstra is going to kill someone and, as you might imagine, Bart is getting some pressure on this—"

"Wait a second. Let me make perfectly clear I don't give the slightest crap what Bart thinks. If my client has violated the law, have the cops pick him up."

"Believe me, they're looking for him. Despite the fact that he seems to be everywhere, they can't find him. Where the hell is he?"

"How should I know? What I know I told you in court. The guy split, as far as I'm concerned. He hasn't called and he hasn't written. He's not my problem."

"Your client is now facing obstruction, tampering, and possible kidnapping charges."

I laugh. "He's not my damn client. And how do you get kidnapping?"

"Find him and put a leash on him!" she yells, and hangs up.

Mary Godfrey says Dunn called the office, but hasn't come by. She told him he'd have to take a leave from work while he resolved his legal problems. She called me simply because I'd asked her to let me know if he made contact. She encouraged Dunn to call me. He said he would.

"To me, he seemed to be in trouble, Mr. Seegerman. I'm sure I don't have to tell you I have some familiarity with people, especially alcohol and drug addicts, in crisis. I fear the events of the past few days have shaken his foundation. He seems to have lost his bearings."

"Did he say where he was going?"

"No. I am very fond of him, Mr. Seegerman. I do hope you'll do your best to help him."

Phil Dykstra is less loud than Silvie, but his fury shows. He explains that had he been home when Dunn appeared at his house, he would have strangled the wanker. I agree that Dunn should not have come to the house, but there is nothing I can do about it. If Dunn has broken the law, he'll be arrested.

"You just better pray I don't find out you had anything to do with this."

"Mr. Dyks—"

"If you see that sick fuck, tell him he ought to turn himself in, because he's safer in jail than he is on the streets right now."

"I will be sure to pass along the message. But as I've explained to you, Mr. Dykstra—" He hangs up. I continue speaking into the phone anyway. "I am not Harold Dunn's guardian. I was, until yesterday, his lawyer. Now I have nothing to do with him whatsoever. You are more likely to see him than I am, and if you do, please send him my regards." I slam the receiver into its cradle.

What a complete prick. Dunn's harmless. So what, he shows up at the house. No one's said anything about him taking off his pants in the front yard.

I'm pissed, so I call Silvie and leave a message.

"Do me a big favor and tell Phil Dykstra that if he ever threatens me on the phone again I'm going to file a complaint with the bank, the FDIC, the SEC, the FBI, the CIA, and the United Nations. And by the way, Harold Dunn is innocent."

Terry reminds me that while Dunn visited the Dykstras, he only called Marjorie Styles. We decide to see if we can catch him at Styles's place. As we drive into her apartment complex, a beat-up old yellow Cadillac, about the size of my living room, pulls out of a parking space on the street and screeches around a corner. Terry and I turn our heads.

"Dunn," I say, shaking my head. "If I had any sense at all I'd call the cops."

"You want to follow him?"

"He's gone. Let's make sure he didn't whack the witness. That would really ruin my day."

Styles stands in the doorway of her apartment. She seems thrilled to see Terry again. Women are commonly thrilled to see Terry. He introduces me. She does not invite us in. I ask about Dunn. She speaks rapidly.

"You just missed him. I think he is one of the nicest men I've ever met. There are so many really mean people in the world, it is so great to meet someone really nice. You know what I mean? Not fake nice, but like really nice, like he means it."

"He was in your apartment?" Terry squeezes in.

"I didn't know he worked at G-O-D. I wouldn't have caused him all this trouble. I can't believe it's the same man in that store. I just can't believe it. I really can't. He doesn't seem like the same man. I don't know, I really don't know anymore."

"Mr. Dunn shouldn't be talking to you, because you are a witness in his criminal case. Is this the first time he's been here?"

"He called, but—I didn't know he knew Mary Godfrey. Oh, my God. If I'd known I would never have made such a big deal about it. It wasn't a big deal. I mean, not really. Kind of embarrassing, is all. I mean I don't even know if it was the same man now. It seemed like it in the store, but I really don't know. He's so nice."

"You might want to inform the police that Mr. Dunn was here," I say.

Dunn appears to have badly confused her. She has no idea what to do or think. She says she'll wait to do anything until her boyfriend returns.

"Can you tell us anything else Mr. Dunn said? We've been trying to contact him."

"Not really. No. Not really. Just that he was trying to stay on the program. You know he's been straight for five years? Did you know that? That's amazing. I think that's just amazing. Don't you? You don't know how hard it is to do that. If you haven't tried you don't know how hard—I've tried, believe me, I know. It's hard. It's basically impossible it's so hard."

"If he comes back, would you please give him this?" I hand her my card.

"Are you a real lawyer? You don't look like a lawyer. Can I ask you a question about my daughter? Because they're trying to take her away and I don't understand what's going on. I got a job and everything, but there's still some kind of problem and I filed the paperwork on it, but I'm too damn dumb to understand and you're a lawyer and everything do you think you might be—"

We back away slowly. Sorry, Ms. Styles. Thank you very much, Ms. Styles. Be sure to call if Mr. Dunn should come by again. She keeps talking. She is talking when we reach the bottom of the stairs. She is talking when we open our car doors and wave good-bye. She is talking when we pull away.

"*She'll* make a good witness," I say.

"She's cranking. Did you see her eyes?"

"Seems to have changed her tune on Dunn."

"Maybe he gave her a little present," Terry says.

"Please don't say that."

"You totally missed it, huh?"

"What?"

"This is why you could never be an investigator."

"What are talking about? I'd be a great investigator."

"You are insufficiently observant. It's like athletic ability."

"What?"

"To her left, inside the apartment. Cash on a chair. Several hundred, at least."

"Unbelievable."

"Accountants don't like mess. He's cleaning up."

I've had more than enough of Dunn for the day. I slide down in the red leather seat of Terry's car. As Santa Rita's familiar landscape rushes by, I slip into fantasy mode. I'm at the piano, onstage at Ted's, looking out into the audience, past Ferdy and my dad in front, Ted and Max at the bar, the standing-room-only crowd, to a table in a far corner of the room, near the door, where a thin man dressed in black sits with two colleagues sipping a club soda with lemon.

I'm tempted to introduce him, but I don't. Exposure is his prerogative; should he want to move from observer to participant, he'll come forward. Finally, after we finish a song, he walks toward the stage, clapping enthusiastically. When I'm certain he's not headed for the bathroom, I wave shyly in his direction, and say, "Ladies and gentlemen, what an extraordinary honor: Mr. Barry Manilow." The crowd looks around, missing him. MBM? Here? Where? I don't see him? Such a prominent person, such a familiar face, they've never seen him out of the spotlight, off a stage in Vegas or on television. They forget he is middle-aged now, slightly hunched, slightly less bright-eyed, a human being. He climbs the three stairs to the stage, walks to the microphone, shakes my hand, and says "Mr. X, the honor is mine."

Our hands joined, I have to use all my strength not to slip back into being little Gordy Seegerman. Waiting for my mom to come home from the hospital after surgery, listening to *Barry Live*—"Looks Like We Made It," "It's a Miracle," "This One's for You." Dancing around our living room, thinking the louder I sing the better my mom will feel. King yells at me to turn it down, but I don't. I don't care if he comes down and pounds me. I don't care if the neighbors complain. I hope the whole world is listening. I turn it up and up and sing at the top of my lungs. Tears streaming down my face, I sing. I am eight.

Barry waves to the crowd which is beside itself, which cannot believe its four hundred eyes. He is buoyant, greeting the Mandys.

"Let's see, it's Maeve, right?" She wails on the drums for an instant and then gives Barry the bear hug of his life. "And you must be Terry?" He bows slightly and shakes the man's hand. "And how could anyone forget Preet?" Preet's skin is dark, but his blush shows anyway. He waves demurely from behind the keyboard.

The audience cheers and comes to its feet. Barry whispers into my ear, the name of a song. I alert the band. Together. Two voices, one tune. Preet attacks his keyboard for the intro, a sweep of violins. My voice is shaky, but Barry has his hand on my back. I look down at

Ferdy and my dad. I raise the microphone up, in the direction of their table, as if it's a glass of champagne. "This one's for you, Pop."

"Don't worry. He'll show," Terry says.

"Of course he'll show. Who's worrying?"

"You look stressed. If he was planning on splitting, he would have been long gone by now."

"Who?" I ask.

"Dunn. What's wrong with you?"

"Nothing. I'll be disappointed if he *doesn't* take off. Why are we going this way?" He is headed away from our office, back into West Santa Rita.

"He's going home. I have a hunch," Terry says.

"I would really prefer not to."

"I don't doubt that."

Terry stops half a block from Dunn's duplex. The wanker's car is parked in front.

Terry, looking stunningly self-satisfied, says nothing.

"Fine." I unbuckle my seat belt. "I'll go tell him to get his ass to court tomorrow."

He puts his hand on my shoulder. "No way."

"We've been looking for this joker all day. He's about to get busted for witness tampering and obstruction of justice. The least I can do is give him a heads-up."

"We sit. If he moves, we follow."

"And if he wanks?"

"We avert our eyes."

I can see Dunn moving from room to room inside the apartment. Maybe ten minutes later, the lights go off. He walks out toward his car. A black sedan whips past us and skids to a stop with its nose to Dunn's Caddy.

"SRPD?" Terry says.

"I certainly hope so."

The sedan has the generic look of a police car, but lacks any official markings. I can't make out the plates. Dunn does not try to take off. He walks calmly up to the vehicle and has a brief exchange with the driver. Then he walks back to the Caddy, locks the driver's-side door, returns to the black car, and gets in the backseat.

We tail the sedan to a McDonald's. The driver, a man of about my age, tall, dressed casually, returns with enough food for several people. The guy looks like a cop, but I have never seen him before. They drive into the downtown area and for a moment I figure they are on their way to the county jail. But before it reaches the city center the car turns into the garage of a high-rise apartment building.

"What the hell?"

"Maybe it's Don's place," Terry says.

"Time for one last massage before going back to jail. Heartwarming."

"You want to go in?"

"There's two hundred apartments in there."

"True."

"You may additionally recall, I didn't want to go to Dunn's."

The lights have come on downtown.

"So?" Terry asks. "Now what?"

"I have no idea."

16

SATURDAY NIGHT. BAND practice.

Behind the Singhs' store in downtown Santa Rita—one of five Get It Here, Now convenience stores sprinkled around the city—is a garage we use as a rehearsal space. This is also where Preet operates a slew of Internet-based businesses of unknown purpose and dubious legality. As for Preet's digital activities, we have settled on a sensible "Don't ask, don't tell" policy. In other words, he does not ask me about the legality of his businesses, and I don't tell him that a soft, round young Sikh man might not fare so well in state prison.

The studio is filled with homemade computers, interconnected monitors, keyboards, recorders, phone lines, and many other electronic gadgets I cannot identify. Worn oriental rugs, muted reds and browns, cover concrete floors. The space is cluttered with amps, drums, a broken Coke machine, a refrigerator, and a couch. Theosophist tracts and a huge collection of paperback diet books pack a wall of tottering bookshelves.

This is our clubhouse. This is where we end up after dates, where we hone our sound, and where we retreat to when our families drive us crazy.

Preet paces the room, thinking out loud. I am hungry. Maeve, whose teenage lover is waiting for her somewhere, looks horny and impatient. We have already rehearsed for a couple of hours, but the man is on a roll.

"We must talk about *meaning*. What does it mean to us, to face this challenge? It is not enough to play, my friends, even to play well. This is Barry bloody Manilow we're talking about."

Preet emigrated with his parents from England when he was a kid. He still affects some of their English manner.

"If we ever go metal—like, seriously hardcore—that would be a totally cool name for the band. Bloody Barry Manilow," Terry says.

"That is your contribution?" Preet humpfs.

"Come on, guys. It's late. Let's do a 'Weekend' and wrap it up," I say. We always finish rehearsal with "Weekend in New England."

"I'll tell you what it means. It means you guys better not fuck up," Maeve says. She spreads herself out on the couch, forcing me off.

"Do you see this?" Preet beseeches me. "This is what I cannot tolerate."

"We just play," I say. "As well as we can. We make sure it's packed. If necessary, we pay people to come. At least, we buy drinks."

"Drinks, definitely," Terry and Maeve agree.

"A defining moment demands not simply excellence and an audience; it demands presence. It requires us to be fully aware, fully conscious. I am simply suggesting that the more we provide meaning to the event, the more likely we are to appear meaning*ful*. We must be one."

"One what?" Maeve says.

I walk behind Preet and massage his shoulders. I guide him over to his command post—a large wicker rocker, filled with pillows, surrounded by keyboards, monitors, and the sound of many fans cooling many motherboards. "Maeve, give me a name," I say.

"Riona Simpson," Maeve says. "Last known address, 56 Singleton Road, Clemson, South Carolina."

We entertain ourselves for hours this way. Preet has access to a frightening array of confidential information through various Web-based relationships. Is he a CIA agent? Probably not. Are there a handful of computer guys with high-level clearances at the CIA—and the FBI, and the DEA, and the IRS—who use his code, whose butts he's saved, who owe him a favor? I don't want to know. But if you give Preet the name of your high school girlfriend he can tell you what kind of birth control she uses and whether she's already done her Christmas shopping.

"Forty-six. Blond, five-four. Hundred ninety pounds. Middle name Hope?" Preet says, looking less agitated already.

Maeve lifts herself onto her elbows. "One ninety? Holy shit," which she pronounces like it is at least a two-syllable word for something that covers a mattress. "Where's that cunt now?"

"Texas. Dallas, Texas. Three DUIs. And a fondness for expensive chocolates."

"Is there a picture? I gotta see this." Preet brings it up, transfers it onto a huge flat panel on a shelf above his head.

"She's a motherfucking house." Maeve squeals with glee.

"Ex?" Terry says.

"Excuse me. Do I look like I'd be with that bloated bitch? She's my sister. Though I'd happily push her off a cliff."

"Close family," Terry says.

"How many more of you are there?" I say.

"Several, or many, depending whether you count the halfs, the steps, and the ones in prison. Try Myla Miravich," Maeve says.

"No, no, no. You know the rules, O'Connell," I say.

"Come on, Preet, tell us if our boy here's gonna get some."

"Don't do it, Preet. I'm serious," I say.

"You haven't even gone out with her. What are you scared of?" Maeve says.

"I'd like to preserve some of the mystery, right?"

"Something's wrong with this one," Maeve says. "Not that something hasn't been wrong with all the other ones. But I just don't think you oughta be getting involved before the gig."

"How about Harold Dunn?" Terry says. He gives Preet the address of Dunn's Santa Rita duplex.

"This your disappeared client?" Maeve says. I nod.

"Why didn't you call me before?" Preet asks.

"We did. This is the guy with the phone numbers. I'm sure he's still around. Just nervous about going back to jail," I say. "Anyway, I'm sort of hoping he's gone."

"I get nothing," Preet says. "You have another address?"

"What do you mean, nothing? We were at his house today," I say. Terry and I walk toward Preet's command post. He raises both his hands as if to say, *If you come any closer I will have to kill you.*

"Preet, there's a warrant out on the guy in this county. You're losing it," Terry says. Preet gives him a dirty look and types some more.

"He has a prior in Portland, early nineties," I say. "Try there."

"No, no, no. No Oregon record for Harold—H-A-R-O-L-D—Dunn—D-U-N-N. If such a person was at any time more than a figment of your imagination, as of now he's wiped. Digitally speaking, no such person exists."

"What the hell is going on?" Terry is getting amped—not the way to convince Preet to try again. They are like brothers slightly too close in age.

"You both need psychiatric care," Preet says.

I pull up a chair. "Let's try this again. Harold Dunn. Former accountant," I tell him. "Probably in Portland. Did county time there on an exposure case ten years ago. Comes here, goes into the G-O-D rehab program, works there for a few years, in their administrative office, gets popped on another exposure, spends a couple of days in county jail here, bails out on ten grand, paid by someone named Gerald M. Fitzgerald, a lawyer, maybe. If he is, he's admitted in California."

Preet types furiously. He has three different screens going at once. "No lawyer Gerald M. Fitzgerald in California or anywhere else. Unless you're looking for the fifteenth Earl of Desmond."

"You're positive you don't show a Santa Rita arrest?"

"Gordon. Do you see that, and that, and that?"

On each screen is a line saying "No record found."

"What about county jail records?"

"I don't have that access. What else? Tell me more." Preet is hungry for data, angry that something doesn't, won't, compute.

Another couple of minutes. Maeve is getting antsy.

"Can someone tell me why I should care about any of this?" she says.

"It is a black hole, Gordy. Your man is a nil."

"Let's say, just for the sake of argument, there is a person named Harold Dunn who lives in Santa Rita, who is my client. And say a Superior Court judge issued a bench warrant for this guy in my presence. Can you think of any reason—"

"Most likely you and Terry have concocted this person in an attempt to drive me insane."

"Preet—"

"Another extremely disturbing possibility is that Mr. Dunn's electronic data is protected at a very high level. In other words, it is there, but I cannot obtain it."

"Why?"

"Perhaps he is in a witness protection program or is some kind of government agent," Preet says, staring at me. He pauses for a few moments and then whips around, back to his keyboards, and starts smacking the keys furiously. "But I feel certain you are about to tell me that Mr. Dunn couldn't possibly be either of those, right?" He speaks twice as quickly and twice as loudly. "Because that would pose certain problems for the *idiot* looking for such a person in highly confidential databases on behalf of his even more brainless friends."

"No. Calm down. Extremely unlikely," I say.

"Perhaps you simply have the wrong name."

"I'm sure that's it."

Maeve walks over and offers Preet a cigarette. He takes it and places it between his lips, but waves away her offer of a light.

"What the hell is this?" Terry says.

"Who could do it?" I say.

"Has to be federal, they are the only ones with the reach," Preet says. He looks as pale as someone with very dark skin can look. He looks grayish-green.

"Let's do the witnesses," Terry says.

"Have you completely lost your mind?" Preet barks.

"Let's do 'Weekend' instead," Maeve says, sensing a crisis in the making. "Even if y'all are in jail, I'm going to be singing for Barry Manilow in three weeks, and I need all the practice I can get."

"Gordy, something is going on here. Don't you think we ought to try to figure it out?" Terry asks.

Preet thumps at his keyboards, no longer looking for Dunn. Now, as he mumbles hysterically, he hopes to cover his tracks. Then he says, "Karma is both merciful and just. Mercy and justice are only opposite poles of a single whole; and mercy without justice is not possible in the operations of Karma."

"What in God's name is that supposed to mean?" Maeve says.

"It is supposed to mean that I will be very fortunate indeed to avoid a painful rash."

17

SAIGON HAT IS a grease-blotched hole in the wall in Santa Rita's Little Vietnam neighborhood that serves unrivaled food on stained plastic dishes with splintery wooden chopsticks wrapped in flimsy paper napkins. The walls are covered with an oily film, the remnants of a million fried imperial rolls. The cooks, as grease-ridden as the walls, hang cigarettes out of their mouths and squint their eyes in the smoke. The ashes fall regularly into the food. A perfect first-date venue. Great food. Loud enough to afford a couple total privacy despite the twenty tables packed into a room the size of a large van. And it's a great filter, too. Any woman who isn't positively thrilled by an evening at the Hat isn't worth a second look.

Myla Miravich sits across the table from me. She is taller than me by an inch and has the thick musculature and V-shaped back of a competitive swimmer. She has lively green eyes and a raspy voice. I can see her tongue bounce around her mouth while she listens to me because her mouth hangs open when she is listening. Every so often she taps her right index finger at the middle of her forehead. I have no idea why. I am on a date with a beautiful woman. I have shown extraordinary strength of character in getting up the nerve to call her in the first place. Life, momentarily, is good.

The general rule that one should not date people one meets at a gig makes sense. Casual sex, yes. No harm there. But to try to have a romance with someone whose first impression of me is as the leader of a Barry Manilow cover band seems utterly cliché-ridden and wrong. I

104

always fall for the girl singer. God help me if she can also play the sax. Conversely, if a woman under the age of forty who happens to admire Barry Manilow wanders into a Barry X show, she's mine. It seems like artifice on my part, a trick. And wrong the other way, too, because she wants to have dinner with Barry X, or thinks she does, and my name is Gordon.

Anyway, my first date with Myla Miravich makes perfectly clear that rules are often pointless. She detests Barry Manilow. She tells me, smiling, she thinks a Barry Manilow cover band is about the stupidest idea she's ever heard of. I tell her, smiling, that at some shows Terry steps out in front and we do a set as the Neils—an all-Diamond-and-Sedaka duo. She thinks Barry X is worse.

At first, this is unsettling. I came prepared for a groupie. I set out to break the rule. But it quickly becomes clear that Myla approached me because—Well, I don't have any idea why Myla approached me, and I'm not going to worry about it. Her interest in me has nothing to do with MBM, and that is fine. The best kind of romance is one that presents an interesting challenge. How can this intelligent, musically aware, seemingly open-minded person not share the central passion of my life? She simply has to be educated. And if there's a person on the planet better equipped than I am to engender in a skeptic a heartfelt interest in and appreciation of Barry Manilow, forget it: I'm the guy.

I tick off Barry's accomplishments. "Emmy, Grammy, Tony. Academy Award nomination. Who else? Twenty-five singles in a row in the Top Forty. Thirteen number one hits. Who else? No one, that's who."

"So he's commercial. Lots of bad music has been commercial," she shoots back.

"Five albums on the charts in one year. Five albums. Can you imagine?" She sucks noodles off her plate with the force of a Shop-Vac and an alluring lack of regard for the curry stains sprouting on her blouse. "Only ones ever to do that are Sinatra and Johnny Mathis. One album; two, three, maybe. You put five records on the charts in

105

one year, something exceptional has happened. Not just commercial, either. Five albums is transcendent."

"Transcendent. Like Mozart."

"Exactly."

"No, no, no. Please don't say you think Barry Manilow is the same as Mozart."

"I didn't say 'the same.' Equivalent."

"Not equivalent. One is heavenly music. The other is cheese."

"You're wounding me here. I'm bleeding heavily."

"You're the one on the mission. I *said* I sort of like Neil Diamond."

"Neil Diamond is fine, pleasing, fun. Good, even. Barry is glorious. Barry is sublime. Barry is matchless."

She pauses for a moment and looks at me as if she might really like me, maybe even want to sleep with me.

"You realize that's insane, right?"

"It's like art. You can look at a painting and say, 'Nice,' or 'Ugh,' but you didn't see it. You looked at it. You have to spend time with it. You have to understand it. Figure out its pieces. See where it came from and what it led to."

"Did I mention that I have a degree in art history?"

"So you should understand. You can't come to art with your eyes closed and a big zero between your ears."

"Barry Manilow is not art."

"You've been listening to Barry, here and there, for what, twenty-five years, but you haven't heard one song."

"Believe me, I've heard. My mother listens to him."

The worse it gets, the more hopeless it seems, the better I feel. We click. I give her my best work stories—the male prostitute with erectile dysfunction; the guy who shoplifted single shoes. She works as an investigator for Insuron, which specializes in covering doctors for medical malpractice. While she tells me the story of the surgeon who left his Walkman earphones in a patient's abdominal cavity, I think:

This is the first time I've been around anyone, since Silvie and I split, who makes me forget, even for just a moment, that there is a 50 percent chance I won't be able to remember my mother's name ten years from now.

And then there is her hair. Tonight it hangs behind her ears in two braids, thick as mooring rope, the color of eighteen-karat gold shined to a shimmer.

I thought I'd turned off my cell. I should have turned off my cell. Heads turn. Sneers appear. This is not the right place for the shrill summons of a digital communications device. I am thankful our dinner is through so I won't have to endure the scorn for much longer.

"Sorry."

It is Don. Dunn is at her apartment.

"Put him on," I say.

"He's in the bathroom," Don whispers, which makes it hard for her to cover up the gruff, low, unmistakably masculine tones knocking at the walls of her voicebox, desperate to escape.

"Is something wrong?" Myla asks.

I put my hand over the phone. "It's a work thing. That client who disappeared." She nods and heads for the bathroom.

"He doesn't know I'm calling," Don says. "I think he's in trouble."

"Did he say something?"

"No, he's just acting weird."

"Is he on his way out or in?"

"In."

"Don't let him leave. I'll be over in ten minutes."

I hang up the phone and realize I have no idea where Don lives, or practices, or does whatever it is Don does. Luckily, my cell records incoming numbers. I click through a few menus and arrive at the "Received Calls" screen. I recognize the most recent, from Don's cell, as one of the two on Dunn's cellular bill we were unable to account for.

107

Myla is back from the bathroom a minute later.

"I have to deal with this—I have to go try to talk to my client. I'm really sorry. You could come for a ride."

"I should go."

We struggle over the bill for a moment.

"It is my pleasure," I say.

"I just don't want there to be any misunderstanding," she says.

"What could I possibly misunderstand? I had a great time and I feel like buying."

"I just don't need any weirdness in my life right now, okay? I had a nice time and you seem to be a nice guy."

"Good. The feeling is mutual."

"You think I'm a nice guy?" she says.

"A wonderful guy. The best."

She sticks out her hand. I'm sure the whole restaurant is watching, rooting against me, no doubt.

"I could use a new friend," she says.

"Consider it done," I say. I take her hand with both of mine and give her a squeeze instead of a shake.

I lean back against my car and watch her walk away. Friends. Wonderful. Then my cell rings. Don. He says Dunn got a call right after we hung up. The wanker left two minutes ago.

I order Maeve to keep it to herself when she opens the door.

"As my friend, I am asking you for this small favor. My date was nearly ideal and I am still savoring it."

"You get laid?"

"You are already draining my pleasure. You are sucking it out of me like a vacuum."

I turn around to go. She grabs my arm and drags me to the couch. Maeve's house is small, but surprisingly pleasant given its owner's often vulgar and repellent, although curiously lovable, manner. Every time I come over I half expect to see porn magazines and empty Budweiser cans laying around. But the house is tidy, filled with family photographs, shots of MBM in concert, and those little clay statues of animals and dwarves you can buy only on television shopping shows.

I say hello to Aineen and Max, who are watching television in the family room.

"So, Harold Dunn whipped out his thing in public?" Max says. He doesn't see any humor in it. To Max, the whipping out of a thing in public is a serious matter.

"That's the charge. Looks like he doesn't want to deal with it though. He bailed out, and no one's heard from him since. You know Dunn?"

"He's part of the squad."

I look at Maeve. "Translation?"

"G-O-D squad."

"A and I met over there, you know," Max says.

"I didn't know that," I say.

"We were in the program together round the same time as Dunn," Max says. "They run a pretty decent program. Saved a lot of lives. Maybe even mine. But I'll tell you one thing: Mary Godfrey—now there's a scary chick."

Aineen has not said a word. She stares at the television as if our conversation is in Swahili.

"It's sort of like a cult. As long as you toe the line, they love you. But if you mention you don't appreciate something, you're out. You don't like something one of the squad says about pretty much anything, you're out. They got enforcers and money to burn. And political power in this town? The mayor, the DA, everyone's over there all the time licking her boots. She's in with the churches too, the black ones, Latino, Asian. She funds their programs, she controls their votes. You can't get elected to shit in this city without Mary Godfrey's say-so, and if you want to stay elected you better not piss her off."

109

"And Dunn."

"G-O-D squad all the way. I heard he's the guy who works the money. I wasn't around enough to get a handle on anything in particular, but the way that dude acted you knew he was in with Mary."

"Anything else weird about the place? You know we're playing their holiday fund-raiser."

He looks at Maeve. "No shit?"

"Shit," Maeve says.

"That's cool. Dunn's an unusual dude, that's all I know. Didn't talk to anyone. Stayed to himself. Went straight into the office after he got out of the program and basically disappeared."

"I went on a date with him," Aineen says.

"What?" Max says, with an air of indignation.

"What? That was before you. I thought he was kind of cute."

"He didn't show you his dick, did he?" Maeve says.

"I didn't see anything. I wasn't really looking, though." Mother and daughter think this hilarious.

"What about Selmer Godfrey?" I say. "What's his deal?"

"I couldn't really say. I never knew the man. Seemed like your basic mama's boy to me. I saw her flipping out on him once."

"You ever hear noises about Selmer or anyone at G-O-D laundering money?"

"Not that I heard. Selmer didn't seem smart enough for anything like that. It's a weird place, though. I was only there long enough to get straight and get Aineen and get out. My cellie from Quentin works security over there. I could make some inquiries."

"Maybe later. Right now, Dunn's not my problem. If he shows, maybe."

18

I HAVE NO IDEA what to expect when I walk into the office on Monday. Maybe the feds will be waiting for Terry and me, now that we have maybe–sort of stumbled into something we shouldn't have, although we've no idea what it is. Maybe Dunn will be back in jail and I'll be back in court. Maybe Phil Dykstra will have put Dunn into intensive care and I'll be off the hook. Maybe Myla will call. But nothing happens. No feds, no Dunn. Silvie calls to check in during the week, to see if I've had any word. But after a couple of days it looks like the wanker has really jumped ship this time.

Turkey Day, morning.

In recent years, Thanksgiving at the Seegerman household has been an explosive affair. Put three men—one with quickly deteriorating cognition, another at risk for same, and a slovenly alcoholic in training—and their eightysomething progenitor around a badly set and drably decorated table in a chilly, falling-apart mansion, feed them a store-bought, defrosted, and reheated version of the traditional Thanksgiving meal, and you will see the meaning and joy of the day gutted, blown to bits, and then picked at, as if by crows at a dump. So we go elsewhere for Thanksgiving dinner.

We do have a Thanksgiving Day tradition of sorts, though. The unofficial county football championship is played Thanksgiving morning at the Santa Rita municipal stadium. The public high school—our team—plays the leading private school squad. None of us except S. has ever taken an interest in sports—and he has little notion of what's happening on the field anymore—but we've been in this town for three generations and civic pride compels our attendance.

The Turkey Bowl is nothing if not perfectly emblematic of Santa Rita. Even at ten in the morning, the fans are riotous and the peppermint schnapps flows generously. The private school fans and players are mostly white. Our side reflects the racial and economic realities of the public school system: mostly black and Latino and Asian, mostly low income, and mostly living in the flats. We've won the Turkey Bowl five years running.

King shows late, as usual, and makes clear he ought to be working. Ferdy is in a rare sour humor. We'd rehearsed late at Preet's and I'm exhausted. My dad, though, is in a fine mood, very talkative, although not particularly coherent. He has the sense that something important is happening, but can't quite get his arms around it.

"I'd like you to sit next to me at Bea's," he says. Later in the day we'll be heading to Ferdy's girlfriend's—if "girlfriend" is the right word for a woman with twenty-six grandchildren—for Thanksgiving dinner. Beatrice lives in a huge, elegantly manicured Victorian in a dodgy area of West Santa Rita, not too far from Dunn's place.

"That's fine, Pop."

"I always get stuck with dark meat."

The fact that Beatrice and her progeny are African-American imbues this remark with a high wince factor, though my father usually manages to curb his racial insensitivity at Bea's house. Anyway, in this case he appears to be talking about food.

"Don't worry, I'll get you the whole breast."

We make it several steps past the front door before S. stops in his tracks.

"Aren't you going to bring the wine?"

"We're not going to Bea's now, Pop. We're going to the Turkey Bowl. Remember?"

"Now?"

"Nine-thirty. You want something to eat before we go?"

Too much data. S. withdraws into silence. Memory is like a Rolex. When it's on the wrist, you can consult it confidently. Its weight alone is a comfort, a reminder of the logic of existence, even when the time is of no interest or use. When you don't need it, you store it in a box on your nightstand; you rely on its being there. Not until you open the box and discover the treasure gone is the loss manifest.

For the past several years, the Turkey Bowl has been the Seegerman family's way of letting the rest of Santa Rita know we're still here, we hear the snide remarks, we're taking down names. And also our way of explaining. We march our dad into the stands, show him off to the police dignitaries and elected officials. Let them see their golden boy wasn't a failure after all. It was his brain on a dangerous frolic of its own. Anyway, that's our story, and we're sticking to it.

A balding, mid-forties, pudgy Asian man with a thick black mustache sits down next to S. and says hello. My father has no idea who he is, but seems happy enough to be talking with anyone not named Seegerman. There are many aspects of my father's illness I do not understand. This is one. When he is able and willing to talk at all, he seems far happier—less grumpy, less critical, less depressed, less distractible—when speaking with someone unfamiliar to him.

The man holds my dad's gloved hand, tenderly, and nods patiently while S. rambles on about how he was a police detective and how his wife died of breast cancer and he'd raised his boys alone. S. even comes up with the name of our street, which is damn impressive. After a few minutes, the man walks away without introducing himself or even acknowledging King, Ferdy, and me.

King looks agitated. "You know who that guy is?"

"No. Dad seems to like him."

"Which proves he doesn't remember shit. He's SRPD. That's the

113

guy that fucked him at the Garfinkels' and that's the guy that fucked him at the inquiry."

"How the hell do you remember all that?"

"I read the file."

"Really?"

"I want to know who my enemies are."

I'd heard enough of the story from my dad and Ferdy and others to absorb the gist of it, but I was busy at college in Los Angeles when the whole mess went down, so I was spared the local media coverage. King lived at home. And he was S.'s boy. My father and I have never been particularly close. I suspect my mom pushed for a second child, and S. left her to deal with me. I should thank him—had he expressed more of an interest I might have missed my Manilow moment. But King and S. were constant companions then, and he takes my dad's undoing, both by his quarrelsome brain and by his traitorous colleagues, personally.

"Your enemies."

"That's right."

"What's his name?"

"Marty Hong."

Early 1989. My father sits in the living room of our house watching the most exciting Super Bowl game of the decade, San Francisco 49ers versus the Cincinnati Bengals. S. is a rabid Santa Rita fan and thus hates the Niners and their pretty-boy quarterback, Joe Montana, with a scalding intensity. He drinks gin and tonics through four quarters to chase down the bile that climbs his throat every time Montana comes a step closer to his third ring. I am glad I didn't see him when the Niners came from behind in the final seconds of the game. S. was a maniacal loser.

So, he's swilling gin, yelling obscenities at the television, and generally having a pleasant afternoon when someone knocks frantically at our front door. S. answers it. Five minutes later he's up the street involved in a hostage situation. Although S. could not have known it at the time, two men had attempted to abduct the six-year-old daughter of a prominent developer named Sheldon Garfinkel. Garfinkel, his wife, and several others are in another part of the house whooping it up for the Niners. The daughter is in the playroom. An older child, a boy, walks into the room just as the Bad Guys are making off with her. He screams and Bad Guy 1 takes a shot at him, but misses. The adults hear it and scatter, some toward the playroom, some outside. Shortly, Bad Guy 1 is out in front, trying to get to his car with the girl. Bad Guy 3, the driver, sees the crowd emerging from the house and splits.

Bad Guy 1 now has his gun in Daughter's ear in the front yard and is spewing invectives at the posse of stunned rich folks on the front steps. Bad Guy 2 is hiding around the side of the house. Into this chaotic scene walks S. I wish I had a videotape of it, because in the events that followed my dad climbed to the apogee of his police career, balanced briefly on the peak, on one foot even, and then tumbled down the other side, which, to his and our dismay, turned out to be bottomless.

S. is calm. He orders the small crowd that has gathered on the street and on the front steps back into their houses. The situation improves. Standing across the yard from one another, they speak. Bad Guy 1 takes his gun away from Daughter's head. S. places his on the ground. Several minutes pass. My dad testified that they talked about the game—Bad Guy 1, a fellow Niner-hater, otherwise occupied, had missed the second half. Bad Guy 1 says he wants a helicopter. S. says that is a possibility. They talk about making sure the girl does not get hurt—that is in everyone's interest.

Then the cavalry begins to arrive. My dad doesn't have a radio, so he has no way to keep the others away. Officer (now Detective) Martin Hong, patrolling nearby, is the first to show. There are sirens approaching from all directions. Hong screeches to a stop, sets up behind his car door, gun aimed at Bad Guy 1, and yells to my dad that he's covered. A couple of other squad cars pull up moments later. S. needs to communicate with Hong, get the patrolmen to back off. He tells Bad Guy 1 he's going to pick his weapon off the ground and walk back to the street.

S. reaches down for the gun. His eyes are on the lawn. Bad Guy 2 steps out from the side yard. From the street, Hong yells—well, now it depends on whose story you buy. Hong said he yelled "On your right." My dad heard "Gun, right" or "Gun to the right." Hong testified he saw no gun, there was no gun, and he never yelled "Gun." But S. heard "Gun."

In one motion, my dad hits the ground, grabs his gun, and twists onto his left side to cover Bad Guy 2. S.'s gun goes off and hits Daughter in the head. Bad Guys 1 and 2 end up looking like Swiss cheese.

In the following year and a half my dad stopped being a police detective—which was his central reason for living—and assumed a variety of other roles: witness at an inquest; subject of a police department internal affairs inquiry and a grand jury investigation; focus of constant media attention; and eventually, defendant in a civil suit. A child was dead and, with Bad Guys 1 and 2 in hell, and Bad Guy 3 God knows where, S. became the man to blame. The conclusion drawn in all these settings was that my dad was intoxicated, that he had no business responding to the call, and that he should not have been handling a gun.

Most of the guys in the department did not believe this for a minute, and neither did anyone who really knew S. before he got sick. I have never seen my father drunk. It just didn't hit him that way. The more he drank, the more focused, attentive, aware he became. It seems clear to me that on Super Bowl Sunday, 1989, the AD hit, maybe for the first time, disorienting him, and screwing with his judgment. I can't say whether it messed with his hearing or his shooting or his ability to make his own split-second decision about the threat, if any, posed by Bad Guy 2. But I'm sure it wasn't the liquor that sent my dad down the wrong side of the mountain.

When King says Hong fucked my dad during the investigation, what he means is that he told the truth. Had Hong wanted to back S., he could simply have agreed that he used the word "gun" at the scene. He could have justified my dad's response by claiming that he believed Bad Guy 2 had a weapon. I don't know that it would have made any difference. S. killed the Garfinkel kid; given the politics of the situation, and my dad's elevated blood alcohol level, it's hard to see how S. could have walked away intact.

The amazing thing, looking back, is that the girl's death wasn't enough to destroy my father. After a while people stopped mourning her and started to feel bad for Pop. As flawed as the logic was—S. had always been a big drinker—the department guys and politicians who matter in these things drew a line from my mom's death to the booze to the shooting. It wasn't his fault, really. He'd been dealt a miserable hand. No reason to overlook nearly twenty years of service. And no reason to deprive Santa Rita of one of the best police minds the county had ever known. After the SRPD settled with the Garfinkels and my dad accepted a demotion and therapy and AA, they stuck him at a desk and told him to keep his head down. In a year they'd have him back in the field.

The thing that finally ended my dad's career? Sex.

19

THE NEXT MORNING it takes me longer than usual to rouse my dad and convince him to spend the day at the Stonehenge Senior Center. It's Friday, Pop. I know that. Friday means you go to Stonehenge. Why? Because Lillian doesn't come on Fridays, and I have to go to work. Where's Lillian? She has another job, you know that. You tell me, where is Lillian on Fridays? How the hell should I know? Dad, come on. I got to go to work—what do you want to eat? Nothing. You have to eat, because otherwise you'll become invisible. Where's Lillian? What do you want to eat? I'm not hungry. And so on.

On the road, Duke calls my cell to tell me the chief public defender—my boss-in-theory's boss-in-fact, which I suppose makes him my boss, though I rarely interact with him—is waiting in my office to discuss the Dunn matter. Like, in my chair? He's hoping you might have a few minutes to spare for a chat. I'm not even close. I'm just getting my dad out the door. I'll be at least twenty minutes. Duke covers the phone with his hand. Then he comes back. Conference room at ten.

My dad begins to chuckle quietly to himself in the car. Nice to see the man smile. Nicer still to see him smile at me, look me in the eye, seem to connect on even a semiconscious level. Then again, this is S. we're talking about.

"What's so funny, Dad?"

"You don't know?"

"Um, I don't think I know."

"You wouldn't have been a very good police officer."

"I consider that a compliment. What is so damn funny?"

"You don't know?"

"If I knew, probably I'd be laughing too, right?"

No response, but he is still smiling.

"What the hell?"

"You have a tail." He is thrilled to give me this news, and seems disappointed now that he can never do so again. I look in the rearview.

"What are you talking about? I don't—" I do. A couple of cars back. SRPD, a marked squad car. I turn. They turn. I pull over. They do, too. They aren't trying to hide and they aren't trying to stop us. I get back on the road and make my way quickly to the senior center. By the time we get there my father has vanished into an impenetrable fog.

S. appears badly out of place at Stonehenge. It is filled nearly to overflowing with hunched and hobbled old people, many in wheelchairs or bent over walkers. But a significant portion of the day-timers are, cognitively, in excellent shape. Dad isn't sixty yet, and he looks more like a staff member—a doctor come to make rounds, maybe. But his deterioration is such that he is able to partake in only the most elementary activities. I sit with him for a few minutes. Friends came up to say hello, but S. scarcely acknowledges them.

"We had a tail," he says. The humor and excitement are gone. He seems desperate to hang on to the experience.

"That's right, Pop. You caught it, too. I wouldn't have seen it if you hadn't been in the car with me."

"I know," he says. "I was a police detective."

"Santa Rita PD."

"That's right."

"The best, or so I've heard."

He is gone.

*   *   *

119

So, sex.

In his present state it's hard to imagine, but my dad at one time had sex. I am proof, but there is additional evidence too, some of it not very flattering.

Several months after the Garfinkel shooting, S. returned to work. He did desk duty for a while, and when he seemed to be off the juice, they let him take care of jobs in the field that no one else wanted. One of those jobs was to drive around California to pick up state prisoners who had business in the Santa Rita courts.

Sometime in 1990 he traveled to a women's prison in the Central Valley and took custody of a woman named Angel Fisch. Ms. Fisch had been serving a ten-year sentence for bank robbery, but her conviction was overturned by the state Court of Appeal. She was to be returned to Santa Rita and retired. After four hours in the car together, S. and Angel took a liking to each other.

As far as I knew, my dad hadn't fallen in love after my mom died. He dated. Every so often, with no warning, a woman would appear for dinner a few times, then disappear just as unceremoniously. But when the AD symptoms hit—particularly during the year of the Garfinkel proceedings and publicity—I suspect my dad felt so despised and confused and terrified that he would have fallen for almost anyone who showed him the slightest regard.

A romance of sorts ensued. They spent hours on the phone. Daily visits, letters. On three occasions, S. used his police credentials to visit Angel inside the jail. He took her each time to a small supply closet where they had sex. Or made love. I think there probably was something like love between them. S. still talks about her, though these days not intelligibly.

Angel revealed her affair to nearly everyone. When she pissed off an inmate in her unit, the woman informed a deputy, who discovered S. and Angel, engaged, on a computer cart in the supply closet. Hence the endless and unfunny cracks about hard drives and floppy disks and viruses and joysticks and so on.

Not a comely end to a mostly dazzling police career. To add insult to termination—which followed quickly—Angel sued my dad and the department for civil rights violations and won—or, at least, the SRPD settled to tie a tourniquet around the hemorrhaging gash my father's conduct had inflicted on its reputation.

Sex. The destroyer.

After the SRPD tossed my dad, he went on a multiyear bender. I lived elsewhere and kept my distance. With S. drinking morning to night, for a few years, no one made much of the holes in his memory, his absentmindedness. The guy hadn't hit fifty; AD happens to old people. Anyway, that's what we thought. By the middle of 1995, he had his diagnosis. A little while later the doctors tied it to a gene.

When I walk outside Stonehenge, two patrol officers stand at the curb, leaning on the cruiser that followed us. I ignore them and walk to my car. In moments like this, I always feel like ambling nonchalantly for a few steps and then taking off running. Too much *Hawaii Five-O*, I guess.

I head for work. They follow. I take a few random turns here and there. They stay with me. There's something sort of fun about being chased—all right, fine, perhaps "chased" is an overstatement; how about "pursued"?—by the police. Who knew anyone cared?

I call Terry's cell. "Where are you?"

"Work. Where are you?"

"Getting rid of S. Can you think of any reason the SRPD would be following me?"

"You serious?"

"All morning."

"Hold on a second." I hear Duke's voice, and then Terry say "All right, all right," sounding annoyed. Then nothing for a minute.

121

Terry returns. "You there?"

"What the hell's going on?"

"Are you on your way?"

"Yeah. The Chief has something on his mind. I'm supposed to be there at ten."

"I'll meet you in there."

"What is it?"

"Dunn."

"What—"

"I'll see you in there." He hangs up. I dial the main number for my office. The cops are right on my tail. I wave at the rearview. They—two of them—wave back. An escort. I feel so much safer.

"Hey, Aineen, it's Gordy. Can you get me Maeve?"

"Everyone's looking for you, Gordy. Are you coming in?"

"Yes. Is she there?" Aineen must forget me because I am on hold for at least two minutes. Then Maeve picks up the phone.

"Santa Rita Public Defender's Office."

"Maeve, what's the word?"

"Darling, where the fuck are you?"

"What's going on over there?"

"Got me, only everyone on God's earth is looking for you."

"I haven't even had coffee yet. I had to drop my dad."

"Hold on."

"What's the big deal? Did they pick up Dunn?"

"Hold on."

"Maeve."

"Seegerman, where are you?" It's Duke, sounding like Chicken Little.

"Duke. You're popping up everywhere like a noxious weed."

"The bullcrap is hitting the wall, Seegerman. I advise you to check your bad attitude and get the hell in here."

* * *

122

"Jesus, who died?" I ask no one in particular as I walk into the office. The usually imperturbable Aineen looks freaked. Silvie Hernandez, Detective Martin Hong, and District Attorney Garland Fischer stand around the waiting room. The Chief, Duke, Terry, and a senior public defender named Francine Horiuchi, all looking very solemn, sit in a conference room a few feet away with the door closed. The look on Silvie's face says, "Do me a favor, don't act like we're friends." The Chief pokes his head out of the conference room door.

"Garland, why don't you give me a few minutes with my people and then we can all have a chat."

Inside, with the door closed.

"Sir, let me just say I'm sorry I was not here earlier. My father is—"

"Not interested, Mr. Seegerman. We've a complicated situation here and I'm trying my best to keep your sorry ass out of jail." The Chief's accent is indistinguishable from Groundskeeper Willie's, on *The Simpsons*. He always sounds like he's on the verge of declawing a cat with his teeth.

"Jail."

"You're familiar with a young woman by the name of Marjorie Styles." He looks down at a page of handwritten notes. "Sixteen Simonton Way?"

"Sure." I look at Terry. "One of the witnesses in my misdemeanor case."

"Not anymore, she isn't. She washed up out at the end of Seventh Street about eight hours ago. They picked up your fella Dunn this morning."

Fuck.

20

FORGET EVERYTHING YOU think you know about Barry Manilow and listen carefully. Please. Forget, if you possibly can, every snide remark, every cheap joke. And for God's sake, try to separate the unpleasant feelings you may have had at the dentist or during a job interview from the tunes you heard, beforehand, in the waiting room or elevator. Drop your attitude and disapproval and misconceptions and listen.

Barry Manilow doesn't need you. And Barry Manilow doesn't need me. When he brushes his teeth in the morning, the guy staring back at him is the most successful recording artist in the history of popular music. Frank Sinatra may be swanker. Elvis fans may be more fanatical. Madonna may, once, have been more fashionable. Michael Jackson's name may evoke more enthusiastic nodding in Outer Mongolia. Some have sold more records and some have earned more critical acceptance. But no one, ever, has put it all together—and held it together for thirty years—like Mr. Barry Manilow.

Let me tell you something, though: you need Barry. We all need him. Barry is us. He's Barry Alan Pincus, a skinny Brooklyn boy, a mutt—mostly Jewish, partly Irish—with a big nose and an absent father. He's a mailroom clerk at CBS Television who sneaks into a soundstage to play the big Steinway in the dark, terrified someone will find him and fire him from his good, stable job. He's the guy at the piano who is too shy, too unsure about his own voice, to step out in front. Even when he becomes the biggest recording star on the planet, you can still hear the bashfulness in his voice; you can still see he has no idea how he got there or how long it will last.

Listen to the music. I dare you. Barry is hope and hopelessness. Barry is love, desire, passion. Barry is exuberance and heartache. He is falling down and beating your palms against the ground and hollering about the unfairness of it all. And he is getting up, dusting off, and walking away. He is jumping up and down and pumping your fists in the air and spinning in dizzying circles. The reason he has sold tens of millions of records and has adoring fans on every continent and sells out concerts in hours after thirty years of touring is because, better than anyone else in popular music, in a simple, direct, unpretentious way, he reflects the essential, wondrous workings of human existence.

My friends, listen carefully: Barry Manilow is the truth.

So why is he still a punch line in some quarters? Why, if Elvis is cool, is Barry uncool? Why, if Tony Bennett is hip, if young pop stars line up to perform with him, is Barry the guy it's safe to malign?

Maybe he deserves it. Maybe this music—which eased my mother's blinding pain, which is familiar to an astounding fraction of the earth's population, which remains hugely popular after all these years—is just bad music. Maybe Barry's shows are bombastic and his audiences insipid. Maybe the songs are maudlin schlock.

Or maybe when we hear Barry we hear ourselves, a little nasal maybe, a bit south of flawless. Maybe when we see him we see us, with our blemishes and wrinkles and pants that fit too snugly around the middle. Maybe, some of us, sometimes, can't stand the sight of him, just the way some of us, sometimes, turn off the light when we walk into the bathroom. Too much information in that mirror.

You can hardly blame people for finding reasons to spurn him, to slander him, to ignore him. Barry is the daunting, overwhelming, terrifying truth. And a lot of people can't handle the truth.

21

TERRY IS RARELY cowed. But these circumstances—the violent death of Marjorie Styles, Dunn's arrest—have that effect. For a moment, before it dawns on me that this is *our* problem, I enjoy it.

The Chief waves at the DA's group in the waiting room, indicating we will be a minute or two. Or twelve.

"As you can see, Mr. Seegerman, there's a wee posse waiting, so let's get right to it. Mr. Fretwater asked us to wait until you arrived, which I think is right. You're the lead on the case. We have to be damn sure we're on the same page here. We certainly owe Dunn every allegiance. But we've institutional interests as well, don't we? So, please, bring us up to speed."

If I had an hour to think about what to say, I still would have felt lost. I have an obligation to my client, to protect him, but also to Terry and the court and my career. And to the truth. To Styles. Could we have done something to protect her? Could we have known Dunn would go off the deep end?

Did I step over any lines? What did we do exactly? We looked for him. We made inquiries. In the context of the exposure case, it meant nothing. But now everything we know—Terry and I—makes us potential prosecution witnesses in a murder case. And if I'm a witness, I'm not the lawyer on the misdo. Which wouldn't be so bad. But would I be obligated, or even allowed, to take the stand against Dunn? Would something I might reveal to the Chief and the others now hurt the wanker, or me?

We know Dunn had access to enough money to pay Don. Is that relevant? We know he'd been to see Styles. Could he have supplied her with the crank that she'd used shortly before we saw her? Did that have anything to do with her death? Could he have paid her to change her tune on the misdemeanor case? She was nothing if not alive when we left. Did that make us defense witnesses? Maybe she demanded more money and Dunn killed her.

"Terry interviewed Styles and the Dykstras on the misdo," I say. "I guess it was the next day or the day after that Dunn bailed out. Then he no-showed at a status in front of Heymann. I became concerned. I thought I might have forgotten to tell him about the appearance.

"Terry and I looked around a little. I hoped to avoid a bench warrant, but we couldn't find him. Then the deputy on the case, Ms. Hernandez, informed me that Dunn had contacted the witnesses himself. Apparently he called Styles and went to the Dykstras' house. I spoke with Mr. Dykstra after that, but I never met with him."

"That's it?" Duke says, deeply skeptical of my story. "What about a transvestite prostitute called Don?"

I laugh nervously. "Don. How could I forget?"

"Hernandez asked me whether we had contact information on him," Duke says. "Do we?"

"We found a phone number at Dunn's house. That got us to Don's management and eventually to Don. Dunn's a regular. Don contacted me a few days ago, Sunday night, when Dunn was at her place, but he left before I could get over there."

Not the whole truth, but not horribly misleading, either. I only left out the important stuff, and facts—like our decision to open Dunn's mail—that could result in our immediate arrest.

"And neither of you had any direct contact with the victim after Dunn bailed?" the Chief asks. He looks just like a Chief should look—tall; thick head of white hair; large, powerful hands; patrician bearing.

Silence floods the room.

"Sir, I have never been in this situation before, and I have great admiration for you and this office. But, with respect, I don't think Terry or I should answer that question."

"And your theory on that would be?" He is interested, not angry.

"In the context of the misdo, we see Styles, no big deal, right? She's an ID witness in a pending case. If she gets killed later, are we obligated to come forward with inculpatory evidence if, in the course of investigating the misdo, we came across such evidence? I think the answer is no. Even if Heymann orders me to say what I hypothetically know, I don't see complying. My primary obligation is to Dunn."

"And how bad is the evidence you hypothetically possess?"

"On a hypothetical scale of one to ten, I'd give it a four. Not meaningless, but not real significant, either. My guess is they already have the same and worse. Plus, I have to believe that no matter how little they need Terry or me, if they know we have anything, we'll be on their witness list. Meaning we get bumped from the misdo and the murder. That's not in Dunn's interest."

"Francine?" The Chief turns to my colleague in the homicide division for comments. Horiuchi is around my age, attractive, short hair, bangs, serious—unless intoxicated, and then she is lewd and hysterical.

"I agree. We ought to try to stay on these cases. Let's take a hard line and see what they have. Unless and until they get a judge to enforce a subpoena, why say anything? We hide behind privilege and work product. Fischer won't want a big fight on this, especially if they've got Dunn otherwise nailed. They shouldn't need anything we have. Unless for some reason Gordon's description is incomplete." Everyone laughs nervously.

"And staffing? How do you propose to handle that?" the Chief says.

Suddenly I sense a way to dump Dunn. "Most likely, Heymann will want to trail the misdo now, sir. Homicide should probably handle the whole package. Once the murder resolves, one way or another, the

314 is bound to disappear. I'm sure Terry will be happy to stick with the case." He forces a smile from across the table.

"Fine with me," Francine says. Relief. Then trouble, from the alien.

"Sir, I think Gordon ought to stay with the misdo until we see what Judge Heymann decides," Duke says. "He knows the file, he knows the client. For continuity. As soon as we start getting substantial action on the murder case we can make the transition." The Chief and Francine don't think this is a preposterous idea. Which leaves me with little choice.

"That's fine with me. I just assumed Francine would want me out."

Greetings all around. Slaps on the back. Very friendly. Marjorie Styles is on ice in the morgue. Harold Dunn's back in the tank. My life has become infinitely more complicated. And Garland Fischer acts like he's at a fund-raiser. Detective Hong gives me an awkward look and then remembers me from the Turkey Bowl. Detective Seegerman's boy. Good to see you. Yeah. Whatever.

Fischer speaks first. "Well, gentlemen and ladies, we've got a bit of a sticky situation here and we thought we'd better iron it out before we're in court on this thing."

Fischer, African-American, early fifties, struts around like a peacock in expensive suits and luminously shined wingtips. He is not a large man—thin and less than five and a half feet—and he stumbles when he speaks, but he is a gifted hand shaker and room worker and backroom deal maker. Everyone with whom Fischer speaks for more than a few minutes believes, forever after, that he or she is on the DA's A-list.

"Silvie, why don't you explain the situation?" Fischer says.

"As you probably all know, Marjorie Styles was murdered, almost certainly in the last twenty-four hours. She was probably strangled; we'll know more in a day or two. Without getting into too many details, we have evidence that Harold Dunn called and then visited

Ms. Styles at her home during the past week. We have evidence he supplied her with drugs. We have his fingerprints in her house. He had opportunity and motive. He's our guy."

"I would have been surprised if you'd arrested Dunn for murder without any evidence," I say, snidely.

"We didn't arrest him for murder. He turned himself in on the misdo warrant." She turns to Hong, who nods. "Actually, as far as I know we still haven't formally arrested him. We're holding him on the misdo."

Fischer speaks up.

"The thing is, Mr. Seegerman, we have information you had contact with Dunn after he failed to make an appearance, after a bench warrant was issued."

"That information is false," I say.

The Chief turns to me. "Mr. Seegerman, can we stick to the script, please. Hmm?" Then, to Fischer: "We'll be of whatever help we can. But I can't be in the position of having my deputies interviewed on pending cases. Unless you have a court order, of course."

The DA responds. "I'll be frank here. We're looking at obstruction charges. A woman is dead and Dunn may well face the death penalty for killing a witness. Your guy was all over town and these fellas were right behind him. If they saw something relevant, and failed to turn it over, that's obstruction. If we discover evidence that they prevented his rearrest, or helped him evade the police in any way, we have a big problem."

I draw blood from my lower lip in an effort to stay silent.

"We're all adults here, Garland. If you find illegality, we'd expect you to move on it. But let me be clear, too. I'm confident these men were operating well within their duties, ethically and professionally."

S. is everywhere in this room. No one need mention him. His misjudgments; the dead girl. Am I my dad? Did I screw up and cause Styles's death? Hong, Fischer, even Silvie—all of them suspect they'll discover malfeasance. They are here to put me on notice: this Seegerman won't get a second chance.

"Sounds like maybe you're really here because you don't have enough to make Dunn on the murder without our help," I say.

"We have a confession," Hong says. He couldn't help himself. Challenged, baited by a Seegerman, Hong walks right off the end of a pier. That is not something Silvie wanted me to know.

"Silvie? The police talked to my client without my knowledge?" I stand up.

"Sit down, Gordon. It's a different case, different investigation. We don't have any obligation to inform you. Read the law sometime."

Her point is legally correct. But still, she knows it's the kind of thing that simply isn't done. Like peeing on the dish of madeleines at a tea party.

After making the point, right as she is, Silvie sinks into her chair. She doesn't look happy with the situation and, if I know my ex at all, I know she would never pull a stunt like that.

"If he asks for a lawyer, we'll call you," Hong says.

"What do you mean 'asks'? You're still interviewing him?" Hong says nothing. "If my client is being questioned, I demand that it stop." He doesn't move. "Silvie, help me out here."

"Garland?" Silvie wants to help, but she needs backing.

"It's a police matter," Fischer says. "If you have a complaint, I think it behooves you to take it up with the SRPD or the court. It's out of our jurisdiction."

"Don't worry, Seegerman. Mr. Dunn's been real cooperative. He's not worried about Styles one bit. He's been trying to get us to dump the exposure charges."

Hong thinks the notion of Dunn trying to help himself on a misdemeanor while confessing to a potential death penalty crime is downright hilarious.

*   *   *

131

Dunn's telling the truth. That's what I decide when I walk out of the conference room. For the first time since I laid eyes on the wanker I believe his story. The whole thing must be a setup. The misdo, the murder. Dunn knows something—maybe it has to do with G-O-D, maybe with money laundering, maybe with drugs—that makes someone, somewhere, very nervous. Maybe it is the feds; maybe not. Anyway, for this person or persons, killing Dunn is an inadequate solution. For some reason, this person has chosen to frame him first for a misdemeanor and then for murder, no matter how much more complicated and time-consuming and seemingly ineffective that approach is compared with, say, shooting him.

I come to this conclusion for two reasons. First, too many bad and inexplicable things have happened to Harold Dunn in too short a period. Some people attract misfortune, but not this much. Someone is out to get this guy.

Also, Dunn may well have taken his pecker for a stroll at the Cullen's store, but he didn't kill Marjorie Styles. It wouldn't make sense. Anyone can kill in the heat of passion. But to kill a witness in order to prevent her from testifying in a misdemeanor case—particularly when there are two other witnesses—takes a very unusual mix of folly and savagery. Dunn is manic, and nerdy, but he isn't stupid, and he isn't the sort of violent it takes to crush a young woman's windpipe like a toilet paper tube. Anyway, who turns himself in on a misdemeanor warrant after strangling a witness?

Something extremely weird and highly unkosher is happening. I don't know who's responsible or why Dunn has become a target. And I really wish I didn't care.

22

BUT I DO. It's Hong's arrant self-righteousness, the thought that the police would interrogate Dunn without informing me, the idea that Silvie Hernandez, my Silvie, would work with these people. I cannot help myself. I don't really know whether Dunn is a psychotic killer or a harmless wanker, or both, or neither, but suddenly I care about the case. Which is not to say that I have any idea what to do next.

My office, twenty minutes later.

"For my birthday, I would like you to have Duke killed," I mumble.

"Let's go see Dunn." Terry follows me back to my office.

"He's still confessing," I say. "Can't you let a man confess in peace?"

"You want to bet he didn't confess to shit?"

"Hong did say 'confess,' right?" I say.

"Yes, but the way he said it. Something's wrong. They're missing something. If I had to bet right now, I'd say it was the boyfriend."

"Whose boyfriend?"

"Styles's. He's a crankhead. He looked psycho."

At the police station they tell us Dunn is back in jail. At the jail they say he is at the police station. The truth is that while we are wandering around downtown Santa Rita looking for my client, Silvie puts the case on for a status conference in front of Heymann that afternoon. So Dunn is in a holding tank in the basement of the courthouse, waiting for the hearing.

"Sorry I didn't make the court appearance, Mr. Seegerman. I swear it won't happen again." Quite a concession from a guy whose next trip out of jail may well be in a pine box. "I had a few things I had to take care of. I hope it won't hurt our chances. I feel real bad about Marjorie." Marjorie, like they'd been miniature golfing just yesterday.

"Harold, I'm not exactly sure where to begin. Can you tell us where you've been for the past few hours?"

He looks the same—unkempt, a bit manic. Not quite sure what he's done to deserve all the attention, but not entirely unhappy with it.

"Over at the police station talking to Detective Hong and then some others—Blunt and another guy. You want me to—" He has some crumpled papers with him and he starts shuffling through them.

"No, that's fine. Were they asking you questions about— Well, tell us, what did they ask you?"

"About Marjorie. They think I killed her." He laughs at that. "They arrested me again. Can they do that, Mr. Seegerman?"

"They can arrest you again if you committed another crime."

"They don't believe me. I told them I was there, I talked to her, first on the phone and then I went over twice. But I didn't kill her. I really liked her. She was G-O-D, you know."

"Really? How'd you find her?"

"Phone book."

"Ah, the phone book." Terry and I nod. "And the Dykstras, the same?"

"Yeah."

"Just in case we go through this again, please don't talk to the witnesses in your case," I say.

He is embarrassed. "Sometimes I get it in my head and—"

"What else did you tell the police?"

"That's it. There's nothing else to tell. They wanted to know where I've been for the past week. I said I mostly walked around. Saw some

134

friends. I didn't do much of anything. I was going to come back. I just needed time to think."

"Who is Gerald Fitzgerald?"

"Gerry? Oh, he's an old friend. How do you know Gerry?" He seems pleased to learn that his circle of confidants has closed rank.

"His name was on the bail receipt and it looked like he'd seen you in jail."

"Yeah. A rich friend. The best kind."

"And a lawyer, too."

"A lawyer? Is that what he told you?"

"That's what he told the jail, to get in to see you. He must have had a state bar card, too."

"I don't know anything about that." Dunn's brow scrunches together.

"Do me a favor and tell him to stay out of the jail, all right?"

"I don't think he'll come around anymore."

"Not too concerned about his ten thousand dollars, is he?" I say.

"Don't worry about Gerry. He's got it coming out of his boots."

"You understand you've been charged with murder. I won't be representing you on that."

"Why not? I don't want another lawyer."

"Well, we all have our specialties, Harold." For example, you are a wanking accountant. "I do smaller cases, but we have a very experienced homicide lawyer who'll handle the murder case. You'll love her. In any event, most likely Judge Heymann will want to put off trial on the misdemeanor until the murder case is resolved. And that will be in front of another judge."

"Don't worry about the murder charge. They'll never take me to trial. I didn't do it."

"They arrested you, so they must not only think you did it, they must have pretty good evidence."

"All they have is my prints in her house. I told them I went there, I talked to her. Why would I admit that if I killed her?" As he speaks he becomes more agitated. His cuffed hands flex up and down ceaselessly. "Why would I kill her?"

"Because she's a witness."

"That's ridiculous. I didn't do the other thing, either. It's all a big mistake. Marjorie said it herself. She said she didn't think I was the man she saw. I wish I had a tape recorder, because she said she'd tell the police she'd made a mistake."

Terry speaks up. "After you gave her a few hundred bucks." Dunn doesn't miss a beat. If he is not telling the truth about this part of it, he is a damn skilled liar.

"She was about to lose her child. She had to pay for a lawyer. I had it and she didn't. I wasn't trying to get her to help me. I was helping her."

"Why don't we forget we ever heard that, okay? As far as we know you never paid Styles a dime. Good."

I collect my things and am ready to go. Terry has other ideas.

"What about the setup, Harold? You think maybe someone at G-O-D killed Styles? You think Selmer Godfrey had something to do with it?"

"I can't talk about that." He looks humiliated, like a fifteen-year-old whose mother not only finds a package of condoms in his underwear drawer, but also wants to give him advice about a cheaper brand.

"That was all bullshit?" Terry says.

"I can't—"

I rescue him. "It's all right, Harold. Don't worry about it." The guy is deeply, painfully chagrined by his earlier accusations. He must really be manic, unable to stop his imagination from hijacking his mouth.

"So you're ready to plead on the exposure case," I say, hoping I can neatly tie up my end of the package this afternoon.

"No. I won't do that."

"And what defense would you propose?"

"It wasn't me. If I had just exposed myself, why would I have kept shopping? Why wouldn't I have left the store?" Not a bad point. Not enough to win a trial, but not completely idiotic either.

Terry and I get up to leave. Right before we walk out of the interview room I startle Dunn back to attention.

"Harold."

"Yeah?"

"What's Foghorn Trading?"

He shrugs. "I don't know."

"Never called there. Never stopped by."

"No. Am I missing something?"

"Don't worry about it. I'll see you in court."

We walk through the lobby. Just before we reach the door, Terry turns to me.

"A guy like Phil Dykstra doesn't list his address in the phone book."

I take out my cell and confirm just that with 411.

"Dunn's about ninety-seven percent full of shit," Terry says.

"Are we having fun yet?"

"I am."

"I can see that."

23

SILVIE SITS ON a bench outside Heymann's courtroom looking through a three-ring binder. I look at her from around the corner. It would probably be healthier to remember her in some entirely compromised position, giving it her all, as it were. But I always think of her singing. Maeve has a wonderful voice, but she treats Barry's ballads the way the Williams sisters handle tennis balls. Silvie's a finesse singer—less power and more poetry. I suppose I should be grateful to remember at all, but the reminder that she no longer sings—or no longer sings with me—is depressing.

She slams the binder closed when I arrive.

"Come on, let me have a peek. It's not my case anyway."

"Well, it's my case and I don't plan to screw it up," she says.

"Congratulations. Now you're probably glad you did Fischer that favor."

"It's hard to celebrate Ms. Styles getting throttled. Dunn's a psycho."

"I still think you got the wrong guy, but I'll let Francine worry about that."

"We have his prints in her house, on a bag of meth. We have him calling. He admits to being there twice. He told us he gave her four hundred dollars." She smiles, raising one eyebrow.

"That was nice of him."

"Her prints are in his car. *And* they found strands of hair, long hair, in the trunk."

"You guys don't screw around, do you? You must have had a very early morning."

"As a matter of fact, I did."

"You going to charge specials?" Which would make Dunn eligible for the death penalty.

"Probably. Fischer has the final say, but I can't see a reason not to."

"I guess this means you'll be glad to deal the misdo now. I mean, now that you have bigger fish to fry."

"Forget the misdo, Gordy. It'll be irrelevant in half an hour."

"I certainly hope so."

In court.

"Mr. Dunn, nice of you to stop by." Heymann seems to be in a chipper mood. His voice is squeakier than ever. "There are judges in this building who take these things personally. But the way I see it, everyone misses a dentist appointment or a haircut now and then. So let's just see that it doesn't happen again, shall we? I'm inclined to leave bail where it is, Ms. Hernandez, seeing as the original figure was on the high end."

"Your honor, the situation has changed considerably since our last appearance. This morning we arrested Mr. Dunn for the murder of one of the witnesses in the misdemeanor matter, Marjorie Styles."

The news stuns Heymann. "Mr. Seegerman?"

"From what we've seen so far they won't get past a prelim."

"Nevertheless, that changes the landscape considerably. How do you propose to proceed here? We have a trial date, when, December 18, right?"

"That's correct, your honor."

"Ms. Hernandez?"

"I think because the cases are related we probably ought to trail the misdemeanor. I'll be representing the People in both cases, but I believe another public defender will be handling the homicide."

"That's correct. I'll submit it, your honor," I say, figuring in fifteen seconds my Dunn days will have come to a troubling end.

Heymann puts his head down for several moments, looks through the case file, and whispers to his clerk. Then he looks at Silvie.

"How long to do this trial?"

Oh no. Please, don't do this to me.

"Two days," Silvie says.

"Mr. Seegerman?"

"I agree."

"No reason to trail that I can see," Heymann says. "We have the dates. We have the space. We'll have the jurors. Is there any reason the exposure matter can't be tried first? I assume it will be months before the murder case is ready to go."

"I'm sure that's right, your honor," Silvie says. "We may seek to join the cases in whatever court presides over the homicide. They arise out of the same circumstances, and I think joinder would be appropriate. If that occurs, the existing trial dates would be moot."

"And why wouldn't you file that motion here, Ms. Hernandez? I've sat on a few murder cases, you know. Or don't you think you'd get a fair shake?" He is baiting her, but affectionately. Or so it seems.

"Well, I suppose I— You are absolutely right, your honor. No reason at all. We will file the motion here."

"I'll save you the trouble, Ms. Hernandez. I'd be inclined to deny it. The presumption in favor of joinder applies only when the crimes are alike, or they arise out of the same circumstances. Even if Mr. Dunn was stupid enough to kill someone to avoid prosecution on the 314, that is a course of conduct entirely separate from exposing himself in a clothing store. What you've got here is a misdemeanor with one less witness."

"I understand, your honor."

"So. Bail is reimposed at $10,000. Of course, Mr. Dunn, you should understand that has nothing to do with your other situation. Until you get that one resolved, you'll be the county's guest."

Dunn smiles. He likes the judge. The judge seems not to have it in for Dunn.

"Mr. Seegerman, do the recent events change your mind about my ability to sit on the case? Perhaps you'd like a minute with your client."

"No, your honor. We're happy to stay here."

Outside the courtroom.

"You know what's happening, don't you?" Silvie is pissed.

"I rarely know what's happening."

"He's mad about his assignment, the misdo department. If he trails the 314, everything goes bye-bye. He says adios to Harold Dunn forever. If not, he figures Judge Reasoner will send the whole package to his court. He doesn't give a shit about the 314. He wants the murder."

"Really."

"Really. And let me tell you something. I'm not trying anything in front of Heymann. He acts like he's my damn father or something."

"He seems like a judge to me, albeit a judge who sounds like he's on helium."

"Well, you don't know him. He's a patronizing SOB. I'll have to get approval from Fischer, but we'll give you a break on the 314. Standard package."

"Really."

"Really."

"What happened to the sheet?"

"I have no intention of trying a misdemeanor while preparing my first murder case."

"And the prior? Your multiple-victim theory?"

"We'll amend. He pleads to one 314. Six months county."

"Three."

"Gordy, what difference does it make? He'll do the time long before the murder trial. He'll probably be in county jail for two years."

"I don't know. Three months just sounds better than six."

"Fine, three."

"Wow. I feel like I won something."

She walks off. "I'm so pleased I could make your day."

My victory lasts an hour.

Silvie gets the okay to make the offer. And a damn fine offer it is. She has a strong case on the misdo, even without Styles, because she would be entitled to inform the jury about Dunn's Oregon exposure conviction. And then there's the kid. Why would an eight-year-old lie about seeing some old guy's peepee? For a whole hour, I figure we got the offer because Fischer and Silvie lost interest in the misdo. But on my way over to the jail, to beat Dunn on the head until he agrees to plead, I change my mind.

Whatever physical evidence they might have against Dunn on the murder case, which so far isn't overwhelming, the DA will still have to have a theory as to Dunn's motive. If he pleads guilty to the misdo, he'd practically be making the prosecution's case for them. If he's guilty on the 314, he has a reason—hardly an adequate reason, but a reason nonetheless—to take out a witness. But if he's innocent, and if he should manage to beat the 314 before the murder case ever goes to trial, the DA will have a serious problem convincing twelve people that Dunn's their guy. Trying a murder case without a convincing motive theory is like cooking without salt. It's not that it can't be done, it just doesn't work very well. I call Silvie.

"You're slick, but not that slick," I say.

"I'm really busy right now, Gordy."

"No deal on the misdo," I say. "You want your 314 conviction, you'll have to come and get it."

"Your client's nuts."

"I haven't seen my client. It just occurred to me that your offer sucks."

"What? You want an apology? How much lower than three months do you want me to go?"

"Nice try, my dear. You have to get up pretty early in the morning to put one over on a Seegerman."

"Good-bye, Gordy."

I feel pretty proud of myself, dodging that one. Until I start to think maybe I have it backward. Or inside out. If a conviction on the misdo is a near certainty anyway, why not take the deal? At least that way at the homicide trial he'd have an argument he was just trying to get it over with, that he pleaded guilty on the exposure in order to focus on the murder prosecution. If a jury convicts him at the misdo trial, which they probably will, then Silvie will really have her motive argument.

In the end, my confused thinking about the issue is immaterial. I figure I will leave it up to Dunn.

"It wasn't me, Mr. Seegerman. They got the wrong guy."

The man is in a terrible situation. His life might very well be all but over. A few years from now he might be strapped down to a bench, poison-filled tubes sticking out of his arms. But he appears to be, not relaxed exactly—he still has the excited energy of a man with something important to say whose mouth is stuffed with food—but optimistic.

"Maybe you should call me Gordy."

"Gordy." He looks honored. He sticks out his shackled wrists to shake.

"I think you should think seriously about taking the offer. It is a very generous deal, and in my opinion we will most likely lose at trial."

"No way. It's a case of mistaken identity. It happens all the time. Everyone knows that."

"Even still, Harold. Think about it."

"There's nothing to think about. You're a great lawyer. You'll figure it out."

24

I'M NO BARRY wannabe, but there are parallels. They're not what brought me to him, but they're part of what keeps me interested. His dad wasn't around much. Mine, either. His grandmother played a central role in his childhood. Ferdy filled in for my mom after she died. Mothers with big, strong personalities. Astounding musical abilities obscured by dead-end day jobs.

And we are sons of Jews who married Irish-Jews. S. is Jewish. My mother was Mary McNamara. Her father was John McNamara. Her mother was Judith Rosenfeld. Barry's mother was Edna Manilow. His father was Harold Pincus. Harold's father, called Harry, married Ann Sheehan, an Irish girl from Brooklyn. After Barry's father split, his mother married William Murphy, another Irishman.

What does all of this mean? I don't know exactly, except that it isn't meaningless. There is something to it—say, three parts paranoid exuberance mingled with one part stubborn, acerbic wit. A breakfast of bagels, cream cheese and lox, with a Jameson's chaser. You can't even really call it a *mix* of religions and heritages and cultures. Oil and vinegar don't *mix*. But if you shake them together long enough, you get an emulsion, an imperfect blending, a semipermanent suspension. That's what it's like to be me. And Barry, too, maybe.

The day the SRPD arrests Harold Dunn for the Marjorie Styles murder also happens to be the first day of Chanukah. I walk into my house falling-over exhausted. Our cavernous living room is dimly lit. A fire

145

burns angrily in the stone hearth. Ferdy, dressed in a suit, stands at the mantelpiece, prepared, as if he's been standing there waiting for me for hours, to recite the prayer and light the first candle on the menorah. S. stands next to Ferdy, mesmerized by the wood popping and crackling in the fireplace. Ferdy has the traditional takeout Chinese food on the table. He looks at me and knows I have totally forgotten the holiday. I have nothing for anyone—no gifts, no energy.

My grandfather has been holding our family together for years. He moved into an apartment above our garage after my mom died. He played mother and father to King and me. He took care of my dad. He encouraged me to move back home after Silvie and I split, to spend some time with S. before he drifted out of reach. And although he is a vocal atheist and a nonbeliever in things incorporeal, he hangs on to Passover and Rosh Hashana and Yom Kippur and Chanukah because they tie us—S. and King and Ferdy and me—together, if imperfectly and momentarily, and not always joyfully.

"I'm late. Sorry."

"Go put on a jacket," Ferdy says, annoyed.

I am not about to argue.

"Hey, Dad." I say, kissing his cheek. "Is King coming?"

"Go put on a jacket. Your father is about to keel over."

King shows up halfway through dinner and quickly finishes off several beers. With my help, S. eats a little; then he wanders up to his bedroom. Ferdy eats silently. To say this is uncharacteristic is to understate the matter considerably. He says nothing of the most recent outrages of the Bush administration. He does not offer the usual lecture on our generation's failure to comprehend the meaning of liberal democracy, to defend civil liberties, to take to the streets to defend the poor and disenfranchised. Something is more wrong than usual. And then it comes. The end.

Ferdy puts down his chopsticks, takes a swig of beer, and puts his hands on the edge of our nine-foot-long dining room table. "Beatrice and I are getting married."

"When?" King and I say, in stunned unison.

"How about 'congratulations,' you little bastards? Soon. Although she needs to kick out a few of her kids to make room for me."

The end. I can't stay in the house with S. alone. King long ago made it clear he isn't coming back. We will unload the manse and stick Dad in a high-priced nursing home for as long as the money lasts. And then we'll see.

"That's good news, Grandpa." I am mournful.

"You'll be all right."

"I guess. Who's best man?"

"Your father, if he's up to it." He seems enormously relieved—to have told us, and to have finally accepted that he can no longer take care of his son.

After dinner, Ferdy and I trade places at the piano and sing folk songs and show tunes and standards. King slumps into the living room couch.

"It's hard to believe someone else will live here," I say.

"You'll be fine."

"I know. I suppose it's best for S. I just didn't think this would ever be a place I couldn't come to. Growing up never seemed an appealing option. Can I move in with you?" I said.

"You go find yourself a girl. Enough of me."

"Easier said than done, Gramps. I have a liability or two."

"What?"

I raise my eyebrows.

"Listen, you're a catch no matter what," he says.

Later, Ferdy has gone to sleep. King stares at my back while I play the piano quietly.

"I hate the idea of leaving here. I mean, I know we'll have to eventually, I'm just not ready."

147

There is no answer. I assume he has passed out, but then his voice startles me.

"This place gives me the creeps."

"But familiar creeps, right?"

"No, just the creeps."

"And what about S.? You really think moving him to a home is going to help?"

"Nothing's going to help, Gordy. The sooner you accept that, the better. Honestly, I think the best thing for S. would be to go someplace where they know what the hell they're doing."

"We do all right."

"I guess. It's not that I don't appreciate it. I do. But you have to know when you've been hit enough, when you should stay down on the mat. It's enough already. He's gone. You—we all—have to move on."

"I don't know."

"Well, I do."

25

BACK AT PREET'S garage, days later. Preet is at his computer, with headphones on, doing his best to stay out of our mess. Maeve lies on the couch scouring a teen fashion magazine for pictures of young girls in their undergarments.

Terry balances on one leg on a plastic milk crate. He wears an electric guitar around his neck and hits power chords to emphasize his thoughts. "I don't think we're as lost as it seems," he says. "We are missing at least one important piece of the puzzle." He is increasingly obsessed with Harold Dunn.

"We're missing the box with the picture of the puzzle, and half the pieces," I reply. "And you are missing several dozen IQ points."

There is no defense, no way to try Dunn's 314 with a straight face, absent real evidence the wanker was set up. What am I going to do, demolish an eight-year-old on cross? "Isn't it true, Ms. Dykstra—if that's your real name—isn't it a fact that you make believe all the time? You expect us to believe someone who runs around in a witch's costume, pretending a broomstick is a flying machine?"

There is something to the case, something more than Dunn's public naughtiness. With a year, a team of investigators, and a lot of money, maybe we'd find out Dunn was framed or, far more likely, we'd find nothing. In any event, I have two weeks before jury selection, no money, and Terry—a stellar investigator, friend, and bass player, but not the world's most pragmatic man.

Maeve snarls at me from across the room, without looking up from her magazine. "Don't think I haven't noticed you checking your messages every ten seconds. I now pronounce you Husband and the Hair. You may brush the bride."

Admittedly, Myla has been on my mind. Perhaps I have been slightly distracted during rehearsal, though I tend to be a highly focused person and, unquestionably, eighty percent of my attention is worth all of Maeve's. She has the focus of a six-year-old hopped up on Froot Loops.

Ms. Miravich and I had another lovely dinner two nights earlier and, I think, safely passed out of that awkward early phase in which sex is altogether out of the question. She did not complain too loudly when I put my arm through hers as we hiked through the wooded Santa Rita hills on a sunny Sunday afternoon. We have spent several hours together without access to our cell phones. We get along. That is the important thing.

I've left a couple of messages and yes, I am anxious to hear from her. My anxiety manifests as me glancing at my phone every few minutes to make absolutely sure I have not missed her. And that the battery is still good. And that the ringer is on.

"What is your problem?" I say.

"Nothing, except it is obvious the little head is at the wheel. Too bad the little bastard can't see over the dashboard."

"You spend your life in totally unworkable, often felonious relationships and do I say a word? N-O. I do not. That is because it is not my proverbial fucking beeswax who you sleep with."

She looks at Terry. "Can I get some help? Is this the right time?"

"Can we come back to the point?" Terry says.

"Gladly," I say.

"We have to figure out the motive behind it. What would setting him up accomplish? It occupies him—gets him off the street for a while, even if eventually he walks on the charges. Whoever is responsible needs breathing room. Something important is about to happen and Dunn is, or was, in the way."

"Okay," I say, drawing out the last syllable.

"What about the holiday party? The G-O-D fund-raiser."

"And?"

"I don't know. Something's going to happen there and they need Dunn gone."

"That makes perfect sense," I say. "Except for the bit about the—everything you just said."

"I'm just trying to get us out of the box here, man. What else?"

"The charges could hurt his credibility, I suppose."

"Right."

"Just seems like a lot of maintenance. If I wanted him out of the way, I'd shoot him, puncture his stomach, tie a bunch of weights to him, and drop him in the bay. Adios, Señor Wanker."

"But if you're the federal government you can't really do that, now, can you?" Terry asks, a crafty smile sneaking across his face.

"What do they want with him, and in jail? It doesn't make any sense."

I sit down at Maeve's drum kit and whack around for a few seconds. She looks over, annoyed. I wave a stick at her. "What do you think, Ms. I Have an Opinion About Everything?"

"I think Dunn isn't the only guy with his dick in his hand."

Terry walks over to Preet and lifts off his headphones.

"We need help, man. We're getting close to the waterfall."

"Go find a barrel."

"Come on."

"No."

"What's the big deal?" Terry says. "Obviously there was no problem last time, or we would have heard something, right? I'll get you a hooker."

Preet is uncommonly shy, sheepish almost. We wonder if he has ever had a date. We assume he is a virgin. We do not talk about it.

"We'll let you sing?" I say.

151

"No fucking way." Maeve is off the couch. "I draw the line at Preet singing in public."

Preet is a master musician, the sultan of samplers, the overlord of orchestration. And a damn fine songwriter. But he can't carry a tune.

"You think I would sing anyway, with this kind of support from my so-called friends?"

He puts the headphones back on. Terry removes them.

"Gordy and I think you have a fine voice, overflowing with, with what?"

"Fiber," I say.

"Exactly. Your voice is incredibly fibrous. If Bob Dylan can sing and Lou Reed can sing, surely you should be able to get out in front once in a while."

I smile and say nothing.

"My own song."

Terry looks at me. I shrug.

"Fine with us."

"Two."

"One of yours and one backup."

"Miracle?" Preet says. In other words, "It's a Miracle." A sly choice, because it's a crowd-pleaser and the backups stand out.

"Deal."

Terry looks at me. "Deal?"

I nod. Maeve is miserable about the arrangement, but she's been outvoted.

"Try Dykstra," I say.

"Why?" Terry asks.

"Because that's the key to the misdo. At this point, without the kid the case goes away. If someone set up Dunn, he got to the Dykstras. Don't you think it's a little ridiculous, though, framing someone for pulling out his penis in a clothing store?"

152

"Someone who knows he has a prior? Who maybe knows a second conviction could land him in state prison for a few years?"

"I suppose."

"What are we looking for?" Preet wants guidance.

"G-O-D connections, I guess; that's where his past was known. Actually, see if you can get a board of directors list for G-O-D."

I step on a pedal, which smacks the bass drum and drives Maeve to her feet. "Could you not do that?"

"Sorry," I say. "Read out the names."

He goes through the list. Some I recognize, but only because they'd be familiar to anyone who spends time in bars filled with city employees or who has lived in this town forever—a junior city council member, two women with prominent last names. And Bartholomew Setz, Sr., chairman of G-O-D's board.

"What's Selmer Godfrey's position?" Terry asks.

"Executive director," Preet says after a few seconds.

"And Mary Godfrey?"

"Not in the annual report," Preet says. "She's all over the website but it doesn't look like she's official in any way. Look at that—pretty low for the son of God-frey."

Preet chuckles, extraordinarily pleased with himself, and points to a line in the report. Selmer Godfrey receives an annual salary of $29,000.

"It's a nonprofit," I say. "Go back to the Dykstras. Criminal stuff, credit reports. Tell us who these people are. Maybe the eight-year-old kid has a juvenile record."

"Nothing. Nothing. Boring. Whoah. Look at that."

I walk over to Preet's cockpit and peer over his shoulder at a credit report. The Dykstras have no money. What they have, in heaps, is debt. Including major borrowings from Santa Rita Mutual.

Terry points at my head, with a eureka look in his eyes. "Selmer Godfrey is up to something, just like Dunn says."

"Said," I add.

"Something Mary wouldn't approve of. So, he brings in Setz."

"Setz is doing fine. Why does Setz need Selmer?"

"Who knows? Maybe Selmer's blackmailing him. Maybe Setz likes little boys. Who cares? All I know is, Selmer and Setz are up to something huge. Dunn figures it out. He's a liability. They need him out of the way. Something's about to go down. And Dykstra's deep in the hole. He owes Setz big time. Selmer goes to Setz, and Setz goes to Phil for a little favor."

"You are—I've never—I can't—" I cut myself off with applause, unable to find the words to describe Terry's brilliance.

"We're out of the clouds and we see the damn airport. I'm not saying we're sipping cocktails at the airport bar yet. We're getting closer."

"To what, exactly? And what about Marjorie Styles? She's the one who first identified Dunn. And what about the feds? Remember them?"

"In this room there are at least two heads up as many assholes." Maeve has held on for quite a while, listening while the boys miscalculate endlessly and find themselves nowhere in particular. Plus, we have come close to impugning someone who helped her kid. Not a safe course. "G-O-D is one of the few organizations in this city worth shit. I don't care what you or Max says about Mary Godfrey. My daughter has her life back."

"No one's saying—"

"Did I sound like I was through?" We freeze. Silence. "Fine, I'm through."

Preet speaks up. "Did you know Bartholomew Setz and Mary Godfrey are an item?"

"What?"

26

"**C**HECK THIS OUT." Preet points to a computer screen. For the first time, he seems genuinely interested in the case. This scares me. Terry I can handle. But together, Terry and Preet will tie themselves, and me, into a knot that can be undone only by police officers, firemen, or doctors.

There they are—fat, square-headed Bartholomew Setz, in a tux, looking every bit the local mogul, and helmet-hair Godfrey, five inches taller—holding hands, caught by a photographer from the *Journal* at a Santa Rita Mutual–sponsored charity gig.

"Holy shit," Terry says, nodding wildly while his dreadlocks toss against thin air.

"Pretty strange," Preet adds.

"Mary Godfrey's getting laid. That's your conspiracy? Dunn is so, so guilty," Maeve says.

No. We are no closer to figuring out why Dunn landed in jail, but it isn't because he flashed little Callie Dykstra three weeks earlier. Guilty people are rational. They may say a witness is lying; they may ask me to file a suppression motion; they may complain about the DA's plea offer. But in my experience, when it comes down to it, guilty people take the deal. Or if they go to trial, they have a good reason to do so: they know the key witness has problems, they figure the evidence is thin. Guilty people analyze the situation and arrive at a sensible solution. If they choose to roll the dice with a jury, it's because they think they might win.

Innocent people, like Dunn, often are not at all rational. Dunn wants a trial. But he has no reason to think he can prevail. He refuses to plead out, although given the murder charges, he'll almost certainly serve the time on the misdo before he resolves the homicide. And it isn't as if pleading to the exposure will hurt his reputation, because he already has the Oregon conviction. The reason a guy like Dunn goes to trial is because he didn't do it.

My cell rings, and my heart skips. But it is Ferdy. It had been raining steadily for a couple of days. Our house desperately needs a new roof. Actually, it desperately needed a new roof years ago. Now, in some places, it requires the installation of skylights because there are holes big enough to appreciate a full moon through. S. thought he'd do some repair work, in the dark, and in his bathrobe.

Fifteen minutes later I am on the terrace outside my room, under an umbrella, shouting up at S., who is doing God knows what with a power drill on the steeply pitched roof, three stories above our cement drive-way. He either cannot hear me or chooses not to, so I climb up, through the attic, out a landing, and up an aluminum ladder S. has somehow perched on a lip of the roof. I do not like ladders. I believe I might die.

"Hey, Dad," I say, my curly mane limp with rain.

On his knees, cordless drill in one hand, he looks at me as if I have interrupted him on the verge of a Nobel-worthy discovery. He says nothing. The drill whirs loudly, but there is no bit or screwdriver attachment in it. My cell rings. Ferdy from downstairs, probably.

I answer. "I don't know what the hell he's doing but—"

It is Preet, sounding uncharacteristically inflamed.

"I thought you were going home," he says. "Ferdy said to try your cell."

"I am home."

"Why are you on your cell, then?"

"Because that's where you called me, Preet. Did you want something?"

"Setz Senior has an old tax case. He pleaded guilty to evasion in the late eighties."

I squat on my feet and brace my rear against the roof. A street lamp across the yard illuminates the rain like a spotlight. My rubber heels make islands in the water that washes down the roof in rivulets.

"Don't you think we should do 'I Am Your Child' straight for Barry?" I ask, not really hoping to kill the conversation, but maybe to slow it down a little. "Seems like to soup it up would be disrespectful. The guy really loved his mother."

Terry is in the background, demanding to talk to me. He can't abide the chitchat. Preet manages to get in a few more words and then Terry grabs the phone.

"It's out of L.A. From the original charges, it looks pretty ugly. Mail fraud, wire fraud. And, get this—money laundering."

"But he pleaded to the tax count."

"Looks like it."

"Which means they didn't actually have any evidence on the other charges. They just stacked the indictment to scare him."

"We're getting close, Gordy. I can smell it."

"What you smell is your own foul breath. We have nothing. Or, let me take that back. I have nothing. I am the one who has to try this case, and so far I have zilch."

"We need to get into G-O-D somehow."

"Talk to Duke. I'm sure he'll approve an undercover op."

"Your negativity is unproductive."

"Your dementia is worsening."

My dad seems immobilized by all the activity in his work area. He sits down next to me and stares down into the yard. He pulses the drill rhythmically.

"Just agree with the idea in principle," Terry begs.

"Fine. Without regard for possible criminal liability, loss of my law

157

license, job, and dignity, sure. It would be interesting to spend a couple of days going through G-O-D's files."

"Maybe you should put off the trial. We need more time to figure this out."

"Heymann won't do it. Not without a good reason."

"What about Ferdy? He could volunteer at G-O-D."

"Good-bye."

I sit for another few minutes, alternately watching my dad and staring at Myla's name and number on the screen of my cell phone. I press the "call" button, while my stomach does a couple somersaults.

"What's that noise?" she asks.

"A cordless drill."

"What are you drilling at nine-thirty at night?"

"My father's drilling. I'm just supervising."

"What's he working on?"

"I don't exactly know. My dad always has some kind of project going on."

"It's raining really hard over here." In San Francisco.

"Oh yeah?" I look up from underneath the umbrella, which doesn't quite cover me and S. The wind picks up, the rain hits me sideways. The ladder slides an inch along the top of the roof. "It's not too bad here."

Drops of water drip off my eyelashes and large, fleshy earlobes. I shield the phone as well as I can and wonder whether there is enough power in a cell phone to electrocute a person. She talks. I talk. I wonder whether she will run if I tell her I might lose my mind in a few years. I watch S. drill nothing. I get wetter and colder and begin to shake. S. is oblivious. Every so often Ferdy shouts up. I cover the mouthpiece on my cell and tell him we are fine. Just fixing the roof.

I walk into my office the next morning to find a stack of legal motions on my desk. *People v. Dunn*. Prosecution's Motion to Offer Evidence of Prior Misdemeanor Conviction; Motion to Introduce Evidence of Marjorie Styles Homicide to Prove Defendant's Consciousness of Guilt; Motion to Offer Evidence of Statements Made by the Deceased Witness.

Silvie does not mean these motions to gain advantage at trial. She means them to bury me. To compel Dunn to take the offer, any offer. She means them to make a statement: *Wake up, Gordon, you and your wanker are about to be roadkill.*

There are lawyers who love motions work, who relish the hours in the library. I am not one of those people, which is one reason I've stuck to misdos. Most DAs don't even file motions in misdemeanor cases. Too much bother. But Silvie wants this case to go away. And if she wins these arguments—if, for instance, she gets to offer evidence of the Styles killing at the exposure trial—there will be even less reason for me to pitch the case to a jury. She wants to focus on the murder prosecution, and that means putting me out of my misery early in the 314 proceedings.

Duke walks in while I am fingering the papers, flipping through pages aimlessly, hoping to find a reason to file nothing in response.

"The Dukester," I say, jovially.

"What have you got there?"

"The DA filed a bunch of paper in the Dunn 314 case."

"Anything interesting?"

"She wants to prove Dunn killed Styles."

"In the misdo?"

"Yup."

"Heymann will never go for that. She's reaching."

"I guess."

"You know, if you'd quit sniveling you might see the case is triable."

"With an eight-year-old star witness."

"Seegerman, I have an eight-year-old. Cindy has a memory like quicksand. She couldn't pick a wanker out of a lineup if her life depended on it. You make an *Evans* motion yet?"

"No."

"What about a motion to exclude the kid's testimony?"

"Who turned you into a lawyer all of a sudden? Anyway, on what ground?"

"I don't know, Seegerman. It's not my case. Overly suggestive? Incompetence? Due process? Figure something out. It was the dead woman who identified the guy first, right?"

"I think that's right."

"Well, what do they have, really? The kid doesn't identify your guy until they already have him in custody. The guy was probably cuffed. Of course she's going to say he's the one she saw."

"I suppose."

"Don't look so depressed, Seegerman. Grab the bull by the legs. Do your job. You're a public defender. Act like one."

I contemplate laughing. I try to sneer. But it isn't in me. He's right.

27

TWO BLOCKS FROM my office, in a narrow, garbage-strewn alley, there is an enormous bar and steakhouse called Department 13. Every courtroom in the Santa Rita Superior Court building has a department number, but there is no 13, just as some buildings have no thirteenth floor. Hence Department 13. Each evening, the court crew—lawyers, cops, judges, clerks, deputy sheriffs—fills the place. Like most of its patrons, it is coarse, crusty, hoarse, haggard, slouching purposefully toward Gomorrah.

Terry, Maeve, and I often meet here after work. Sometimes Preet joins us. Sometimes he complains about the noise, the smoke—illegal in California, but cops smoke bloated cigars at the bar, so who's going to complain?—the nonvegetarian fare. Once in a while Ferdy drags my dad down here for dinner and a reminder of his former life.

I sit at the bar, sipping bourbon, smoking a once-in-a-while cigarette, and pretending to read Silvie's papers. A large mirror across the way catches me like a callow buck in a hunter's scope. Gotcha, Seegerman. You can run, but you cannot hide. I run my fingers across Silvie's name in the caption of her motion: "Silvie R. Hernandez, Deputy District Attorney." It can't possibly be as bad as I expect. I'm not a terrible courtroom lawyer. Juries like me, even when they convict my clients. So I'll lose a trial to a woman I used to love. So what?

I look in the mirror and slip back into fantasy mode. I see me, at the piano, onstage at Ted's looking out into the audience, past Ferdy and my dad in front, Ted and Max at the bar, the standing-room-only crowd, to a table in a far corner of the room, near the door, where a thin man dressed in black sits with two colleagues sipping a club soda with lemon.

I'm tempted to introduce him, but I don't. Exposure is his prerogative; should he want to move from observer to participant, he'll come forward. Finally, after we finish a song, he walks toward the stage. My heart pumps violently. I get ready to introduce him, but he ducks into a hallway next to the stage to use the restroom. Every head in the room turns to watch the man's back. They believe in me, in us, but we all await word from Barry. We require his imprimatur.

As he emerges, I take a chance. "Ladies and gentlemen, what an extraordinary honor, Mr. Barry Manilow." The audience cheers and comes to its feet. He waves and smiles, but returns to his table. During the set I glance back several times to check on him. The crowd is with us, but Barry is not. He's bent over in close conversation with his friends. He shakes his head a couple of times during "I Write the Songs," laughs, and slugs down his soda. All we can do is play our hearts out. We're together, as good as we've ever been, but we're not reaching him. He seems bored.

The night wears on and the crowd begins to sense our fear, our disappointment. The energy evaporates. We try a couple of up tunes—"Miracle"; a medley of advertising jingles Barry wrote or sang—but nothing works. Some people at the back leave. Desperate, I hesitantly ask him to join us for a number. He rises halfway out of his seat, acknowledges me, but declines. *Thank you. Thank you very much. Perhaps some other night.*

I huddle with the band and tell them to go into "Weekend in New England." By consensus—the Mandys', our audiences'—it is our strongest song. Usually we hold it until the end. But we have no time to waste. I put my head down, close my eyes, think of my mom, Silvie, Myla, S., Ferdy, the band, my life, and belt it out like I've never done before. The chatter at the bar quiets. The waitresses stop in their tracks. The clinking of beer bottles and jangling of keys and tapping of feet cease. It is up to me. There is nothing left to do but sing—"I feel the change coming, I feel the wind blow, I feel brave and daring, I feel my blood flow." The song ends and I bow my head.

When I look up, the crowd is on its feet. After a minute, they sit. There is an empty table where Barry was. A waitress is clearing away glasses. We've lost him.

Ferdy walks in with my dad, who is dressed in black slacks, a sport jacket, a white shirt, and a loosened tie, like he might have been after a day of interviewing witnesses or testifying or meeting with department brass. One of the curious features of AD is the absence—relative to many other neurological diseases—of physical symptoms. If we can get S. to shower and shave and put on a decent outfit, he looks pretty good, better in some ways than he did when his primary source of calories was gin.

We sit in a booth and order dinner. Ferdy rants about the president of the United States, a man he calls The Tush.

It has not been an easy century for my grandfather. His family ran out of their village in the Ukraine with a few suitcases, at the urging of some unfriendly bearded guys on horses. Failing to thrive in New York, they started west, shedding members in such unlikely places as Memphis and Reno. Great-Grandma and Great-Grandpa Seegerman kept moving and settled in Santa Rita, the terminus for the transcontinental railroad. By the time Ferdy started to consider growing up, the Depression had hit.

If the Seegerman clan had a coat of arms, it would say, in Latin, "Hounded, Trounced, and Luckless, but Still Cautiously Optimistic."

Ferdy sought refuge in leftist politics. He became a socialist, then a communist, until Stalin made fools of the American reds, at which point he became a labor activist, then a civil rights activist, then an antiwar activist, and then an antinuke activist. These days he opposes

163

nearly everything and believes, correctly no doubt, that pretty much everyone is out to screw pretty much everyone else. His gloomy political views, his sad family history, and his rotten back, knees, and hips notwithstanding, he is a remarkably cheerful eighty-eight-year-old.

"You know," Ferdy says, dropping his volume, glancing around warily. "Somebody's buying up property in West Santa Rita, over by the freeway."

"Oh, yeah? Where'd you get that?"

"I got my sources. You ever heard of an outfit called Foghorn something, Foghorn Management, I think?"

Oh, God.

"No. You sure it's Foghorn?"

"Absolutely." The "o" is accented and slightly overlong, a product of his years at the docks. "They're the boys doing the buying."

Myla is supposed to show up in a couple of hours. I am not ready to expose her to my dad, so I try not to engage. But when Ferdy happens upon a worthy topic, he's like a bulldog with his teeth around an old shoe.

I cut my dad's steak and potato into tiny pieces and watch as he slowly feeds himself. No myoclonus tonight. He is sluggish, but the food makes its way into his mouth. I have no clear sense where he is— listening, not listening. Aware of his former colleagues milling around the bar, the occasional glances, the eyes averted, the almost imperceptible air of grief that attends his public appearances. Or not.

"Is that a fact?"

"They're paying way above market for vacant lots, crap houses, and then renting them back to the owners. Something big is happening and I'll bet you it ain't gonna be good for the little guy. I'll tell you, Gordy, once upon a time this was a working-class city. The rich bastards stayed on their side of the bay, in Frisco. It's that damn bridge." He swings his head from side to side mournfully. "They never shoulda built it."

The bridge Ferdy detests, a structure he may well have planned to dynamite in his more radical days, his personal windmill, is the Bay Bridge, an elegant span from San Francisco to the East Bay, the Santa Rita side, completed in 1936. The bridge cost more to build than any single structure in modern history. Its piers, sunk deep into San Francisco Bay, contain more concrete than the Empire State Building. Ferdy was twenty-two when it opened.

He worked the docks and played nights in big bands around town. The Pyramid, the Excelsior, the Santa Rita Lounge. He stayed home during the war because of a leg injury, but he entertained the shipyard workers and sailors on leave. Ferdy married Annie Gold in 1941. They had a daughter the next year, who died before she turned one. S. appeared in 1945. Annie passed before the decade was finished.

I wouldn't blame my grandfather if he holed up somewhere and licked his wounds. Life hasn't been particularly kind to him. But he'd rather fight.

"I guess not."

"Damn right," he says, in a warning tone, stuffing a piece of rare T-bone into his mouth, which is already filled with fries.

"Do you mind not proselytizing and chewing at the same time?"

"I'll tell you what I think. I think they got plans to build the stadium over there."

"Where?"

"West Santa Rita. Where those Foghorn boys are buying property. Are you listening?"

"I thought the stadium was supposed to be near the lake."

"That's what everyone thinks. But just wait. Out of the blue the council's going to change its mind. West Santa Rita. Freeway access. Cheap land. Good views."

"Nowhere near a train station. Filled with toxic waste." From the shipyards that closed after the war.

"There's no reason anyone would buy those houses except to tear them down and build something for the entertainment of rich people."

My dad's best pal at the department, Michael Bacon, walks up to our table, squeezes himself into our booth, steals a handful of my fries, and stuffs them into his mouth.

"What a happy-looking family." I stab at his hand with my fork before he can raid my plate again. "What's happening, Seegerman?" S. looks up and smiles, nodding hello. "How is the old bugger?"

"See for yourself," Ferdy says. He doesn't like cops. He doesn't trust cops. I give him a stern look.

"He's fine, Mick, thanks. Hey, Pop, you remember Mick Bacon, don't you?"

S., sensing it is a social moment, sticks out his hand, and knocks over my beer bottle. Its contents dribble down the front of my suit pants. S. keeps his hand out across the table, hanging on to the moment for dear life, while I head for the bathroom. When I return, Mick has finished off half my steak.

"So, Gordon. Looks like you got yourself a live one with this Dunn character."

"Oh, yeah. What's the word?"

"The word? The word is that the lovely and talented Silvie Hernandez is going to clean your clock."

"I'm not trying the murder, Mick. I'm on the misdemeanor."

"What misdemeanor?"

"Obviously you've been paying close attention."

"I know what I hear, and I hear you're in deep doo-doo."

"That's very encouraging," I say, using my butt to push him out of the booth and away from my food.

"Hold on, hold on. I'll tell you one thing." His usually animated, fleshy face draws in for a moment. He speaks very quietly. "You ought to have plenty to work with, believe me."

"That's very helpful."

166

"Keep your damn voice down. You got a bad cop on this one." He shakes his head. "Bad, bad, bad. The worst in the department, maybe."

"This doesn't have to do with my dad, does it? This isn't about a grudge?"

"Good steak."

"Mick."

"Needs more salt. Ferdy, pass the salt, will you?"

"Hong?" I whisper to him.

"Nice city, Hong Kong," Mick says, smiling. "I heard they got good deals on jewelry."

Terry and Maeve pass Mick as he threads his way through the jammed bar toward the door. Both sit down and start picking at the scant remains on my plate. My dad perks up whenever he sees Maeve and her abundant bust. She does her part for the demented, smiling at him and leaning slightly forward.

I tell them what Mick said, about a dirty cop in the Dunn case. I doubt it will help, but at least now I will have something to make Silvie miserable. I'll file a *Pitchess* motion, which asks the court to reveal the contents of Hong's personnel file. The documents are usually confidential, but if there is relevant impeachment material—say, evidence he planted evidence or suborned perjury by a witness—I'll be entitled to use it against him at trial.

After a while Ferdy and S. leave.

"Did you talk to Ted?" I say.

"Why?" Terry says, nervously. "What happened?"

"I don't know. That's why I asked if you talked to him."

"I talked to him," Maeve says, coming back to us after a few minutes ogling the after-work, XX chromosome crowd.

"And?"

"And nothing. There's no and."

167

"What about Barry?" Terry says hungrily.

"Barry who?" she says, but her smile means we're on. Terry and I slam hands above the table. Then Preet walks up and squeezes into our booth.

"I might have something interesting for you," Preet says. "You remember Foghorn Trading?"

"Ferdy just told me some supposed source of his told him a Foghorn Management company is overpaying for real estate in West Santa Rita."

"He's quite a sleuth, your grandfather," Preet says, handing me a crumpled section of the day's *Santa Rita Journal*. It contains a short article laying out the information Ferdy detailed minutes earlier.

"Unclear whether it's the same company. But Foghorn Management is definitely a subsidiary of Santa Rita Mutual. Bartholomew Setz, Jr., is the president."

"Where is all this coming from?" Terry asks.

Preet stands, waves off the question, and heads for the restroom.

28

AN *EVANS* MOTION goes like this: Sally robs a convenience store wearing a Bill Clinton mask. But before she takes off in her orange and white 1971 VW bus, the vehicle of choice for armed robbers with a retro flair, she removes the mask. Two witnesses see her face, briefly. They tell the police Sally is a white woman, mid-twenties, with short blond hair. They identify the bus. Three days later, the cops stop Sally for speeding. They think she might be good for the robbery, so they put her in a lineup with several other women. The two witnesses identify her. She is, as we say, busted and disgusted.

But Sally's lawyer discovers there were some serious problems with the lineup. For instance, of the six women who stood with Sally, five were black and one was Chinese. Three of the women were about Sally's age, but they had long black hair. The others were all over the age of seventy. This, the lawyer tells the court in her *Evans* motion, was a suggestive identification process. The witnesses knew to choose Sally because she stood out like a trumpet in a bluegrass band. What we need here is a do-over. Get everyone together for a fair lineup, and then see whether the witnesses pick out Sally.

In chambers with Judge Heymann.

I'd hammered out responses to Silvie's motions thanks to a very long day in the library. I'd also made my *Evans* motion, at Duke's suggestion, figuring that even if Heymann denied it, in the process I'd be forced to read the file carefully for the first time, to figure out how to try the case. And I made my *Pitchess* motion to get Hong's personnel file. I even let the alien see my papers, to let him know I'd heard him. Time to buckle down. Enough shaking my fists at windmills. Time to be a lawyer.

"I have read your various motions, counsel, and before we begin I thought I'd make a few preliminary remarks." Heymann is not in a good mood. He still sounds like Mickey Mouse, but he is gruffer, more surly—sort of like Mickey with a nasty hangover. Quickly it becomes clear that he is aiming at Silvie. "This, as you may recall, is a misdemeanor case which, by your own estimation, will last two court days, including voir dire."

"That was before—"

"May I?"

"Sorry, Judge," Silvie says.

"Two days." He sticks up his long fingers in a V. He does not have peace in mind. "Your basic eyewitness ID case. I expect Ms. Hernandez will put her investigating officer on the stand, and her percipient witnesses. They will say Mr. Dunn displayed his penis. I expect the defense will put on Mr. Dunn to say he did not. Perhaps Mr. Dunn will choose to remain off the stand. That is his decision. I would nevertheless expect a competent lawyer like Mr. Seegerman here to have something for us—perhaps a character witness or two; perhaps an expert to explain the deficiencies in eyewitness identification."

I nod. I'd figured I might be able to get Mary Godfrey on the stand to say what a good guy Dunn is.

"Ms. Hernandez. Here is what we will *not* be doing at this trial, should you choose to go ahead with these minor charges while a murder case is pending."

"Judge, we've made a very generous offer on the case. Mr. Seegerman turned us down," Silvie says.

"Mr. Dunn turned her down, your honor. There's nothing I'd like more than to settle this case," I respond. "Dunn wants his trial."

"So be it. At that trial, which will occur come hell or high water on December 18, the prosecution will *not* offer evidence that Harold Dunn killed anyone. You will not offer evidence that Harold Dunn attempted to obstruct justice or paid witnesses. There was no stay-away order in effect, as far as I know, and I don't think you have evidence from any *living* person that Dunn tried to change anyone's mind. It may have been stupid for him to visit the Dykstras' residence, but it was not illegal. And you will not offer statements, no matter how inculpatory, from dead people. The word, as we all learned in our first year of law school Ms. Hernandez, is 'hearsay.' It would also amount to a confrontation violation. Tragically, Mr. Seegerman never had a chance to cross-examine Ms. Styles, and that means her statements are out. I've read your authorities on all of these issues, Ms. Hernandez, and I'm unconvinced. You'll have your chance to prove all of those things in another courtroom at a later date."

"Your honor, may I be heard?" Silvie asks, not sheepishly at all.

"Ms. Hernandez, I expect you'll want to put your argument on the record later. I just thought I'd give you the benefit of my thoughts so you wouldn't waste a lot of time in your trial prep."

"I understand the court's concern about the length of the trial. But consciousness of guilt is a relevant subject of prosecution evidence. If we can show that Dunn acted as if he knew he was guilty, the jury should hear that. We have powerful evidence that he not only knew he was guilty of the misdemeanor, he went so far as to kill a witness who, he knew, was critical to the prosecution's case. We're going to have a tough time without her, and without her statement in the store. If that's not consciousness of guilt, I don't know what is."

"We agree. If Dunn killed her, that would be very strong proof he believed he would be convicted in this case, and therefore evidence that he knows he is guilty. But who's to say he did it? Another jury has to make that call, and until they do, Dunn didn't kill anyone. If I let you get into the Styles case here, Mr. Seegerman will have a right to challenge that evidence, and I'm sure he would do a thorough job of it. A two-day trial thus becomes a two-month trial. And the jury's attention is diverted far from the issue before them. You want to writ me on this, go ahead. I'm confident the Court of Appeal is going to see it my way. What else was there?"

"The Oregon prior." Silvie sulks.

"Mr. Seegerman," the judge says, looking at his shoes, or something on the floor. "Seems like section 1108 is right on point."

"I understand, your honor. I still think it's in this court's power to exclude a ten-year-old prior. The jury is going to kill my guy when they hear that."

"No argument there. But in its wisdom, the California legislature has determined that"—now he is quoting—"evidence of the defendant's commission of another sexual offense or offenses is not made inadmissible by Section 1101."

The O.J. law. In the Simpson case, there was a big fight over whether the prosecution could offer evidence that O.J. beat Nicole to a pulp several times before he killed her. Under California law at that time, the rule was that the prosecution shouldn't be able to make the argument that if you did it before—whether "it" was abuse your wife or display your penis in a clothing store—you probably did it again. I can't remember how Judge Ito ruled, but in any event, after O.J., the legislature changed the rule in sex and domestic violence cases. So now Silvie could offer up the old exposure conviction, and make the argument that Dunn isn't just a person who wanked; Dunn is a wanker.

"I understand that, your honor. But you still have the power under 352 to keep this jury focused on these charges."

In other words, Heymann can simply exclude the evidence of the old conviction because letting it in would be unfair or too time-consuming. But having barred proof that Dunn strangled Marjorie Styles, and having excluded her statements to Hong in the Cullen's store, I don't think the judge has any favors left in him.

172

"And I decline to do so. It's not that old, and from the police reports in the Oregon case, the circumstances are nearly identical. Big store, ladies' clothing area. Anything else?"

"My motions. *Evans* and *Pitchess*," I remind him.

"Oh, yes. *Evans*. I don't have an objection to a new lineup if you're entitled to one. But so far I don't see anything wrong with this ID. Marjorie Styles leads the security guards to Dunn, not the other way around. Once they have that identification, wouldn't you agree it made sense to have the girl look at him?"

"Sure, but what's she going to say? Dunn's cuffed up. He's flipping out. Hong has him up against a bin of Adidas. There's a crowd of rubber-neckers gathering on both sides of the size 10 men's shoes. Lorraine Dykstra leads her eight-year-old daughter by the hand into this scene, points to Dunn, and says, 'Is that the man?' Come on, Judge. What could be more suggestive? I'm not saying Styles's ID is bad. I'm saying the kid wasn't given any option other than touching my guy."

"What about the mother?" Silvie puts in.

"All the mother says is she saw Dunn in the area. That means nothing. He's entitled to be in the store."

"Ms. Hernandez, anything further on this?"

She sounds exhausted. "I think the ID is fine and the court should additionally consider the interests of the child. This has been an extraordinarily traumatic experience, as you can imagine. Not simply the offense, but Mr. Dunn's visit to the house as well." Silvie is reminding the judge he ruled against her on that evidence. "I think we should keep in mind it's an eight-year-old girl. He'll have his chance to put her on the stand."

"Your honor—"

"Mr. Seegerman. You are on the verge of winning something. Don't screw it up."

"My lips are sealed."

"I am inclined to grant the motion. It does seem to me, though I cannot imagine excluding the child's testimony as the product of an unduly suggestive identification process, that there are grounds to make that argument to a jury. In that case, I think it makes sense to bring her in for another look. Let's make sure it's quick and painless, hmm?"

"We'll set it up, your honor. Does Dunn have to be there?" Silvie asks.

"Counsel?" The judge looks confused.

"I think it would make life easier for the child if Mr. Dunn were not there," Silvie says.

Now I am lost, too.

"Ms. Hernandez, it's a lineup. How do you propose Mr. Dunn be left out of it?"

I've never seen Silvie so momentarily lost, and then so thrown by her own cluelessness.

"Of course, your honor. Of course. My mistake."

"Good. As for *Pitchess*, no reason for me not to take a look at Detective Hong's file, is there, Ms. Hernandez?"

Under the *Pitchess* case, the judge is permitted to review a police officer's personnel records before deciding whether it should be revealed to the defense. If there is nothing relevant in the file—in other words, nothing the judge would allow us to use against him at trial—we get just that. If Hong is dirty, then we ought to get the dirt.

"No, your honor. Keeping in mind the Court's admonition about keeping the case on track, I think that makes sense," Silvie says.

"Are you suggesting I keep in mind my own admonition?"

"Only that cross-examination of an experienced detective on marginally relevant matters would take a lot of time."

"I'll try to remember that. Thank you very much, counsel."

We shuffle out. Silvie does not speak. She looks to be on the verge of tears. I make the mistake of asking her if she is okay. She tells me to go away.

Back at the office. Duke loiters around Aineen's desk, waiting for his troops to return from battle. I walk in and give him a full bear hug. It feels very much like hugging a human being. He does not hug back.

"What the hell's wrong with you, Seegerman?"

"You absolutely saved my life. Heymann ripped Silvie Hernandez a brand-new excretory passage this morning. He granted my *Evans* motion and my *Pitchess* motion."

"Good. Now all you have to do is try the case."

"You know I'd love to, but I really don't have the time," I say, walking away. "This part was fun, though."

29

FRIDAY, DECEMBER 13. The Dunn murder case, preliminary hearing.

Whether because Alexander the Great had divinity in mind when he built a thirteenth statue near his capital and subsequently died young because he angered the gods, or because there were thirteen people at the Last Supper, or because Christ was crucified on the thirteenth, or for no reason at all, people get jittery on Friday the thirteenth.

Silvie, for example, looks nervous. I sit in the back of Judge Caroline Saltzman's Superior Court department, watching my ex flip through the pages of the Dunn homicide file. Every few seconds she clears strands of black hair out of her face and tucks them behind her ears, only to have them fall almost immediately back onto the papers in her hands. Her first murder prelim. Screw it up and word will spread quickly: good lawyer, but not good enough for the giant step into homicides.

Four jumpy sheriff's deputies charged with court security pace around the room, eyeing everyone circumspectly. The case has received significant attention in the press. A television camera crew sets up in the jury box. The gallery is nearly filled.

Francine Horiuchi, the public defender representing Dunn in the murder case, bounces her right leg up and down like a nine-year-old before a big gymnastics meet. It looks likely her client will face the death penalty at trial, and this is her best chance to derail the prosecution.

Judge Saltzman, a small, bird-faced woman in her mid-fifties with thinning brown hair, worked for twenty years at Santa Rita's largest corporate law firm. She spent her days lunching with bankers and sitting in board of directors meetings. She rarely saw the inside of a courtroom. But she contributed so much to the state Republican party that the governor had no choice but to make her a judge when she set her sights on the bench. A week after donning the robes, several years back, she took a six-month leave of absence for what were described as health reasons. She lost it is what happened. The position appealed to her, but actually judging—putting people away, writing legal opinions, handling jurors, dealing with loudmouth lawyers—sent her over the edge. I don't think I have ever seen anyone less suited to the Superior Court bench. She is fidgety, impatient, smart but not thoughtful, quick-tempered, and commonly completely irrational in her decisions. She looks nervous this morning. Then again, she always looks nervous.

I am jittery, too. Not only because the Dunn misdo trial and our chance to play for MBM are rapidly approaching, or because the wanker, for whom, inexplicably, I now sort of care, looks likely to go down for the Styles murder, or because Terry seems bent on unearthing the source of all the weirdness that swirls around the case even if I am driven insane in the process, but also because a few minutes after I sit down, Stone Van der Geist and his pal with the sawed-off shotgun park in the row behind me.

Dunn, apparently not the superstitious sort, looks totally relaxed. Having swapped his orange jumpsuit for a red one, indicating he has been charged with murder, his wrists bound and shackled to his legs, he raises his head in my direction in lieu of a wave.

"Howdy, counselor." Van der Geist leans forward and puts his face within nibbling distance of my right ear.

"Mr. Van der Geist."

"Murder. Can you believe it?" He says the word like Jack the

Ripper might have, had Jack been sitting in the gallery at the Simpson trial.

"You think he did it?"

"I don't know," Van der Geist answers. "He seemed the gentle type."

I try my best to disengage, open up a file, but Stone is back at my ear.

"You know what worries me? It's that all this is going to hurt my business."

"That would be unfortunate."

"Suddenly the police have taken an interest in me. I'm nice enough to help you out, and next thing I know I'm being threatened with arrest myself. A guy in your line of work can understand how upsetting that could be."

"I really appreciate your help, Mr. Van der Geist. Believe me, I didn't contact the police. Dunn gave them your name." That seems to calm him, or at least flummox him temporarily.

"Why would he do that?" I raise my hands to indicate our shared disbelief.

I'd only seen a partial transcript of Dunn's long interview with the police, but in it he described in great detail his activities after he got out of jail. He told them about Van der Geist and Don; he told them about his visit to the Dykstras. He told them about talking to Styles and then seeing her twice. He even told them about the cash he gave her. He gave the prosecution almost everything they needed to convict him and kill him: a motive, a means, an opportunity.

The clerk calls the Dunn matter. It feels strange to hear "*People versus Dunn*" and not get the ping in my stomach that always attends the calling of my cases. It's not as if I'm disappointed not to be in Francine's shoes today, but still there are times I wonder whether I should be more ambitious. Those times are, mercifully, brief.

In California, for the prosecution to force someone to sit through a felony trial, it has to demonstrate at a preliminary hearing that there is a good chance, or "probable cause," to believe that he or she is guilty. What is probable cause? No one has any idea.

In practice, probable cause is defined by whatever judge is presiding over a given preliminary hearing. In this case, no matter how thin the DA's evidence that Dunn actually strangled Marjorie Styles, there is zero chance Judge Saltzman is going to dismiss the charges. She is as gutless as she is dithering. And her chances of remaining on the bench are best if she curries favor with the cops and prosecutors.

In the next hour, Silvie makes public the state's proof, so far, that Harold Dunn killed Marjorie Styles. A parade of cops, a deputy coroner, and Lorraine Dykstra take the stand and obediently tell the DA's story.

I watch Silvie pace in front of Judge Saltzman's bench, focusing on a report, while the witness follows her, waiting for the next question. It is a relief, finally, to have another love interest. Now I can see that Silvie has flaws. A perfect rear end does not an ideal partner make. She is stubborn. She is quick to judge. She has little patience for human foibles—especially my human foibles. Sometimes it surprised me that she thought so highly of MBM, because he is the champion of the forlorn, the dreamers, the sort who are trying their best but not quite making the grade. Silvie is a toughy, which sometimes made her a difficult girlfriend, but also makes her a hell of a prosecutor.

Here is the picture she paints at the prelim.

The police arrest Dunn in the late afternoon of November 13. One week later he bails out. Angered, and fearing the loss of his job, he visits the Dykstras. Ms. Dykstra tells him to get lost. Undeterred, he approaches Callie Dykstra, but the child scurries into the house. Later, Dunn contacts and eventually visits Marjorie Styles. Dunn's fingerprints are all over the apartment—on a glass in the kitchen, on a table in the living room, and on a plastic packet filled with methamphetamine, found on the nightstand next to Styles's bed. And Styles must have been in Dunn's car, too: the police find her prints on the window beside the front passenger seat of Dunn's Cadillac.

In a sense, Dunn testifies, too, because Silvie makes much of his admissions in the taped interview—to visiting the Dykstras once and Styles twice; to giving Styles money. He told the police he gave Styles a ride to a residence in the Santa Rita hills—although he couldn't or wouldn't give the cops an address—the day before Thanksgiving, which was his explanation for the prints in his car.

Less than forty-eight hours later, an early-morning fisherman spots Styles's body washed up under the Seventh Street pier. She has died from a lack of oxygen to her brain, a lack produced by manual strangulation.

Francine insists that Silvie play the entire interview, and so Judge Saltzman hears Dunn deny emphatically that he had anything to do with Styles's death. But overall the statement does far more to hurt Dunn than to help him. He cannot accurately account for his whereabouts for much of the period between his release and Styles's murder. Knowing him even as little as I do, it's obvious he is trying to protect Don, and maybe others, who kept his cover while he decided if or when to go back to jail. But in the interview he sounds like he's dodging. Given the other evidence of contacts with Styles, and his motive to remove her as a witness from the misdo case, Dunn cannot avoid a murder trial. Judge Saltzman would as soon streak through the Hall of Justice cafeteria as she would dump this case.

30

B UT FROM THE gallery it seems to me Silvie's presentation raises
more questions than it answers. Where was Styles's boyfriend? He
must have known about Dunn's visits, but he doesn't testify. Why
would Dunn kill Styles to avoid the misdo prosecution when he knew
the Dykstras could sink him? What about the hairs in the Cadillac's
trunk that Silvie mentioned before our last meeting with Judge
Heymann? Francine identifies these holes in her cross-examinations,
but it isn't going to do her any good.

And then there is Don. My sense as I watch her testify—she is
tastefully dressed for the occasion in a gray pants suit with a large
American flag pendant pinned to a lapel—is that she is the only person
in the courtroom who really knows Harold Dunn. I move to the edge
of my seat, ready for some insight after a long morning of hearing
what I already know.

"Edward Slaughter," Don tells the court. "But I prefer to be called
Madonna." Her voice is perfectly pitched to a courtroom drama:
demure, but solid and direct. She aims her answers, to begin with, at
Silvie, but mid-response she leans back in the witness box and looks at
the judge. This is a person who has seen a lot of *Law & Order*.

"Ms. Slaughter," Silvie says. "Please tell the Court what you do for
a living."

"I'm an actress."

"What else?" It is near the end of a long morning, and Silvie has no
intention of dancing with Don.

"Well, I work as a waitress to pay my rent, but I really consider myself a professional actress."

"Permission to lead, at least for the next few questions, your honor."

"Granted."

"You're a prostitute, right?"

"Excuse me, Ms. Hernandez. I am not a prostitute."

"You receive money from—"

"In addition to my theater and restaurant work, I am a professional escort."

"The defendant"—Silvie points at Dunn—"is one of your clients, right?"

Don smiles at Harold, who smiles back. "One of my favorite clients and favorite people." The whole thing is positively heartwarming.

Don says Dunn stayed with her regularly after he got out of jail. Yes, Dunn told her he'd been arrested. Yes, he'd described the charges.

"Did he seem bothered by his arrest and the charges against him?"

"He was very upset. He swore they had arrested the wrong person."

"Did you understand there was a bench warrant pending for Mr. Dunn's arrest?"

"His lawyer told me that." Silvie turns momentarily and throws me a disagreeable look. "I don't know if Harold knew it or not. But I told him when I found out."

"And what did Mr. Dunn say when you informed him of the warrant?"

"He promised he'd take care of it."

"But he didn't return to the jail."

"No. Well, I don't know what he did all day. But he came to my place most nights."

Silvie leads her through the days after Dunn's release. Dunn told Don about his visit to the Dykstra house. He told her about meeting Styles.

182

"Did Mr. Dunn say why he went to the Dykstra residence?"

"He wanted the girl to see his face. He said he didn't do it, expose himself."

"And what did he tell you happened there?"

"The lady slammed the door in his face is what he told me."

"Did he talk to the girl?"

"No. The mother started screaming or something."

"And what about Ms. Styles? Did he mention why he wanted to talk with her?"

"Same reason, I believe. But after they met the first time, I think they became friends. Harold is a very generous person, a very kind person. It sounded to me like she was going to change her mind."

"Did Mr. Dunn tell you that's why he was going to see her, to change her mind?"

"He said he wanted to talk to her."

"Did he tell you he gave her several hundred dollars?"

"Yes. He said—"

"Did he tell you he gave her drugs?"

"No."

Silvie ought to leave it there. She has her probable cause. She doesn't need Don at all. But Silvie is a neat one. Nothing drives her crazy like loose ends. She figures she will just run Don through the period in which the killing occurred, to emphasize Dunn's lack of a clear alibi.

"When was the last time you saw Harold Dunn before his arrest? Or his rearrest, I should say."

It is the only really inviolable rule of witness examination. If you don't know the answer, don't ask the question.

"A couple of hours before, I guess," Don says.

By now Silvie is seated at the counsel table. She looks up from her notes.

"And where was that?"

At this point, Silvie knows she is in trouble. The confidence she has

183

exhibited throughout the morning evaporates. But she has to go on. If she cuts herself off, Francine will be sure to finish the questioning.

"In my apartment."

"Mr. Dunn was in your apartment on the morning of November 29. Friday."

"Yes."

"When did he arrive there?"

"The day before. In the early afternoon sometime. We spent the night together watching movies I rented. We had Thai food delivered. Curried sea bass and tom kai gai soup." An enchanting image—no turkey and football for those two.

"But that isn't what you told the police."

Before Don can answer, Francine jumps up and asks for a bench conference. I am thirty feet away, but I know exactly what happens. If the next answer is yes, Don will be confessing to a crime—obstruction of justice, lying to police. But if she told the police the truth when they interviewed her—in other words, if she told them she had no idea where Dunn was between November 28 A.M. and November 29 A.M.—then she has committed perjury in her prelim testimony, in an effort to give Dunn an alibi. In either case, she is in trouble, and the court has an obligation to halt the proceedings, inform Don of her rights, and get her a lawyer.

Bedlam ensues. The court cautions Don, who begins to weep quietly into a pearl-colored handkerchief. Stone Van der Geist flees the courtroom to call his lawyer. Fifteen minutes later, the lawyer appears and tells the court that if further questioned, Don will assert her Fifth Amendment right to remain silent. Silvie gives up, packs her things, and departs in a cloud of disgust.

31

A PALL HAS FALLEN over 4200 Candlewood since Ferdy announced his marriage plans. I am glad for him, and it may make sense for S. to move somewhere where the care is more consistent. But the house itself understands it will soon be abandoned, to be reoccupied by a cheerful young couple and a gaggle of recklessly lighthearted children. Into the Dumpster, along with the old sinks and tubs and appliances, will go the disease and affliction and tragedy that have filled the house for thirty years. The manse is a very old person—a person who once loved children and flowers and the smell of baked things. Now it is content to rest, quietly, amidst the sickly and forgetful and dysfunctional. I doubt it has the energy to start over.

The night before the Dunn prelim, Myla came to dinner. It seemed about time to expose her to S., to show her the house, before real estate agents started ordering the walls whitewashed and the shingles repaired. Lillian cooked and ate with us. S. was friendly, talkative, and slightly lecherous. Myla didn't seem bothered by it, and I felt proud to bring home the kind of girl for whom my father would emerge from his fog, if only to leer.

Ferdy grilled her mercilessly and she held up well. She seemed to enjoy the banter. She defended the insurance industry skillfully. She stuck up for doctors. She told us some stories about her parents' lives before they emigrated from Russia. I sat quietly as she and Ferdy and Lillian and S.—in his way—acted like some sort of family.

"She's a doll, Gordy. Don't screw it up." Ferdy and I stood over the

185

sink doing dishes while Lillian and Myla sipped coffee. S., overwhelmed by the excitement, had retreated to his bedroom after a gallant exit in which he remembered Myla's name and told her for the ninth time that he had been a police detective. Myla, for the ninth time, looked interested and impressed.

"I know. She's not into Barry, though."

"A catastrophe."

"I can't figure out how to tell her about the Alzheimer's."

"Tell her. If she goes, she goes. Don't waste your time or hers."

I looked out at her. I wanted to kiss her once before weighing the whole thing down.

"I know."

We are excellent companions. We talk easily, we laugh well. We are comfortable with the silences that punctuate our conversations. And although she insists with some frequency that she is not looking for love, it seems clear to me she either is or shortly could be inclined toward a romantic relationship. Perhaps even with me.

I gave her a house tour, showed her rooms I hadn't been in more than once or twice in years. A hall filled with dust-caked furniture. A grand piano Ferdy started restoring years ago, before he fell in love. Huge green garbage bags filled with my mother's clothing. We walked out into the yard and sat huddled together on a stone bench looking at the brightly lit house from the back.

"Your dad seems to be in good spirits," she said.

"He's in good shape tonight. Sometimes he's an incredible pain in the ass. Sometimes he's almost like an infant—totally dependent, doesn't talk."

We sat in silence for an awkward minute. I was desperate to lean over and kiss her.

"Myla."

"Yeah."

"Do you want to kiss me?" I hadn't actually intended to say that. I got confused. What I meant to say is "Do you want me to kiss you?" She tittered for a moment and then got very quiet.

"I think you're a really nice person, Gordy. I hope that's obvious."

"I like you too. A lot." I was shivering. It may have been the cold, or it may have been the moment.

"Are you okay?" she said.

"I guess—I'm fine. I just really like you."

She smiled. "I thought—" She put her head down.

No matter how many times I've been in this situation, it doesn't get any easier. She wants me to kiss her. She must. What the hell is wrong with me?

"So?" I said.

"This is really awkward," she replied.

Ferdy walked out the back door and yelled at us.

"Gordy, you out there?" We did not answer, but he walked down the steps and spotted us. "Preet's on the line."

"So?" I said. But Ferdy's hearing isn't what it used to be and I figured it would be quicker to run in and get rid of Preet myself. "Don't move," I ordered Myla.

I ran into the house and grabbed the phone.

"What? I'm in the middle of something."

"In the middle of something or someone?"

"Did you need something, or are you just calling to ruin my life?"

"For all intents it's one company, the Foghorns. It's a real estate deal. Apparently Setz Senior does this all the time. Santa Rita Mutual loans money for a housing development or office building. On big projects like that, they're usually one of the smaller lenders. After they decide to lend the money they set up an outside company to buy up real estate in the area. It's a sure thing. Like insider trading, but with property. Setz doesn't want the developers to know, so he doesn't do it through SRM."

"Where the hell are you getting this stuff?"

"I have a friend who has been kind of looking into it." His tone said there is something deeply embarrassing or illegal about his source, but with Preet it's best not to push too hard.

"Someone's going to build an office building in West Santa Rita?"

"If Foghorn is the company buying property in West Santa Rita, apparently Setz has his reasons. From what my friend told me, Foghorn doesn't even own the property. It's a nominee for someone else."

"And who's that?"

"My friend didn't know."

"Why would Setz use a nominee to buy the property?"

"The buyer stays anonymous."

"Can you find out who it is?"

"Maybe. I'll try."

I ran out back, but the moment was gone. Myla and Ferdy were in the garage looking at a half-rebuilt 1959 Studebaker. She looked pleased—relieved, even. By the time Ferdy finally took one of my hints to leave us alone, Myla seemed in a rush to leave.

"You want to go for a walk?" I said, desperate to try again.

"I really have to go."

We walked to her car. She opened the door, but did not get in. I went in for the kiss. She turned her head. I got the cheek. Then, crushed, I hugged her.

"I'm sorry," I said, though I hadn't a clear idea why I was sorry—S.'s lechery, Ferdy's ranting, my inability or unwillingness to accept that she wasn't ready to kiss me, might never be ready—but I figured a general statement of regret would cover the necessary bases.

"Don't be sorry. You have a great family. The house is amazing."

"Yeah?"

"Yeah." She stuck out her hand. "Friends?"

"Friends."

Then she peeled my hand off the car door and left. Or fled.

*   *   *

I headed to Terry's for solace, and alcohol.

"Weird," Terry said.

"Exactly."

"Dunn must know something about this Foghorn deal. He's covering for someone."

"And my romantic situation?"

"What about it?"

"Don't you think it's a just a little suspicious that I got the cheek?"

"What's the rush?"

The rush is I might only have ten or fifteen good years left. At this rate, the chance of my getting laid before I forget Myla's name and number is remote.

"There's no rush. I just want to know if I'm wasting my time. I really like her. I find myself thinking about her constantly."

"Is Dykstra involved in Foghorn?"

"Preet didn't mention that. You were going to tell me something?"

"The fourth number on Dunn's cell bill."

"The guy who claimed I had a wrong number."

"No longer in service."

"Which means what?"

"Got me. Are you enjoying hanging out with her?"

"Definitely."

"Then how are you wasting your time?"

32

TERRY AND I walk into the lobby of the county jail. A man sitting in a corner, talking on a cell phone, looks familiar. Terry doesn't recognize him. I sign us in to the visitors log. A few lines above appears "Gerald Fitzgerald, attorney." He was in to see Dunn. In fact, it looks like he's still in with the wanker: the log has a time-in entry of one-ten P.M., but no time out.

I ask the deputy checking in visitors where the interview is taking place. After a minute at his computer he says Dunn is back in his unit. I point to the log. He shrugs and shows me others who neglected to fill in the time-out blanks. Apparently people leave the jail in a rush.

I turn around and stare for a moment at the man on the cell phone. He looks a lot like the man I saw three weeks earlier driving the dark sedan, who picked up Dunn at his house, stopped for food at McDonald's, and then pulled into a downtown high-rise. Fitzgerald. I walk to within a few feet of him. He is still on his cell. He looks perturbed.

"Can I help you with something?" He has a thick Southern accent.

"You're not Mr. Fitzgerald, are you?"

"Sorry, pal." He returns to his call. I look at him for another few moments. It's him—same mustache, same cocksure bearing. It's the same guy, and he's definitely a cop. "Is there a problem of some kind?"

"No, sorry." I scurry off.

In with Dunn.

"I thought we agreed Fitzgerald was going to talk to me before acting like your lawyer," I say.

"Don't worry about him. He's just a friend. Tell me how things are coming along with the case." The misdo. This from a man seriously in jeopardy of lethal injection.

"Why does he come here?"

"To make sure I'm okay, I guess. He's just a friend."

"But you don't talk about your cases."

"No."

"So what do you talk about?"

"I don't know. Nothing. You know, bullshit."

"And Fitzgerald's not a lawyer."

"I don't know, Mr. Seegerman. If you say he is, then maybe he is."

"I don't have any idea what he is, Harold, I just can't figure out what he's doing pretending to be your lawyer. Can you help me here? Is he a cop? Is he from G-O-D?"

He shakes his head emphatically. "Nothing like that."

"Tall guy, mustache, mid-thirties. Good-looking. Southern accent. Sound like Fitzgerald?"

Dunn looks down at his cuffed wrists.

"How about this? Is he the guy who picked you up outside your apartment after you bailed out, bought you dinner at McDonald's, and took you to a building a few blocks from here?"

"I swear to you, he's just a friend. That's all. What's the big deal?"

"You seem to have very good friends," Terry says. "Don, for example. Nice of her to step up like that."

"I don't know what she was thinking. That was embarrassing to watch."

"Not true?"

"I didn't kill Marjorie Styles, but I wasn't with Don."

"And where were you?" I say. Then I cut myself off. "No. You know what, I don't care where you were. That's a conversation

191

you might want to have with Ms. Horiuchi. Let's talk about our case."

I fill him in on the recent developments—Judge Heymann's rulings; my plans for the lineup. He asks me if I can win the case. I tell him to take the DA's offer, but only because I know he won't. I am beginning to think we have a sliver of a crumb of a chance, and it's clear he'd be much better off in the murder case with an acquittal on the exposure charges.

"How did you find the Dykstras' house?" Terry hardens, tired of chasing his own tail.

"I told you, the phone book."

Terry slowly shakes his head. "Unlisted."

"I'm telling you, it was in the phone book. Maybe I had an old one or something."

"Harold, do we look like cops?" Terry says. "You don't have to bullshit us. If you got set up, we want to know. If Phil Dykstra or Godfrey is behind it, we'll nail them. But we're running into walls. Help us out. Give us a lead. Anything. You want to beat the misdemeanor, we need to give the jurors some reason to believe you and not to believe an eight-year-old girl."

"I'm sorry. I don't know how to help you. All I can tell you is she picked the wrong guy."

"That's not enough. Why did they get the wrong guy? Why did they pick you?"

Dunn flushes. "I don't know. I don't. I was just looking for shoes."

I sit back in my chair, frustrated. Actually, I don't care that much—clearly we'll never have enough evidence of a setup to offer it as a defense at trial—but Terry is bent on breaking the guy, so I fold my arms and let the master work his magic.

"Why don't I tell you a story, Harold, and you see if it helps."

"All right."

"A guy gets arrested for exposing himself in a store. He tells his

192

lawyer he got set up, mentions some names; the whole thing's pretty hard to believe. The lawyer figures the guy for a nut case, but when he noses around a little, there seem to be a lot of weird connections, too many coincidences. The lawyer starts to think maybe there's something to it." Terry rattles through what we know, the ties between Setz, Dykstra, and Santa Rita Mutual on the one hand, and G-O-D on the other.

"Then it turns out the bank is behind a company that's buying up cheap real estate all over West Santa Rita, for no good reason. A hundred properties, maybe. Millions of dollars. For old crack houses and vacant lots filled with garbage. And lo and behold, the client has calls to that company on his cell phone bill. Then the client gets arrested for killing one of the witnesses in the misdemeanor, but he doesn't seem to be worried about that case at all, even though he's looking at the death penalty. And after he gets arrested for the murder, for some reason he won't help his lawyers in the misdemeanor case by telling them how to prove he got set up. Crazy story, huh?"

Dunn's agitation quiets for a moment. "I've heard crazier."

"Are we close? Can you give us a hint?"

"I can't. I'm sorry." He seems to be.

"Can't? Won't? Sorry, we're not close, or Sorry, you can't give us a hint?" Terry says, exasperated. "You know what I think? I think you're scared. Someone got to you when you were on the street. Selmer Godfrey. Or Fitzgerald, maybe."

Dunn's head does not move. He does not appear scared, or disturbed by Terry's recitation, or in any way affected by our entreaties. He either cannot or will not give us anything, and he doesn't feel bad about that.

Terry gets up to leave. "We're not the enemy, Harold. Right now the Santa Rita Public Defender's Office is all you've got."

We walk down the front steps of the jail.

"We get paid way too little for this shit," I say.

"He's close, Gordy. A couple more tries and we'll get him."

"You're out of your mind. He's totally locked up. Find Fitzgerald and you might have a shot."

"How am I supposed to find fucking Fitzgerald? We don't even know if there *is* a Fitzgerald. Maybe Francine can get to Dunn—tell him stories about the joys of death row."

"To me, the weirdest thing about this whole mess is Dunn. Silvie is sure she's going to convict the guy. Francine would gladly deal the case for an LWOP"—a sentence of life without the possibility of parole— "and Dunn seems genuinely not to give a shit. Death penalty or no death penalty, he wants to beat the damn misdo."

"So, can you beat it?"

"No."

Somehow Terry has found time between our afternoon jail visit and the early evening to reveal my romantic issues to both of the other Mandys. The minute I walk into rehearsal, Maeve wants to talk about Myla.

"Did I not say something was wrong with that girl? Species name— *Womanus frigidalis*. Say it with me, guys."

"*Womanus frigidalis*," they repeat robotically. A nitwit chorus.

"She's not frigid, Maeve," Preet says. "She's simply not jumping into something without giving it the thought it deserves. I respect that."

"What the hell do you— Fuck me." That is, "Fuh-uhk may."

"He's right. Or at least, I think he's right," I say. "If she weren't interested, why would she stick around? Why wouldn't she just tell me to go away?"

"I don't think I've heard such complete bullshit in my entire life. Why does she stick around? Why the fuck does she stick around? Because she has your balls in one hand and your wallet in the other. Who's been buying dinner?" I point at my chest. "Thank you very much."

194

"I didn't realize it was group therapy night."

"There's nothing worse than a weak man. I think I'm gonna be sick."

After two hours of whacking her drums furiously, Maeve calms down. She lies on a carpet, staring up at the exposed rafters, while Terry and I toss a Nerf football back and forth across the studio.

He walks through the Dunn case, over and over again, pointing out every possible alliance and connection and coincidence.

"I really appreciate what you're doing on this," I say.

"No problem, man. It's driving me nuts. It's almost like someone put all this stuff out there just to confuse us. There's a simple answer, and I'm missing it, because there's too much information, too much noise."

"Hey buddy, we do what we can do."

"We'll get there. Just a matter of time."

"But not tomorrow." The G-O-D holiday gig. "Tomorrow we're a band."

"I know."

"He's lying," Maeve chimes in.

"Shut your trap, Maeve," Terry says.

"Seriously, Terry. They're paying us good money. Tomorrow night is about Barry, not about Dunn."

"I know."

"We have a reputation to protect. In less than two weeks we're going to play for Manilow. I don't give a shit what happens to Dunn. Nothing is going to screw that up."

"All right, I hear you."

"He's still lying," Maeve says.

"Will you shut up?" Terry says. "I'll be onstage with the rest of you. What am I going to do, sneak off in the middle of 'Copa'? Quit your whining. Talk to me about Dunn."

"Look at it this way," I said. "Say he never opened his mouth and we got into this thing with no reason to believe everything isn't kosher. Say all you have is what you have—executives of the largest bank in the country are on the board of a local nonprofit. You have some real estate deals you don't understand. And a child of a bank executive happens to see a guy expose himself, and that guy happens to work at the nonprofit. It's a coincidence. Life is filled with them. You have nothing. Without Dunn's original allegations, you have zilch."

"That's bullshit, and you know it. What about Dunn being in High Power for a misdemeanor? What about suddenly he's loaded with cash? What about Fitzgerald?"

"All that is curious, yes. But, what's really making you see a big plot isn't proof, it's Dunn's original allegations. Which, I should add, he's basically retracted."

"Not retracted, just won't talk about. Can't you see the dude's scared out of his mind?"

"What you're not getting is that *I* have to get up in front of a jury on Wednesday. All this stuff is fascinating, and maybe in the end it will turn out to mean something; probably not, but either way *I* have to try the case."

"All right, all right."

"Time's up. I can't be distracted by all this anymore. It's been a hell of a lot of fun playing Scooby-Doo for a few weeks. Now it's time for me to hang up the gumshoes and be a lawyer. Get it?"

"All right, relax. I hear you."

"He's still lying."

"Maeve!" Terry shouts. "Shut the hell up."

33

I SIT AT THE out-of-tune upright in my living room, brushing up on the Christmas songs we're obliged, by the season, to perform at the G-O-D gig, and waiting for the Mandys. It's Saturday, fourish. They are late. We have to set up the G-O-D gig, sound-test, and get out of there before cocktails at five-thirty. Then I have to come home, relieve Lillian for two hours, feed S., hand him off to Ferdy, and rush back to G-O-D by eight-forty-five.

Ferdy trudges through the front door dressed in rubber boots, an overlong black trench coat, and a red knit hat. "You look like you're either going duck hunting or to a porno movie."

"I've been for a walk. It's called exercise. You oughta try it."

"Do I have to wear the boots?"

He tosses a newspaper on the coffee table. "There's more in here about that Foghorn mess. As usual, I was right about the whole thing."

The same reporter who earlier had identified a company called Foghorn Management as the buyer of a slew of decrepit West Santa Rita real estate now describes a massive upscale mall-and-condominium development, the size of a small town, slated for West Santa Rita. At first glance it seems an unlikely place to sell zillion-dollar lofts and Mercedeses. The plan is to build a gleaming consumer and residential mecca with its eyes on the freeway and the bay, and its ass to what would be left of West Santa Rita.

The article suggests that the plan is to level a nearly mile-long, half-mile-wide stretch along the freeway. Much of the area is uninhabited, or inhabited by people who don't count—homeless, addicts. The value of the properties now owned by Foghorn would likely skyrocket if the development goes through. As would the value of G-O-D's campus, three blocks outside the condemned area. The article notes in conclusion that the plan has the support of the present mayor and District Attorney Fisher, a candidate for the job.

When Preet pulls up, Max, looking as bald and burly as ever, sticks his head out the front passenger window. He greets me enthusiastically. Perhaps too enthusiastically, especially for Max, who typically has an extremely flat affect.

"Howdy, counselor."

"Hey, Max. What's happening?"

"Not a whole lot." I climb in the back. Maeve looks like she hasn't gotten much sleep.

"Hey, Maeve." She moans.

"I figured we could use the help," Terry says, attempting to explain Max's presence.

Max turns his head back to talk to me. "I thought I'd check out the old scene at G-O-D, you know what I'm saying. See if things ain't what they used to be and all that shit."

"Kind of like homecoming," Terry adds.

"Exactly."

What is obvious from this inane jabber is that something is going on that ought not to be going on, and it almost certainly has nothing to do with Barry Manilow. I choose to ignore it.

When Preet pulls the van over at G-O-D, a large group, perhaps fifty people, plus a slew of television cameras, crowd the steep front steps of a building at the edge of the campus, a towering Victorian brightly painted in shades of yellow and purple and blue. Mary Godfrey is giving a press conference.

Terry hops out and joins the crowd. We listen to St. Godfrey rail against the planned development. She notes "the sad coincidence that on the very night G-O-D will celebrate its contribution to the future of West Santa Rita, we have discovered that perhaps West Santa Rita has no future at all."

In a few minutes, all is lost. Someone hands Terry the newspaper article. There is no explosion, but I can see the information sputtering around his head like popcorn in a pot of hot oil. His eyes dart back and forth. I see his brain clicking. I see him wonder where Dunn fits in. I see him wonder who the bad guys are. But he doesn't say a word about it. After a couple of minutes he hops back in the van. We follow.

I'd heard that the G-O-D holiday gig is the social event of the year in Santa Rita, but I am not prepared for its scale. Three enclosed tents take up most of a block. The tents are filled with red and green balloons and enormous Christmas trees, fully adorned. Fake snow covers the pavement inside the tent. Hordes of Santa Clauses roam around aimlessly. Bartenders and waiters in black tie organize their stations. On each table—and there are at least fifty—is a centerpiece consisting of a three-foot pile of wrapped and ribboned presents.

The entire party area as well as the main G-O-D building is surrounded by a temporary chain-link fence. This party is for donors and luminaries and politicians, not for the organization's wretched clientele. The fence is meant to keep out anyone without a fat wallet or some other legitimate reason for being there.

Mary Godfrey's goons have multiplied and seem now to be everywhere. One particularly gruesome fellow—he looks like the guy in a cartoon whose nose has been flattened with a cast-iron pan—in a red SECURITY jacket waves Preet over and demands to know who we are. Eventually we convince him that we are the entertainment and he issues us passes. We receive five, one for each of the band members and one for Max.

While we set up, Max disappears. Afterward, we go for an early dinner. Max does not join us. I go home to deal with S. and return with my car. We mill around outside for an hour before the show. Max is nowhere in sight.

"Hey, Terry," I say.

"What's up?"

"Where's Max?"

"Don't know. Haven't seen him."

"Terry, please tell me I have no reason to worry about anything other than our performance this evening."

"You have no reason to worry—"

I walk away.

34

WE TAKE THE stage at nine-fifteen and it quickly becomes clear that this show is going to be different. We've played to hundreds. Here are nearly a thousand. Why had it not occurred to me to become nauseated? We have played, mostly, for people who understand and appreciate what we do, friends. But here is much of the Bay Area's elite—media, agents, God knows who from the music industry. It simply had not occurred to me before I walked in through a flap in the tent that this, rather than our date with MBM next week, could be the most important performance of our lives. And not one of these people is here because of a fondness for Barry Manilow.

Preet does the usual introduction into the opening of "Tryin' to Get the Feelin'." I hear a stunned silence from inside the tent.

"Anybody *get the feeling* we're fucked?" Maeve says.

When we jog onto the stage the crowd looks at me as if we are four squeegee men come to soil its pristine new Jaguar. We finish the first tune. A scattering of polite applause. But the looks on the faces I can see, in the front, say, "Thanks very much. How much do we owe you?" We try our upbeat reggae version of "I Write the Songs." Slightly more action from the people up front, but not enough to carry us through a whole set. I have not felt so acutely the threat of total failure and humiliation in a very long time.

Shrink from it, piss on it, or dance with it. Those are our options with this crowd. I look at each of the Mandys, and they understand perfectly what is required. Time to boogie. We trash our carefully designed set list, with its gradual crescendo, and break out the cannons. Maeve steps to the front and belts out a note in her busty soprano—a note seemingly untethered to any song. That gets their attention. We build a musical bulwark behind her. Preet is working the drum machine and the keyboards. Terry and I step up next to Maeve. Her voice flies to the back of the tent, turning every head. When it finally lands, we dissolve into "Rudolph the Red-Nosed Reindeer." But only for a few lines. Then Preet sends the drums into a fast Latin beat and we morph without a break into "Copacabana."

Even this crowd can't resist a really hot "Copa." We push the song to its limit, acting out the parts. The dancing. The music, the passion. The point is not to win every heart in the joint, not with one song. The point is to convert a core group. Once they are with us—and, after "Copa," they are—we can rely on them, on the energy flowing back from the front of the room, to suck in the skeptics.

We relax into it after the initial battle, weaving Christmas songs in and out of Barry tunes. The tent becomes more and more crowded, particularly in the area closest to the stage. We play three dance tunes and then a ballad. I am good. I am adequate. But Maeve and Terry are absolutely on fire. Every time Terry moves to the front of the stage there is a surge of women toward us. I make a crack about auctioning off Terry's underwear and we start getting cash hurled at us. When we hit "It's a Miracle," with a "Jingle Bells" lead-in, we own the place. As promised, Preet joins us on the vocals, the spotlights on the front of the stage illuminating his bright red turban. The crowd doesn't seem to notice his sour notes here and there.

A thousand people dancing or tapping their feet or waving their arms around, swearing they've always loved Barry Manilow.

*　　*　　*

Herewith, the top five complaints about MBM and simple rejoinders that ought, once and for all, to secure his rightful place in the artistic stratosphere.

Five. *We don't like his clothing, and we really don't like his hair.* Seriously, the nastiest review Barry ever got began not with a discussion of his performance or his music, but with the claim that a man who would go on to sell more than fifty million records "has his hair done at the Clip and Snip Poodle Salon." The thing is, Barry came of age in the seventies, a decade not known for its tastefulness. He was a star, and stars at that time were expected to push the stylistic envelope. Think of Elton John, for God's sake. Anyway, every music critic ought to have a plaque in her or his office that says, IT'S THE MUSIC, STUPID!

Four. *The fans are middle-aged housewives who worship Barry because he reminds them of their little boys.* The obvious response is that MBM's most recent greatest hits compilation quickly went to Number 3 on the charts and sat there for half a year. So there must be a whole hell of a lot of middle-aged housewives out there. And in any case, sure, the core audience is made up of people who fell in love with Barry in their teens and twenties, who are now in their forties and fifties. So what? That would have included my mother, and I know you're not disrespecting my mother.

Three/Two. *The songs are overwrought and the sentiments are sappy. The purpose is exclusively commercial.* Taste is taste, and there's no use trying to convince someone who simply doesn't care for Barry Manilow to like his music. But it is another thing entirely for someone who holds himself or herself out as an authority to dismiss or belittle the music, to suggest that on some objective level it is bad. It is another thing entirely to claim that hundreds of millions of people all around the world, over three decades, for whom Barry's music has been a source of inspiration, joy, encouragement, reassurance, and exhilaration, have no taste. That they are wrong. We are not wrong. We love what we hear and we won't apologize for what we love.

And the number one most popular reason for criticizing Barry Manilow? *A man made famous, in part, by singing a song called "I Write the Songs" did not, in fact, write many of the songs that made him famous, including "I Write the Songs."* Uh. So? Let me put it this way. Do you know who Melissa Mathison is? Ever heard of Joseph Stefano? No? That's strange, because they are responsible for writing two really famous movies, two of the most critically acclaimed and commercially successfully films ever. The reason you don't know their names is because most scriptwriters, like most songwriters, don't get enough recognition for their work. That, it ought to go without saying, is not Barry Manilow's fault. He has gone out of his way to acknowledge songwriters because, unlike many singers, he is a composer and so appreciates where credit is due.

Also, many of the songs written by others have become so popular because Barry arranged them, Barry orchestrated them, and Barry performed them. The song, like the screenplay, is a skeleton, raw material. It falls to the arranger and the singer, as it does to the film director, to add the flesh, to mold the clay, into something brilliant. Joseph Stefano wrote *Psycho*, but Alfred Hitchcock made it shine. Melissa Mathison wrote *ET*, but Steven Spielberg gave it life. And though Bruce Johnston deserves credit (and royalties) for composing "I Write the Songs," Barry Manilow ought not to be dismissed because he made the song immortal.

I drink beer steadily throughout the set, and as we come to the last few songs my head is tingly and my emotions spasmodic. The spotlights are blinding. It is not for me to say we are brilliant. I can only say that we have made a convincing argument for the music. That a huge crowd, an hour before skeptical, uninterested, dismissive, is now almost silent, transfixed, watching Maeve, who sits at the edge of the stage, her legs crossed, her head down, a microphone to her lips, doing her best Judy Garland imitation. The song is "Sandra," one of the saddest songs I know, about a faithful housewife and mother who grew up and settled down too quickly. It is about the challenge of finding meaning in, and appreciating the fragility of, a life lived in an ordinary way.

I have heard her sing this song a hundred times. Tonight, for reasons that are beyond me, tears begin to stream down my face as I pound on the keyboard. I think of Ferdy moving out, of packing up and leaving the house at 4200 Candlewood, of my walking away and having nowhere to go. I think of where Silvie and I might have ended up had I not been so fearful. Of what my mother might think if she were in the audience tonight, drinking, dancing, cheering, whistling. She would have been more than proud. She would have been glorious.

I decide that I must tell Myla. How I feel. About the AD. I will stop running from it. I am thirty-three years old. I am a lawyer. I am a musician. I must stop running.

We leave the stage after "Weekend in New England," but the crowd has no intention of letting us go. We return. Terry sings "White Christmas." I do "Even Now." And then Preet sets the computers to autopilot; we four join hands and walk to the front of the stage for "Can't Smile Without You." After we whistle the intro, there isn't a person in the audience sitting and there isn't a person in the audience not singing along. It's thunderous. And utterly preposterous—a thousand rich folks standing, holding hands, arms hooked together, swaying back and forth, in the midst of a Santa Rita slum, surrounded by an eight-foot-high chain-link fence, singing at the tops of their lungs.

From the corner of my eye, I see Max slip in through a flap at the side of the tent. A light twinkles off his lustrous crown.

35

THE CROWD GOES cuckoo when we finish. None of us can quite believe the reaction. It's the season and the occasion and the free and free-flowing booze and the slightly unnerving juxtaposition of black tie and ghetto. But we are overwhelmed, even slightly embarrassed. The frenzy is almost like a collective apology for failing to appreciate us from the start.

Often after a performance the last thing I want to do is mingle with the audience. But this show is a breakthrough. This kind of response is certain to give us a major boost. Before we walk off the stage, I plug the December 20 show at Ted's, which now should be packed. I feel so good about these people that I am anxious to shake a few hands. I step into the tent and am quickly swarmed by well-wishers, suddenly-out-of-the-closet Mani-lovers, and maudlin drunks of all stripes. On the other side of the twenty people who surround me I see Myla. After, believe it or not, signing a few autographs, I free myself.

"Hi."

"Hi."

"Hi."

"Hi."

I take her hands and then give her a slightly-too-long hug.

"What are you doing here?" I say.

"You didn't say you were playing tonight."

"You didn't mention you were a G-O-D contributor."

"Not me. Insuron."

"Of course. So, what'd you think?"

"I hate to admit it, but I was singing there at the end. People really got into it."

"A convert."

"Don't push your luck."

A DJ takes over. We are near the stage, crowded in by several hundred drunk and bejeweled people in tuxedos and high heels shouting at one another above the din. It is nearly impossible to hear her.

"Are you here with someone?" I'm glad she can't hear enough to answer that one. "You want to go get a drink?" I yell. She nods. I take her arm and lead her into a jam of people, every one of whom now believes he is my best friend. It is almost impossible to move. We cover ten feet in five minutes. From my left, Max breaks through the crowd like a defensive lineman, grabs my arm, and pulls me to the side of the tent. He almost breaks Myla's ankle in the process, because she is attached to my arm.

In a minute we are outside in the nippy night air. The thick canvas muffles the clamor from inside. Terry stands fifteen feet away, in front of the van. He sticks up his thumb, signaling what? "Everything is okay"? "All systems go"? "Keep on truckin'"?

"Max, Myla. Myla, Max." They shake. Terry walks up and greets Myla.

"Can we have a few minutes? Band business."

"Forget it. I need a drink." I take a step away, but no one follows. Terry and Max have peculiarly serious looks on their faces. Myla must think they are completely nuts.

"I'll get the drinks and meet you back here in ten minutes," she says.

"No. What's the—"

Terry puts his hand on my back and cuts me off. "Ten minutes."

They don't talk. They escort me around the side of the main G-O-D building. The three-story Victorian now stands between me and my love. I am buzzed from the beers and the show and the thrill of seeing Myla. I feel a powerful urge to turn around and punch Terry in the head. I don't really know why. Adrenaline, probably.

"Should I ask?"

"You're about to be enlightened," Terry says.

"And if I'm not interested in enlightenment?" There is no answer.

We climb down several concrete steps to a patio area, maybe fifteen feet square. There is almost no light on this side of the building. Terry and I sit on a bench on one side of the patio.

"We good?" Max says.

"Yeah, good," Terry answers. Max disappears up the stairs.

"Terry."

"Max has a friend, his cellie at San Quentin, who works for G-O-D. I thought—"

I get up to go and have made it halfway up the stairs when Max appears with one of the G-O-D security guys. He may be one of the goons I saw trailing Mary Godfrey when she first showed me around. Then again, the goons are not easily distinguishable. Some are white, some are not. But otherwise, they all look a lot like Max's friend. Which is to say, big, ugly, mean, dangerous, and somehow on the verge of tearing off their clothes and starting a rousing Chippendales routine.

"This is the guy I was telling you about," Max says.

Terry steps up and shakes his hand. The man looks over his shoulder, in the direction of the party tent, every few seconds. I do the same. "This is Gordon Seegerman and Terry Fretwater."

"I enjoyed the show," the man says. "And I fucking *hate* Barry Manilow."

"Thanks a lot." I think.

"So what do you want to know?" the man asks. I look at Terry.

"Gordon and I work in the public defender's office. He represents a man named Harold Dunn. You know him?"

"Sure, I know Dunn."

"He's been arrested for exposing himself in a clothing store."

"And murder, too."

"That's right. Dunn told us that Selmer Godfrey or someone at G-O-D is involved in something illegal. Money laundering, maybe."

"Oh, yeah? He should shut the fuck up."

"He also had a pretty crazy story about being set up by Mr. Godfrey, on the exposure case."

"Okay."

"I guess we're just trying to figure out whether Dunn is a mental case or whether anything he told us is true."

The man looks at Max, who nods.

"Dunn's nuts, if you ask me. I've been around for a while and I don't know anything about any laundering. I'd be very surprised. Too many eyes on the money for anything like that. Dunn should know. He was the one keeping the books."

"The place does seem to have a lot of security," Terry says.

"Mary Godfrey has a lot of enemies, pal. She runs a pretty tight ship. There's a lot of losers who pass through here, fuck up, get kicked out, and go away mad. I don't know what Dunn's problem is, because I know for a fact he'd be dead without Mary Godfrey."

"He seems to think it's Selmer's deal."

Max's friend thinks this comical. "Selmer? Fuck, man. Selmer doesn't change toothpaste brands without his mother's say-so."

"What about Mary Godfrey?"

"She's the real thing. That's all there is to it."

"The real thing," Max says, aping his friend.

The man points a warning finger at Max and says, "I'm done here, man." They hit their fists together, hard.

"I really appreciate it," Max replies.

"Be cool."

We hear footsteps and voices from the corner of the building, maybe twenty feet away, approaching. I turn to look, and seconds later Max's friend evaporates through a small door at the corner of the patio area. It's a few security guys and Selmer. We sit still. Most of them pass by, but one dips down the steps.

"Mr. Godfrey. Over here."

Max stands. Prepared for God knows what. There's no problem. What's the problem?

We're quickly surrounded. Selmer has the usual gleeful look on his face. A gaggle of goons stand behind him, at the top of the five steps out of the sunken patio area.

"Mr. Seegerman, Mr. Seegerman." He shakes his head in joyous incredulity. "What a gorgeous performance. I really don't have the words."

"Thank you very much, Mr. Godfrey."

"Selmer, please. I insist that you call me Selmer. I am sure you will go on to riches and fame and I'll be proud to say I knew you when." He has taken, and refuses to cleave himself from, my left hand.

I force a smile. "Thank you so much."

"What are you doing hiding down here? There are a million people waiting to meet you." He finally lets go of me and sticks his hand out to Terry, who takes it, hesitantly. "I don't think we've met."

I introduce Terry.

"You were all just beyond wonderful. And how is Mr. Dunn? I was shocked to hear about Ms. Styles's death. She was a client here, you know."

"Really?" I say.

"Tragic." The grin never leaves his face.

As we emerge from the patio area, Myla approaches us. I am relieved to see her. I apologize for abandoning her. Selmer introduces himself. Smiles all around.

"Gordon, can I talk to you for a second?" Terry says.

"No."

I drag her off, away from Terry and Max, away from Selmer and his goons, away, away, away, to the relative peace of the party tent. We dance for a while, drink some, and reemerge into the night.

"I've been waiting all night to say this, Myla. I have a feeling I'm falling in love with you." She searches valiantly for a look other than crushed, but she fails. "What?" I say.

"That's not fair at all. I told you I'm not looking for a relationship right now. I've really enjoyed spending time with you, but—we hardly know each other."

"I know."

"You're just in love with love. That's why you like Barry Manilow."

"That's not true. I don't feel this way very often." I try to kiss her, but there's no mistaking it now. She holds me off.

"It's the wrong time for me. I like hanging out with you, but I don't want that right now."

"Are you sure?"

"Yes."

"You have a boyfriend?"

"Sort of. It's complicated."

"Why didn't you say something?"

"I did. I told you I'd like to be friends."

"But, I don't know, you just seemed—" I am whining. I cannot stand the sound of my own voice, drunk, pitiful.

"I have to go." She stands up and backs away.

I find Maeve on the dance floor getting jiggy with it—"it" being five gorgeous, scantily clad twentysomethings.

"I've been dumped," I say.

"What?" Her arm is hooked around the arm of one of her girls and she is twirling around and around, and so she hears none of my lament.

"Dumped. Rejected. Broken up with."

"I can't hear you."

211

I give up and throw myself into the music and the twentysome-things. And I continue to drink.

Without intending to be self-hating, anti-Semitic, or otherwise bigoted, I believe Jews do not make good drunks. My father is, was, an exception. I am the rule. We are good with brisket—not everyone can handle that much boiled beef. We like our lox. We cannot hold our liquor.

Too much alcohol and I feel as if, and behave as if, I am on an emotional roller coaster, with my head braced against the side of the car, preparing to puke. I love everyone, and the next minute I hate everyone. One moment I'm buoyant, and the next wretched and hopeless.

None of the twentysomethings seems likely to demand that I come home with her. And the longer I stay at the party—that is, the more time between my Barry X performance and the present—the less I can count on affirmation from the crowd. What, at ten, was "You are so talented" at twelve turns into "Barry fucking Manilow, man, Barry fucking Manilow." Preet is gone. Maeve is busy choosing a bedmate. Terry is who knows where. I should go.

36

I EMERGE FROM THE party tent. It is no less loud within than earlier. But it is now nearly deserted without. I sit for a few minutes on the dry ground. The cold leaks through my white tuxedo into my torso and I shiver. It sharpens my thoughts, though, sops up some of the beer.

Myla is gone. She was never here. I will miss her. Dunn must be nuts. Perhaps I've been set up, played for a fool. In any event, win or lose the trial, in six days I will stand on a stage and play for Barry Manilow. My stomach churns. My head pirouettes. I need nicotine. I return to the tent. Maeve has disappeared.

Outside again. I turn to look up the street. From the side of the main G-O-D building, where we'd had our discussion with Max's friend, Terry and Max appear. They walk hurriedly toward a parking lot nearby. A half-circle of G-O-D goons follows them, two feet behind. Terry and Max have no car. I have a car. I take a few quick steps. I nearly topple. Shit.

I wobble quickly toward them. Terry and Max get in the back of a large sedan. A goon joins them. Two goons get in the front. Two others stand outside until the car's doors are closed. Then they quickly walk back toward where I am standing, and then up the alley on the side of the G-O-D building.

There are many cars crowding the street, so the sedan cannot leave quickly. Which is fortunate because in my inebriation it takes me a minute just to get my car door open. They are three cars ahead. I feel my pockets for a cell phone, which I left at home. Whom would I call anyway?

I follow them out of West Santa Rita to the outskirts of downtown. I must both keep my friends in view, and drive, while drunk. Driving by itself would be a chore, although I suppose it wouldn't be a disaster to attract some police attention. The double yellow lines in the middle of the road keep weaving under my car. The streets are deserted.

The sedan pulls in to a large, street-level parking lot and around a jog left at the back. I cannot drive into the lot because there is no reason for anyone to be there this time of night except to commit a violent crime or to follow someone who has that in mind. As I am not the former, the goons are sure to gather that I am the latter. I ditch the car at the curb and stumble up the side of the lot, along a building, away from the floodlights, to save my friends. Or, perhaps, to further shame the Seegerman name. When I poke my head around the corner, Terry and Max are still in the back of the sedan with a goon. The front-seat goons are now at the trunk, removing items that might, under other circumstances, have benign purposes—a tire iron, an aluminum bat—but now seem certain to be intended for no good.

There are not many people who know I am at risk for early-onset AD. My closest friends, my family. Silvie. It doesn't seem the kind of information I ought to have on my résumé. Too easy for me to use as a crutch. Too easy for others to write me off or to pity me.

But I have had the testing conversation with all sorts of people, those at risk for AD and other genetic illnesses, those not. And my un-scientific survey yields what may not be obvious results. A significant percentage of those at risk for genetic illness choose not to be tested. Many marry, have families, jobs, ordinary lives. And then either they develop the disease or they do not. They simply choose not to know.

But that's not the surprise. The surprise is that uniformly, if you ask someone who's *not* at risk what he or she would do in my situation,

the response is immediate and unequivocal—"I'd want to know";
"How can you live your life?"; "It would be impossible to have a
relationship otherwise"; "Better to know than to live in the dark"; "I'd
always be wondering, if I forgot my keys, is it because I forgot my
keys, or is it the Alzheimer's. I'd definitely get tested."

We are all going to die. Some of us sooner than later. Some of us will
fall out of buildings and some of us will die of an infection. Some of us
will know our time is short and some of us will be caught unawares. I
may have the rogue AD gene and, nevertheless, die moments from now
in a heroic effort to save my friends from violence at the hands of the
G-O-D squad. Or I may lose my memory and, like S., rely on my loved
ones to care for me while I slowly, ineluctably, fade away. If I do not
have the rogue AD gene, I may be bludgeoned to death by the goons,
or I may die of Alzheimer's anyway.

For me, right now, not knowing means having hope and taking life
extra seriously and not wasting my time. Not knowing means aligning
myself with my dad, feeling like we are part of the same struggle. Not
knowing means not being flippant about living or about dying.

I may change my mind. I may get tested tomorrow. I may not. I'll
just have to see.

Now that it seems clear Terry and Max have offended G-O-D in some
profound way and are about to have the buckles beaten off their belts,
I still don't have my cell phone. And I still don't know what the hell to
do. Inside-the-car goon gets out and joins his buddies, though he does
not take up an instrument of pain. There is discussion among them.
They are deciding on an approach? A burial site? Terry and Max are
still. It is not possible to tell whether they are talking. I hope they are
talking. I hope they have a plan. I do not.

"Please get out of the car," a goon says, with surprising courtesy.

Max and Terry oblige, though they do not appear to be in any rush.
Why do they not run? Their legs seem unbound. Then I see: the

backseat goon has a gun. Better to be beaten than shot. Definitely. I decide to wait until it is absolutely clear that a beating or murder is about to occur, and then to scream, make myself obvious, and run. Seems like a reasonable idea. I cannot fight them, but I can draw their attention, make it clear that I know what is going on here and that I won't stand for it.

I am still intoxicated, but the adrenaline has now overwhelmed the liquor. The result is that I am shaking badly, and banging my head rhythmically into the concrete building. A trickle of blood falls onto my cheek. No, wait, it's sweat. It is forty degrees out, I am not wearing a jacket, and I am sweating profusely. My heart is pounding. I do not want my friends to die, and I do not want to die. Not tonight. Not before we play for Barry.

"You think you're pretty fucking smart, don't you?" backseat goon says.

When is a question not a question? Answer: when the person asking it does not require a response *and* is holding a weapon.

"Barry Manilow," backseat goon spits out. He is obviously in charge. "Barry Manilow sucks. Now, Chicago. That's some serious shit. Earth, Wind and Fire. The Commodores. Even the motherfucking Bee Gees. But Barry Manilow. That's just totally incorrect."

To his credit, Terry does not attempt to save himself by abandoning Barry. All fine groups. But please, the Bee Gees? You're going to compare "Could It Be Magic" and "If I Can't Have You." Ludicrous.

The gunner goon herds Terry and Max back along the car to the side of the building. Driver and passenger goons follow. They are nearly out of view. I inch around the corner and tiptoe, one foot, then another, toward them. I need to be within screaming distance. But also able safely to escape. A foot further. I swipe a can. The noise startles them. I drop to my knees. I am still ten yards away, out of the light, so they don't see me. Driver goon is anxious to take action. He is behind the others, with a bat above his head. Time's up.

I yell at the top of my lungs, but I hear nothing. Well, actually, I should say I hear nothing of my yell. That is because behind me, suddenly, is the wail of a police siren. A black, unmarked sedan with a temporary siren on its hood wings across the lot and begins its skid around the corner. In an instant all three goons fly into their car and screech out of the lot, away from the alarm, down an alley, and into downtown Santa Rita. When it rounds the corner, I expect the police vehicle to begin a high-speed chase. But it does not. Rather, it slips to a stop feet from Terry and Max, who are still pinned against the building. Two men in casual dress emerge from the car. One I do not recognize. The other is Gerald Fitzgerald.

37

OVERJOYED THAT THE crisis has passed, I start running toward Terry and Max. I am still conspicuously plastered, so I stumble and fall a few feet from them. They are confused to see me, but have no time to make inquiries. That is because shortly after they emerge from their vehicle, Fitzgerald and his partner draw their guns and order us to lie on the ground. I am already there. Terry and Max are increasingly baffled. Terry starts to ask what's happening and the man who is not Fitzgerald swears he will shoot him (Terry) in the ass if he says another word. They cuff us. I had begun to feel nauseated while standing. Being prone helps. Although I believe my hair is now wedded to the ground by a wad of chewing gum.

"It'd be much easier to shoot them, don't you think? Who the fuck's gonna know?" I cannot see him, but it's Fitzgerald. Or at least I'm sure it's the guy I saw in the jail, whatever his name—same syrupy Southern drawl.

"Do me a favor and aim. Last time you got brains on my pants."

"I really don't feel like filling out reports for three arrests."

It is as if they are trying out for a bound-to-be-canceled police drama on a failing cable network. Their routine is not even that believable.

Again, Terry speaks up—"Arrests for what?"—and again the not-Fitzgerald man warns him not to speak.

"We'll still have to file the firearm discharge reports. This big fella might take more than one shot."

"True."

"Let me ask you a question." The man I believe is Fitzgerald kicks the underside of my shoe. "What the fuck is it with Barry Manilow? You're not serious, are you? It's all some kind of Jewboy faggot lawyer irony, right? You're not going to tell me you actually like Barry Manilow, are you?"

When is a question not a question?

"Are you going to shoot them or not? I'm hungry."

"You fellas got anything to eat?"

"No," we moan in unison.

Again, inexplicably, Terry views this as an opening to speak.

"Terrence Fretwater, shut the fuck up. What's this big one's name?"

"I don't know."

"What's your name, Mr. Clean?"

"Max Lichter."

"Good. Max Lichter. Gordon Seegerman. Terrence Fretwater. You are under arrest for obstructing a police investigation, conspiracy, and the murder of Marjorie Styles. Anything else?"

"I think that's it."

Terry cannot be contained. I think he might have felt relieved to be shot.

"What are you talking about? Gordon's the lawyer for the guy who murdered Marjorie Styles."

They laugh. "Oh, yeah? Who's that?"

"Harold Dunn."

"Never heard of him."

I roll over, suddenly clear that we're being played. "What's going on? Are you SRPD?" They think this hilarious.

"You starting the interrogation now, counselor? Because if you are I'm gonna have to call my lawyer," the not-Fitzgerald guy says. He is a small, tidy man, balding, with a buzz cut elsewhere, about forty, older than Fitzgerald, accent from someplace in the Northeast, but not New York or Boston. Baltimore maybe, or Philadelphia. He has a soul patch, the thick clump of hair at the middle of the bottom lip that ordinarily is worn by men who also favor berets. He wears penny loafers with no socks. The tops of his feet are extremely white and extremely hairy.

"We just saved your pathetic asses, and this is the thanks we get?" Fitzgerald says. "I really think we should shoot them."

"How did you know we were here?" Terry says.

"Terrence, my friend, we know when you take a shit. In fact, I'll tell you a little secret. Seegerman here likes to hum show tunes when he's on the toilet."

I am stunned into sobriety. Which show tunes exactly? Never mind.

"You're Fitzgerald, right? I saw you in the jail last week. You're Dunn's friend," I say.

"I don't know what you've been smoking, Seegerman. My name's Frank Foster. This here's Carl Evenrude. I've never heard of anyone named Dunn. And I've never seen your sorry ass before in my life. Who are we? We are the fellas come to tell you that if you so much as go within a mile of G-O-D, we're gonna shoot you. You will not investigate. You will not research. You will not ask questions. You will not interview witnesses. If you do any of these things, we will shoot you. And then we will arrest you. And then we will shoot you some more. Get it? And tell your turban-headed pal that if we find out he's accessing any confidential databases, we will shoot him, too."

"It's all a little confusing," Terry says.

Foster steps on Terry's back and does something to his gun, cocks it or clicks it or something, which makes clear that he is one step closer to killing my bass player.

"Moreover"—Evenrude has taken over—"you will not discuss the events of this evening, any of them, with anyone, including yourselves. You won't even think about it. You have never seen us. You were never here. If you do not follow these instructions, we will shoot you."

"And if Selmer Godfrey happens to stop by with his friends for a chat?" I say.

"Then I guess you're fucked," Fitzgerald says as he pops off our cuffs. Then they get in their car and screech off.

"Thanks for dropping by," Terry says, waving from the ground.

Max and I sit in my car, recovering. I lean against the steering wheel. I nod off and the horn blares, startling me back to life. The front passenger door is open. Terry paces back and forth furiously.

"We've got the tip of an iceberg shoved up our asses," he says.

"That is downright poetic," I say.

"It's all bullshit," he says.

"That, I agree with."

"They must be feds."

"What the hell happened back there?" I say.

"Where?"

"What do you mean, 'where'? At the party. With the goons."

Max speaks up. "Terry wanted to take a look around the business office."

Terry takes over. "We didn't get ten feet in the building before the security guys came after us. Fifteen minutes later we're here, about to get our heads bashed in. Then you're here. Then those cops or whoever they are show up."

Next thing, we hear the shriek of tires, Foster and Evenrude's sedan, no siren this time, backing up the alley at high speed. They skid to a stop, but not before putting a dent in the side of my car. Foster rolls down the driver's-side window. His gun is drawn.

"Gentlemen. Was there something unclear about our instructions?"

When is a question . . .

He sings, in a raspy monotone: " 'We see you when you're sleeping, we know when you're awake.' " He stops singing. "Shut the fuck up. Clear?" He backs up, turns around, and speeds off in the opposite direction.

221

"What about my car?" I yell, to zero effect.

We walk into the middle of the lot, away from the car, which we have finally guessed is wired.

"Definitely feds," I whisper.

"SRPD wouldn't know how to get a wiretap if their life depended on it," Terry adds. "They must have the office, too. Can they do that?"

"No. But that doesn't mean they haven't done it."

"Why us, though? It makes no sense."

We drive home.

"Pretty good show tonight," I say.

"Maybe the best ever," Terry says, staring out the front passenger window.

"We're gonna pack Ted's next week."

"You think?"

"Totally." There is a silence.

"Myla dumped me," I say.

Terry turns his head. "You serious?"

"Yeah."

"I'm surprised. You guys seemed good together."

"Never even got a kiss."

"Could be worse."

"How?"

"You don't think it's worse if you *do* get a kiss, or more, and *then* she dumps you?"

"No. Maybe."

"She say why?"

"The usual. Wrong time. Wants to be friends. Something about another guy somewhere. Though if I had to bet, I'd say it's Barry. She can't handle the depth of my commitment."

"It's a beautiful burden."

"I really liked her, though. I haven't felt this way about anyone since Silvie."

"Don't even go there."

"I know. I'm just saying."

We drive in silence for a few minutes. Santa Rita is sleeping. It is hushed and the streets are empty. The street lights stand like imperturbable guards, an escort for our ride home.

"You know what bothers me?" Max says.

We whip around and glare at him, silently, from the front, trying to shut him up. I've had enough of Foster and Evenrude for the evening. The last thing I need is them showing up at my house and freaking out S.

He continues: "What bothers me is all these late converts. I appreciate what you guys are trying to do and everything, but my fear is that soon it's going to be hip to be a Manilow fan."

38

SUNDAY, I SULK. I ignore calls from the Mandys. I read *The New York Times*. I try to forget about Dunn. Late in the day, I take S. and LeoSayer for a long walk. My dad stays several steps behind, like a teenager out for a stroll with his parents. Terry meets up with us along the way, for the purpose, apparently, of ensuring that I end up in a mental institution before I can fulfill my lifelong ambition of playing for Barry Manilow.

"This is definitely going to hurt. I don't say it lightly, but—"

"Do you say something lightly or take it lightly?" I say. "How can you say something lightly?"

"You're being played."

"Me."

"It's Hong."

"Hong."

"Hong. What the hell is he doing in a clothing store on a Wednesday night?"

"Shopping."

"And he just happens to be standing next to Dunn, who just happens to be the guy who knows everything there is to know about the money flow at G-O-D." He speaks under his breath and glances around every few moments. "Your cop friend said he's dirty, no?"

Pay attention now. Martin Hong is working with or for Selmer. For reasons unknown, and perhaps unknowable, they want Dunn out of the way, but are unwilling to kill him, which would save me a whole lot of time and energy. So, in a manner unexplained, with the help of a crank addict, a housewife, and an eight-year-old girl, they set him up for the exposure charge.

Hong, increasingly worried that I or we will uncover the apparently purposeless frame-up on the misdemeanor, drops a wire on me, or us. At his direction, or Selmer's, or his and Selmer's, the G-O-D Squad goons kidnap Terry and Max, threaten violence, and then, in a piece of pure theater, are chased away by two people, perhaps officers working for Hong, perhaps feds, who discourage us from continuing our entirely unproductive, chaotic, and harebrained investigation by suggesting, without actually saying, that they are law enforcement.

The problem with this analysis is not that it has no logic whatsoever. The problem is that it has just enough logic to make it sort of possibly possible, while still being utterly senseless. There is just enough to it to give me a stomachache, but not nearly enough to help me help Harold Dunn.

"That is utterly senseless," I say.

"It gets worse."

"Appalling."

"Hong did Styles."

"In what sense?"

"Dunn said Styles was about to change her story. The question is, what was she going to say?"

"Is that the question?"

"Maybe she was going to flip on Hong, reveal the whole deal—"

"What deal?"

"So—"

"So he kills her."

"Or has someone else do it. You don't really think it was Dunn, do you?"

"No, but—"

"I have one more. I don't like it, but I won't keep you in the dark."

225

"You are a true friend."

"How does Hong drop the wires on you, your house, your car?"

"He doesn't."

"Just say he does. How does he do it?"

"He doesn't. How do you know there even *is* a wire? Evenrude and Foster were just making a point. We don't really know they were listening."

"And how did they know where we were?"

"We don't know anything, Terry. We know nothing. Period. Maybe they followed me. Maybe they just happened to be passing by."

"Just say they did wire you. How?"

"They didn't."

"Gordy."

"Fine. I have no idea. Perhaps you'd like to tell me, Terrence?"

"Myla."

Myla.

"Myla?"

"Myla."

"Now that is a truly bizarre theory," I say.

"She had the opportunity. And you said you thought it was strange between you."

"I never said that. I'm an idiot. She was clear she wanted to be friends. I just imagined the rest."

Terry looks at me like I have just suggested France is a city in England. "Friends. She wanted to be your friend."

"That's what she said."

"Whatever." He is drooling incredulity.

39

SILVIE AND DETECTIVE Hong and Garland Fischer meet us at Central Station on Monday morning. Why the DA wants to attend a lineup in a misdemeanor case is beyond me, but there he is, all five feet two of him. Standing with them are Lorraine Dykstra and the little girl who is my target at Dunn's trial. I imagine her with a bull's-eye on her forehead. I am in trouble. She is not four feet tall. The word "adorable" blinks brightly in my head, like news of a disaster flashing at the bottom of a television screen.

We file into a small room with one-way glass filling half of a wall. Hong makes a call and after a minute he raises a screen on the window. The wanker is second from the left. His face is frozen. He frowns slightly. There are seven men. Each one has a number hung around his neck.

Callie Dykstra stands with her mother at the back of the room, away from the window. Hong turns to her.

"None of the people in that room can see you, Callie. It's a trick. You can see them but they can't see you, all right?"

I am praying for some smart-alecky response. Some reason to feel okay about going after Callie at trial. When do children become sarcastic buggers? Apparently it's older than eight, because she nods demurely and moves gingerly to the window.

Lorraine Dykstra stands next to me, several feet behind her daughter. She can see the lineup, but she cannot see Callie's face and Callie cannot see hers. No chance for Mom to do any coaching.

"Take a careful look at the faces of each of the men, Callie. Don't say anything until you're done looking at all seven. Don't look back at us. When you're through, let me know." He turns to Lorraine. "Ms. Dykstra, if you can, tell us the number of the person you saw by holding up a number of fingers." The mother picks Dunn without a moment's hesitation.

Callie stands on both feet, hands at her sides, no fidgeting, no obvious discomfort. She moves her head a few centimeters when she is done studying each member of the lineup. As far as I can tell, she doesn't spend more or less time looking at Dunn. Callie looks as if she is studying number seven, the final subject, and is about to make the ID. I brace myself for the hammer blow to the back of my head—if she makes the right call here, she'll be that much more convincing in court. But she says nothing. Instead, she starts back the other way, man by man, several seconds on each. This kid is brutal. Not only is she four freaking feet tall and cute as a button, she's prudent and serious. She knows this is important.

We wait. No one says a word, though it's obvious the delay is killing Silvie and Hong as much as me. Callie makes her way back, seven, six, five. She stops there and stares for several moments.

"Cal? You okay?" Lorraine Dykstra says. The kid nods, says nothing, and does not take her eyes off number five. Of the seven, he looks least like Dunn. For a moment I think, That's it, case over, but then she moves on—four, three, two—my stomach drops—but then one, and back again, one, two, three, four, and so on. She can't do it. She has no idea. Fischer moves toward Callie. Silvie looks at me and then at Hong and then at Callie.

"Garland, why don't we give her room?" I say.

Fischer looks at me as if I've just called his mother a mongrel.

"I am giving her room, counsel."

"Well, it looks as if you're stepping next to her, and I just want to make sure there isn't any communication or coaching."

"Are you accusing me of something, Seegerman?"

"Come on, I'm just protecting my client here. Let's just give her—"

"Shut *up!*" the kid yells. We are silent, but she still doesn't pick anyone. Another minute passes.

"If you don't know, that's okay, Callie," Silvie finally relents. "It's important for us to know now if you can't tell us which one it is."

I'm positive the kid is about to say she can't do it. She is staring at the subjects, but doesn't seem to be focused on one in particular. From the side I can see her eyes move across the row of men more quickly now. And then her head begins, faintly, to move from side to side. Her lips come together as if she is about to speak. *Sorry. Sorry, I just don't . . .*

Then Dunn's face changes. Perhaps he senses the confusion in the booth. It isn't a grin, exactly. It's the beginning of a smirk, only on the left side of his face, but it's enough. He must have had the same look on his face when he presented his member to the young Miss Dykstra.

The kid looks at Dunn and points.

"That's him." No ambivalence at all. "That's the man."

Silvie is gleeful when we leave the building.

"Your guy is going down hard on the homicide. It was Styles's hair in the trunk."

"Good job, Silvie. I'm sure we'll all be able to sleep better when they execute Harold."

"I will. I still don't want to try the misdemeanor. Tell your guy to take the deal."

"Believe me, if I could make it go away, I would."

She hands me a thick envelope.

"Cullen's finally got me the surveillance tape. It's edited down to the relevant time frame. You'll see."

Gulp. "And?"

"The coverage in the store is pretty limited—they have cameras on the registers and near the dressing rooms, but Dunn isn't on either. There's another on the entrance that has him walking in at around quarter to five. His penis is not on film."

To hear an ex-girlfriend, especially an ex with whom I had excellent and at times wild sex, talk about another man's member is disconcerting to say the least. I don't even like to hear her use the word, let alone to contemplate what she must have done with one or more penises since our sad split.

"So why are we having this discussion? The video is irrelevant."

"I'll play him walking in, to show how long he's in the store."

"I'll stip to it"—in other words, agree that Dunn entered the store at a particular time.

"No, I want to show him on the tape. He looks terrible."

"That's nice."

"You know what they say, all's fair in love and trial," she says, walking off.

40

FRANCINE HORIUCHI IS in my office when Terry and I return. She looks grim. She hands me a lab report.

"The hairs in Dunn's trunk were Styles's," Francine says.

"I heard."

"What about the boyfriend?" Terry says.

"He's a truck driver. He leaves for a job on Tuesday morning, drives to L.A. and isn't back until Friday midday. The dispatch records have him on the road, out of the Bay Area the whole time."

"So much for the boyfriend."

"I thought we might have a shot at a 995," Francine says. "But once Judge Saltzman finds out about the DNA test, we might as well forget it." A 995 is a motion by the defense to dismiss before trial for lack of evidence. In other words, it argues there should be no trial because there isn't even probable cause that Dunn killed Styles, let alone proof beyond a reasonable doubt. Given who the judge is, it was a long shot to begin with. The hair in the trunk of Dunn's Cadillac makes filing the motion a complete waste of paper.

"You ask Harold about it?"

"He told me what he told the cops in his interview. The day before Thanksgiving, she put a duffel bag in his trunk and he drove her to an address in the hills."

"And Dunn doesn't have an address."

"He says he can find it. Judge Reasoner ordered the sheriff to take him up there tomorrow." She stands up. "You better talk to him,

Gordy. We'll see what happens, but I gotta tell you, this case is becoming less triable every day. Your guy—"

"*My* guy? Since when did he become my guy?"

"He seems to like you, that's all. Talk to him. I think I can get Hernandez to drop the specials." Meaning Dunn pleads to a life sentence and has a shot at parole. In twenty years.

After she leaves, I toss Terry the surveillance videotape and relay Silvie's spiel on its contents.

"Feel free to watch it and report back," I say.

"Why?"

"I have no idea."

Afternoon, in chambers with Judge Heymann for the pretrial. Silvie updates him on the progress of the murder case, and on the lineup in the morning.

"Any chance of a resolution?" the judge says.

Silvie looks at me. "No, your honor," I say. "Mr. Dunn is pretty clear about wanting a jury trial."

"What's the present offer?"

"Three months, your honor," Silvie says.

"Three years to three months. You must be one hell of a lawyer, Mr. Seegerman."

Silvie wasn't about to let that one sit out there for very long. "Given the murder charges, frankly we don't view this case as very important. We would agree to dismiss the 647.6 and accept a plea on a single 314 count."

"Even if we do go to trial, I don't see how there's more than one 314. With no testimony from Styles, only one witness will say she saw Dunn's penis," I say, rather purposelessly.

"And your client isn't willing to take the three months?"

"Nope."

"Your client is a fool. On the *Pitchess* motion, Detective Hong's personnel record will stay sealed."

"Is your honor ruling that there is nothing relevant on the impeachment issue in the detective's file?"

It must be fun being a judge. He is right simply by force of position—because his decisions, for the most part, are not subject to review.

"If there were more to this case, maybe. But even if Hong's the worst cop in the world, the case doesn't depend on him. Either the girl sees Dunn or not."

"Well, he's the one who arrests Dunn—"

Silvie jumps in. "Because Marjorie Styles IDs him. Hong just happens to be standing there."

"And he's the one who sets up the suggestive ID," I say.

"It is what it is, Mr. Seegerman. You get to make that argument to the jury, but I don't think there will be any dispute about the facts. Your guy is under arrest, he's cuffed, right?"

"Right," both Silvie and I say.

"He can describe what he felt like, if he wants to take the stand. The only question is what it all means—does it make the girl more likely to say the person under arrest is the person she saw expose himself. How is Hong's credibility at issue?"

"I understand the ruling," I grumble.

"If you have a theory on this I want to hear it," Judge Heymann says, and then turns to Silvie. "I don't think I'm stepping out of line here to say Hong's record is a mess. I can't see how he's still investigating serious crime in this county. And I'd be very nervous about putting him on the stand in a murder case. But there's no investigation here, really. No significant interviews beyond confirmation of the original IDs. His credibility makes no difference in this case, so I don't think I can let the defense go after him."

Back in my office, late afternoon.

My speaker phone beeps. There is no one on the other end.

"Hello."

"Hey, Gordy."

"Hello, Maeve. How are you?"

"I heard your dick flicker is screwed."

"Something like that."

Silence, but the speaker phone light remains on.

"Was there something else?" I say.

"What?"

"Did you want something else, or can I go back to work?"

"How are you gonna try the case if the kid IDs Dunn?"

"That is an excellent question. If you have any thoughts, I'd be pleased to hear them."

"Not really."

Silence. Then I hear her chair squeak and a grunt or two.

"What are doing right now?"

"Painting my toenails."

"Are we through?"

"Huh?"

"Maeve, I'm—"

"The Hair is on 72."

"Gordon Seegerman here." You should hear me. So composed. So smooth. Cool even. Always a degree cooler. It's the only way. I made some serious mistakes, opening up, falling fast. But now the brakes are on. If I have a chance at all, I have to make this a conversation she won't, can't, let be the last.

I tell Myla to hold for a moment. I kick my door closed, hard, thus giving Maeve—panting from her run to my office—a concussion. Although Myla is the one who calls, I speak almost without pause for two minutes. I was out of line. I was drunk. I was spinning out after the show. And there's all this stuff going on, the Dunn trial, other stuff I can't really talk about, my dad, stuff that has nothing to do with you

234

but—I just went a little nuts. Of course, I understand, we all have attachments, we all have complications. If there is someone else, that's fine. We're not talking about marriage here. I just like you. It's that simple. I look forward to seeing you. I hope I'll see you again.

Cool. Well, all right, not cool entirely. Lukewarm, say.

"I understand. Don't worry about it."

"Right. So what are yours?"

"What are my what?"

"Your complications."

"That's not why I called, Gordy. I just wanted to make sure you were all right. You seemed a little, I don't know, crazy on Saturday."

"I'm sorry. I really am."

"No problem. I'm glad you're okay."

"Can we get together?" Yeah. Real cool.

"You have a trial coming up. And the show. Why don't we talk when things aren't so busy. All right?"

"All right."

"I hope everything works out."

"Thanks. Can I just ask you one question?"

"I don't know. Try me."

"Do you happen to know a Santa Rita police detective named Martin Hong?"

Myla doesn't say no. She says "Why?" Why does she say why? My question is a simple one. It does not require an explanation. Why "why"? "Why" is a time buyer. "Why" is a speed bump. "Why" is a punt from the ten-yard line.

"Forget about it. Call me when you're ready." Stunningly cool. But inside, I think, "Why?"

"Call the paramedics. Romeo is bleeding," Maeve says, squatting on the floor of my office.

"I'm fine."

235

"You look like shit."

"That's because I have a trial in a few days and I've done everything to prepare except everything."

"Can I help?"

"Sure. Tell me how to convince a jury that just because Dunn wanked once, ten years ago, that doesn't make him an incorrigible wanker."

"Just go back to your Bible, X. It's all in the Good Book."

"Maeve."

"Don't Maeve me. Corinthians 1:30, 'But of him are ye in Christ Jesus, who of God is made unto us wisdom, and righteousness, and sanctification, *and redemption.*' People find the Lord. People change. People in glass houses have hard nipples." I shake my head. "Seriously, glass houses are hard to insulate so the people who live there are always cold."

"I may be able to use the redemption thing."

"Good. Plus, make sure you make that little girl cry. The jury will love that," she says, walking toward the door.

"That's very helpful."

"No problem." She exits. Terry walks in.

"Did you want something?" I say.

"What's going on?"

"Work."

"You think more about what I said?" he says, under his breath, sure Evenrude and Foster are listening.

"No."

"Be careful."

"Thank you very much. Now, if you don't mind."

I'm at the office until nearly eight, reading cases and articles on eyewitness identification. I speak for nearly an hour with my expert witness, Dr. Phyllis Strong, a psychologist at the Santa Rita campus of the California State University, and an expert in the areas of memory, suggestion, and identification. She speaks well and ought to make a fine witness. Silvie won't have any idea what to do with her. With Dunn's prior, and the kid, it won't make a difference. But I'll be able to look the wanker in the eye and say, "Everything that could be done was done, Dunn"—and then try my best not to laugh hysterically.

I noodle around on the Internet for a few minutes, deciding whether I ought to check Insuron to see if Myla is legit. I am enormously relieved when she shows up just where she ought to, a name and a number on the company's website, in the claims investigations department.

I am appalled at how easily Terry cast doubt on Myla's legitimacy. Call him Iago.

41

THE NEXT MORNING, Terry, Francine, and I squeeze into Terry's
Mercedes and follow Detective Hong, a deputy from the jail, and
Dunn in a SRPD cruiser out of downtown Santa Rita. It is a brilliant
day, and when we hit the hills the sun is blinding. It looks as if we are
going to my house, same right off Santa Rita Avenue onto Doyle
Street, same left up Francis Lewis Lane. But we pass Candlewood and
climb for another minute.

We stop at an address on Francis Lewis, but I cannot see the
residence from the street. There is a seven-foot cement wall covered
with ivy. And an elaborate iron gate, through which I see a stand of
pine and a small pond. Woven into the ironwork of the gate is the
name "Silverstone." There are the Santa Rita well-to-do—their houses
are like mine, only without the holes in the roof, the falling shingles,
and the mudslide in the backyard. And then there are the Santa Rita
zillionaires—huge mansions, five-acre lots, tennis courts, pool houses,
Hummers and Jaguars crowded into eight-car garages. And views
forever—across Santa Rita to the Bay and San Francisco and out past
the Golden Gate Bridge to the Pacific.

We stop the car and walk up to the cruiser. Hong drops Dunn's
window.

"I pulled up right here. She got out and got her stuff from the trunk
and walked toward that gate. I didn't see her go in. I can't even say she
went to this house. She waved and I left," Dunn says.

"Are we done here?" Hong asks.

"I guess. You don't want to knock on the door?" Francine says.

"I already know who killed Styles."

He raises Dunn's window and peels off. Terry pushes a button on an intercom box. The communication is difficult, but eventually someone buzzes us in. We walk for a couple of minutes, up a long blacktop driveway, past a garage and a guest house to a large oval turnaround in front of the house, a classic brick Georgian mansion, with towering columns and a front door approximately the size of Rhode Island, with glistening brass fittings.

"Are you Mrs. Silverstone?" Terry says, turning it on for the older woman who answers the door. She is obese. She has little hair. She looks gravely ill.

"Yes."

"Thank you for seeing us." He hands her a card. "I'm Terry Fretwater and these are my colleagues from the Public Defender's Office." He introduces us and I shake her hand, which feels something like an unrefrigerated trout. "We're looking for some information about a woman we believe did some cleaning here."

"Who's that?"

"Marjorie Styles." Francine takes out a picture.

"What's this all about?"

"Did she work here?"

The woman backs several feet into the house and reaches for a phone. She punches a few numbers, mumbles, and walks away. We do not see her again. Two minutes later, a short man, perhaps forty years old, lumbers down the grand stairway into the grand foyer and stands in the grand doorway, looking bothered. He is extraordinarily pale, ghostly. He wears shorts and shiny black alligator shoes without socks and a green Izod polo shirt. He has remarkably long fingernails.

Terry shows him a picture of Styles. She may have been there in the past to clean. Was she there the day before Thanksgiving? No. Why so sure? I'm just sure. Call my lawyer if you have other questions.

239

He slams the door, nearly severing two of my fingers, without giving us his name or his lawyer's name or saying good-bye.

"He's the guy," Terry says.

"What?" Francine and I say in unison.

"He killed Styles."

"That's obvious," I say.

"He admits she's been to the house. How does Dunn pick this address? Whoever this guy is, he's lying about Styles being here on the twenty-seventh. Why would Dunn lie?"

"Because he killed her?" Francine says.

"It makes no sense. She'd changed her mind about the ID. She thinks he's the world's nicest man. We talked to her, Francine. She was practically in love with the guy."

"That I agree with," I say. "She would have been our witness. Not the world's most convincing witness, but I think there's a good chance she would have recanted her original statement."

"Also, a place like this?" Terry says. "They have staff. They have full-time cleaning people. They don't hire Merry Maids to come in and steal all the silver."

In the car, before he turns the key, Terry taps out a number on his cell. He shushes us and waits for an answer.

"This is Terry Fretwater. We met—" Pause. "Great. I hope you'll be able to help. I don't want to—" Pause. "Okay, terrific. What I'd like to do is say a name. My question is whether you have any reason to believe it is the name of the competition. You say 'yes' or 'no' or 'I don't know,' and the conversation ends. Either way, Harold Dunn is forever in your debt." Pause. "I understand, of course—if you don't know, you don't know. He's looking at the death penalty and this may be extremely important." Pause. "You ready?" Pause. Terry says the name very slowly: "Merry Maids." Pause. "You won't be hearing from us again."

240

"The always accommodating Stone Van der Geist," Terry says, deeply satisfied with himself. "Cleaning lady, my ass. Marjorie Styles was a hooker, and that freak"—he points back at the estate— "whoever he is, killed her."

S. chooses the night before the Dunn trial to fall apart. I get home at nearly nine o'clock. My father has locked himself in his room and refuses to emerge. Lillian is outside, staring at his bedroom window, which is wide open. I can see him pacing.

We ought to have moved him downstairs long ago, but we feared the change would throw him. He moved into his small room shortly after my mother died. The master bedroom suite has not been occupied since. It is a museum, crowded with half-packed boxes and covered in dust. It has remained essentially untouched for nearly a quarter of a century. Same chifforobe filled with my mother's dainty dresses. Same pictures—of King and me, of the McNamara clan—on the night stand and dresser and walls.

I consult with Lillian and then walk inside.

Ferdy is visibly shaken. Not a common sight.

"He thinks we're trying to kill him."

I can't make out most of S.'s ranting.

"How'd he lock the door?" I removed the hardware months ago after a similar, though less hysterical, episode.

"I don't know. He's got it jammed somehow," Ferdy says. "You want to call the police?"

I raise my eyebrows. The right thing to do under normal circumstances. Maybe we'll get there. But the SRPD can't necessarily be depended upon to treat my father with the care and tenderness he deserves. I try the door. I kick at it. I bump into it and bruise my hip. I back up the hallway, fifteen feet. I run at the door. I make it about halfway when my right ankle collapses under me and I topple. The pain is fierce.

Luckily, events do not permit me to ponder my agony for very long. Lillian screams from outside. We race—Ferdy races; I hobble—out front. LeoSayer yaps incessantly. S. has one leg out the window. We yell up to him. *Stay put. We're coming in.* I rush up.

If my father commits suicide, I will certainly be entitled to a brief continuance of the Dunn trial. Why am I trying to save him? I don't know. Anyway, with his luck and ours, he'll leap out the window and instead of putting himself out of our misery he'll break both his ankles and I'll end up waiting on him day and night. I wish my father had been nicer to me. Maybe I wouldn't have such foul thoughts.

"Dad, would you step away from the damn window?" I yell from outside his door. I try it. Still stuck. I punch it with my palms a few times. Nothing. "Police, open up."

Grunts and movement inside the room. Incomprehensible yelling from outside.

"I don't want to die," S. whines.

"And I don't want you to die, Dad. Open the door."

"You're all going to be sorry—" He trails off.

"What's wrong with you?"

"Sorry. Sorry."

"Dad, please open up." More shouting from outside. "Dad, open the fucking door right now."

Silence. For some reason the hush is too much to bear. I start to weep. Real tears. No feint, no tactics. I ask him again, quietly, and a few moments later the door opens.

"You're all going on a trip," he says. He has been crying. It is the first time I have ever seen this. Ever. I hug him.

"No, Dad, we're not going on a trip."

Yes, we are.

42

EIGHT-THIRTY A.M., December 18. Department 26. Trial.

Webster's Unabridged has seven entries for the word "trial." Number four seems to fit my present circumstances best. "Trial: a source of annoyance or irritation."

I am twenty minutes early, but Silvie is already there, divining elaborate ways to punish me in public. My files are sandwiched between my arm and torso. She has a cart. My worn Evidence Code book is stuffed with blank legal pads and notes and reports. I have folded down the corners of pages containing relevant sections. Hers has no crease in the binding; colorful printed tabs sprout from every side. My suit is wrinkled and encrusted with LeoSayer hair. Hers—a bright red designery sort of getup—is not.

"Morning, Gordy. What's with your leg?"

"S. completely lost it last night. I had to wrestle him to the ground."

"Are you okay?"

"I could not possibly be better."

"If you need the weekend, I'm sure the judge—"

"Let's get this thing over with while I'm still standing. I was sort of hoping for the sympathy vote, anyway."

"The whole thing is ridiculous, a colossal waste of my time and yours, and it all has to do with one thing—Rufus Heymann's ego. Every other judge in this building would have trailed the case."

"Why don't you just dismiss?"

"You know, it was Styles's hair in the trunk."

"You already told me that. The evidence doesn't get any stronger because you repeat it, Silvie. Dunn says she had her bag in there."

"I'm sure the bag was covered with her hair."

"It's not impossible."

"No, but it's not enough for reasonable doubt where he has motive, opportunity, his prints are all over the place, and he admits being in the house and giving money to a witness."

"He didn't do it, Silvie. I'm not saying you don't have plenty of evidence, but you have the wrong guy."

"And what makes you so sure?"

"You remember Venn diagrams from school?"

"A little."

I put down my materials and hold up my left fist. "Over here you have the set of men who expose their genitals in public." Then the right. "Over here is the set of people who are capable of putting their bare hands around a woman's neck, squeezing until she stops breathing, and then tossing the body into the bay." I wave my hands around. "There's no intersection between the two sets. Rapists and murderers, yes. Robbers and murderers, yes."

"But not flashers and murderers?"

"A flasher is looking for love, Silvie. He's looking for affirmation. He may have a strange way of knocking, but he's trying to get inside the house where the party is. The person who killed Marjorie Styles lives in a shed behind the house. He has no interest in going to the party."

"This is fascinating."

"Plus, Dunn turned himself in on the warrant for the misdo. You think a guy guilty of murder does that?"

"Dunn doesn't strike me as the swiftest kayak on the river. Anyway, you've all but admitted your guy is good for the 314."

"I admit nothing."

*   *   *

244

Trials. Annoyance and irritation. And boredom. Trials proceed at the pace of a slug on downers. Trials are profoundly tedious. A trial lawyer spends two thirds of his career standing in the hallway outside the courtroom, waiting. Even when court is in session, mostly, nothing happens. An expert testifies and spends an hour talking about his qualifications. A witness takes the stand to say something simple: She saw the defendant steal a car; the defendant told her he bought a gun. How long can that take? If you've been on a jury, you know. If not, take my word for it: Hours. Days.

Trials, too, are uniquely ill equipped to reveal the truth about anything. If a defendant is really guilty and the prosecution has the evidence, he's going to plead out. If a person obviously is not responsible for a crime, he probably won't be charged in the first place. It's the ones in the middle that end up in front of a jury. And there is no reason whatsoever to think that a process in which twelve people selected at random, thrown together without experience or training or preparation, barraged with testimony, evidence, and instruction on the relevant legal principles, and then forced immediately thereafter to discuss the case and arrive at a verdict, are any better at divining the truth of a given situation than a coin flip.

Actually, it's worse than a coin flip, because jurors come to court with biases and preconceptions. Often they are more focused on the lawyers' hairstyles or apparel than on the evidence. Often they are wondering whether they left their irons on or whether their wives are cheating. They are not paying attention. They don't care. Trials are neither revelatory nor enlightening. They are neither exciting nor amusing. They are rarely momentous—except for the defendant— and if they are notable, it is for all the wrong reasons. People are engrossed by criminal trials for much the same reason my job is often a comfort to me: There is solace in the realization that it is someone else's catastrophe.

*   *   *

Bernard, Judge Heymann's clerk, calls the case. "People of the State of California versus Harold Dunn, for trial."

I lean over. "You all right?" I want the potential jurors behind me immediately to see me conferring with my client.

"Yeah, fine," Dunn says. But his face is white and his knees knock frantically.

I quiet his leg with my hand. "Relax," I tell him. "You look like you might combust."

"Sorry."

"These people want to like you, Harold. Don't give them a reason not to."

"Counsel," Bernard says. "Please state your appearances for the record."

There are perhaps fifty people in the gallery. Judge Heymann introduces himself and asks anyone who is not a potential juror to leave the room. One person leaves, a reporter from the *Santa Rita Herald*.

The judge reads the complaint. Because Silvie justifiably believes Dunn is going down in the murder case, she has dismissed the Penal Code 647.6 charge, annoying or molesting a minor. The complaint alleges a single count—that on or about November 13, 2002, in the area of 4200 Songtree Avenue, Santa Rita, California, Harold Larry Dunn did willfully and lewdly expose his person, or the private parts thereof, in a public place, or in a place where there were present other persons to be offended or annoyed thereby, in violation of California Penal Code Section 314.

"The law guarantees to each side the right to a jury that will act with complete fairness, with strict impartiality, and without favor to one side or the other," Heymann says. "In a moment we will commence the process of voir dire to determine whether there is anything in your background or experience that might impair your ability to sit fairly and impartially in this case."

Voir dire. Truth telling. Heymann reads from a form on his desk, while I slide slowly down into the uncomfortable wood chair at counsel table.

"But preliminarily, if there is anyone here who cannot, for reasons of health or family responsibility or any other good reason be here for the next two days and perhaps Friday, please raise your hand."

Of the fifty potential jurors, all but a few raise their hands. Heymann is not pleased.

"Ladies and gentlemen. Jury service is a responsibility of citizenship. The following are not acceptable hardship excuses: You have to work; you were planning on going skiing; your mother-in-law is in town; you have a term paper due." Heymann goes on, and gradually most of the hands recede.

"I'm doing you a favor, believe me, because if I let you go you'll end up on a six-month asbestos trial over in Department 19." Heymann releases a couple of the legitimate hardship cases. Then he tweets through the preliminaries. He explains how the case will proceed, from opening statements to evidence to closing arguments to deliberations. Then he begins introductory instruction on the law.

"As jurors, you must determine the facts of the case from the evidence received in the trial, and only from the evidence received in the trial. You must not base your decision on or allow yourself to be influenced by mere conjecture or guesswork. You must not discuss the case or anything connected with the case among yourselves or with anyone else, and you must not permit anyone to speak to you about the case or about anything connected with it until the case has been finally submitted to you for decision. You must keep an open mind about the case. You must not form or express any opinion about the case or about any issue connected with it until you have heard all the evidence, the attorney's statements and arguments, and my instructions on the law, and the case has been submitted to you for decision. As jurors you will be the sole and exclusive judges of the credibility of the witnesses and the facts of the case. I will be, among other things, the judge of the law of the case. You must accept the law as I state it to you in my instructions even if you disagree with them or any one of them. You must not be influenced by pity for the defendant or by prejudice against him. You must not allow yourself to be influenced by sentiment, sympathy, passion, or public opinion. You must not be biased in any way against the defendant because he has been charged with the crime set forth against him in the complaint or because he is standing trial on those charges. Neither of these facts is evidence of his guilt. The law requires instead that you presume the defendant to be innocent of each of the crimes charged against him and that you not find him guilty of any count unless his guilt is proved beyond a reasonable doubt."

The jurors are behind me, in the gallery, but it is obvious they are already, at best, bewildered, and at worst, somnolent. Heymann takes a deep breath, blows it out, and continues.

"Reasonable doubt is defined as follows: It is not a mere possible doubt, because everything relating to human affairs is open to some possible or imaginary doubt. It is that state of the case which after the entire comparison and consideration of all the evidence leaves the minds of the jurors in that condition that they cannot say they feel an abiding conviction of the truth of the charge."

Right. So, one of the more serious flaws in a criminal trial is the generally accepted notion that someone, somewhere, knows what reasonable doubt is, or that any two people who believe they know what it is define it the same way, or that a group of twelve people, none of whom has thought about the question for ten seconds in the past, can meaningfully agree on what it is. To ask those same people to use that standard to judge the guilt or innocence of a person charged with a crime, whose liberty is at stake, is something like sitting a four-year-old at the helm of a four-hundred-foot-long container ship in Santa Rita harbor and telling her to head for Japan. She might make it. Who knows? Stranger things have happened.

"A defendant in a criminal case has a constitutional right not to be called as a witness in his own case. In other words, he may choose not to testify. If the defendant in this case should choose not to testify you must not discuss that fact in deliberations or draw any negative inferences from that fact or hold it against the defendant in any way."

Did I mention that criminal trials make no sense? Is there a better way to guarantee that jurors *will* think about, talk about, and use a defendant's silence as evidence of guilt, than telling them not to do so? If a defendant does not take the stand to give his side of the story, jurors think one of two things: He's hiding something, or he's hiding something. Either way they consider it powerful evidence of guilt. Can you blame them? Believe me: The reason a criminal defendant does not take the stand to give his side of the story is he's hiding something.

The issue, in Dunn's case anyway, is irrelevant. The wanker can hardly wait to testify.

43

JUDGE HEYMANN COMPLETES reading the printed form, takes off his reading glasses, and looks out at the gallery.

"If you make it onto this jury, you become a student again. This is the university of this case, and when you graduate, in two days, you'll be qualified to decide whether the prosecution has proven the charges beyond a reasonable doubt. Do me a big favor, don't discuss the case with your husband or your daughter. Don't go read a book if you're confused. This is the classroom. If you have any questions, write them down and hand them to the bailiff and we'll get them answered as best we can."

Bernard calls fourteen names. Twelve sit in the jury box. Two sit in the alternates' seats outside the box. Six are white. Four are black. One is Asian. Three are something else. There are six women and eight men. They are all staring at Harold and me. And they look angry.

Judge Heymann orders each one to provide some basic information—name, job, immediate family members, details of prior jury service. He asks them to indicate whether they have anything in their backgrounds—a wanker in the family, perhaps?—that could interfere with their judgment. I try to pay attention while each of the potential jurors has his or her moment in the spotlight. For some of these people the experience is excruciating. For some it is a rare chance to address a large and captive audience.

Frankly, I don't like jurors. They scare the crap out of me. I have heard that an experienced trial lawyer develops an instinct for the types of jurors who might favor his client in a given case. I have no such power. They all look mean to me. And dumb? Please. If a reasonably intelligent person wants to avoid jury service, it's not real tough. Which means that people who end up on a jury haven't the intellectual wherewithal to avoid it. Or, worse, they affirmatively want to serve, which is even scarier—anyone who chooses to spend many unpaid hours sitting in an overheated room to take part in a proceeding distinguished by monotony and confusion has an agenda. And it is a rare circumstance indeed in which someone wants to serve to *help* a criminal defendant.

I work up a fancy smile and walk over to the jury box.

"Good morning, ladies and gentlemen. My name is Gordon Seegerman, and I have the honor of representing this man"—I turn—"Harold Dunn."

Just as I am set to launch into my voir dire spiel, a woman in the jury box raises her hand enthusiastically.

"Yes, ma'am," Judge Heymann says. "What is your name?"

"Joan Greene."

"What can we do for you, Ms. Greene?"

"I believe I may know Mr. Seegerman, only by another name."

"An alias, Mr. Seegerman; how mysterious. What is that name, Ms. Greene?"

"Barry X."

"Counsel?"

"I am an amateur musician, your honor. Barry X is my stage name."

"Oh, believe me, he's no amateur," Ms. Greene assures the court. "He's the best Barry Manilow imitator I've ever seen."

I really hate being called an imitator. But probably this isn't the right time to get into that.

The courtroom suddenly comes to life. There are laughs, and one or two gasps, though I suspect those are from people startled awake by the commotion.

251

"And do you believe your familiarity with Mr. Seegerman in the other context will influence your ability to serve as an impartial juror in this case?"

She pauses for a moment to think. "Well, I *am* sort of in love with Barry Manilow. It might be hard."

Good-bye, Ms. Greene, and fare thee well. Bernard calls another name and a new victim meanders into the jury box.

"Any other jurors familiar with Mr. Seegerman's musical career?" No takers. "Very well, you're up, Barry X."

"Thank you, your honor." I stand behind Dunn with my hands on his shoulders. "My client has been accused of a crime. He has pleaded not guilty and he's here today because we contest the charge. We say Harold Dunn hasn't broken any law. He is an innocent man, wrongly accused. As the judge told you, if you make it onto this jury, then, after listening to the evidence, you—each of you, individually—will have the job of saying whether the prosecution has proven the charge beyond a reasonable doubt. That's not an easy job. You have to listen very carefully to the witnesses. You have to think about the judge's instructions on the law. You have to listen to me and the district attorney tell you our views of the facts. And you'll have to sit in a little room, right through that door, for as long as it takes, to carefully discuss the evidence with eleven people you don't know, who may think about things differently than you, and arrive at your own conclusion. If you can't do it, please let us know now. If the charge bothers you, if you think anyone who gets arrested is probably guilty, if you have trouble presuming my client is innocent, speak up. All we can ask for is fairness."

I let that sink in for a moment before I begin to question the jurors. Every time I do this I am reminded of the dating game. Juror Number One: If you were a color, what color would it be, and why?

"Ms. Englander. Good morning. Can you tell me whether you may have read something about this case in the newspaper?"

"Yes."

"And do you think what you read might have an impact on your ability to be fair to Mr. Dunn?"

"It might."

"Your honor? I can continue, or the court—"

"Ms. Englander." Judge Heymann takes over. "Let me address this to everyone. How many of you have read about this case in the newspaper?" Every hand in the jury box goes up. "What about in the audience?" Most. "Ms. Englander, generally speaking, what was the information you gathered from the articles you've read?"

"That Mr. Dunn killed one of the witnesses in this case."

Heymann stands up. "Counsel, my chambers, please."

"Thoughts?" The court reporter has joined us. This is too important for an off-the-record chat.

What all three of us are thinking is that Silvie was right: Heymann ought to have trailed the misdemeanor case. The Styles killing had received considerable attention in the press, and every article connected it to the exposure charges against Dunn. It will be impossible to find twelve jurors who haven't heard about the murder case. But Heymann can't very well delay the misdo trial now—not and save face.

"At a minimum, your honor, I think it makes sense to start with a new group. You could confront the problem from the start, tell the venire that no matter what they may have read or heard in the press, there is no evidence that suggests my client is guilty of any crime, including the Styles killing."

"You want to start over?"

"Well, no, I don't really *want* to start over. But I don't think it's fair to Mr. Dunn to seat anyone who heard Ms. Englander's comments. And I think we'd better head off the issue from the get-go."

"Ms. Hernandez?"

253

"I think your honor can address the issue with this group as well as any other. From the number of hands, I expect the majority of any group we seat will have heard about the Styles case. The *Journal* had it on the front page for a couple of days at least. I think the best we can do is tell them they should put it out of their minds. Legally, that's sufficient."

"Why haven't I heard about your musical career, Mr. Seegerman? I'm quite fond of Barry Manilow."

"I hope that won't lead the district attorney to seek your recusal, Judge."

He scrunches his face into a forced smile. "I agree with Ms. Hernandez on this. I doubt we'll do any better bringing in a new venire. I'll instruct this group to ignore the other case. And I'll permit as much voir dire as you like on the question. Okay?"

"For the record, your honor, I think this group has been tainted by Ms. Greene's statement. I'd ask the Court to dismiss the present venire and bring in a new one."

"Denied. But let me know when your next show is—Barry."

Back in court.

"Ladies and gentlemen," Heymann begins, "one of the things you may already have gathered from today's proceedings is that we are doing our best to pick twelve of you who can consider the evidence in this case, and this case alone, and do so fairly and impartially. Both the district attorney and Mr. Dunn are entitled to that under the law. Many of you have read newspaper articles and perhaps seen reports on television about another case involving Mr. Dunn. Please listen very carefully now. You will assume, I am ordering you to assume, for the purpose of this trial that the charges in that case are false, that there is no evidence that Mr. Dunn has done anything wrong.

"There will be no evidence offered in this case relating to the other. And as I have explained, you must base your decision in this case on the evidence you hear in this courtroom and only in this courtroom. I cannot emphasize this strongly enough. The defendant is innocent until proven guilty beyond a reasonable doubt of the charge in this case, which is a violation of California Penal Code Section 314. That is the only charge you will be asked to consider. You must put entirely out of your mind anything you have read or heard about that charge or any other. It's not easy, and we understand that. But that is what we ask you to do. If you do not believe you can do it, please say so. You will be excused."

The Styles homicide issue thins out the jury pool considerably. I am left to voir dire a group of people who either do not read the newspaper or watch the TV news, or who are so utterly self-deluded that they believe they can banish from their consideration of the misdemeanor charge news that the wanker strangled a witness in the case, or who are not at all deluded, but claim to be able to set aside the murder accusation because they want to get on the jury for the sole purpose of putting Dunn away.

Among these slim pickings I must find one person, one extraordinary soul, who believes that flashing should be made legal or that eight-year-olds are preternatural prevaricators. Who has no use for evidence that Dunn has an exposure prior. Who so distrusts the legal system that she or he will assume the murder charges *and* the misdemeanor charges are utterly bogus.

The voir dire process is as sketchy and flawed as the rest of a criminal trial. I ask the potential jurors what TV shows they watch, where they shop for food, who their heroes are. From this I am expected to determine which jurors might naturally distrust the authorities, which might be closet fascists.

But in truth, my decisions are guided by less bland factors. The dirty secret of all criminal trial lawyers—prosecutors and defense counsel—is that the most effective proxies for jurors' leanings for or against a person charged with a crime, for or against the authorities, are things that most people believe ought not be factors in a judicial system: sex, age, class, race. African-Americans and poor people make good defense jurors because, historically, they have been mistreated by cops and the justice system. Engineers like order and trust authority, so they are better for prosecutors. Young people are less offended by minor sex and drug crimes.

"Mr. Singletary," I ask an older white juror, "is my client guilty?"

"How should I know?"

"Your honor, I move to excuse Mr. Singletary for cause."

"Denied."

"Mr. Singletary, and the rest of you, the correct answer to that question is no. My client is not guilty, because, as Judge Heymann has explained, you must presume that he is innocent until and unless Ms. Hernandez has offered proof beyond a reasonable doubt to the contrary."

"Ms. Jones. Is my client guilty?"

"No."

"Excellent."

Mr. Singletary wants to strangle me. But no matter, I'll dump him with one of my peremptories. Each side gets to dismiss four jurors for any cause or none. The point of this exercise is to educate the group, drive home the key point. This case is Silvie's problem. It's her burden to overcome. Dunn and I are spectators. All we have to do is sit here and watch.

44

WE HAVE TWELVE jurors and an alternate. There are at least two I believe could, conceivably, go our way. One is a twentysomething Latino fund-raiser for a tenants' rights organization. The other I'd normally expect to be pro-DA. She is a white homemaker in her sixties, who lives not five blocks from my house. She remembers when my father shot the Garfinkel kid. She even remembers my mother. She knows my life has not been easy. She will not forsake me. Anyway, she seems like a nice lady, certainly no worse than the rest of the monsters in the box.

Judge Heymann continues to read from the book of pretrial instructions. He lectures on the subject of opening statements. They are not evidence. They are not argument. There is nothing to argue about yet, because there has been no testimony or other evidence. The lawyers will simply describe what they believe the evidence will show. It may show what they predict, or it may not.

When Heymann nods at her, I expect Silvie to jump out of her seat. But she does not. She takes her time. She is relaxed. I have never seen her address a jury before, but I am not surprised that she is extremely effective. She can be harsh and arrogant, but here she uses her looks and small stature to her advantage. She thanks the court, walks around to the front of the counsel table, and leans her gorgeous rear against it. *Let's chat*—she tells the jurors with her smooth, lips-together grin and her easy manner—*about Harold Dunn.*

"This case is about as simple as they come. The evidence will show that on November thirteenth, that man"—she points generally in the direction of Dunn, although she could be pointing at me—"walked into the Cullen's store on Songtree Avenue and exposed himself to an eight-year-old girl. Her name is Callie Dykstra. She will testify that she saw him with his penis in his hand. She will tell you he smiled at her and then walked away. She will tell you she identified him about ten minutes later. She also identified him in a lineup weeks later. And I expect she will identify him here, in front of you, as the man who exposed himself to her.

"Callie's mother, Lorraine Dykstra, will tell you she saw Mr. Dunn, shortly before Callie did, in the same area. A Santa Rita police detective named Martin Hong will tell you that he arrested Mr. Dunn, and he will also confirm that Callie identified Mr. Dunn in the store and in a lineup not too long ago. And, finally, you will learn that this isn't the first time Harold Dunn has exposed himself in a clothing store and been caught and prosecuted. He's done the same thing before. That is it. A simple case."

We're absolutely dead. What the hell am I doing here?

"Mr. Seegerman," Judge Heymann says.

"Thank you." I look over at the jurors. "Simple, but not so simple," I say, still seated.

Then I stand and limp to within a few feet of the jury box. My right hand is in my right pants pocket. I have no idea what to do with my left. I must remember not to pick my ears or nose.

"The evidence will certainly show that Callie Dykstra saw *someone* expose himself to her in the Cullen's store on November thirteenth. The evidence will also show that the person she saw was not Harold Dunn. You will learn from an expert witness, Dr. Phyllis Strong, a professor at the California State University at Santa Rita, all about the problems with eyewitness identification. You will learn about how suggestible an eight-year-old, and all people, can be under stressful circumstances. In other words, Dr. Strong will tell you that an

258

identification can be influenced by many factors and that it is often extremely unreliable.

"You will learn that Harold Dunn, like so many Americans, suffered for many years from alcoholism, and that many years ago he made a stupid mistake. He was prosecuted, as he should have been, and he went to jail. But then he turned his life around. You will learn all about how Harold Dunn moved to Santa Rita, how he sobered up and remains sober, how he went through the Giving-Out-Dinner rehabilitation program and became so trusted by that organization's founder, Mary Godfrey, that she hired him to work as a bookkeeper.

"Most important, you will hear from my client." I walk back to the counsel table and stand behind Dunn with my hands on his shoulders, praying he does not smirk. "Mr. Dunn will take the stand and he will tell you about his life, about the mistakes he's made, and about the dues he's paid. And he will tell you, in no uncertain terms, that, yes, he was shopping for shoes at the Cullen's on Songtree on November thirteenth, that Detective Hong arrested him, and that Callie Dykstra identified him *after, after* he was already in handcuffs, *after* a crowd had gathered, *after* he had been shoved up against a rack of wingtips and sandals, and *after* he had become so upset by the situation that he was sweating profusely and felt nauseated and faint. The evidence will show, ladies and gentlemen, that Callie Dykstra's identification is so tainted, so much the product of suggestive circumstances, that it is worthless. And the district attorney will offer no other evidence, not a stitch, that Mr. Dunn did anything wrong. Not so simple."

The one item of evidence I do not mention is the only one that has any significant chance of getting Dunn off. After the openings, the court breaks for fifteen minutes. I run outside, to a private corner, and call Mary Godfrey. We'd traded messages before the G-O-D show. She had expressed a willingness to help Dunn. But now, given the recent events, I have no idea.

"Mr. Seegerman. I'm so sorry I haven't had a chance to call you since the show. I cannot tell you how pleased we were. I have heard nothing but praise."

"Thank you very much. We enjoyed it."

"I hope you'll return next year."

"That's very kind. I look forward to it. I'm actually calling about Harold Dunn."

"Of course. How is he?"

"I assume you're aware of all the developments?"

"Only what I've read in the paper. You know, Marjorie Styles was in the rehabilitation program here. Twice, according to our records. I cannot say I remember her."

"We're in trial in the misdemeanor case. I am not representing Harold in the other matter. But I was hoping you would be willing to come in tomorrow and testify on his behalf."

"What could I possibly say? I don't know anything about Harold apart from his activities here."

"That's exactly what I need. The case against him is quite weak, except for his prior conviction. I guess I'm looking for someone to tell the jurors that people can change. Maybe that Harold changed after he went through your program. Perhaps to say something about his character."

"To my knowledge, he has an excellent character. We miss him around here. Frankly, we've been in a bit of a state since all this began."

"That's exactly what I need. It would be a huge help."

"I don't mind telling you, Mr. Seegerman, the media attention has not done us any favors."

"I understand. I hope when all of this is over and Harold has been fully exonerated, he can return to work."

"That would be wonderful. You believe he is innocent."

"I do."

"Well, I have a good sense about you, Mr. Seegerman. If you say it will help, I will do what I can."

45

THE JURY IS OUT, but we are back in session. Before the jurors return, Judge Heymann addresses us.

"Counsel, after giving the matter some thought, I have decided to withdraw my ruling excluding examination on Mr. Dunn's visit to the Dykstras' house. The meetings with Ms. Styles will remain off limits. I find, contrary to my original view, that the jurors could validly consider Dunn's trip to the Dykstra residence as evidence of a consciousness of guilt. Having said that, I think this is a mine field for both of you, and I am not sure how it cuts. But do with it what you like."

Before, we were dead. Now we are completely dead.

Callie Dykstra takes the stand. Silvie is smart. The kid is the key to her case. Silvie could try it and win it with Callie's testimony alone. No reason to piss the jurors off by making them wait for it. And from the fifteen minutes I spent with her at the lineup, it is clear she will make a terrific witness. She will stumble, she will be nervous, but that is what the jurors expect. What she will not do—both because she is smart and because Silvie will have prepped her—is expand on the story she has already told.

"Mr. Seegerman, it would be my preference to do the initial examination on competence. If you want to add anything, why don't you approach and we can discuss it."

"That's fine, your honor."

The jurors are still waiting in the hall. The kid is on the stand. The witness box is built for adults. When she sits back in the chair, we cannot hear her and can scarcely see her. So the judge asks her to stand. Callie reaches up and pulls down the microphone so it is at the level of her mouth.

"Testing, one, two, three, testing," she says into it, forthrightly.

"Callie," Lorraine calls sternly from the gallery.

The judge breaks up and then recovers. "Will Ms. Dykstra be standing with the witness as a support person?"

"No, your honor. I think Callie can handle this on her own," Silvie says, like a proud parent.

"Callie, my name is Rufus Heymann and I'm the boss of this court. I get to tell everyone what to do. If at any point you have a question or problem or you need to go to the bathroom, or you just want to take a quick break, you look up here at me. Okay?" The kid nods.

"Also, that lady over there is copying down everything we say and she can't see you too well so instead of nodding your head if the answer is yes, just say yes into the microphone."

"Yes." She has her small mouth right at the mike and her response is booming. Bernard swears her in. Then Heymann introduces everyone to Callie and begins the competency examination. There is no chance this kid is unqualified to testify, no chance that she could not perceive Dunn holding his dick in his hand, that she cannot understand the oath. But we have to go through this exercise.

"Do you know the difference between the truth and a lie?" Judge Heymann asks her.

"Yes."

"If I say I am nine years old, what's that?"

"A lie."

"And if I tell you that you are extremely cute, what's that?"

"Your opinion."

We all smile. What a cutie. Dunn's finished.

"How about if I tell you that we are in the Santa Rita courthouse?"

"True."

"So when Bernard told you to tell the truth, the whole truth, and nothing but the truth, you understood what he meant?"

"Yes."

"In a minute the jurors are going to come in and sit over there. It is very important that after that you make sure to answer every question asked by either Ms. Hernandez or Mr. Seegerman or me truthfully. Okay?"

"Yes."

"Counsel?"

"Nothing, your honor."

"Good. I find this witness more competent than most of the adult witnesses who testify in this courtroom. Let's bring in the jury."

Silvie's examination could not be more effective. She asks four preliminary questions—What is your name? How old are you? What is the name of your school? What street do you live on?—and then launches into the events of November 13.

Callie and her mother were shopping for Thanksgiving outfits. It was the late afternoon. They had been in the store for a while, looking at jewelry. Later, in the girls' clothing section of the store, Callie walked by herself over to an area near the dressing room, to return some items. She turned around to rejoin her mother. A few feet in front of her was a man. The fly to his pants was open.

"He had his hand like this." The kid demonstrates, palm up.

"And what else?"

"His peepee was in his hand. I looked at him and he smiled. Then he walked away."

Silvie has Callie step out of the witness box and demonstrate. The kid is not the least bit shy. She places Silvie's left hand, palm up, at crotch level, and then parks herself less than three feet away.

"Like that."

"You saw his hand and his penis first?"

"Yes."

"And then what? Why don't you return to the witness box, Callie?"

The kid climbs back into the box.

"And then I looked up and saw him."

"Did you see his face clearly?"

"Yes."

"Do you remember the face today?"

"Yes."

"Do you see the man you saw at the Cullen's store in court today?"

"Yes." She points at Dunn. Mercifully, he does not wave back. I grab a glance at the jurors. It's a nightmare. They love the kid. They hate Dunn. They really hate me.

"What did you do then?"

"When?"

"After the man left."

"I went and told my mother."

"Were you scared?"

I jump up. "Objection. I don't see why the witness—"

"Mr. Seegerman, if you have an objection, state it. I will then either rule on it or I will ask for argument outside the jury's presence. Understood?"

"Relevance, your honor."

"Overruled. Do you remember the question, Callie?"

"Not really."

"Were you scared after what the man did?" Silvie says.

"Not really. A little, I guess."

She told her mother, who reported the incident. What the jurors do not hear is that in the meantime Marjorie Styles had snitched off Dunn and was roaming the aisles with a store manager looking for him. They found him in men's shoes, and Martin Hong made the collar. A short time later Callie and her mom showed up.

"Did you see the man again in the store?"

"Yes."

"Was the man with some other people in another area of the store?"

"Yes."

"Is the man you saw standing with those other people in the courtroom today?"

"Yes." Again, she points at Dunn.

"And then you went to a police station with your mom just a few days ago?"

"Objection. Leading."

"Sustained."

Silvie turns away from the judge and throws me an irritated look.

"Did you go with your mom to a police station a few days ago?"

"Yes."

"Did you see the same man at the police station a few days ago?"

"Yes."

"Was he standing in a room with some other men, with numbers around their necks?"

"Yes."

"Is the man you saw at the police station standing with the other men in court today?"

She points at the wanker.

"I'm almost through, Callie. A few weeks ago, do you remember seeing a man talking to your mom in front of your house?"

"Yes."

"After the man got through talking to you mom, what did he do?"

"He started walking across my front yard. He waved his hand at me."

"Is it the same man you saw in the store and at the police station?"

"Yeah."

"That's all I have, your honor."

"Mr. Seegerman."

46

"**T**HANK YOU. GOOD morning, Callie. My name is Gordon Seegerman and I'm going to ask you some questions about what happened in the store. If you don't understand something I say, be sure to let me know, okay?"

"Okay."

"Now, think back to the day you were out shopping with your mom. Actually, can you tell me if you've been back to that store, to the Cullen's store, since November thirteenth?"

"Yeah."

"How many times, do you remember?"

"Once, I think." She looks at her mom, who now sits with Silvie at counsel table.

"What about other times? Had you been to that store before November thirteenth?"

"Uh-huh."

"Callie, try to answer with either a yes or a no," Heymann says.

"Okay."

"How many times have you been to that store, total?"

"Lots."

"So you know the store pretty well, right?"

"Yeah."

"Do you remember what the weather was like that day?"

She shrugs. "Not really."

"Do you remember what you were wearing that day?"

"No."

"What about your mom? Remember what she had on that day?"

"No."

The jurors start fidgeting.

"Okay, let me ask you about what happened on November thirteenth. When you saw the man the first time, you said the first thing you saw was his penis in his hand, right?"

"Yeah."

"And then you looked right up at his face?"

"Yeah."

"Do you remember what he was wearing?"

"No."

"Did he have a hat on?"

"Objection, she already—"

"Sustained."

"You didn't look at his face for very long, right?"

"No."

"A second or two?"

"Yeah."

I have her stand up and repeat the demonstration. As she did the first time, with Silvie, she uses my left hand to demonstrate, with my palm held up.

"Was that the hand the man used to hold his penis?"

"Yeah."

"You said you were a little scared after you saw the man."

"Yeah."

"Nothing like that had ever happened to you before."

"I saw my cousin's once at the pool."

She may as well have written each of the jurors a check for fifty grand. The kid is in.

"And when you told your mom, how did she look?"

"Mad."

"But not at you. At the man, right?"

"Yeah."

"Was she still mad when you saw the man a little later, standing with some other people?"

"Objection, your honor. Speculation."

"I'll rephrase. Did your mom look mad when you saw the man a little later?"

"Yeah."

"Now, Callie, all the questions I'm about to ask you are about the second time you saw the man, in the group of people, but still in the store, in the shoe area, okay?"

"Yeah."

"How many people were standing around the man when you saw him the second time?"

"Lots."

"And did you see Detective Hong holding the man by the arm?" Hong is at counsel table with Silvie. I point to him.

"Yeah."

"Did you know that the person holding the man was a police officer?"

"I don't know."

"Could you see that the man had handcuffs on?"

"Yes."

"And you know that police officers carry handcuffs."

"Yeah."

"Did your mom tell you Detective Hong was a police officer?"

"I don't remember."

"Did the man in handcuffs look scared?"

"Yeah. He looked like he was about to cry."

Really? I pause, let the jurors think about that for a minute. I definitely like this kid.

"You thought he looked like he was about to cry?"

"Asked and answered."

"I'll withdraw it. Tell me, Callie, what did the man look like?"

"His face was all red and his hands were shaking."

"You saw his hands shaking?"

"Yeah."

"Were you scared then?"

"Kind of."

"Were you about to cry?"

"No."

"And what happened next? Did Detective Hong ask you if the man whose arm he was holding was the same man you saw earlier?"

"Yeah."

"Did Detective Hong look mad?"

"A little."

"But not at you. He looked mad at the man, right?"

"Objection, spec—"

"Overruled."

"Did Detective Hong look like he was mad at the man?"

"Pretty mad."

"Only one last question, Callie. You remember when the man came to your house and talked to your mom?"

"Yeah."

"You're not really sure whether that was the same man who showed you his penis, right?"

"Pretty sure."

"That's all I have, your honor."

Silvie does some minimal redirect, has Callie say she's sure Dunn is the guy who flashed her. The whole thing goes so quickly I have no idea what I've accomplished, if anything. And I have no idea if I've escaped without engendering so much hatred in the jurors that they will write my name next to Dunn's on the verdict form and convict us both. I figure I have what I need to get Dr. Strong started, and pray the jurors will make the inferences we need. Truth is, it was a lousy ID. Whoever flashed her, the kid sees him momentarily, and then she identifies Dunn in the most suggestive circumstances possible.

47

L ORRAINE DYKSTRA IS NEXT. She doesn't hold a candle to her kid on the stand, but her testimony is not critical to Silvie's case. Dykstra testifies that some minutes before Callie reported the exposure to her, she saw Dunn in the area near the dressing rooms. She did not see him again until after the arrest. She tells the jurors she refused to speak with him when he came to the house, and she picked him out at the lineup.

"How's Callie's vision?" Silvie asks.

"Fine, as far as I know."

I am barely listening, but this catches my attention.

"Just one last question. Would you say Callie is the kind of kid who makes up stories?"

"Objection."

"Sustained."

But the damage is done. With the jurors jostled out of somnolence by my objection, Lorraine Dykstra shakes her head back and forth. *Not my kid. No way.*

After that move, I throw a little more attitude at her on cross.

"You didn't see anyone expose himself on November thirteenth, right?"

"No."

"Ms. Hernandez asked you a question about Callie's vision. You said it's fine as far as you know. Do you know?"

"It is fine."

"When was the last time she went to the eye doctor?"

"I don't recall."

"Has she ever been to the eye doctor?"

"Objection: She says she doesn't recall."

"Overruled."

"I don't believe she has. Kids don't—"

"How did you feel after Callie told you a man had exposed himself to her?"

"I felt furious."

"And did you stop feeling furious between the incident and the identification in the men's shoe area?"

"Absolutely not. I'm still furious."

"I can completely understand that. Harold Dunn didn't threaten you when he came to your house, right?"

"Not exactly."

"He did not threaten you."

"No."

"Didn't say you should change your story."

"No."

"He told you he was at your house because he thought if Callie had a close look at him she might realize she'd been mistaken."

"Basically."

"That's all, your honor."

Heymann sends us for lunch.

Every prosecutor puts her investigating officer on the stand. It's the way things are done. I suppose the idea is that it builds confidence in the case somehow. Often it makes no sense, though. And it makes no sense here. Hong has nothing of significance to offer. Dunn made no incriminating statements. There is no physical evidence, which is admissible only through the investigator. But I suppose a prosecution without testimony from a police officer feels, to a DA, like walking out of the house in the morning with no pants on.

Hong runs through the events of November 13 and the lineup a few days back. He says the kid identified Dunn at both. Hong then describes Dunn's 1991 offense. The wanker goes into a clothing store and loiters outside the women's dressing area. He exposes himself. Three people see it. He pleads guilty. Silvie also authenticates the Cullen's surveillance video through Hong, though she doesn't play it.

Cross.

"You have the court file from the 1991 Oregon case in front of you, Detective?"

"Yes."

"Can you tell me what Dunn's blood alcohol level was at the time of the offense?"

"I can tell you what it measured after the arrest."

"Fine."

"Point one five."

"And would that make him legally intoxicated in California?"

"It would make it illegal for him to operate a motor vehicle. I don't know that there's a law against shopping while drunk."

The jurors chuckle politely.

"What about public intoxication?"

"Well, there's no evidence that he was acting drunk."

"Other than the exposure offense."

"Objection."

"I don't know that there's a question pending, Ms. Hernandez."

"I'll move on, your honor," I say. "When you asked Callie Dykstra to identify the man who exposed himself to her, that was after you'd arrested my client, right?"

"Correct."

"Had him in cuffs."

"Yes."

"Read him his rights."

"Not yet, I don't think. It all happened in a matter of a few minutes. I think I Mirandized him after."

"Okay. But there was no question in your mind that he was under arrest."

"I told him so."

"He was not free to leave."

"No."

"His hands were cuffed behind him."

"Yes."

"You had his arm in yours."

"Yes. Well, we weren't dancing. I had one of his arms in one of my hands."

"He was up against a rack of shoes."

"You make it sound like his face was buried in a pair of loafers. He was standing there. I had a hand on him. I'd just finished cuffing him when Ms. Dykstra and Callie approached the aisle. So his back was turned. He turned around for the identification."

"Lots of rubberneckers."

"Some."

"Twenty?"

"I don't recall exactly. Less than twenty. There were one or two in the aisle, and some at the ends of the aisle."

"How did Dunn look?"

"What do you mean?"

"I don't know, anything remarkable about his appearance? You heard Callie's testimony."

"I don't recall anything remarkable. He looked like he wasn't too happy to have been arrested. Most people aren't."

"He look like he was in shock?"

"No."

"Was his face red?"

"That I don't recall."

"Was he shaking?"

"I don't recall that."

"Did he look like he was about to cry?"

"Objection."

"Overruled."

"Did Mr. Dunn appear to be on the verge of tears?"

"No."

It is nearly four when Hong walks off the stand. Silvie rests. Judge Heymann dismisses the jury and then the parties. I go home.

I don't hate my father. Unless I choose someday to take a close look at my fourteenth chromosome, and I discover that it is my mother's and not S.'s, our fates are tied too closely for loathing. If I did, though, you could hardly blame me. He wasn't any kind of father. When he wasn't absent, he was drunk. When he was sober enough to have an opinion of me, it was dismissive or slighting. He approved of Silvie, but made it clear he couldn't quite understand what she was doing with me.

But I hated him when I was a kid. Not because of how he treated me, or the abuse he leveled at King while my older brother clung to him like a sloth wrapped around a tree trunk, too sluggish and fearful to distinguish predator from pal. Even the way he all but abandoned my mother when she became ill—even as a child, I understood that he had no idea what to do with her, or with what must have been his overwhelming anger at her slow decline and premature exit.

I hated my father because he was a cop. Every night when he came home I watched from the top of the stairs while he proudly unloaded his hardware and stored it on top of our refrigerator, out of reach. I watched him swagger to the liquor cabinet, spill out a shot, down it, and pour another. I sat with him while he stared at the television and shushed me if I asked a question or tried to tell him about my day. And I watched him at the dinner table while he stuffed his face and drowned us out with work tales of crazies and bad guys. He was extraordinarily powerful, autocratic even. But I sensed that it was a thin veneer, that his rule, his sense of authority, depended on the trappings of his job. That beneath the cop costume my father was as rickety then as his neurofibrillary tangles and senile plaques have rendered him now.

I know police officers are necessary. And I know that most of them are decent, hardworking people who risk their lives to keep the rest of us safe. I know the feelings I have about Martin Hong, how good it felt to slap at him on the stand, and the yearning I have every time I walk past a police cruiser to slash a tire, have to do with my dad. I am wrong to feel these things. I must get some therapy.

48

NINE-NINETEEN A.M. December 19.

Next morning. Harold Dunn is on the stand. For the first time since we met, his wrists are cuffs free. I fear he will get carried away with his newfound emancipation, wield his arms too grandly in the witness box, let his charged temper leak from beneath the thin finish I have given him in preparation for his testimony. Speak slowly, Harold. Listen to the question. Count one thousand one, one thousand two, and then answer. Do not expand unnecessarily. Do not extemporize. If a yes or a no is possible, that is the preferred response.

Dunn is in the witness box before the jurors enter the room. They do not see that his legs are shackled. He is wearing a shabby blue sport coat and a pair of my khakis. All his own pants were seized by the SRPD looking for the blood or hair or skin of Marjorie Styles. The slacks fit badly—they are too short and too wide—but the jurors see only his left thigh. And his left thigh looks fine. He wears a red-and-green-striped tie, in the spirit of the season.

He tells the jurors that he was born in eastern Oregon and received his bachelor's and accounting degrees at the University of Oregon, Eugene. He was a CPA. But also he was, is, an alcoholic, and the two mixed badly. He lost his license automatically when he pled guilty in the 1991 exposure case.

"Do you remember what happened when you were arrested in 1991?"

"I don't remember it very well, I'm very embarrassed to say. I was loaded all the time back then. I remember riding in the back of the police car and being in jail. I don't really know what happened in the store."

"But you don't deny that you committed a crime."

"I pleaded guilty. If they said my pants were down, I'm sure they were. I don't think they had any reason to lie."

"But you don't remember."

"I'm sorry."

"You went to jail?"

"For three months. It was really the best thing that ever happened to me. It was the beginning of the end."

He got out of jail and spent the next few years drunk, and in and out of hospitals. His body was crumbling. A friend told him about the G-O-D program and he moved to Santa Rita in November of 1994. By the end of 1996, he was sober and working for Mary Godfrey.

"There are no rehabilitation programs in Oregon?"

"There's no Mary Godfrey and no G-O-D in Oregon."

"And how were you employed when you were arrested this time?"

"I was working at G-O-D. As far as I know, I still am. I'm not a licensed accountant, but I do all the bookkeeping and financials. It's a fifty-million-dollar operation over there. Most people don't realize that."

I glare at him for a moment—Did I ask you about the finances at G-O-D?—before asking the next question.

"Mr. Dunn, when was the last time you tasted an alcoholic beverage of any kind?"

"June 1995. Seven and a half years clean and sober."

"Let's talk about November 13, 2002. Have you ever been to the Cullen's before?"

"First time and last, I promise."

"What made you go there?"

"I think someone in the office said they had pretty good deals on shoes. Mary said I ought to get a new pair because mine were pretty old. I didn't really want to."

"Mary Godfrey?"

"Right."

"And so you went there on November thirteenth."

"Yes."

"Do you remember what areas of the store you were in?"

"I know it took me a while to find the shoe section. I walked around a bit. I didn't pay that much attention really."

"Were you around the women's dressing area?"

"I could have been. Like I said, it probably took me ten minutes of walking around to find the shoes. I mean, I wasn't inside the dressing area, but I may have passed by the entrance."

"Do you remember seeing Callie Dykstra?"

"I don't. I'm sorry. I can't say she didn't pass me, but I was pretty focused on finding the shoe area."

"How about Lorraine Dykstra?"

"I do not remember seeing her."

"Then what happened?"

"Then I found the right section of the store and spent a while walking up and down the rows. They have all sorts of shoes but in bins, so it takes a while to sort through them all. And they're only single shoes. You have to go to this other part of the store to get the other shoe to try it on."

"Did someone confront you at some point?"

"Well, Detective Hong—I didn't know he was a detective at the time, because he wasn't wearing a uniform. I saw a few people talking at the end of the aisle, and then Detective Hong, he walked over to me and asked me my name and told me I was under arrest."

"How did you respond?"

"I asked him, 'For what?' He said, 'You know for what,' and then he handcuffed me and pushed me up against the bins of shoes with his back."

"How did you feel at this time?"

"Objection: relevance."

"Overruled."

"How did all this make you feel?"

"Like I might pass out. I've been sober for a long time and it made me feel like all of a sudden I was slipping back down the hill."

"Were you sweating?"

"That happens to me when I get nervous, I start to perspire heavily."

"Were you shaking?"

"Yes."

"You still had no idea what you had been arrested for?"

"No. I kept asking what was going on and he told me to shut up."

"What did he say, exactly?"

"He told me, he sort of whispered, 'Shut the fuck up.'"

"More than once?"

"Several times."

"What happened next?"

"I was still pressed against the bins of shoes. Hong told me to turn around. When I did, I saw the girl and her mother and some other people. They stood several feet away, with Hong. I couldn't hear what they were saying. Then they left and I went to jail."

"Mr. Dunn, did you expose your penis to anyone at any time at the Cullen's on November 13, 2002?"

"No, I did not. I was looking for shoes."

"So Callie Dykstra is lying when she says she saw you with your penis in your hand."

"Objection."

"Overruled."

"I don't think she's lying, no. I think she is mistaken. If I had done it, why would I stick around?"

"Objection, nonresponsive. I would ask that the last part of the response be stricken."

"Sustained and granted. The jury is to disregard the last sentence." As if any one of the jurors could say, if asked, what the last sentence was.

"You went to the Dysktras' house on November twenty-first?"

"Yes?"

"Why?"

"Now I see that I wasn't supposed to go there, but at the time I just figured maybe if the little girl saw my face she might realize it wasn't me. I just wanted to try to help myself, is all. I'm sorry."

"Did you threaten anyone?"

"No."

"Did you urge Ms. Dykstra to change her mind about what she saw at the Cullen's on November thirteenth?"

"I spoke to Ms. Dykstra for less than a minute. I just asked her if she'd mind if I showed the girl my face. She told me to leave."

"Did you talk to Callie?"

"She was running across the yard when I was leaving. After Ms. Dykstra told me to leave I didn't try to talk to her."

"That is all I have on direct, your honor. I'm sorry, there was one other thing. Mr. Dunn, which hand do you use to write?"

"My right hand."

"You're a righty?"

"Yes."

"Nothing further, your honor."

"Ms. Hernandez."

49

"**YOU WERE NEVER** in the Cullen's store on Songtree before November 13, 2002."

"If I was, I don't recall it," Dunn answers.

"You testified you'd never been in the store. That was incorrect."

"I don't believe I've been in the store another time."

Silvie walks over to the defense table and hands me a photocopy of some Cullen's receipts with Dunn's credit card imprint on them. She takes a step toward the witness box.

"May I approach?"

"Yes." Silvie and I walk up to the bench and whisper to the judge.

"Your honor, I have never seen this document before," I say. "And I don't see what relevance it has to this proceeding."

"Is that an objection?"

"Objection as to relevance, and motion to exclude it because Ms. Hernandez never bothered to turn it over in discovery."

"Denied and denied. You opened it up, counsel."

Silvie hands Dunn the receipt.

"That refresh your recollection, Mr. Dunn?"

If trials, in real life, ever come close to Perry Mason moments, they are about as meaningful as this. Dunn either doesn't remember or for some reason didn't want to admit having been at the Cullen's. I don't even know why I asked him the question. It was a throwaway. For some reason, Silvie had the store run a check on prior visits, and she happens to have the document with her. So she scores a point. Big freaking whoop. If the jurors are smart, they will see it for what it is, trivial. Of course, jurors are not, as a rule, smart. Which, I suppose, means Silvie has just proven beyond peradventure that Harold Dunn is the lyingest man in the county.

The rest of the cross-examination isn't much more exciting. She takes him through the events of November 13. She gives her version of events, and then says "Right," as in:

"You saw the little girl and decided to expose yourself, right?"

And in response Dunn says "No" or "Wrong" or "That isn't what happened." He says several times, "I was looking for shoes," which has become a kind of mantra.

She tries to get him to talk about the details of the Oregon prior, but he maintains he cannot recall them. She becomes increasingly frustrated. He is better on cross than on direct. He seems to like her less than he does me—why, I do not know—and that makes him less gregarious. Overall, I am pleasantly surprised by his performance. I expect at least one or two real screw-ups, and there are none. He sounds like he is telling the truth. I suppose he may be.

Silvie intelligently plans to finish her cross-examination with the surveillance film, leaving the jurors with a grainy image of Dunn entering the store. He will look like a criminal, as all people do on low-quality video. Given the limited purpose Silvie has for the evidence— to show that Dunn was in the store for a significant period, to argue that he was preparing to wank, not looking for loafers—I have not even bothered to watch the tape. She wheels a cart with a large television monitor into the center of the room. The judge reminds the jurors that the tape was admitted into evidence earlier, through Detective Hong. The jurors wake up. *Mmmmm, television.*

Silvie plays the clip, perhaps five seconds long. The camera seems to be mounted halfway up a post of some kind outside, and slightly above, the store's entrance. I watch from counsel table. Dunn is in the witness box. Silvie stands by the monitor. I'm sure that when the clip ends she asks Dunn questions about the time stamp on the film, about what he was doing in the store for thirty minutes before his arrest. I am sure Dunn answers the questions. I hear none of it.

"Your honor, could we have the clip played again?" I say, sounding stunned.

"Ms. Hernandez?" She rewinds the tape and plays it again.

I get up and walk to within two feet of the monitor. It may be that no one else in the room can see past me. I do not care. It is Dunn. The shot is of the top of his torso and head, from the left side. The fingers of his left hand, unmistakably, curl around the handle of a case of some kind—perhaps a briefcase—although it is possible to see only the handle. There was no reference to it in any of the witness statements or in the police report. Perhaps three steps behind Dunn are two men I easily identify as G-O-D goons. One is the man who had the gun on Terry and Max in the backseat of the car.

In the film Dunn's head is down, his body is hunched forward. His right arm is up, at the level of his upper chest. He is running.

I have now lost interest in the proceedings. I need to get with Terry. After I conduct a perfunctory redirect of my client, Heymann hesitantly grants my request for a break. Ten minutes later we are in the courtroom, Terry and I and Dunn. We are alone. I play the video. I stand back to see how far the dreadlocks on Terry's head will stand on end when he sees it. He pauses the tape, walks up to the screen, and touches the face of one of the goons.

"I don't believe it."

"Look there." I point out the handle in Dunn's fingers.

"They're chasing you," Terry says. Dunn knows exactly what is happening. A purple wave of shame washes across his face. And a few tears begin to fall from his eyes. "Right?"

The wanker does not speak. His head is down.

285

"Play the rest," I say. Dunn rushes in the store, but the goons do not follow. They mill around the entrance. Then they walk out of the camera's purview.

"Harold," I say, attempting not very successfully to remain calm. "Game over, man. We're going to lose this case. And, more important, you're going to be convicted of killing Marjorie Styles. And maybe executed unless you tell us what the hell is happening here." I point to the screen. "Tell us what happened."

"They would have killed me, Mr. Seegerman."

"Who?"

Now he points. "Them."

"They're from G-O-D."

He nods.

"What's that?"

"A briefcase."

"Containing what?"

"Financial documents. Evidence."

"Of what?"

"I told you."

"Selmer. Some kind of corruption at G-O-D." Dunn nods.

"What happened to the papers? There's no reference to them in the reports."

"I left them in the store, before I got arrested."

"You were in there for a long time. What were you doing?"

"Walking around. Trying to figure out what the hell to do."

A deputy enters the room and insists that Dunn be returned to the holding area outside the courtroom. The judge wants to reconvene.

As the deputy leads him away, Dunn says, "I'm sorry."

Terry and I are again alone in the courtroom. I lie down across the counsel table, on top of notepads and pens and books.

"What the hell am I supposed to do with this?" I say.

"It was self-defense."

"What?"

"He flashed to get arrested."

"I don't know."

"What else could he do? Otherwise he walks out of that store and gets whacked, and G-O-D gets the docs."

"The only proof we have of any threat to Dunn is from Dunn, and he's already testified he didn't do it. He told the jury he didn't do it. He was pretty freaking convincing, too. He can't get up now and say, 'Oh, wait, I committed perjury an hour ago. I did do it, but only because I needed police protection.' It sounds ridiculous. The whole thing is crazy."

"Crazy, but true."

By now Silvie and the court staff are in the room. I drop my voice.

"Maybe. None of it matters now."

50

DR. PHYLLIS STRONG is younger than I'd expected, only a few years older than I, and more attractive than any expert witness ought to be. I am used to wrinkled older men who come to talk about blood alcohol tests, and matronly psychiatrists who are draped with turquoise and testify about delusional thinking. Strong is perhaps thirty-five, slightly taller than I, with long ringlets of brown hair, firmly built. She has extraordinarily large brown eyes. She holds her mouth open in a perfect, half-inch-high "O" when listening to my questions. I have never seen anyone do such a thing before and it is entrancing—not the right state in which to undertake examination of a witness on a complex scientific topic.

After I walk her through her background—Harvard BS; University of California PhD; full professorship, California State University at Santa Rita—her areas of research, her familiarity with the professional literature, her membership in various professional organizations, and her experience testifying in court, Judge Heymann qualifies her as an expert in the area of visual memory and eyewitness identification.

"Before we get into the substance of your testimony, can you tell the jurors how much you're getting paid to be here today?"

"One hundred seventy-five dollars per hour. I receive one hundred fifty dollars per hour for out-of-court preparation. Altogether I believe I've spent six hours looking at materials and preparing for my testimony today."

"Thank you. You mentioned that you often testify in court?"

"Many times. Over fifty by now."

"Typically in criminal cases?"

"Three quarters, I would say."

"And of those, how many were as a defense expert?"

"All."

"All?" I pause. Let it sink in. "That sounds like a bias in favor of defendants."

"Objection."

"I think the witness understands the question. I'll allow it."

"I do, thank you. I don't typically receive calls from prosecutors. Usually what happens is a defense lawyer calls me and says, 'I think the eyewitness identification in my case has problems.' I take a look at the circumstances, and most of the time I disagree. When I find difficulties or flaws in some aspect of the identification process, I make myself available to testify. But there are many situations, most actually, where I refuse to testify because I don't see any flaws."

Under California law, Dr. Strong can't tell the jurors that in her opinion Callie Dykstra didn't see the man who flashed her long enough to identify him, or that the stress of the situation made an accurate ID unlikely, or that the circumstances in which she picked Dunn were highly suggestive. A trial expert is a teacher, educating the jurors on topics relevant to their review of the evidence.

"My research is primarily in the area of visual memory, how we remember things we see, people or sequences of behavior, or events we observe."

"Does the study of visual memory apply to eyewitness identification in the criminal justice context?"

"Absolutely. The same principles that I study generally in the area of visual memory apply to testing the accuracy of eyewitness identification or eyewitness memory in criminal cases."

Most people believe that memory is like a video camera—you see something; it is stored, intact; and then at some later time you access the memory of the event, whole, like regurgitating a grape right after you eat it. Strong says that memory is more like information stored in a computer, in small pieces that require internal organization and recombination when accessed.

"Can you tell the jury the sorts of things that may influence a person's ability to accurately perceive an event?" I ask.

"The better question is what factors may influence perception of a face or another person, since we are talking about eyewitness identification."

"Believe me, if the court would permit you to ask the questions *and* answer them, we would both be much better off. In any event, tell us about those factors."

"Perception is by far the most important aspect of memory, because the quantity of information input has the greatest impact on a person's ability later to retrieve the information. The most important factor is time—how much time the witness spends actually looking at the person's face. If you look at me for an extended period, and there are no distractions, and you are close enough to see me, you can take in a fair amount of information about my face and what it looks like: cheek structure, nose, size and position of eyes, hairstyle, jawline, and so forth."

I watch as she moves her hands around her face, like one of those models on *The Price Is Right* presenting a refrigerator or patio set. She is a phenomenal witness. Totally in control of the room. She looks mostly at the jurors, and occasionally at the judge, just to check in.

"When a witness sees someone's face for three to five seconds, that permits perception of general features, race, gender, and perhaps a distinguishing feature or two. There is not enough time to see the specific features of a person's face. Also, stress plays a critical role. When a witness perceives someone during a period of great stress, the reliability of their memory goes down sharply. And there is another factor, which we sometimes call weapon focus, which usually means that when there is a gun involved in a crime, witnesses tend to be focused on the gun. Their perception of the face of the person holding the gun is less clear."

"What about in a situation where a person is surprised by something, say the exposure of someone's private parts in public?"

"I wouldn't go so far as to say it's the same as a gun, but it could lead to a level of distraction that reduces input or perception." It takes every ounce of my small store of decorum to move on. The one-liners dart around my head like caged finches on speed.

"What is recall?"

"Recall is simply a person's ability to remember a face or a sequence of events. The question I study is what factors can have an impact on that and lead to false memories. The ones we are most concerned about, particularly in the criminal and eyewitness identification contexts, are where people truly believe they are recalling a memory but do so incorrectly because of various factors."

"And what kinds of things can have that impact?"

"Usually a person's ability to get the right answer, say, in a lineup procedure, depends on how hard the question is. So, for example, if I ask you what the capital of Uganda is, maybe you will remember, maybe not."

"Not."

"But how about if I put it this way. Which of the following is the capital of Uganda—Paris, New York, Rome, or Kampala? You'd probably get it right."

"Don't be so sure." Out of the corner of my eye, I can see Heymann is not amused. My witness rescues me.

"Same situation in an identification process. If the witness is essentially given the answer, the ID is not reliable."

"What is suggestion?"

"That is closely related to what I am talking about. It is just what it sounds like. An eyewitness identification procedure, like a show-up, as occurred in this case, or a photo display, is suggestive if it makes the answer obvious, if it relays to the eyewitness in some way that the police believe a particular person is responsible for the crime, or if it leads the witness to select a person on the basis of factors other than his or her recollection."

Strong then listed a series of factors that might lead to a suggestive identification, all of which were present when Callie Dykstra identified Dunn: It was a single-person physical show-up; the defendant was visibly nervous; there were a group of strangers in the area looking on; and, most important, the police gave the victim verbal or nonverbal cues that indicated they believed they'd apprehended the right guy.

"Would a person being handcuffed be a nonverbal cue?"

"Definitely."

"What about if the person is being held by his arm in a semiprone position?"

"Again, if the person looks as if he has been arrested, the chance of a misidentification is considerable. It all has to do with the perceived expectations of the police. If the eyewitness senses that the police believe they have arrested the person who committed the crime, identification of that person is highly likely."

"But what about if the eyewitness later identifies the same person at a lineup and in court? Doesn't that make up for any problems at the original identification?"

"No, the opposite is true. Once an eyewitness makes an identification, whether or not it is the result of a suggestive procedure, the witness is unlikely to change his mind later. The original ID is imprinted on the person's brain. That's particularly true because at the time of the subsequent identification the witness is likely to have observed the subject for a much longer period than at the time of the offense."

"So a person can actually come to believe in an incorrect identification?"

"Events become part of a person's memory because they were suggested. People are not able to distinguish between what they actually remember, because they observed it, and what is in their brains because it was suggested. Suggested information is just as real in memory as information that was actually perceived."

"Do children make good eyewitnesses?"

"Sure, once they reach the age at which they can understand what is going on and relate it, they have excellent memories. But they are subject to all the factors I've described. They must perceive an event or a face long enough to be able to make an accurate identification. Like adults, they remember less well in stressful situations. They are subject to the weapon focus phenomenon."

"And what about suggestivity?"

"In that case, the research is very clear that children are far more subject to suggestive circumstances than adults. The younger the witness, the more highly suggestible and the greater the effect of contamination. Also, unlike many adults, children very strongly want to comply with the expectations of an authority figure such as a police officer. They will attempt to make their answers consistent with what they see as the intent of the questioner rather than consistent with their perception of the event."

"You're saying kids lie?"

"Not at all. As I said, suggestion leads to imprinting on the brain. If a child receives a strong enough message from an officer, he or she quickly comes to believe that the suggested information is an actual memory."

Silvie's cross is competent, but I can see the effect Strong's testimony has on the jurors. The child has morphed from a perfect little eight-year-old who must be telling the truth into a lab rat subject to influences beyond her control. And Hong is now the bad guy. He shouldn't have permitted Callie to identify Dunn under those circumstances.

After hammering Strong on her obvious prodefense bent, Silvie does what she can with the testimony.

"You are not suggesting to us that everyone who makes an identification in a stressful situation or after seeing someone for a short time is wrong?"

"No. But the research is fairly clear that those factors have a significant influence on an individual's ability to perceive an event correctly."

"People often make accurate identifications in stressful situations, right?"

"Sure." Strong is in control, not the least flustered. She gives where she must and does not overcompensate.

"And children, too, often accurately identify their assailants in stressful situations, right?"

"The factors I discussed, including suggestivity, are at work, but yes, of course they do."

"And you can't say, no one can actually measure whether any person or child in any given situation has accurately identified an assailant, right?"

"No. I can only say what factors influence accuracy."

For the first time, I have an inkling that the case can be won. There it is, in the distance, a nimbus of doubt. I cannot say it will reach the jury box. I cannot say they will see it. And I have no idea whether it will overcome the impact of Dunn's prior. But there is hope.

And there's this other thing, too. I am beating up on Silvie a bit. The case is getting away from her. The DA's star, my ex, the lovely Mrs. Setz—Dunn and my expert have flummoxed her. Win or lose, I have discovered that seeing her flail makes me feel, at the same time, faintly contrite and strangely satisfied.

51

DURING A BREAK, I walk outside the courtroom. Mary Godfrey, roast beef in a goon sandwich, is sitting on a bench talking on a cell phone. I recognize one of the goons, the one with the aluminum baseball bat above his head. He does not appear to know me. Godfrey waves me over and ends her call. She looks stern, less cordial than in our previous meetings.

"Mr. Seegerman."

"Thanks so much for coming today, Ms. Godfrey."

"I must admit I'm having some reservations. Are you sure it's necessary?"

"It would be very helpful."

"There are other interests at stake here. The reputation of our organization has suffered, which means our important work has been threatened."

"All I'm interested in are your impressions of Harold. His transformation, his work. This isn't about G-O-D, Ms. Godfrey. I just want the jurors to know a little bit about him."

"I will agree to testify, Mr. Seegerman, but I want a few minutes alone with Harold before I do."

"You understand he is in custody?"

"Yes."

"There will be a deputy present."

"That's fine. Unless you can arrange it, I don't think it will be possible for me to appear today." That's it. No sign-off, no apology. She goes back to her phone.

I run it by Silvie. She isn't thrilled with the idea, but doesn't have any legal ground to object.

In a cramped holding cell next to the courtroom, fifteen minutes later. The courtroom deputy stands inside the door with a baton in his hand, ready to take out the wanker should he try to strangle anyone else. I sit in one corner. Ten feet away, Dunn, cuffed and shackled, sits with his head down, listening to Mary Godfrey. She is whispering. I do not hear a word. Her back is to me. I can see Dunn's eyes. There is no fear in them. He looks like a child being chastised for biting a younger sibling. She talks at him for several minutes. He nods. He understands. He says nothing. I cannot see her face but her head movements are emphatic.

"Okay, Mr. Seegerman." She turns to me. "I'll testify." Dunn does not thank her or react visibly.

"It is an honor to have you in our courtroom, Ms. Godfrey," Judge Heymann says.

"Thank you very much. It is my pleasure to be here."

Silvie winces.

"Carry on, counsel."

Godfrey briefly explains who she is and describes the G-O-D organization. She gives something like the speech I heard when we first met. She is used to making speeches, to being completely in control of the flow of information, so she makes a lousy witness. But none of it makes any difference to me. The jurors know who she is. I wouldn't care if she testified about her hairspray bills. I just want the jurors to know that St. Godfrey thinks enough of the wanker to be here.

"Harold was much like all the others who come to G-O-D. He was dependent on alcohol. He was ill. He was lost. But he was enough of a man to know that he needed help. Our rehabilitation program is voluntary; I believe it says a lot about our clients' characters that they show up in the first place."

"Did Mr. Dunn successfully complete the rehabilitation program?"

"Yes, he did."

"Did you get to know him through that program?"

"Now we are fortunate enough to have several programs going at any given time, but at that time I was more intimately involved in the process. I entered the church late in life. I was married and had two sons. One works closely with me at G-O-D. But another I lost to drug addiction. I suppose Harold reminded me of my son, and I took to him."

"Did he eventually begin to work with you at the organization?"

"Yes. We gave him a chance and he did remarkably well. For several years, we have worked closely together. He has significant responsibilities for the financial side of our organization." She smiles and looks at the judge. "We are looking forward to having him back at work."

Silvie could object. She could have much of Godfrey's testimony stricken. But it would seem petty and it wouldn't prevent the jurors from getting the message. *Acquit him. Mary Godfrey will be personally grateful.*

"Did you know about his criminal record when you took him on as an employee?"

"Absolutely. We believe in redemption, Mr. Seegerman. We believe in the ultimate good in every person. We believe that people can change. And I have seen great change in Harold. I have never regretted taking him on."

"Never had any complaints about him at work?"

"Never."

"Good employee?"

"I can say that I trust him completely and that without him watching over our finances . . . well, let's just say we're better off when he's around."

"Did you see any evidence that Mr. Dunn had begun to drink in the period before his arrest?"

"Absolutely not. I have a keen sense for these things after so many years. And it is an offense punishable by banishment. I would have fired him immediately."

"What about stressors—any indication Mr. Dunn was having a hard time before the arrest, whether at work or otherwise?"

"Objection: relevance."

"Overruled."

"I did not see any change."

"Only one other question, Ms. Godfrey. Did you tell Harold Dunn he ought to get a new pair of shoes?"

She smiles. "Yes, as a matter of fact I did. I thought the ones he was wearing were appalling."

"Thank you very much for appearing today. Nothing else on direct."

Cross.

"Ms. Godfrey, you don't know whether Harold Dunn exposed himself to an eight-year-old girl in a Cullen's store on November 13, 2002, right?"

"I do not. But I would be extremely surprised if he did."

"Nothing further, your honor."

It is nearly three-thirty. After St. Godfrey floats out of the courtroom, I tell the court my case is complete. Judge Heymann makes it clear he is unhappy that we have gone over schedule, but there is no way to argue the case today. He apologizes to the jurors and orders everyone back to court at eight-thirty A.M.

The term is "brain dead." My brain is no longer alive. My ankle is badly swollen, but my body is still essentially functional.

It is nine. Twenty-four hours from now, should I make it through my closing argument, should I have the energy to shower and brush my teeth and gel my hair and put on a white tuxedo and drive to Ted's and set up and sound-check and avoid vomiting or fainting or both when I take the stage, I will perform in front of Barry Manilow. It would be a dream, if it were not such a nightmare.

The Mandys and Ted are sitting in a circle on the floor, arguing about the set list, when I arrive. They scarcely acknowledge me. Preet feels strongly that we should play a few original songs. We are musicians, not puppy dogs. We won't do ourselves any favors by groveling. Spirited, not obsequious. They look to me for guidance, or at least for an opinion. But I have none. If I wake up on Saturday and can remember my own name—even if I have lost the Dunn case and have alienated MBM and have ruined my friendships—it will be a victory.

We settle on a set list. One of Preet's songs, near the beginning of the show. And we rehearse a last time. I watch Ted for a response. He is pleased. Though my voice is at half-mast and I am sick with exhaustion, he tells us we're as good as we've ever been. It is true. The months playing and hanging together, even the stresses of recent weeks, have worked for us. There is nothing like four people wanting the same thing with all their might. It is a nod we are after, a tip of the hat from a single human being. A man. All we can do is play.

52

NINE-FORTY-FIVE A.M. December 20. Friday morning. Closing arguments.

A juror is late. I sit in the gallery and review my notes. Sweat stains on my starched white dress shirt creep outward to where, soon, they will be easily visible to the jurors. Terry takes a seat on the bench behind me.

"How you doing?"

"I'm resigned to failure."

"Dunn made a call from inside the store."

"You raided his mail again."

"Nah. Francine laid a subpoena on Cingular. One call, about fifteen minutes before he gets busted. Not two minutes long."

"Weird."

"Very weird."

"Who's it to?"

"No idea. The number's dead. We'll get it, but it'll take a while."

"It didn't match any numbers on the old bill?"

"No. You ought to ask him."

"Who?"

"What do you mean who? Your client."

"Why?"

"You're not curious?"

"I am slightly curious. But, as you may not be aware, I have a more pressing matter just now."

*   *   *

Silvie stands and walks to the middle of the courtroom. She looks totally poised. She is going to destroy me.

"I told you two days ago this is a simple case and I still believe that is true. A young girl and her mother go into a clothing store to shop for Thanksgiving outfits. I think it is obvious from her testimony that Callie Dykstra is an unusually intelligent child. Very independent. She goes to the ladies' dressing area to return some clothing. And what happens? That man"—Silvie glares and points her luscious right pinky at Dunn—"has the gall to confront an eight-year-old child, to take his penis out of his pants, and to expose himself to her. Make no mistake about it. That is something she will not forget the rest of her life. To suggest that she forgot it in the few minutes between the crime and her identification of him, just a few minutes, isn't only preposterous, it's offensive.

"Did she react irrationally? No. Did she act like a person under great stress, whose memory or ability to identify her assailant is unreliable? No. Did she become hysterical? No. She walked calmly to her mother and reported the incident. If Callie Dykstra's identification in this case is no good, there's no such thing as a good identification."

Silvie explores the definition of reasonable doubt for a few minutes. She goes through the judge's instructions on the law. She explains the elements of the crime. She cudgels Phyllis Strong every way she can imagine: The expert is biased toward criminal defendants; we bought and paid for her testimony; Strong can't say whether Callie correctly identified the man who flashed her, because Strong wasn't there.

And she emphasizes that it is not the jurors' job to worry about Harold Dunn, to think about what might happen to him if they convict. That is the judge's job. They should not sympathize with him or acquit him because he overcame alcoholism. He should be commended for his accomplishments. But those are not the issue.

"The only relevant question, and it is a simple question, is whether Harold Dunn exposed himself to Callie Dykstra on November 13, 2002."

Silvie says my client's full name over and over again—Harold Dunn, Harold Dunn—with such repulsion that by the time she is through I feel faintly nauseated by sitting next to the man.

"He did, ladies and gentlemen. Callie was walking to the dressing area to return some clothing. She saw a man holding his penis in his hand. She looked up and she saw his face. The lighting was perfectly adequate. She said she saw his face clearly. He was standing still. He had no gun. She observed his face for several seconds. And no matter what Dr. Strong says, it doesn't take an expert to know that if you see someone's face for several seconds, you can easily identify that person a few minutes later. She did. No one told her what to say. She clearly knows the difference between the truth and a falsehood. If it wasn't him, she would have said so. She is that kind of girl. She knows her mind. She identified Harold Dunn because his was the face she saw a few minutes earlier. It was Harold Dunn. Pure and simple. Thank you."

Exhale. Gulp. Cough. Swallow. Inhale.

"Good morning, ladies and gentlemen. This is the last time I will be able to address you in this case, and I want, first, to thank you for your service. It is no easy task, listening to the evidence"—I pause. The jurors are looking at me. Which is appropriate under the circumstances. But it nevertheless results in a surge of perspiration and nausea—"listening to the evidence, to Judge Heymann's instruction, and trying to make sense of it all. But it is one of the most important things you will do in your lives." I walk behind Dunn and put my hands on his shoulders. "What is at stake here is this man's liberty."

"Objection." Silvie flies out of her seat.

"Sustained," Heymann says, shaking his head. "Mr. Seegerman, please. The jury will disregard the last remark."

"My apologies, your honor."

Hardly. I always say this, the DA always objects, the court always sustains the objection and tells the jury to disregard the statement, and the jury never does. I'm setting the tone, hoisting the scenery before delivering my devastating soliloquy. Before I start in on the evidence, I want the jurors to focus on the grim prospect of locking a man away. I want them to look for a way to acquit as if their lives depended on finding one.

"In any event, it is one of the most important decisions you will ever make, so please, I ask you, make it carefully.

"Reasonable doubt is something we hear about our whole lives. And even though it's a little mysterious, it's not that hard to understand. Every day you look outside and decide whether you need an umbrella. If it looks cloudy, or if the weather report says rain's expected, or it's February when rain is fairly common, you have reasonable doubt that it is going to be sunny the whole day. If it's a perfectly sunny day, and the weather report says no rain, and it's the middle of the summer in Santa Rita when there hasn't been any rain in years, but your nutty neighbor says he's sure it's going to rain because his dog hasn't barked all day, you have no reasonable doubt. Hey, maybe you have a tiny little smidgen of a doubt, but you know it's not reasonable."

"Let me tell you something." I look up and point at the ceiling. "You take one look at the evidence in this case and there's only one rational conclusion. Get out your galoshes because it's already raining."

The jurors look lost and bored. The analogy is idiotic. My fingers are clinging to the rim of a huge toilet bowl, my legs are dangling in the bowl, inches above the water, and Silvie is yelling at the top of her lungs, "Flush, flush!"

"There are three sources of reasonable doubt in this case. Each one of them ought to be enough for you to acquit Mr. Dunn. Together they are a mountain of doubt.

"Mary Godfrey, one of the pillars of this community, explained to you that when my client arrived at G-O-D he was a broken man. He'd made serious errors in his past, including the offense Detective Hong told you about. But he was ready to change. And change he did. He not only successfully kicked alcohol, something I'm sure you know isn't easy, he engendered such trust in Ms. Godfrey that she took him on to handle the books. A pretty responsible position. An important position. Not the kind of thing a person who has beaten alcoholism, who has changed his life, is going to throw away so easily. And Ms. Godfrey told you she saw no indication—and she's the one who could say if there was any—no indication whatsoever Mr. Dunn had started drinking again. Certainly if my client was drunk on November thirteenth, Ms. Hernandez would have introduced evidence of that. Detective Hong didn't say he smelled of alcohol. No blood test. No evidence at all that Mr. Dunn has had a drink in years. She told him to get a pair of shoes, and what happens? He gets arrested for a crime he didn't commit. He should have kept the old shoes.

"Next there was Dr. Strong's testimony. I won't take you through it all, but let me say this. Every possible factor against a reliable ID is present in this case. An eight-year-old girl—a smart girl, a good girl, but still, *eight*—is shocked when a man exposes himself to her. She must be stressed beyond belief. She looks up, maybe for two seconds—not several, as Ms. Hernandez said, but two—to see his face. And then he takes off. That's it. Dr. Strong says no one can really identify a face in that short a time. Can't do it. She also says the penis was a huge distraction, sort of the way a weapon would be. She called it weapon focus. I don't think I need to say much more about that. Obviously it was a distraction for an eight-year-old girl. Short time viewing the subject, stress, and distraction. All of these interfered with Callie's ability to perceive.

"Dr. Strong also told you the kinds of things that can lead to a suggestive identification. She told you that children are far more suggestible than adults. Detective Hong, the authority figure, practically ordered Callie to say Mr. Dunn was the man who flashed her. My client is in handcuffs, up against the wall. He is sweating. He is in shock. He looks like a criminal, ladies and gentlemen. He isn't one, but he sure looked like one on November thirteenth, cuffs on, his back to everyone, Detective Hong holding his arm. There are people standing all around. Lorraine Dykstra is furious. She drags Callie into this pumped-up scene. What was Callie going to say? No? The man whose arm you're holding, who has cuffs on, who looks like he's about to pass out—an eight-year-old girl is going to tell the big police detective he has the wrong guy? I don't think so.

"And once she identified him in the store, just as Dr. Strong explained that people do—once they get it in their heads that this is the guy, no matter how wrong they are, that's where it stays. So Callie identified him again, in the lineup and here in court. If the first ID was bad, the rest are bad, too. This was the most suggestive identification imaginable. This was an experiment in suggestivity, ladies and gentlemen. And it worked.

"Finally, you heard from my client. I won't tell you he is the smoothest witness I've ever seen. He stumbles a bit. He talks a lot. He gets excited. But he didn't try for one second to cover up his past. He admitted his mistakes. He admitted he used to be a drunk. He admitted he broke the law and paid for it by going to jail. And he changed. He got sober. He climbed out of the gutter and got a job and won Mary Godfrey's trust and now oversees millions of dollars. And let me tell you something, ladies and gentlemen: not for some corporation. Not to make himself rich. To help people like himself, who are struggling with addiction, who are sick or abused or who've lost their families and jobs, who have nowhere else to turn. That is Mr. Harold Dunn. What Ms. Hernandez is asking you to do is to punish him again for what happened more than ten years ago. That's not fair.

"It wasn't him, ladies and gentlemen. Someone exposed himself to Callie Dykstra on November thirteenth. No doubt about that. But it was not Mr. Harold Dunn. It's not Callie's fault. She's a smart kid. And—remember, imprinting, just as Dr. Strong explained—I know she really believes she picked the right guy. But she didn't. She picked the wrong man. She picked an innocent man. Thank you very much."

I walk very slowly to counsel table, pull out my seat, put my arm on Harold's shoulder, and shake his hand. When his hand is in mine, it occurs to me I have completely forgotten to mention Callie Dykstra's testimony that the man who flashed her held his penis in his left hand. Dunn is a righty. But Silvie is already halfway across the room. She has wounded us repeatedly, but perhaps not fatally, in her initial argument. Now she aims to finish us off.

The single most unpleasant experience for a criminal defense lawyer is a prosecutor's rebuttal argument. Good DAs typically give a very bland initial closing. They save the big guns for rebuttal. Because, although I can move around in my chair and wince and object during Silvie's final remarks, I cannot respond. Ever. She is a tight end who looks behind, twenty yards from the goal line, and realizes no one can catch him. I am the backfield defender, the one who missed the last tackle, down on the ground, sucking wind, beaten.

"Mary Godfrey likes Harold Dunn. So what? Dr. Strong says eyewitnesses make mistakes. So what? Neither one of them was in the Cullen's store on November thirteenth. Neither one can say anything about what took place in that store. Neither one can tell you what Callie Dykstra saw.

"Only three people who testified in this courtroom were there. Detective Hong was there. He arrested Dunn. He told you that Callie Dykstra identified the defendant as the man who flashed her. Lorraine Dykstra was there. She told you Harold Dunn was in the women's dressing area, just where Callie says he exposed himself minutes later. Minutes. What is he doing there? He was just shopping for shoes? In the women's clothing section? That's ridiculous."

Her volume increases. She is baiting the jurors—challenging them. *Go ahead, let yourselves be duped by the criminal. Acquit the pervert.*

"And Callie Dykstra was there. Remember—if you're all not under too much stress—remember what she looked like when she testified. Remember how she sounded. She didn't look like a person who would have been confused. She didn't look like a person who would have been subject to suggestion. She was perfectly clear. She didn't make up extra details. She was totally believable."

Silvie stops. It is over. She takes a step or two back toward counsel table and then spins on her heels.

"Wait. I made a mistake. One other person was in the Cullen's. That was the defendant, Harold Dunn." Silvie points at him, but takes a couple steps away, toward the jury box, as if he is contagious. "He admits he was in the store. He admits he was in the area of the women's dressing rooms. But he says, 'It wasn't me, ladies and gentlemen. It wasn't me.' Callie Dykstra has no motive to lie about what she saw. She doesn't know anything about Harold Dunn. She just pointed to the man who flashed his penis at her and said, 'That's him, that's the guy'—three times: in the store, at the lineup, and in court here, in front of you.

"But Harold Dunn *does* have a reason to lie. He doesn't want to be convicted. He doesn't want to pay the price for terrifying an eight-year-old girl, for scaring and scarring her. And what do we know about Harold Dunn? What does everyone in this courtroom know about Harold Dunn? What we all know is that he's just the sort of person who walks into clothing stores, goes to the area near the women's dressing rooms, and takes out his penis. He got caught in Oregon, and he got caught here. It's as simple as that."

53

B Y THE TIME Judge Heymann issues his final instructions and sends the jurors off to deliberate, it is twelve-forty-five. I cannot imagine that deliberations will last more than a couple of hours. I run back to the office to return a few calls and snarf down a limp cheese sandwich. I check in with the Mandys, who are all at Ted's. I'll be there by two-thirty.

I check back into Department 26 around two-fifteen. Still no word. I explain the situation to Bernard, the court's clerk. He says he will reach me on my cell if something happens. I rush home, grab my tux, and drive to Ted's. Less than seven hours. I have nothing to do except set up, sound-check, shower (at Ted's), dress, and worry, but it feels like way too little time. The Mandys are there, sitting at the bar. They appear disturbingly relaxed.

"How'd it go?" Terry says.

"I don't care," I say. "Don't talk about it. You want to hear something completely insane?" They nod. "Sometime in the next several hours, Barry Manilow and I are going to be standing in the same room, and *he* is going to be listening to *me* sing. It doesn't get any weirder or more astoundingly excellent than that."

"Something like having Britney Spears going down on me and having my nails done at the same time," Maeve says.

"Like courtside seats at the NBA finals," Preet says, becoming excited. "Santa Rita is up four points in the last ten seconds, and my brothers are stuck on a long line waiting for nachos."

"Like—"

"Enough. Are we ready?" I say.

By four o'clock, I have completely forgotten about Dunn. We check and recheck the sound. Ted is nervous. I have not seen him so before. He consults with me about the lights. We expect a big crowd, after the G-O-D show, so he clears out several tables at the front. We discuss where he will put Barry and his group. We have no idea whether MBM is coming alone or with an entourage. Will he want to be right up front and visible, or hidden in the back? Should we buy him a nice bottle of champagne? Does Ted even *have* a nice bottle of champagne? We make several contingency plans. I call Ferdy to make sure my dad is being cooperative.

At four-thirty Bernard calls. There is a question from the jurors. It is not a verdict. This is good. This is fine. An hour or two back at work, in court, will calm me.

When I walk into Department 26, Foster and Evenrude are sitting in the last row of the gallery. It is otherwise empty. They throw me huge smiles and wave enthusiastically. I respond, hesitantly.

Bernard calls the case.

"Counsel, Mr. Dunn. Welcome back. The jury has sent the following question, and I would like some input on how to respond." Heymann then unfolds and reads the jury note: " 'We would like to know why Dunn was arrested before Callie Dykstra identified him. How did Detective Hong know to arrest him?' "

Silvie jumps in. She's pissed. "Well, very candidly, your honor, that's been the problem with this case from the beginning. There's a huge hole in the evidence, and the jurors have found it."

"Please watch your tone, Ms. Hernandez."

"I apologize, your honor. It has been very difficult to know how to try this case. The reason Harold Dunn was under arrest is that he had been identified in entirely unsuggestive circumstances by Marjorie Styles. We are lying to the jurors if we tell them otherwise."

"There is no authority for the admission of any statement or identification by Ms. Styles," I say. "I looked at the law on this after your honor ruled. In a misdemeanor case, Styles's ID and her statements are out."

"And how do you propose we respond?"

"I think we tell them—"

Duke, who has slipped into the courtroom without my seeing him, leans over from behind the bar that separates the gallery from the parties and touches my shoulder. My head jerks around. He hands me a sheet of paper. I read it, take three steps to my left, and hand it to Silvie. She stares at it for a moment and returns it.

"Mr. Seegerman. What on earth is happening?" Judge Heymann wants to know.

"It's an order signed by Judge Saltzman. May I read it into the record?"

"Be my guest."

" 'On the court's own motion, the complaint captioned *State of California versus Harold Larry Dunn*, alleging a single count of murder in the first degree with special circumstances, filed November 29, 2002, is dismissed pursuant to Penal Code Section 995. The court has reviewed the record and finds that there is an absence of probable cause to hold the defendant over for trial on this charge.' "

Silvie is stunned. She looks at me. I shrug. I have no idea. No idea whatsoever. Francine didn't even file a 995 motion. There was no reason to do so, particularly after the DNA match for Styles on the hair in the trunk of Dunn's Caddy.

"Congratulations, Mr. Dunn. We still have our jury waiting for us, counsel," Heymann says.

"Your honor," I say, "I think the Court will recall that I was very uncomfortable with the exposure these jurors had to the publicity on the murder case. That objection remains. I think, at this point, we are entitled to a jury instruction from the Court that all charges against my client relating to the murder of Marjorie Styles have been dismissed, and that Judge Saltzman has found an absence of probable cause to believe he committed that crime. I think that will make up for whatever prejudice Mr. Dunn suffered at the hands of the Santa Rita media."

Silvie is nearly hysterical. "What does that have to do with anything? This isn't the murder case. This is a misdemeanor."

"Please calm down, Ms. Hernandez. We have plenty of time to work this out."

Uh, actually—

"I am inclined to agree with Mr. Seegerman," the judge continues. "I think we owe it to the jurors to inform them of these developments. I will simply read them the order, and explain what it means. What about the jury question?"

"I don't think this changes things on that, your honor," I say. "The question is simply whether there is admissible evidence in this case that would answer the jurors' question. I think there is not. There is no way to answer that question without going outside the present record and offering the jurors blatantly inadmissible evidence."

"What do you suggest?"

"I suggest telling them we cannot answer the question. That they must rely on what they have before them."

"Ms. Hernandez?"

"I'm stuck. I don't necessarily disagree with the defense. Someone killed Marjorie Styles. Someone prevented her from identifying Dunn in this case. I still think he did it. But that's not relevant here. I'll submit it."

"I'd say you're taking a risk, Mr. Seegerman. Jurors don't typically take no for an answer. Given these peculiar circumstances, I will grant a mistrial should you request it."

I turn to Dunn. He shakes his head.

"No, we want a verdict."

The judge brings out the jurors. He reads them Judge Saltzman's order on the murder case. He explains it. And he tells them he would like to be able to give them a more satisfactory answer to their question, but he cannot. They must rely solely on the evidence presented to them in court. The jury foreman tells the court he believes they can reach a verdict today. They would like to continue deliberating. Heymann orders us to remain within five minutes of the building. As I leave the courtroom I see Evenrude and Foster. Again, they smile and wave. They seem to be having a grand time. It is five-twenty P.M.

I call the Mandys. I do not tell Terry about Foster and Evenrude. I may never tell him. I walk down to the cafeteria in the basement of the Hall. Silvie is there. We are the only ones. I sit at her table.

"Very weird day," I say.

"It makes no sense. I had that prelim nailed. And with the hair? Come on. You know that case goes to trial. I didn't even have a chance to brief the thing."

"It's a mystery."

"Fischer's really going to hate this. He had the idea this was the case that would put him in city hall."

"He'll deal."

"Your guy's pretty slick."

"Dunn? I don't know. All I know is that jury better come in soon, one way or another, because in three hours I have a date with Barry Manilow."

She stands, takes a big sip of coffee, and lifts her large leather bag over her shoulder. Her pitch is unusually shrill. She seems on the verge of tears. "You know what, Gordy? You need to grow the hell up. I know this is going to come as a great big shock, but there are some things in life more important than Barry Manilow."

I am in constant phone contact with the Mandys from the coffee shop. I call Bernard every ten minutes. I promise him free drinks at Ted's for the rest of his life if he can get the jury to convict Dunn, or acquit him, but it has to be soon. It is six, then six-thirty, then seven-ten. They are back. I run, pain shooting up my ankle into my leg, four flights up to Department 26.

"Everyone here?" Judge Heymann glances around the room. "Good. I believe they are ready. Thank you all for your patience."

Dunn is agitated. The bailiff herds the jurors into the box. One is missing. The bailiff goes to hunt him down. He is in the bathroom. He will be a minute. We wait. Several minutes later the juror emerges into the courtroom, smiling sheepishly, apologizing.

"Hey, when you got to go, you got to go," Judge Heymann says. Then he turns to the foreperson. "I understand you have a verdict."

"Yes, your highness."

Stunned silence and then laughter from the bench.

"Mr. Foreman, though at home I am sometimes the king, in this courtroom I am your honor, not your highness."

"Sorry. I guess I'm a little nervous."

The foreman hands the verdict form to the bailiff who delivers it to the judge. The judge reads it, taking absolutely fucking forever in my estimation, and hands it back to the bailiff, who hands it to the foreman.

"What is your verdict, Mr. Foreman?"

"We, the jury in the above-entitled action, do hereby find the defendant—"

For fuck's sake. Will you get on with it?

"—Harold Dunn not guilty of the charge of violating California Penal Code Sec—"

I am already swatting Dunn congratulations on the back, gathering my things, and turning to leave.

"Counsel, do you mind?"

"Sorry, Judge. I have a very important—"

"I don't care if you have a date with Mother Mary herself. You owe these people and this Court some respect."

"I am very sorry, your honor."

"Ladies and gentlemen. I want to thank you for your service to this county and to the parties in this case. Jury service is—"

Blah, blah, blah. After he finally releases the jurors, who take their sweet freaking time to mosey out of the courtroom, Heymann asks Silvie if there is any ground to continue to hold Dunn. She hems and haws, but finally agrees there is no pending criminal charge. The judge orders the bailiff to remove Dunn's cuffs. Then he thanks us and gavels the proceedings adjourned. Silvie flees in disgust. Harold hugs me. I explain I am really late. I will call him. I will see him soon. I'm happy for him. I'm really happy.

Down three flights, ankle pulsating. Out the front door. Into my 1987 Honda Civic Hatchback with Foster and Evenrude's dent in the passenger side. To the Downs. To Ted's. To Barry.

54

S IX DAYS LATER.

It is ten-thirty A.M. I'm at my desk, sipping coffee and eating a box of greasy leftover lo mein while looking over a couple of new files. I should take a few days off. I should be home. But home is packing and explaining to S. for the zillionth time what is about to happen to him, to the house, to his family. I will live underneath my desk like Bartleby. I would prefer not to find an apartment. I would prefer not to sell my mother's furniture and box her pictures and close the door on 4200 Candlewood. I would prefer not to have everything change.

The chief public defender knocks gently and ambles into my office. I quickly vacuum a mouthful of noodles into my mouth, spraying grease over an open file.

"Is that breakfast or lunch?"

"Uh, brunch, sir. Brunch, I think."

"And a disgusting brunch it is."

"Yes, sir. Revolting."

"I noticed you here on the early side this morning, Mr. Seegerman. I suppose you have something particularly pressing."

"Just a little crazy on the home front these days, sir."

"I understand completely. Work is a refuge. I saw a bit of your performance in the Dunn matter."

"I'm honored. A silly case all around."

"I was impressed. May I ask what we're doing in the cellar after all these years?"

"Sir?"

"The cellar, Mr. Seegerman. Why the hell are you still trying misdemeanors after eight years?"

Because I am misdemeanor-man. Because this is where I belong. It is my home.

"I suppose I'm just more comfortable with the smaller cases."

"I understand. Ambition is not for everyone. So I suppose a position on a special team wouldn't interest you. I have the idea to put a few people onto some special projects. It would involve a very substantial salary bump."

"It's an honor, sir."

He gets up and walks to the door. "Nothing sadder than a man afraid of succeeding, Mr. Seegerman. I hope you will try to remember that you are not your father and you need not end up like him." He spins and walks out. I sit, stunned. Then, a few seconds later, I run to the door.

"I will definitely think about it, sir!" I shout down the hall at his back. He raises his hand to acknowledge me, but does not turn or respond.

A few minutes later, my cell phone rings. It is Myla. She insists that I meet her in half an hour at the federal building, ten blocks from my office. She refuses to explain. Nineteenth floor. Courtroom M. Don't ask questions. Just come.

I sit in a back corner, not entirely sure what I am doing. The front of the room is crowded with fancy-looking lawyers. Real lawyers.

Myla, dressed in a suit, walks into the room and up my row and hands me a fifty-page federal indictment. *United States of America v. Giving-Out-Dinner, A Nonprofit Corporation, Mary Godfrey, Selmer Godfrey, Santa Rita Mutual, Inc., Foghorn Trading, Inc., Bartholomew Setz, Senior, Bartholomew Setz, Junior, Philip Dykstra*, and a long list of other names. Corporations; individuals. Money laundering; bank fraud; wire fraud.

"Merry Christmas," I say.

She plops down next to me. "Read." I look up to ask a question; she points at the document and says nothing.

After a few minutes, Myla hands me her cell phone. I look at her, confused. She insists I take it.

"Hello?" I say.

"Yo."

"Who is this?"

"Counsel, how are ya?" Frank Foster. The accent is unmistakable.

"Confused."

"Keep reading, Seegerman."

Myla sits next to me, staring straight ahead. I flip through the pages. Harold Dunn is mentioned in almost every count. He is alleged to have been a key player in the criminal activities. But he is not charged with any offense. In other words, as we'd long gathered, he's a snitch. Dunn wasn't in High Power because of Silvie or Fischer or Selmer Godfrey. Dunn was in High Power because United States Treasury Agent Frank Foster called the Santa Rita sheriff and told him to put Dunn in a safe place.

"We sort of figured he was working for someone. What with the cash he was waving around and the rides he kept getting from government-issue vehicles," I say into the phone.

"Can neither confirm nor deny," Foster says. "But let's just say you did a good thing, counsel."

"Which particular good thing did you have in mind?"

"You miraculously convinced twelve people that Harold Dunn didn't unleash his pecker in public. Let's just say that a federal jury wasn't real likely to believe a convicted child molester about anything."

"I don't see Martin Hong's name on this thing."

"Who's Martin Hong?"

"The detective who arrested Dunn on the exposure case," I say.

Foster laughs. "Arrest him? We should give him a fucking medal. You kidding me? You think I want Dunn whipping out his pecker in front of my kid?" The phone cuts off.

Moments later the judge takes the bench and the clerk calls the case, *United States v. G-O-D et al.*

If the afternoon calendar at the Hall of Justice is a mosh pit—smelly, sweaty, loud, and sometimes riotous—the equivalent in federal court is a night at the symphony. The atmosphere is bookish, hushed, refined. The lawyers are expensively dressed and faintly magisterial. Even the criminals in federal court seem somehow of a better caliber—of a rarer, more civilized, less soiled variety.

The Godfreys, the Setzes, and a slew of others I don't recognize emerge from a holding tank at the side of the courtroom. Foster and Evenrude lead them in. Foster waves at me. I wave back. The defendants look stunned. They have all been arrested within the past few hours. The proceeding is brief and uneventful. The court arraigns the defendants and sets a bail hearing for the next morning.

Myla, next to me, has not budged the whole time. Nor has she glanced at me, or held my hand, or smiled. She has simply watched the proceedings in silence.

We sit there, in the corner of the courtroom, our legs inches apart, until the appearance concludes and the room empties.

"Interesting way to treat a friend," I finally say.

"Come on, Gordon, you're a grown-up."

"That's debatable."

"You represented the informant at the center of a two-year investigation. And the whole thing seemed pretty weird. The daughter of one of our key targets turns up as a witness in a case against our guy. We had to be absolutely sure we weren't missing something. The truth is, I got too close, and I'm sorry."

I look at her. "What the hell is that supposed to mean?"

"It means I'm a human being, all right. I make mistakes. I can't control every situation perfectly. I have feelings."

"Ah, yes, feelings." I smile.

"Yeah."

"Am I allowed to ask you about what happened?"

"No," she says. But she does not move. The courtroom is empty.

"What is Foghorn Trading?"

"All that's in the indictment."

"I've never been a very good reader."

"Setz set it up, but it's just a shell, a way of putting layers between G-O-D and what it owns. Basically Setz and Godfrey bought dirty money at twenty or thirty cents on the dollar, and spread it around at G-O-D. It ended up back at Santa Rita Mutual, squeaky clean. Eventually they had to find a productive use for all the cash, so they starting buying real estate. Foghorn did the deals and the deeds went into the name of another company, which was owned by another, and so on. Eventually it all traces back to G-O-D. Mary Godfrey *used* to be one of the largest landowners in this county."

"How's that?"

"We filed forfeiture papers on everything. Nice of her to help out Harold, though."

"The jurors loved her."

"Well, they ought to. She's a great lady. Setz and Selmer and the others are scum—just looking to get paid. But not Godfrey. I'm not saying she didn't break the law, but as far as we can tell she plowed all the money back into G-O-D."

"And Marjorie Styles? You absolved your snitch for that crime, too?"

"Absolutely not. Dunn was with us when she was killed."

"Dunn was with you."

"We couldn't say anything because of Setz's wife, Fernandez. Her husband was up to his ears in this thing."

320

"Hernandez."

"Oh, yeah." She smiles slyly. "I forgot. You know her."

"In passing."

"Anyway, we weren't ready to indict yet. We still had some loose ends to tie up."

"Of course."

"When it looked like they were serious about going forward with the murder case, we got the judge to dump it."

"You got Judge Saltzman to dismiss the murder case."

"I feel bad about all this, Gordy, but I'm relying on you to forget about this conversation. This is my job."

"You feel bad."

"I got too involved and I'm sorry."

"You didn't get involved. That's the problem. You should have gotten involved, and you didn't. But you really wanted to, which made it obvious that something was seriously wrong with you, although for the life of me, until about ten minutes ago, I couldn't tell you what it was."

I am insane.

"I was just trying to do my job."

"Are you still involved?"

"Leave it alone, Gordon." She jumps up and sticks out her hand. I do not take it. "My name is Myla Miravich. I am a U.S. Treasury agent. I am the number three on one of the biggest federal cases ever to be charged in this county. I am sorry if I misled you. I really am."

"That doesn't answer my question."

"There's no answer to your question. Not now, anyway."

I smile.

She smiles back.

55

NEXT DAY, I AM in my office. Terry has his feet up on my desk and inhales a limp slice of pizza. I am pretending not to be sickened by it, because I am trying to be a nicer person these days. Preet has all but convinced me that karma exists. If it does, I believe mine is in a sorry state of repair. And, with chromosome 14q24.3 to worry about, I can see no reason not to hedge my bets. So I will attempt to be less sardonic. I expect I will fail. But there is a benefit to the effort, or so Preet assures me.

Silvie knocks. She looks lovely, though by all accounts her life has fallen to pieces. Her husband and father-in-law remain in jail.

I stand. "Hey there."

"Sit. I came to tell you we just filed a rape complaint against a guy named Simpson Silverstone. Sound familiar?"

Silverstone—the man we interviewed briefly at his Santa Rita Hills estate, where Dunn claimed he dropped Marjorie Styles shortly before she was murdered.

"The complainant is a prostitute named Joyce Ball." Silvie tries not to smile. I suppose smiling must feel incongruous these days, like a betrayal.

"Ball."

"Believe me, I wouldn't have the energy to make it up. Anyway, Ball knew Marjorie Styles. And they both dated Simpson Silverstone—separately and together. Apparently he's a complete psycho. We're questioning him on the Styles murder."

Terry understands the delicacy of the situation, but he looks about to burst with self-satisfaction.

"For reasons I hope are obvious, I'm not on the case, but the ADA on it asked me to make the initial contact."

"You need Dunn."

"I can't even bring myself to say his name. But yes, he's a key witness if we develop a case against Silverstone on the Styles killing. He may be the only person who puts Styles at Silverstone's house. The investigation is ongoing, but we'd like to talk to him."

I write Foster's name on a sheet of paper, fold it, and hand it to her.

"That's the name of his handler. He's with Treasury. I haven't heard from Dunn since the trial."

"Thanks." She does not move.

"Terry. Leave," I say.

He scampers off. She sits.

"I can't talk about it. All right? I just can't."

"I didn't say anything."

"It's running across your forehead like a ticker tape."

"No, it's not. I'm just worried for you."

"Thanks. Anyway, I should apologize for how I treated you during the trial."

"Please."

"No, seriously. I was a bitch. I was totally buried and Fischer was putting a lot of pressure on me. Which is a reason, but not an excuse. I still think Dunn was good for the exposure, but you did a great job. You beat me fair and square."

"Apology accepted."

She pushes her chair back and stands.

"There *are* some things more important than Barry Manilow, but I will admit it's a fairly short list."

56

FERDY AND S. AND I sit at the kitchen table eating bagels, reading the paper, and not talking. It is Sunday, December 29. Moving day. The silence is our highly ineffectual attempt to avoid completely freaking out S., who senses his life is about to change in big and unpleasant ways. On the front page of the Sunday *Journal* is a story about the release on bail of the lead defendants in the Pearlygates case—as it has been dubbed.

King, driving an enormous rental truck, pulls up the gravel driveway and onto the grass, thus liquidating two large strips of the lawn. He lumbers inside and helps himself to my breakfast.

"You gonna help me or what?" he burps out. I do not look up from my paper.

"With what?"

"With my shit, little brother."

"And what shit would that be?"

He walks out the front door. I go back to the paper. A moment later he enters, carrying a television. He exits and returns with two suitcases.

"What are you doing?" I say.

"What does it look like I'm doing?"

"It looks like you're moving. Possibly *in*." He shrugs. "Really?"

"Can I get some help here?" he says. I trail him out to the truck. "The market for organic pet food is tanking. Did you know that?"

"I did not know that."

He slides a ratty orange armchair to the edge of the truck bed, tips it over the edge, and balances it on his ample midsection. "People simply don't grasp the importance of a well-balanced meal for their animals. I'm too far ahead of the curve right now. Anyway, I need to cut expenses. I assume you haven't changed your mind."

I've been trying for years to get King to move home, to share S.'s care, to relieve some of the burden on Ferdy.

"No. Dad stays, though."

"Fine." He is not looking at me.

"King."

He turns and launches the chair into the middle of the yard.

"What?"

"We share everything, fifty–fifty. 'I'm busy' can't be an excuse. Dad has to be the priority."

"All right, all right. I'll be working here, anyway. I'm thinking about herbal Viagra. It's an aging population, Gordy. You know what I'm saying."

"I know exactly what you're saying."

Late afternoon. King and I return from our last trip down the hill and across town to Bea's. I am exhausted and am looking forward to a beer, a shower, and a nap. We—the four Seegerman men—will dine on steak and martinis tonight, to celebrate Ferdy's move out and King's move back. The phone is ringing when we walk in. It is Frank Foster.

"I've got a bit of a problem, counsel, and I was hoping you might be able to help. About twenty-four hours ago we lost contact with Harold Dunn."

"You lost contact." As if the wanker were a wayward satellite traveling irretrievably into outer space.

A few days before Foster's call, I'd received a postcard from the wanker. He wrote, simply, in shaky capital letters, "THANK YOU," and signed it Harold. I thought nothing of it. The guy deserved a vacation if anyone did. I tossed it into the top drawer of my desk.

"We were hoping you might have something for us."

"No, not really. You try Don?"

"Nothing," Foster says. "He ever mention anything about where he might go, friends, family?"

"He's history, huh?"

"Probably." Foster sounds exhausted. I almost feel bad for him. "We're in trouble without him."

We have become, in many ways, a nation of snitches, of informants, of rats. And snitches are like high-wire acrobats: they flip and roll, they walk the wire while the clowns below—defense lawyers and former criminal associates—throw water balloons and eggs at them, trying to trip them up. They work without a net. Sometimes they sneak off just before the show begins, slipping out the back of the circus tent while the house lights are down, and the spot is focused on the wire strung fifty feet above the hay-strewn dirt floor.

"I'd help if I could," I say.

He sighs. "I figured it was worth a try. He's our boy. We'll get him."

I hang up and smile. No way. Dunn done gone.

I fall asleep the minute I hit my bed. An hour later I wake to strains of MBM seeping, like the aroma of a freshly baked blueberry pie, underneath my door. I walk out and trace the music to S.'s room. He is seated at the edge of his bed. I join him. The music, coming from a rarely used boom box we purchased for him years ago, is slightly too loud for comfort. He seems to be listening attentively. I didn't know he could still operate the machine. I don't believe my father has ever voluntarily listened to a Barry Manilow song in his life.

"What's going on, Dad?" Nothing. Then he turns to me, looking quizzical. "Are you all right?" I say.

"King is moving home."

"That's right. Is that okay?"

"Yes."

"I think it's a good thing for everyone. I really didn't want to move out. I'm glad we'll all get to be together. Almost like a family."

We sit for another minute, listening to the music.

"Your mother thought a lot of Barry Manilow."

I cannot help but laugh.

"My mother was an extraordinarily wise woman."

"I never much cared for him. This is a nice song, though."

I take hold of his hand and put it on my lap.

By all accounts, Barry Manilow had an extraordinarily close relationship with his mother, Edna Manilow, who died in 1994. You might even say he was a mama's boy. The song playing, "I Am Your Child," was on Barry's first album. It is more than simply a tribute—it is a devotional. It is a tune I rarely sing publicly because, frankly, I can't get through it without a picture of my mom popping into my head and my windpipe choking off.

In the middle of the song, Barry sings, "Whatever I am, you taught me to be."

I feel as if someone has whapped me on the top of my head. *Whatever I am, you taught me to be.* Mary Godfrey. Selmer.

I look at S. I return his hand to his lap.

"I am your child," I say to him. He does not respond. I run to the phone.

"You there? Pick up the damn phone, Terry. It's important."

"Hey."

"Where are the Dunn boxes?" I say.

"My office."

"The last cell bill's in there?"

"I assume."

"What about the video? The Cullen's surveillance tape."

"Yeah."

"Meet me at the office."

"Now?"

"Now."

I set up the video monitor while Terry digs Dunn's most recent cellular phone bill out of a box of files.

"I have the distinct feeling we've been looking at the blank side of the puzzle the whole time," I say.

I rewind the video and start it. We watch for several minutes. It begins before the time Dunn enters. There is nothing of note. Then we see the bit Silvie played, of the wanker entering the store, of the goons nipping at his heels, of Dunn holding the handle of something like a briefcase. We watch and watch. The goons mill around and then depart. Eventually we watch Detective Hong escorting Dunn out of the store. Dunn's wrists are cuffed behind him. Hong does not have the briefcase.

"Why are we still watching?" Terry says.

"I don't have a clue."

But we are both glued to the screen, like four-year-olds watching C-Span. Silvie said she thought the video had been edited down to the relevant time frame. I am waiting for it to cut off. But it does not.

"Where's the briefcase?" I say, staring at the screen.

"In the store. If you believe Dunn."

"And what's in it?"

"Documents. If you believe Dunn."

"And is there any reason to believe anything Harold Dunn has ever said?"

Perhaps fifteen minutes after the last film of Dunn—of him leaving the store with Hong—a small, bent man slowly walks up to the Cullen's entrance and goes in. Terry and I both see it and move our faces to within inches of the monitor. Two minutes later, the man appears again, this time on his way out. He is carrying a large metal briefcase in his left hand. It is Selmer Godfrey.

I take out my cell phone and punch keys until I reach "Calls Received."

"What's the number of the call from Dunn's cell when he's in the store?" I say.

Terry scans Dunn's most recent cellular bill and reads the number aloud.

"It's Selmer," I say, staring at my phone. My cell recorded his number when he called, weeks earlier, to inquire about Dunn's bail. I hold it up like an Oscar statuette. "He called Selmer to come get the briefcase."

I punch in Frank Foster's number.

"You find Dunn?" I say.

"No."

"I may have something for you."

"I'm listening."

"Your indictment is the world according to Harold Dunn. That's why you need him so badly. He gave you the whole package, documents, accounts. The whole story."

"Seegerman, it's Sunday. You got something for me or not?"

"Come on, Agent Foster, how often do I get to be right?"

"I don't imagine very often."

"What's the basic setup? Who's running the show?"

"The nun and Senior Setz."

"And what about Selmer?"

"What about him?"

"How does he fit in?"

"Our source"—in other words, Dunn—"says Selmer does what Mary tells him. He's a mama's boy."

I slam the desk with my fist, alarming Terry.

"And you believe him?"

"I'm getting bored."

"You didn't bother to tell me Dunn was skimming money off the top of whatever G-O-D was involved in."

Pause.

"Maybe."

"Not maybe. He was ripping them off, yes or no?"

"Is that it? Is that your big news?"

"You let him live large because you needed him to make the case. You let him have his fun with Don. You let him put away something for a rainy day. No harm, no foul, right?" Silence, not disavowal. "What you don't know—and what Mary Godfrey probably still hasn't figured out—is that Dunn was working for Selmer. They had their own thing going. Godfrey had her son and Dunn figured for mama's boys, too, but she figured wrong. Selmer must have been pissed that Setz and the others were getting rich while he had to make it on his lousy twenty-nine grand."

"Fucking conjecture, Seegerman. I'm still waiting for the cum shot."

I wince and pull the phone away from my ear.

"Dunn had a briefcase with him before he got arrested. A big fat metal briefcase. Some of Mary Godfrey's knuckle-draggers were chasing him right before he walked into the Cullen's store. Dunn told us the case had documents in it—evidence for you guys. That's what he wanted us to think."

"And?"

"And. And Dunn is full of shit. He had a load of cash with him, Foster. He flashed the kid because Mary Godfrey's goons were going to pulverize him *and* take the money if he walked out of there without a police escort. A suitcase filled with documents, he had no reason to stash in the store. The SRPD wouldn't have any idea what they had. They wouldn't have cared. But a million bucks?"

"Your point?"

"Guess who Dunn called right before he got busted? And guess who we have on videotape leaving the store with the case?"

"Selmer Godfrey." The skepticism in his voice dissolves into something just short of stupefaction.

"Who bailed twenty-four hours ago, if the *Journal* has it right."

I hear him cover the phone and bark orders to someone to find Selmer.

"You're welcome."

"I'll get back to you." He hangs up.

I reach into the top drawer of my desk, fumble around for a moment, and pull out Dunn's postcard. I flip it over on my desk. On the cover is a picture of the San Diego Zoo.

"It warms my heart to think of them cruisin' for babes in Acapulco."

"No way, man. They seem more the type to settle down together and open a bed-and-breakfast."

We wave at each other. "Adios, Harold."

57

NINE DAYS EARLIER. To the Downs. To Ted's. To Barry.

For fifteen minutes, from the slam of my car door in the parking lot of Superior Court to my arrival at Ted's, my thoughts are like bacon bits in a tornado. Every time an image or notion enters my mind, another flies by that grabs my attention. Each should make me smile, or worry, or feel triumphant or angry or nervous. But none lasts long enough.

Why would Judge Saltzman . . . Your highness . . . Dunn is done . . . Silvie did a great . . . What are Evenrude and Foster . . . your highness . . . I won, I won, I won . . . I beat Silvie . . . poor Silvie . . . did you get tested . . . grow up, Seegerman . . . some things in life are more important than Barry Manilow.

It is nearly eight when I reach Ted's. One hour to go. For reasons I do not pretend to understand, my cerebral zephyrs lull when I pull into the parking lot across the street from the club. It is dark. The lot already is nearly filled. I slump down in my seat for a minute and look in my rearview at people walking into Ted's. I can quit. I have the power. I can choose this moment to drive off and leave this life and these people behind. The thought is soothing. Will I open my door and walk in and face the challenge of convincing my hero to accept me? Or will I flee?

Usually I am upstairs in Ted's living area before a show, in costume. But tonight, in my lawyer's garb, I thread my way through the already dense crowd, greeting friends and fans and well-wishers. Do they know? Is that why these people are here? Because Barry Manilow is coming? No one says a word about it, but the place is buzzing. Ted waves from the bar. I walk over. We shake.

"Sorry I'm late. Did they tell you I had a jury out?"

"I heard. You good?" He hands me a beer. I will drink it in the shower. Alcohol and scalding hot water. Then I will be better than good. Then I will be ready.

Upstairs.

"Gordon Seegerman, one," I say. "Silvie Hernandez, zippo." The Mandys are spread around Ted's loft in various states of undress and frenzy.

"No shit," they say, nearly in unison.

"Shit," I say, and walk into the bathroom.

My mother often wrote Barry after she became ill. She copied the letters and tucked them carefully in her Manilow file. They were simple fan letters. She was a smart lady, a good writer, and so they are entertaining, not sycophantic. In return, she got what I'm sure she expected from a man who, at the time, was the biggest star on the planet—autographed pictures, pleasant form letters. A few months before she died, though, she wrote to tell him about her illness. Her letter is direct. It says she has appreciated his music, that it has helped her to be strong, and that probably he wouldn't be hearing from her in the future.

Someone in Barry's organization must have read the letter carefully, because a few weeks later she received a handwritten reply. This is what it said:

Dear Mary,

Thank you so much for your correspondence. As you know, I get thousands of letters every week and it is impossible to respond to every one personally. But yours was different. You sound like a special lady, and your family is very lucky to have you.

I am so sorry that you are ill. It sounds like you are a strong person and that you have a wonderful family to be there for you. And I am thrilled that through my music I have been able to help, if even in a very small way. I often wonder whether what I am doing makes any difference, whether making the music I love really matters. Then I get a letter like yours and I feel that if I have made even one person's life a little less difficult, I am on the right track. So, thank you, for your letters and for your support.

Yours truly,

Barry Manilow

I am in the shower. The hot spray sears my forehead and scalp. Barry's letter is in the inside pocket of my white tuxedo jacket. It comes with me to every gig. I want Barry to hear us, to approve, to endorse the CD. But even more, I want to thank him. I want to shake his hand and look him in the eye and tell him how much it meant for him to take a few minutes to tell my mother that her support mattered, that he'd heard *her*.

It is nine. Ted's is packed. It is the buzz after the G-O-D show, the inkling that something special might happen tonight. I am dressed. Ted appears at the top of the stairs.

"You guys ready?" he says. We mumble yes.

"Is he here?" we ask.

"No word yet. He'll show. Relax. Do your thing. Don't try to control everything." He walks out.

"Easy for him to say," Terry jabs.

"He's right, though," Maeve says. She is sheathed in a luscious, sleeveless, silver-sequined gown, with a white boa wrapped around her neck. She stands and wobbles on six-inch stiletto heels.

I stand. "Maeve, my darling, I have never, ever seen you look so radiant."

I give her my arm and walk her down the stairs. When we reach the bottom, Terry and Preet step down behind us. I signal Ted at the bar. He kills the house lights. Ferdy and S. and King and Bea sit at a table near the front. Aineen and Max are next to a table filled with Singhs. A group from the Public Defender's Office is at the bar. Preet points a remote controller over my head at the stage. An orchestra swell hushes the last few conversations. Ted handles the introduction.

"Ladies and gentlemen, the moment you have all been waiting for. Tonight we are going to aim beyond the clouds, and rise above the crowds, and we are going to start one hell of a parade; say good-bye to the ringing phone, say good-bye to the old grindstone, they don't write the songs, but you better believe they sing 'em, please welcome Santa Rita's own, Barry X and the Mandys."

The crowd goes wild. Maeve takes half a step forward, but I hold her back. Terry has his hand on my left shoulder.

"Listen to that, you guys." I turn my head to them. "You remember what I said I wanted out of this?"

"You said you wanted to get laid," Maeve says.

"I said I wanted to spread the word. Mission accomplished. No matter what happens tonight, we done good." We share a high-five—Maeve nearly topples over in the process—and jog onto the stage.

The show is effortless. We are surrounded by family. It has none of the charge of the G-O-D gig, but it is smoother. The crowd knows that we know they are with us. We share a vision. No need to convince anyone here. When Barry arrives, it won't take him ten minutes to understand what we have accomplished. He will walk in and he will say to himself, *This feels like home.*

But Barry does not walk in. He does not shake our hands. We do not sing a duet.

Thirty minutes into the show, Ted waves me over to the bar. The charity gig in Tahoe has been canceled because of a winter storm in the Sierra. Barry sends his regrets. He is still very interested. He will definitely reschedule.

My trip back to the stage is unbearable. I know we will get him here, eventually. And, after the G-O-D show, I have the distinct sense we are on our way.

But I have no idea how the Mandys will survive this. By the time I am within ten feet of them it is clear I don't have to open my mouth. They know. I shake my head. Preet hits the first chords of "Somewhere in the Night," which is not the next song on the set list. But I see his point. I have the microphone in my hand and I stand in a small space in front of the stage, staring at my bandmates. And then I sing, first to my friends—"*so glad you opened the door*"—and then to the audience— "*You're my song, music too magic to end, I'll play you over and over again.*" I look out toward the back of the club, to the door, willing it to open. Open, you bastard. And it does. Myla, her head down, ducks inside and then tucks herself into the back of the crowd.

"*Loving so warm, moving so right, closing our eyes, and feeling the light, we'll just go on burning bright, somewhere in the night.*"

It is the maybes that get me out of bed every morning. Maybe next time, Barry will show. Maybe my father's malady will pass me by. Maybe, just maybe, I will pick up the phone a week or a month from now and it will be Myla.

"Hi," I'll say.

"Hi."

"How are you?"

"I'm okay. How are you?"

"I'm fine. I'm good," I'll tell her. "I saw you at the show, you know, before Christmas."

"You did?"

"I did," I'll say. "I saw you tapping your feet, too."

"I was not tapping my feet."

"Oh, yes, you were."

Hope. Everlasting hope.

Acknowledgments

In a fair world my indebtedness to Hilary Liftin, Lydia Wills, and Cullen Schaffer would be declared in four colors and enormous type on the front cover of this book. Hilary got me writing. She shared her agent, her essential editorial insights, and her publishing know-how. She even gave me a title. She is a splendid writer and a great friend. Read her books!

Ms. Wills twice rejected my manuscripts. But she did so in such a uniquely kind and constructive and generous and supportive manner that I felt spurred, not spurned. I am relieved, finally, to call her my agent. I am proud, also, to call her my friend.

Cullen edited me like a pro and loved me like a little brother. At appropriate times over the last forty years he has covered, kicked, and saved my butt. He is the finest person I know.

Colin Dickerman, Lara Carrigan (Go Dawgs!), and the rest of the staff at Bloomsbury USA have cured me of my fear of publishing people. They turned my manuscript into a book. They work very hard. If I had the power I'd give them all long, paid vacations.

Several people suffered through early, gnarled versions of this book. My apologies and thanks go to Chris Botka, Nancy Cohen, Elena Dorfman, Pam Klein, and Lisa Schiffman.

Yvette Molina, the painter, did a good deed relating to this book that is too complicated to describe. Trust me, someday she will be very famous. She doesn't need, but still deserves, my gratitude.

Barry Manilow's music was the primary inspiration for this book. So, thanks to him, too.

Finally, Jennifer Dykes believed she was marrying a lawyer. As it turns out, she believed wrong. She has had to cope with all manner of trying and occasionally obnoxious writerly behavior. And, for the most part, she's handled it all with grace and composure. (There was that one incident in Milan, but never mind that.) She is my love and I don't care who knows it.

KEEP READING!

Turn the page for a sneak peek at the dark and thrilling new entry in the Misdemeanor Man mystery series,

I RIGHT THE WRONGS

Despite his recent successes in the courtroom, Gordon Seegerman is intent on sticking to his low-end practice, handling misdemeanors for the Santa Rita, California, public defender's office. His priority is his Manilow cover band, which is on the verge of hitting it big—if they can find a substitute for their drummer, who's nine months pregnant and on bed rest. But when the cops bust the state's leading high school quarterback for dog-napping and possession of marijuana, and then the dog's owner's wife winds up dead, Gordon finds himself back in the wrong sort of spotlight, and back at work.

And work has never meant so much trouble. The judge assigned to the case has a pathological disregard for the law, the city is on the verge of a violent eruption, and the client looks like he might be the next homicide victim. Forced into the most serious case of his life, Gordon discovers the truth behind a decades-old murder and learns a shocking lesson: he may not be the Misdemeanor Man after all.

The new novel by Dylan Schaffer

I RIGHT THE WRONGS

Hardcover $23.95
Bloomsbury Publishing
Available wherever books are sold

Prologue

"**G**ORDON SEEGERMAN?" A nurse, dressed in scrubs crawling with the sniggering faces of a hundred cartoon cats, pokes her head into the waiting room. "Would you come this way?"

She weighs me and takes my blood pressure.

"Are you all right?"

"I'm fine, thanks," I say.

She gives me a sideways glance. The cats on her uniform gawk at me. I follow her into an examination room.

She looks at her clipboard. "Just the blood draw today?"

I nod too enthusiastically. She stretches a length of rubber around my arm. My veins bulge. I make a fist, she sticks me, and sucks out two vials of blood. And it's done. So simple. Years spent worrying about this moment and it's over in ten seconds.

In two weeks, I'll return. I'll sit in the waiting room and flip through a *People* magazine while my heart tries to pummel its way out of my chest. A nurse will call my name. I'll walk into a doctor's office. And the doctor, having spliced and diced my genes and taken a close look at my fourteenth chromosome, will tell me whether, like my father, I am destined, in the not-too-distant future, to lose my mind to early-onset familial Alzheimer's disease.

That, or I'll let the appointment pass and go on not knowing.

"You have the follow-up visit all set, right?"

I nod. She looks at me for a moment longer and then says, "Try not to drive yourself too crazy, Mr. Seegerman. You haven't quite made it through the rain, but, somehow, you'll survive." The woman knows her Manilow.

I smile. She arches her eyebrows and, before I can thank her, spins out of the room.

1

FORTY-ONE DAYS EARLIER, April 28, 2004.

"Vegas," I say, raising my beer.

"Vegas." My bandmates Preet Singh and Terry Fretwater, join me.

"Vegas can bite me," our fourth, the exceedingly pregnant Maeve O'Connell, grumbles from across the room. She is splayed out on a threadbare, sagging couch, confined upon medical advice to horizontality. "*I* ain't drinking to Vegas."

"*You're* not drinking period," I add.

For her soon-to-be son's sake, Maeve has taken leave of her essential pleasures: alcohol, caffeine, tobacco, young women, and, most agonizingly, the Mandys, our Manilow tribute band. We're gearing up to play a gig at a bar in the Mandalay Bay hotel in Las Vegas, the day before Barry appears in concert there, his first show in two years. It is our shared dream to perform for the man, to receive his blessing, and to take our Manilow mission to unbelievers nationwide.

We're in the wretched, windowless garage, behind one of Preet's father's convenience stores, that serves as our studio and clubhouse. It's nine-thirty P.M. and, though May is two days away, the temperature outside is around ninety degrees. Inside, with our amps cranked and Preet's colossal computer rig whirring furiously, it must be a hundred. I'd like to pour the beer on my head, but we're auditioning girl singers, so I don't dare. It's been some time since I had a proper date.

"Who's next?" I say. Preet glances at his notes.

"Joe."

Maeve, who describes her place of birth as a town where the necks are red, the men are named Ned, and the children are inbred, chuckles and drawls, "This ought to be interesting."

I wipe a line of sweat off my forehead. "If you don't pipe down, Preet's going to snitch you off to Aineen." Maeve's home-confinement-enforcing twenty-five-year-old daughter.

Our ad in the local alternative paper makes clear we're looking for a woman, to temporarily replace Maeve, to get us through Vegas. Joe better be wearing lipstick. Terry kicks open the door.

Joe is not wearing lipstick. Joe has a goatee.

"I sing in falsetto," he says, and shrugs.

Terry looks to me for approval, but it's too hot to have an opinion. We pop a beer for our guest and take him through the introductory drill.

Listen carefully, Joe. We're not impersonators, got it? We don't do dress-up or camp. We don't do irony. And we don't do covers. We do homage. We're a tribute band. We're translators, envoys, mission-aries. Probably you're a wonderful person. You may even be able to sing. But if you don't get what we're doing, if you're not truly and unapologetically on the bus, you're wasting our time.

Joe looks bewildered. He does not appear to have the slightest idea what we're talking about. He glances around the rehearsal space, blank-faced, looking for a bus, I suppose.

"Everybody ready?" Terry asks. We toss the newbie a softball: "Weekend in New England." He has a terrific voice, evocative of Aaron Neville. But there's nothing about the performance that con-vinces me he's here for Manilow, that he shares our vision.

My cell phone, parked on Preet's keyboard, shrilly cuts into the middle of the song, which sputters and then expires. Preet answers.

"Ferdy," he says, holding out the phone. Ferdy is my grandfather. He turns a spry and cantankerous ninety in a week.

I wave away the call.

Preet tries, but fails to cut off the old lunatic, who shrieks his way through some sort of narrative that ends with a series of demands. The content is a mystery to me, but the tone is unmistakable.

Preet folds up the phone and tosses it at me. "The cops just arrested Marcus Manners."

"No shit," Terry and Maeve say.

"Now *there's* a stunner," I say. "Who's Marcus Manners?"

"The leading high school quarterback in the state," Preet reports. "Apparently he's also Bea's godson."

Beatrice Johnson married my grandfather a year ago. She is a charming and accomplished woman of some eighty-three years and two hundred and eighty pounds.

"He's about to graduate from Hills," Terry explains. Hills High School, the most upscale of the city's public schools.

"And why do *I* care?"

"Ferdy says you're the kid's lawyer. They're all downtown waiting for you."

"All *whom*?"

"Not clear."

"Did he say what the deal is?" I ask.

"He mentioned a dog. And O. J. Simpson. It was a bit hard to make out," Preet says. By now Joe seems genuinely alarmed.

I grab my keys. "The name again?"

"Marcus Manners."

I walk to the door. Joe has his back to me. I point at him and then slash my index finger across my throat.

My name is Gordon Seegerman. I'm an assistant public defender for the city of Santa Rita, California. I'm assigned, as I have been for nearly a decade, to the misdemeanor division. Each morning I wake up, drive sixteen minutes to my dank office in the basement of the

Santa Rita municipal building, and settle into my job as a cog in the creaky wheels of the criminal justice system.

A file appears on my desk. A man has been arrested for a petty crime—stealing a slice of pizza, or being drunk in public, or showing his genitals to someone who isn't interested. I meet the man. I pretend to commiserate when he explains: *they got the wrong guy; they planted the evidence; the witness is lying; I was holding the stuff for my cousin.*

I nod a lot. I tell him everything is going to be fine. Later I discuss the case with a deputy district attorney. He or she makes the standard offer: seven months county jail or one hundred hours community service or a stay at a drug rehab outfit. In turn, I make a halfhearted, short-lived, and uniformly ineffectual attempt to improve the deal. I take the plea offer to the client, who yells at me, says he wants a real lawyer, tells me I'm an idiot or worse. And then, in a few days, he pleads guilty.

I take as few cases to trial as humanly possible. I avoid promotion— to the felony division, to the serious cases—as I might the Ebola virus. What ambition I have I save for my music, for my commitment to Manilow. What energy I have I exhaust, mostly, handling my dad, who, perhaps simply to irritate me, ten years ago developed a rare form of Alzheimer's. Imagine a toddler after a few shots of Jack Daniel's—that about describes my father.

My job is my job. I lay low. I try not to attract too much attention. Every two weeks I'm pleasantly surprised to find that the city has deposited a sum of money in my bank account. I can't say I believe this money is earned, but I'm not inclined to return it.

Two blocks short of the Hall of Justice complex—courts, district attorney and public defender offices, Santa Rita Police Department headquarters—I stop my frail, front-bumperless, white Toyota station wagon at a light. The windows are closed, and the air-conditioning is turned up so high it's strafing my forehead. I therefore can see, but not hear, a woman on the corner talking into a cellular phone. She's in her mid-thirties, dressed for work at a place where dress matters. I have seen her before, but I can't think where. She's stick-thin, with a perky but not large bust, heavily made up, blond. Her nose curves abruptly at its end. Her shoulder-length hair hangs straight, at attention, paralyzed by product.

She pulls the phone away from her ear, fixates on the sidewalk for a moment, and then fires her mobile at the pavement. I'm rooting for her to stomp it. But she drops to her knees, returns the phone to her bag, and buries her face in her hands. Meanwhile the driver behind me lays into his horn, and I'm off.

I park across from the Hall. A crowd is gathered out front. TV microwave vans line the curb. A group of people who must be attached to the vans—reporters, camera people, techs—moves toward me as I cross the street. They do not look for oncoming traffic. A reporter—dark suit, microphone in hand, brown helmet-hair, more than his fair share of teeth—reaches me first.

"Are you someone?" He's frantic.

"I don't think so."

The reporter pokes the microphone in my face. The others circle around.

"Ted Garnett, FOX 4. You here on the Manners kid?"

"I'm with the public defender," I say, reaching to shake the reporter's hand to buy a few seconds. The handshake is unexpectedly clammy and limp.

The camera people shove to the front. The lights blind me.

What are the charges?

Are there drugs involved?

Has he lost his scholarship?

Is the family going to make a statement?

Where is Marcus?

Can we talk to Marcus?

A more experienced person would ignore the questions and irritatedly push away. But the spotlight stuns me, as does the notion that someone, somewhere, might care what I have to say. So I stare into the camera and confess my total ignorance.

A NOTE ON THE AUTHOR

Dylan Schaffer is a criminal defense lawyer who has served as appellate counsel in more than fifty murder cases, including death penalty matters. He has represented defendants in the San Francisco dog mauling case, the Billionaire Boys Club case, the repressed-memory murder case, and the John Gotti–Gambino Family prosecution. He lives in Oakland, California. This is his first novel. For additional information, visit www.misdemeanorman.com.

A NOTE ON THE TYPE

The text of this book is set in Linotype Sabon, named after the type founder, Jacques Sabon. It was designed by Jan Tschichold and jointly developed by Linotype, Monotype and Stempel, in response to a need for a typeface to be available in identical form for mechanical hot metal composition and hand composition using foundry type.

Tschichold based his design for Sabon roman on a font engraved by Garamond, and Sabon italic on a font by Granjon. It was first used in 1966 and has proved an enduring modern classic.